CHANGELING- A JADE IHA

You can't always recognize the face of your enemy.

Two thousand years ago, the legendary mathematical genius Archimedes was poised on the brink of the greatest discovery in human history when his life was brutally snuffed out. His murder has never been explained.

While investigating the strange Paracas skulls—believed by some to be the remains of extraterrestrial explorers—archaeologist Jade Ihara receives an unexpected visit from an old foe seeking her help against entities he calls "Changelings" and their plot to manufacture a false chapter of human history.

Hounded by radical extremists led by Atash Shah—a man bent on becoming the Mahdi prophesied to unite the Islamic world—and haunted by the faceless puppetmasters who secretly control the world, Jade must follow the trail of clues to uncover a deadly truth that has been erased from history.

Can she solve the mystery of Archimedes' murder, or will she become the next victim of the conspiracy to hide the truth?

PRAISE FOR THE JADE IHARA ADVENTURES

"I'll admit it. I am totally exhausted after finishing the latest Jade Ihara page-turner by David Wood and Sean Ellis. What an adventure! I kept asking myself how the co-authors came up with all this fantastic stuff. This is a great read that provides lots of action, and thoughtful insight as well, into strange realms that are sometimes best left unexplored." **Paul Kemprecos, author of *Cool Blue Tomb and The NUMA Files***

CHANGELING

A JADE IHARA ADVENTURE

DAVID WOOD
SEAN ELLIS

Gryphonwood

Changeling- A Jade Ihara Adventure
Copyright 2015 by David Wood
Published by Gryphonwood Press
www.gryphonwoodpress.com

Cover by Drazenka Kimpel

This book is a work of fiction. All characters and situations are products of the author's imagination. Any resemblance to actual persons and events is entirely coincidental.

ISBN-10: 1940095409
ISBN-13: 978-1-940095-40-0

Works by David Wood

The Dane Maddock Adventures
Dourado
Cibola
Quest
Icefall
Buccaneer
Atlantis
Ark

Dane and Bones Origins
Freedom
Hell Ship
Splashdown
Dead Ice
Liberty
Electra
Amber
Justice

The Jade Ihara Adventures (with Sean Ellis)
Oracle
Changeling

Stand-Alone Novels
Into the Woods
Arena of Souls
The Zombie-Driven Life
You Suck
Callsign: Queen (with Jeremy Robinson)
Destiny (with Sean Ellis)
Dark Rite (with Alan Baxter)

Bones Bonebrake Adventures
Primitive
The Book of Bones

David Wood writing as David Debord

The Absent Gods Trilogy
The Silver Serpent
Keeper of the Mists
The Gates of Iron

The Impostor Prince (with Ryan A. Span)

BOOKS BY SEAN ELLIS

Mira Raiden Adventures
Ascendant
Descendant

The Nick Kismet Thrillers
The Shroud of Heaven
Into the Black
The Devil You Know (novella)
Fortune Favors

The Adventures of Dodge Dalton
In the Shadow of Falcon's Wings
At the Outpost of Fate
On the High Road to Oblivion

Chess Team/Jack Sigler Thrillers
(with Jeremy Robinson)
Callsign: King
Underworld
Blackout

7 | CHANGELING

Prime
Savage
Cannibal

AUTHORS' NOTE

May 8-August 24, 2015

Since much of this novel revolves around our system of timekeeping, a brief explanation is in order. Most of us are familiar with the usage AD (anno Domini) and BC (before Christ) to differentiate our modern era from the backwards counting system for dates before the last two thousand years, beginning with the assumed date of the birth of Jesus. Because of the obvious religious connotations and the resulting biases, to say nothing of the fact that these arbitrary designations are not generally believed to be accurate—most Bible scholars believe Jesus was born in the year 2 BC—many historians prefer to use CE (common era) and BCE (before common era). As a scholar, Jade would likely use this latter system, but that would not be true of everyone she comes into contact with, thus the reader will, from time to time, encounter references using the more common system.

Just remember AD=CE and BC=BCE.

PROLOGUE

FOUND

An unknown land—202 BCE

The boy became a man but he never forgot what he had seen that day.

Ten years later, the memory was as clear to him as his own reflection in a pool of still water. Ten years spent waiting, but also growing, learning... preparing for this moment.

His name was Apollonius, and his earliest memories were of the siege. He did not remember a time before that, before the Romans came with their ships and their armies. The siege lasted nearly two years, but what he remembered from that time was not the hardship of being bottled up in the city by the armies of General Marcellus, but rather the battles, for they were unlike anything ever imagined by the poets. Marcellus had come with his mighty engines of war—the Sambucae, great siege ladders, taller than the city walls, each borne by a pair of quinqueremes which bristled with artillery weapons to drive the defenders away as the ships made their approach—but the Roman general was no match for the genius of Syracuse, Archimedes.

Under his direction, the men of the city had constructed an enormous claw of iron that reached out over the harbor like the hand of Zeus himself, plucking the ships from the water as a child might pick up a pebble, and then letting them fall to be dashed apart. He constructed a wall of mirrors to focus the sun's rays on the enemy, blinding their artilleryman and even setting fire to Marcellus' ships.

For a time, it seemed that no threat could prevail against the city. The favor of the gods was upon them. Indeed, if not for the withdrawal of support from their Carthaginian allies, the Syracusians might have defeated Marcellus, but even without such assistance, they could outlast the Romans.

The arrogance of the city was its undoing.

Assured of their eventual victory, the citizens of Syracuse proclaimed a festival to honor Artemis, the goddess who had protected them. Marcellus, learning of this diversion, sent his soldiers to scale the walls of the outer city. Caught by surprise, the defenders were overwhelmed. Although the inner citadel remained intact, the survivors holding out for another eight months, the city's greatest weapon was lost.

That was the part that remained etched in his memory.

When the attack began, steel ringing on steel as the Romans swept over the walls and fell upon the defenders, the commander had dispatched Apollonius to the workshop of Archimedes. With the noise of battle in his ears and the smell of death in his nostrils, the boy ran through the streets, desperate to warn the genius of the enemy's approach.

He found the famed mathematician bent over one of the great sand tables where he drew diagrams and performed elaborate computations. The wet sand was the perfect medium for temporarily holding his ideas until a scribe could record them on wax tablets. There was no scribe in the workshop on this night though. Archimedes was alone, drawing furiously with his finger, first in the air and then in the sand, which was already covered with an elaborate design of circles within circles. He did not look up when the boy burst into the workshop.

"My lord, the Romans are within the walls. You must flee to the fortress."

The old man shook his head without raising his eyes, his jaw grinding with determination. "So close." He pointed at the picture he had drawn. "It's almost complete. I must finish it."

"The Romans will kill you if you stay." As if to underscore the urgency of the plea, the noise of fighting echoed in the street behind him. The enemy was close.

Archimedes waved a hand, dismissively. "I very much

doubt that. Marcellus knows I'm far more valuable to him alive."

Apollonius gaped in astonishment. "You would surrender to the Romans?"

"Romans. Greeks. Syracusians. It makes no differences. This…" He held his hands above the table. "This is all that matters."

"You can finish it in the citadel," the boy pleaded. He hastened forward, intending to obliterate the design and force the old man to comply, but a mere glimpse of what Archimedes had inscribed in the sand stopped him.

It was indescribably beautiful. Ten years later, he had no difficulty recalling it to mind, but that was perhaps not surprising since he had spent the better part of those years tracing the design, scratching it in the dirt and on tablets of soft clay, drawing it with ink upon leaves of papyrus.

Archimedes, sensing his intent, deflected him with a backhanded slap. The mathematician had seen more than seventy summers and the siege had left him weak and frail, but the intensity of the blow stunned the boy, leaving little question about the old man's intention.

"Go boy! The Romans will spare me, but I do not think you will be so fortunate." A shriek from the street outside, abruptly cut short, revealed that it was already too late for either of them to reach the citadel. Archimedes grabbed hold of his arm and propelled him deeper into the workshop sanctuary. "Hide," he hissed.

Apollonius hid, scrambling beneath some half-finished contraption that rested on a wheeled platform. He was burrowing deeper into the shadows when he heard the voice.

"There you are, old man."

The boy froze, then with painstaking care, turned around and crept out into the open until he could see what was happening.

A legionary stood in the doorway, blood dripping from the tip of his gladius. He was a tall man with features as shapeless as unleavened bread. That face was the only thing about the events of that night that the man the boy grew up to be could not recall, but the man's eyes—charcoal-black, absorbing the flickering lamplight without even a glimmer of a reflection—those he remembered.

"Yes, here I am," Archimedes said, disdainfully. "You have caught me. Now, run off and tell Marcellus where to find me."

The soldier advanced into the room. His black eyes glanced at the table, scrutinizing the design. "You solved it," he said, his tone grave. "Unfortunate."

"The circles?" Apollonius could not see Archimedes' face, but he heard the surprise in the old man's voice. "You're no centurion. Who are—?"

The man stepped close to Archimedes, so close that the boy could no longer see his bland face or jet-black eyes. "This is not for you."

There was a crunching sound and Archimedes gave a loud sigh as the sword point burst from the center of his back.

Apollonius clamped his hands over his mouth to stifle a whimper of grief. As the old man crumpled to the floor, the killer wrenched his weapon free, and in the same motion, swiped the bloody blade across the design, obliterating it. Then, just as quickly as he had arrived, the man disappeared.

In the days that followed, as the boy scurried about in the darkness, hiding from the occupying Romans, he searched their faces, seeing something of the killer in every one, but none had his eyes.

It had taken him considerably longer to grasp the meaning behind the design that Archimedes had died for, but as he began to do so, peeling away the layers of the mystery, Apollonius understood why the mathematician had been willing to risk capture in order to see his work completed. What he could not understand, even ten years later, was why the black-eyed man would have wanted to destroy it.

Perhaps the answer to that riddle would become clear once he entered the vault.

That it was a vault, a storehouse of secrets, he could only infer. His study of the design had revealed many things to him—secrets woven into the fabric of human belief, hidden in the mathematical precision of the universe—but sometimes those messages were ambiguous, contradictory.

The journey had been long and full of peril, but the design he had glimpsed and studied and ultimately completed had not led him astray. He had found the vault right where he knew it would be. From a distance, he thought he was approaching a city, with great red towers looking out across the wilderness. An abandoned city, surely, for only savages inhabited the land through which he passed—foragers and hunters who moved with the seasons and followed the animal herds. As he drew near, he saw that the towers and pillars were merely rock formations, the citadels and fortresses carved from the landscape, not by men, but by the gods. What better place to hide the secrets of the cosmos?

Unfortunately, where was not as important as when, but there too, the design had not failed him.

He had crossed oceans in ships, and trekked across barren landscapes on foot, always guided by the stars, counting the days. As the voyage stretched out into weeks and months, he began to despair of reaching his destination in time. If he failed, the task would fall to someone else, and perhaps what he had learned would illuminate the path of some distant descendant. Or perhaps not. The design was more than just a map, more than just a key to unlock the door. It was a test of intellect, of worthiness.

A test he had passed, evidently. He was not late.

Apollonius approached the cave on the morning of the vernal equinox. It looked like nothing more than a scalloped recess, scooped out by the elements, a place for wild animals to take refuge from the sun, but up close he saw that it was a concealed passage leading deeper into the great fortress-shaped rock.

He coaxed his tinder into a flame on the end of a brand and crawled into the sloping passage. The red rock seemed to constrict around him, so tight that his shoulders were scraped raw, but he kept moving, kept pushing the torch ahead of him to light the way, trusting that the design had not led him astray. If he was wrong, if the passage closed in even more, he would be caught like a fish in a net, unable to extricate himself.

I'm not wrong, he told himself. *This is just another test.*

He shoved the torch forward again. The smoke from it was filling the passage, stinging his eyes, but it had not been smothered which meant that there was plenty of air to keep it burning. He pushed it out further and was about to squirm forward again when the flame abruptly disappeared, leaving him in darkness.

He whispered a curse, but kept moving forward, groping for the torch. Instead, his hands found nothing, not even the stone of the passage. He pondered this for a moment before grasping the significance of it. He had reached the end of the passage and the entrance to a much larger cave. He felt warm, humid air on his face, and heard the trickling of water all around. The torch, he surmised, had fallen down into the darkness to be extinguished in an unseen pool on the cavern floor.

No matter. He had several more in a sack which he dragged along behind him. He probed the darkness until he found the edge of the precipice. The walls beyond felt smooth, curving gently away, and although the cavern floor was out of reach, from the drip of water, he knew that it was not too much of a drop. He kept crawling until he was able to lower himself down, and then simply let go, sliding the rest of the way to splash into the knee-deep water.

Working by touch alone, careful to keep his equipment dry, he got another torch lit, and in its faint orange-yellow glow, got his first look at where Archimedes' design had brought him.

The cavern was not large, the walls only a stone's throw apart, but the space was completely open. He realized immediately that he was standing inside a sphere too perfect to be the work of nature. Strange relief patterns, squares of varying depth, adorned the walls, forming a maze through which dribbles of water oozed down the walls to accumulate at the bottom of the sphere. At the very center of the pool, where the water was surely deepest, his first torch now rotated lazily.

The water must be draining out there, he thought. *Otherwise, this whole chamber would be flooded.*

After a moment of watching the torch spin, he realized that the water was draining away faster than the seepage replenishing it.

This revelation filled him with excitement. He understood now how his predecessor, the man who had unknowingly launched him on this quest, must have felt on that day when he had grasped the relationship between volume and density while bathing, a day that, if the stories were true, had seen him running naked through the streets shouting "Eureka! Eureka!"

The chamber would be dry soon, and then he would use Archimedes' design to unlock the vault.

"This is not for you."

The voice startled him, nearly causing him to drop his second torch. He whirled toward the opening high on the wall above, seized by fear, his hand instinctively seeking the sheathed dagger that hung from his belt, but there was no one there.

Those words. He remembered them vividly, too. Was that all this was? His imagination running wild? The sound of the water playing tricks on his ears? The ghost of a memory, reaching out across the years to frighten him?

He took a deep breath, then another, and when his racing heart was becalmed, he turned back to the center.

The man with black eyes stood there.

Ten years had passed and the boy Apollonius had grown up, but the man with the face that looked like nothing and no one, and the eyes that seemed to drink the life out of anyone who gazed into them, had not changed at all. He looked exactly the same as he had that fateful night when he had put his sword through the chest of Archimedes of

Syracuse.

The same sword that he held in his right hand.

Apollonius threw up his hands in a show of surrender. "Mercy, sir. Please. I've come so far."

"I know," the man replied, his voice as flat and emotionless as his visage. "I had hoped that you would fail."

"But why? I have passed the test. I am worthy to enter the vault."

"This is not for you."

The blade flashed and the torch fell from Apollonius' hands, plunging the chamber once more into darkness. As his life drained away, along with the water in which he lay, Apollonius heard a sound like the grinding of a millstone. The vault was opening, but he would not live to see what lay within.

LOST

Sydney, Australia—Three weeks ago

First Officer Jeanne Carrera was surprised to see Captain Seth Norris already seated in the cockpit, idly thumbing through a printed weather report. Norris was punctual, always arriving on time but he rarely showed up early and never got to a plane ahead of her.

"Turning over a new leaf?" she remarked as she stowed her carry-on.

"Hmm?" Norris glanced up and offered a polite smile.

"You're early. You're never early."

He shook his head dismissively. "Traffic was lighter than I expected. I made good time."

She settled into the right seat. "How was your weekend?"

"Good. Amelia's birthday was yesterday. I'm still coming down from all the sugar."

Carrera laughed, but her mirth hid a strange disquiet. She couldn't put her finger on it, but something felt wrong, like déjà vu but different. She knew that Norris' had been looking forward to his daughter's party almost as much as he had been dreading having to interact with the eight-, now nine-year-old girl's mother—his ex-wife. Nothing strange about that.

So why do I feel like I stepped into the wrong scene in a movie?

She wondered, for a fleeting instant, if she was dreaming but the moment passed as quickly as it had come and she dismissed her reaction.

Yet, as they worked through the pre-flight checklist, exchanging idle banter, the feeling kept coming back intermittently, like the flicker of a fluorescent light bulb about to die. Eventually, Norris took note.

"Are you feeling okay, Jeanne?"

There it is again. What the hell is going on? She managed a wan smile and a shrug. "Yeah. Just…weird."

The captain straightened in his seat, his expression instantly serious. "What's weird?"

"It's nothing. Just a little spooked."

"A little spooked isn't nothing. Your subconscious might be picking up on something that your conscious mind is missing."

She laughed, though it was an uncomfortable sound. "Since when did you become so superstitious?"

Even as she said it, she realized that the source of the strange feeling was Norris himself.

Amelia's birthday.

Norris never called his daughter by her given name. Whenever he spoke of her, he almost always said, "my little girl" or sometimes "my daughter." When he called her by name, which was rare, he always used the pet name "Mellie." But today, he had called her "Amelia."

Despite the still-unexplained incongruity, Carrera felt an odd sense of relief. Simply knowing what it was that felt out of place had eased her concerns. She felt as if a bothersome sliver had finally been tweezed out of her subconscious.

"It's nothing," she reiterated, and this time she meant it. Maybe the birthday girl had scolded him about his refusal to use her proper name. Carrera could remember when she had demanded that her own parents cease and desist from using nicknames. *I was probably about the same age as Amelia.*

"You're sure?" Norris pressed. "Four hundred and twenty-two people are about to put their lives in our hands, so if for any reason you don't want to fly, you need to let me know."

"Seth, it's fine. I'm good." And she was, even though she didn't know why Norris had started referring to his daughter in a different way, or why he had shown up early when he almost never did, or why he was suddenly insisting that she pay attention to her intuition when she had never known him to do that....

Even though there was no explanation for any of those things, the satisfaction of having figured it out was enough to put her mind at ease.

Mostly.

They concluded the pre-flight checks and finished boarding, and as Norris greeted the passengers and briefed them on the itinerary for the trans-Pacific flight, Carrera made the final preparations for take-off. As she watched him work and listened to his voice on the public address system, she found herself scrutinizing everything he did, every minor perceived deviation from his normal routine. She could not tell if he was acting differently, or if she was merely being hypersensitive, but from a technical standpoint, his flying was spot on.

About two hours after take-off, Norris handed the controls over to Carrera and rose from his chair to stretch his legs. There was nothing unusual about this. Flying, particularly on a long trans-oceanic route, was mostly a struggle against tedium. There was very little for the pilot to do aside from remaining vigilant and ready to respond to the unexpected, which could mean anything from steering around pockets of turbulence to coping with mechanical or electrical failures. Carrera focused her attention on the instrument panel while Norris stepped into the lavatory.

Although her initial discomfort had long since passed, Carrera continued to be plagued by the surreal sense of dislocation she had experienced before take-off. She could not shake the feeling that she was actually asleep and dreaming everything. The phenomena was so persistent that she felt compelled to test the reality of her circumstances by checking to see if the printed weather report made sense. She had heard that, in dreams, written text often changed or was illegible, but the weather reports were completely normal. She was not dreaming then, but she definitely felt like she was in the Twilight Zone.

"Still spooked?" Norris asked from behind her.

"Is it that obvious?" She smiled without looking back and quickly added. "Not spooked exactly, just feeling a bit…odd."

"If I may ask, when did it start?"

Carrera craned her head around to look at him. Norris was standing just behind her, his arms crossed over his chest. The pose was all wrong; he never stood like that. Or did he? She shook her head. "Honestly, it was when you called your daughter 'Amelia.'"

"Ah. And that's not something I usually do." Norris said it more like a statement than a question. He tilted his head back as if embarrassed by the mistake. "Well, as the saying goes, the devil is in the details."

Carrera's forehead creased in confusion. "What do you mean?"

Norris smiled and then moved with the speed of striking viper. Carrera did not even have time to yelp in alarm. The captain clapped his left hand over her mouth, stifling any potential cry for assistance. His right drove something into the side of her neck.

Carrera felt a sharp twinge, like a bee sting, followed by a bloom of icy cold radiating away from the spot. She caught a glimpse of a discarded syringe falling to the carpeted floor, and then his right arm snaked around to immobilize her. She tried to struggle out of his grasp, but whatever he had injected into her neck was already having an effect. Her muscles felt leaden. Even breathing was an ordeal.

She gasped a word, a single question that was muffled

by the hand still clamped over her mouth. *Why?*

Norris however seemed to understand. As darkness closed in from the edges of her vision, Carrera thought she heard him say, "Not for you."

PART ONE
SKULLS

ONE

Peru

"Aliens!"

The familiar refrain echoed across the open stretch of sand, setting Jade Ihara's teeth on edge. "I swear to God," she muttered, "if he says that one more time, I'm going to personally start an intergalactic war."

Beside her, Pete "Professor" Chapman chuckled. "Careful, now. Don't get caught on camera biting the hand that feeds."

"Easy for you to say," Jade retorted. "You're not the one watching your career slowly circling the drain. I can't believe I ever thought this was a good idea."

Nevertheless, she stopped and glanced around to make sure that their conversation was not being captured on video. They were already a hundred yards away from the squat museum complex—Jade thought it looked more like a police station or a military base than a repository of ancient culture—which seemed to be the focus of attention for the camera crew, but she knew Professor's admonition was warranted. With modern technology, it was sometimes hard to tell when the cameras were rolling. While the crew of *Alien Explorers*—a cable television documentary program with a penchant for making elaborate connections between ancient civilizations and little green men—did most of their work with state-of-art video and audio production equipment, she knew they also liked to sometimes fold in candid footage shot with handheld digital video cameras and even smart phones, which in the final edit, gave the finished product a sort of gritty verisimilitude.

The arrival of the video crew still rankled her. Jade realized now that that deal with the production company had probably been in place long before she was hired and there was little doubt in her mind that her sex and physical appearance—the daughter of Japanese and Hawaiian parents, she had been called an 'exotic' so many times, the line made her want to throw up—had played a more important part in her selection for the archaeological crew than had her expertise. Her employer—or more accurately, an attorney from the legal department of the foundation that was sponsoring the dig—had made it clear that she was to give full cooperation and support to the cable television producers who had taken over the site.

Camera-friendly good looks notwithstanding, after two days of watching her carefully excavate tomb shafts, the crew had mostly lost interest in her. The on-site interview with Jeremiah Stillman, publisher of the fringe magazine *Alien Legends*, and esteemed "extraterrestrial astronaut theorist" who had arrived late the previous evening, was much more engaging than watching Jade removing dirt by the teaspoonful. Still, a viral video outing her as a skeptic would definitely not be a good thing.

Aside from Professor, the only other person to hear her was an intern, Rafi Massoud, and he was part of her team, not the production crew.

"You're not going to rat me out, are you Rafi?"

The young man, a second-generation Arab-American and a student at UCLA, raised his hands in an exaggerated display of innocence. "I'm with you, Dr. Ihara. That guy's a kook. No way am I putting any of this on my CV."

"Oh, don't be so Old School," said Professor. He cocked his felt Explorer fedora forward in a near perfect imitation of Harrison Ford playing Indiana Jones. "Everyone craves the spotlight, even the Ivy League guys. Trust me, no one is going to think less of you—academically speaking—for doing your job on camera, even if they edit it to make it look like you're saying something you aren't."

"I know," Jade sighed. "But…" She nodded toward the front of the museum where Stillman was holding up an unusually shaped human skull, which he claimed to have found while roaming the dunes, and gesticulating emphatically. In her best approximation of his voice, she said: "Aliens!"

Professor grinned. "It sells. Better, it gets the kids

interested. Admit it, you're secretly hoping that we do find something not of this world. Otherwise, you wouldn't have taken the job."

"Not true. I took the job for the money. That's why it's called a job."

He was not completely wrong, though. While she had spent the last eight months doing very little that could be described as archaeology—long distance guest lecturing via telepresence and researching possible future projects—Jade had passed up several opportunities to get back in the field simply because the invitations were even less interesting than being cooped up in a library with a stack of dusty old books.

There were other reasons for her professional hiatus, however. To borrow a cliché from criminal parlance, Jade Ihara had been laying low.

Several years earlier, her search for the legendary pre-Columbian city of Cibola had put her in the cross-hairs of the notorious international quasi-religious criminal conspiracy known as the Dominion. She had subsequently tangled with them on numerous occasions, and in so doing, had painted a target on her back. The Dominion, in all its many forms, was obsessed with ancient symbols of power—artifacts that might be used to solidify their grip on the world, and which might, as she had seen more than once, actually possess supernatural attributes. As even more recent events had demonstrated, the Dominion was not the only enemy who might want to do her harm, which was how Professor had come to be her constant companion.

A former Navy SEAL and a genius in his own right—he came by his nickname honestly, with two post-graduate degrees—Professor was now working, in a semi-official capacity, for a division of the Central Intelligence Agency, acting as both a bodyguard for Jade and a sort of watchman, on the lookout for anything that might hint at some new threat, while at the same time, using his own not inconsiderable body of knowledge to buttress his cover as her research assistant. It was not the cush assignment that some of his peers might have imagined. The threats Jade faced were real, and all the more ominous since there was no way of knowing from where the next attack would come. And, if she was honest with herself, Jade knew that she could be a bit... prickly.

She liked Professor, liked him enough to entertain the possibility that their relationship might someday extend beyond the professional, beyond friendship, but she also knew that was a bad idea. He was now her closest friend and confidant, and if they took things to the next level and it went horribly wrong—something that seemed to happen whenever she led with her heart—it would ruin the perfectly acceptable status quo.

On Professor's advice, she had spent the last eight months on what could only be charitably termed as a 'sabbatical.' She had spent a lot of time in the water, snorkeling in Waimea Bay and surfing the North Shore of Oahu waiting for Professor to give her the signal that it was safe to go back to her old life. After six months, the tedium had become unbearable and over his objections—truth be told, he was a bit overprotective—she had started looking for work again, whereupon she had quickly been reacquainted with the reality of just how boring, not to mention political, archaeology could sometimes be.

The offer to work at Wari Kayan, the ancient necropolis of the Paracas culture on the slopes of Cerro Colorado in Peru however had been too intriguing to pass up, partly because the expedition was being underwritten by a not-for-profit foundation with very deep pockets—a welcome change from the miserliness of academia—but mostly because it was a chance to lay her hands on one of the most sensational discoveries in modern archaeology: the Paracas skulls.

The Paracas culture had inhabited the western slopes of the Andes mountain range from 1200 BCE until their eventual assimilation into the Nazca culture which endured until about 750 CE before fading almost completely from history. Although the Paracas produced astonishingly beautiful polychrome ceramic ware and intricately patterned textiles, their greatest claim to notoriety stemmed from the relatively recent discovery of unusual elongated human skulls in Paracas burial shafts.

There was no great mystery to the skulls. The Paracas, like many other ancient cultures throughout North America and indeed, the rest of the world, had practiced a form of body modification known as "artificial cranial deformation." In early infancy, Paracas children would have their heads bound tightly with blankets and sometimes wood planks, which had the effect of distorting the natural shape of the skull as it grew and hardened. The practice had been observed in several extant societies well into the 20th century and was in fact still done in some remote Pacific island cultures. It was generally believed that the reason for the custom was primarily aesthetic; ordinary round skulls evidently weren't considered sexy enough.

The discovery of deformed skulls on the Paracas peninsula would have been simply another footnote, but for the close proximity of another intriguing archaeological mystery. A hundred miles away in the remote Nazca desert, an ancient civilization had created hundreds of enormous geoglyphs—shapes of animals and other elaborate geometric patterns—which were so large that the only way to identify them was looking down from altitude. Some scholars even speculated that it would have been necessary to have an aerial perspective in order to execute the patterns. In the latter half of the 20th century, the so-called Nazca Lines had provided fodder for alien astronaut theorists like Erich Von Daniken, who cobbled together a patchwork hypothesis of extraterrestrial visitors posing as gods, influencing ancient cultures and facilitating the creation of everything from the pyramids of Egypt to the *moai* statues of Easter Island, with little regard for the fact that most of the cherry-picked "evidence" to support the idea was easily explained without the influence of visiting alien astronauts.

Jeremiah Stillman was not the first UFO enthusiast to connect the deformed skulls found at Paracas, which did sort of look like Hollywood's vision of an extraterrestrial creature, to the nearby Nazca lines, but he had been fortunate enough to live in the Information Age, where cable television and the Internet provided a platform for conspiracy theorists and fringe scientists to publicize their ideas without any meaningful scrutiny. Stillman had been quick to glom onto a persistent, and completely fraudulent, claim that genetic testing conducted on the Paracas skulls had yielded alien DNA. When confronted with the evidence, the "expert" had defended his position by alleging a government conspiracy to suppress the truth, a common and completely unassailable strategy for the true believers.

Yet, despite the fact that Jade found Stillman both professionally and personally distasteful, she could not completely discount the possibility that he and other alien astronaut theorists might be onto something. The Nazca Lines, which incorporated Paracas motifs, *were* unusual, and while much of what was generally believed about them was exaggerated—you didn't need to be in orbit to see them—there was no good explanation for why they had been made. Similarly, while artificial cranial deformation was well-understood, it was reasonable to ask why, throughout a thousand years of history and prehistory, people all over the world had made a conscious decision to change the shape of their children's skulls. Was it possible that they were trying to make themselves look more like their "gods"?

Jade knew from personal experience that almost anything was possible. She had seen too many strange things in her travels to dismiss anything out of hand.

It was unlikely in the extreme that she would find anything remotely resembling proof—one way or the other—in her excavation at the Wari Kayan necropolis, located on the Paracas Peninsula of Peru. It was virtually impossible to prove a negative hypothesis—the non-existence of aliens or absence of alien involvement with the Paracas culture—and even if she found something that refuted the popular theories of men like Stillman, such evidence would do little to shake the faith of the true believers. Such was not her intention however. She wasn't looking for proof any more than she was looking for fortune and glory. She was a digger, interested only in finding things that had been lost to the ages.

They made the short trek across the virtually barren sand dunes to the foot of the rocky rise known as the Cerro Colorado ridge, where the ancient Paracas had laid their dead to rest in vertical shafts cut into the summit. Several of these had been found, most pillaged by grave robbers, but several more remained unexcavated.

Jade picked her way up the sixty-foot slope, following a well-trod but unmarked route used by both archaeologists and tourists, and made her way to one of the target sites they had identified during the initial survey a week earlier. She shrugged out of her backpack, removing from it the tools of her trade—a small plastic trowel, an icepick, and a stiff bristled brush—and then squatted down beside the sand-filled shaft to commence digging into the past. Professor and Rafi moved to different sites and did the same.

She worked methodically, spooning out sand quickly without screening it. Unlike a habitation site—a former village or city ruin—there was little chance of discovering artifacts in the upper layers of fill, and in the unlikely event that she did, the plastic blade of the trowel would do little if any damage. The work proceeded quickly as she fell into a familiar rhythm, and soon she had cleared a knee-deep pit nearly five feet across. She was just about to lower herself into the hole when Rafi called out to her. She rose slowly to avoid a head-rush, and then hiked over to see what the student had discovered.

Rafi had made faster progress than she, removing several cubic feet of dirt from a shaft. He now stood in the shoulder-deep pit shining a small flashlight down at the sand underfoot. Centered in the cone of illumination was a brown-gray protrusion that she immediately recognized as the top of an elongated skull.

"Good work," she said, approvingly. "Is it human or…" She arched her eyebrows in an approximation of Stillman's trademarked enthusiasm. "Alien!"

Rafi laughed with her, then bent down and tried to wiggle the skull loose. "I'll tell you in a—"

The skull came free easier than expected, and then, as if he had pulled the plug from a drain, the sand beneath Rafi began to move, sliding into the void the removal had created. He let out a yelp of surprise, and then dropped several inches into a swirling vortex of sand.

Jade threw herself flat on the ground at the edge of the pit and thrust a hand down at the imperiled Rafi. She caught hold of his wrist, but in the instant that she did, the ground beneath his feet gave way completely. He only outweighed her by about twenty pounds, but with no time to brace herself, Jade was yanked headfirst into the pit. She scraped past the rocky edge of the excavation so quickly that she did not even have time to think about letting go of Rafi's arm, and then she was falling headfirst into the yawning blackness.

TWO

The fall lasted only a moment or two and ended with a plunge into chilly brackish water, which was, Jade supposed, preferable to slamming face first into solid rock. An instant after the splashdown, a thrashing Rafi struck her with enough force to knock the wind out of her. For a few seconds thereafter, she struggled to right herself while fighting back the panic of being unable to breathe while enveloped in near-total darkness. She groped for something to hang onto, noticed a spot of light high overhead and oriented toward it like a beacon.

"Dr. Ihara!" Rafi called from somewhere nearby. "Are you all right?"

She tried to answer but no sound came out. Then, with a gasp, she caught her breath. "Okay," she managed. "I'm okay. What the hell just happened?"

It was a rhetorical question, she knew what had happened, but Rafi answered anyway. "The shaft must have been dug right over a cave or a sinkhole. It collapsed. A cave-in."

Jade took several breaths to steady herself, and then stared up at the opening overhead. Judging by its size, she estimated it to be a good fifty feet above them. Her eyes were adjusting to the darkness, but aside from Rafi treading water nearby, there was nothing to see. The walls and ceiling of the cave remained beyond the limit of her vision.

She tilted her head toward the opening. "Professor!"

Her shout rebounded from the unseen walls with a harshness that set her teeth on edge, but a moment later, the light from the opening dimmed, partially eclipsed by Professor's silhouette. "Jade! What happened?"

Rafi started to answer but Jade cut him off. "Tell you all about it later." She grimaced as her voice echoed back, almost painfully loud. "Right now, we could use some rope."

"On it," Professor replied. "Don't run off."

"Haha. Funny guy." The light grew noticeably brighter as Professor moved away, and Jade realized that her night-vision was continuing to improve, though that was about the only bright spot, literal or otherwise, about the situation. She faced Rafi again. "I don't know about you, but I'm sick of swimming. Let's try to find somewhere high and dry."

Rafi nodded, then jerked abruptly as if he'd been stung. He whipped his head to the right and peered into the darkness. "What was that?"

Jade was instantly on guard, searching the unplumbed depths of the cave. "What? What did you see?"

Rafi did not answer immediately, but kept turning his head in fits and starts. "I... I'm not sure. I saw some... thing... moving in the corner of my eye."

"Some*thing*? Can you be a little more specific? Some*thing* bigger than a breadbox? Some*thing* with teeth and claws?"

The intern shrugged helplessly. "A shape. I thought it was a... It looked like a person, but—" He jolted again, spinning nearly halfway around. "There. Did you see it?"

Jade frowned. She had not seen anything and she was fairly certain that there was not actually anything to see, which meant that Rafi was either messing with her—unlikely, since he had not demonstrated the least inclination toward playfulness, and still insisted on calling her "Dr. Ihara"—or he was hallucinating.

Hypothermia?

The water was cold but she didn't think it was cold enough for that. Regardless, immersion was not doing their health any favors. There was a tingling in her scalp and pressure building behind her eye sockets like the beginning of a sinus headache. The sensation had been there all along, probably the result of the impact with Rafi, but it seemed to be growing in intensity. "There's nothing there, Rafi," she insisted. "Come on. Let's try to get out of the water."

He returned a tentative nod and then began dog-paddling toward her. She rolled over was about to head out in a random direction when she caught a glimpse of someone floating beside her. She snapped her head sideways but there was nobody there.

"You saw it, didn't you?" Rafi said, his tone verging toward hysteria. "There's something here. We're not alone."

"There's nothing there, Rafi. We're jumping at shadows." Even as she said it, Jade glimpsed movement again. *Damn. Now he's got me doing it.*

"They aren't shadows," Rafi insisted. "Think about where we are. This was their burial place."

"Ghosts, Rafi? Seriously?" She tried to inject an appropriate level of disdain into her voice but the chilly water and the throbbing behind her eyeballs was taking its toll. The best she could manage was a nervous quaver. "You don't believe in that stuff anymore than I do. You're just psyching yourself out."

She actually did not know what his personal beliefs on the subject of the afterlife were. Religion was a topic they had never discussed. He was an Arab-American, which meant there was a better than average chance that he was Muslim—his cultural heritage had in fact recommended him for the job, since it was extremely unlikely that he would be a sleeper agent for the religious extremists with whom Jade had tangled in the past—but up to this point, Rafi had been very private about the practice of his faith.

"I don't know what to believe. What if he's right? Stillman, I mean. What if the Paracas *were* part alien or something?"

Jade's first impulse was to scoff, but two things stopped her: the terror in the young man's voice, and the presence of a very human-looking shape in the periphery of her vision. She resisted the urge to look directly at it, and to her astonishment, it remained there, hovering at the edge of her perceptions.

She didn't know if it was a ghost, or an alien, or the ghost of an alien, but something was definitely there.

No, she told herself. *There's nothing there. You know better.*

"Ignore them," she told Rafi. "They haven't done anything to hurt us. Maybe they don't even know that we're here. Maybe they're just an echo of something that happened in the past."

She felt foolish talking about the hallucinations—that was what they were, she decided, what they had to be—as if they were something real, but her subconscious mind refused to accept that they were not.

"Yes." Rafi grasped at the explanation eagerly. "That makes sense."

Jade did not think it made a lick of sense, but if it was enough to get her young companion moving, that was good enough. She began swimming again, paddling away from the scant light filtering down into the cave, and into its dark unknown depths. Despite the fact that everything else was shrouded in impenetrable murk, the shapes floating at the corner of her eye remained every bit as vivid, which meant that they were almost certainly some kind of optical illusion—not a true hallucination, but something else, like the visual aura from a migraine or phosphenes, the phenomenon more commonly known as "seeing stars." The fact that both she and Rafi were seeing them, not to mention the sudden onset of her increasingly intense headache, might indicate an environmental factor—toxic gas or fungal spores in the air—which meant it was imperative that they find a way out as soon as possible.

"Ignore them," she said again. "Swim."

She struck out again, stroking and kicking into the shadowed unknown. The ghost images remained with her, but she did her best to put what she was seeing out of her mind. She succeeded only when one outstretched hand brushed against a slick wet but very solid wall of stone.

"Found something!"

Rafi did not answer but she could hear the splash of his strokes, still several feet behind her. She could not see him but the ghosts were still there, haunting the edge of her vision.

She explored the wall with both hands. It was unnaturally smooth, almost certainly the product of human artifice. This was no sinkhole, but a man-made underground chamber, probably a burial crypt used by the Paracas.

Despite the dire circumstances, Jade felt a surge of excitement at the unexpected discovery. She had not dared to hope to find anything like this.

"A way out?" gasped Rafi coming alongside her.

"No. Not yet, at least." She moved along the wall and as she did, her knees bumped against it. The wall was not a sheer vertical surface, but curved toward her like the inside of a bowl.

Curiouser and curiouser, as Alice might say, she thought. But the only thing that mattered now was getting out.

"This is salt water," Rafi said. "This cave must connect to the ocean."

Jade had already come to a similar conclusion, but they were at least half a mile from shore. If there was a tunnel or passage, and if by some miracle it was big enough to accommodate them, it would almost certainly be completely inundated.

One 'if' at a time.

She filled her lungs with air and then ducked her head under the water, sliding along the convex wall. Just a few feet below the surface, she encountered loose debris—pieces of rock, possibly dislodged in the collapse that had deposited her and Rafi in the chamber.

Something flashed just at the limit of her field of vision. Her first thought was that the ghosts had followed her underwater, except that this time when she involuntarily turned her head to look the specter did not disappear. A faint yellow glow was emanating from the floor of the chamber.

It was Rafi's flashlight, still shining despite being immersed in sea water and half-buried under the rock fall. She grasped hold of it and was rewarded with a bright shaft of yellow illumination that revealed the true dimensions of the chamber.

And something else. An opening, as smooth and round as the chamber walls. She kicked toward it and thrust the hand with the flashlight into its depths. The light revealed a smooth borehole that went on well beyond the reach of her eyes.

A long swim, she thought.

Maybe too long. Professor would be back with a rope. The smart thing to do was stay put and wait to be rescued.

She ducked her head inside and swam forward.

Just a little ways, she promised herself. As far as she could go before her lungs demanded she head back to take another breath.

The distinctive sound of a splash reached her ears. There was an air pocket above her. She surfaced, letting her breath out slowly while allowing the unfamiliar atmosphere to waft into her nostrils. It smelled like the ocean.

As she breathed in, cautiously at first, then eagerly, she surveyed her new environment. The air pocket was not an isolated bubble but occupied the ceiling of the passage, stretching out as far as she could see.

Better, she thought. There was no guarantee that this route would not lead to an impassable dead end but there was air to breathe and turning back was always an option.

She filled her lungs again, and dove beneath the surface, kicking hard to reach the chamber where Rafi waited. She broke the surface and found the shivering student ducking away from an invisible assault.

The ghosts.

She had almost forgotten about them, but almost from the moment her head broke the water they were there again, lurking just out of view. Worse, the pain behind her eyes, which she now realized had abated somewhat during her initial exploration of the passage, returned with a vengeance.

It's definitely something about this chamber, she thought. *And whatever it is, I don't want to spend another second here.*

"Rafi! Come on. This way. We're getting out of here." She seized hold of his arm and pointed down, signaling for him to follow.

A few seconds later, they were both in the air pocket. The pain in her skull immediately relented and the hallucinations ceased as well. Jade did not pause to offer an explanation. Instead, she began immediately paddling down the length of the tunnel. Rafi followed along without question but it was plainly obvious that the change of scenery had energized him.

She swam the length of the passage, more than a hundred yards, noticing all the while that the ceiling overhead was getting closer. Her first thought was the passage was sloping down, but when there was just six-inches of air above her, she realized what was actually happening. The water level was rising with the tide. In a few more minutes, the tunnel would be completely filled and the precious air pocket would be gone.

Crap.

"Rafi! Big breaths!" She gulped in air, filling her lungs to their full and rarely used capacity. Her body rose until she was nearly horizontal, her back scraping against the smooth ceiling. "Stay close," she called, letting the breath out and immediately sinking back. "And whatever you do, don't stop swimming."

She took another deep inhalation and then plunged downward, paddling and stroking furiously.

The flashlight revealed the long, smooth-bore tunnel, as straight and perfect as a length of steel pipe, seemingly without end. Her strokes felt sluggish, the effect of the incoming tide pushing against her like a current, but she did not relent.

A faint spasm in her diaphragm reminded her of the need to breathe. She ignored it but knew it was only the first of many to come. Before long, her lungs would begin to burn from the buildup of too much carbon dioxide, and while she knew that she was capable of pushing through even that discomfort, Rafi did not have her experience or training. If she was feeling it, then he was probably already starting to panic.

She did not look back. Salvation, if any existed at all, lay ahead. The exchange of tide water strongly suggested an outlet to the ocean, but how far away that outlet was and whether it would be large enough to let them through were variables beyond her control.

In the glow of the flashlight, she spotted something that gave her reason for hope. The floor and walls of the tunnel were dotted with sea life—anemones and mollusks—just a few here and there at first, but increasing into a veritable ecosystem, supplied with nutrients by the relentless ebb and flow of the tides.

The light suddenly revealed a barrier directly ahead, filling the tunnel from top to bottom. Before she could process what she was seeing, much less even think about slowing, Jade collided with the obstacle which was not a solid mass but rather a collection of fibrous stalks, like slimy ferns. Her momentum carried her through and she found herself abruptly enfolded in a literal sea of green. Daylight, almost intensely bright after the darkness of the submerged passage, filtered down through the water to reveal the blurry tidal zone.

Jade swam for the light, kicking furiously even as her lungs screamed for the fresh air that she knew lay just a few more feet above. The light grew brighter and the water warmer as she neared the surface which remained maddeningly out of reach for several seconds, and then, as if shot from an undersea cannon, she burst through.

For a moment, all she could think about was sucking in fresh air, but after the burning sensation in her chest began to abate, she began to orient herself. An incoming swell lifted her high enough to see the white water frothing on the golden beach and just beyond that, she could make out the museum, a few parked vehicles, and a small cluster of people gathered in front of the structure. Further away rose the rocky ridge of the Cerro Colorado, and somewhere up there, Professor was probably trying to figure out what had happened to them.

"Rafi!" She spun around in the water, calling out and searching for him, but there was no sign of the young intern.

She rotated forward and thrust her head once more beneath the water. Nothing moved in the blurry foreground. Rafi was still in the tunnel.

She kicked hard, clawing back into the depths. A brown

smudge of disturbed silt marked the spot where she had broken through the kelp. Reaching it was a Sisyphusian struggle against buoyancy but she did not give up. After what seemed an eternity, she caught hold of the seaweed and pulled herself into the concealed opening.

Rafi floated motionless, fifty feet away. Jade did not hesitate to swim toward him. That he had drowned was plainly obvious, but that did not mean he was beyond resuscitation. Regardless, she was not going to leave him behind.

As soon as she reached him, she grasped his head in her hands and pulled his face close, pressing her lips to his, exhaling a breath into his mouth. She hoped that would be enough to bring him back, but the air simply bubbled back out, pooling on the ceiling of the tunnel like droplets of quicksilver.

She let go of his head and grabbed the back of his shirt collar instead, dragging him along as she began kicking back toward the mouth of the tunnel. His dead weight slowed her down and before she could reach that intermediate goal, the primal urge to breathe seized her once more, tearing at her lungs like a desperate animal caught in a snare. She fought back, using every trick she knew to fool her nervous system, blundered through the mass of kelp blocking the tunnel and clawed her way back to the surface.

As soon as she broke through, she exhaled another rescue breath into Rafi's mouth, then rolled him over and commenced a one-handed backstroke toward shore. The incoming tide which had nearly killed her in the tunnel now worked in her favor, supplying added impetus to her efforts. Lazy swells propelled her ever closer, but in the sheltered bay on the eastern shore of the peninsula there were no breakers to carry them into shore. She kept swimming until, at long last, she felt the coarse sand bumping against her knees.

Her arrival went unnoticed by the crowd gathered in front of the museum more than five hundred yards away. She tried to call for help but her croaked supplication was barely loud enough for her to hear it over the low murmur of the sea, so she abandoned the effort and turned her full attention to Rafi, dragging him up above the tide line. As soon as there was relatively solid ground beneath her, she started chest compressions.

The next few minutes were a blur. Over the years, she had taken more first-aid and lifeguard classes than she could count but this was the first time she had ever put what she had been taught to use in a real world situation. She had no idea if she was doing it right. What was the ratio of rescue breaths to compressions? Was his airway clear?

She readjusted his head, tilting his chin up, and tried another breath. She felt it go in and then suddenly Rafi convulsed, vomiting a geyser of lukewarm water into her face. She flinched back in surprise and then sagged in relief as Rafi began coughing and retching, and most importantly, breathing again.

Exhaustion crashed over her but she knew her task was not yet finished. She knelt beside him and rolled him onto his side. "I'm going for help. You're going to be okay."

Though still coughing violently, Rafi nodded and she saw the gratitude in his eyes. She stood, fought through the momentary dizziness and lurched toward the museum, waving her arms and shouting as she ran.

Her efforts finally yielded the desired results. Someone noticed her, and then one by one, heads began to turn and the bubble burst. She recognized many of the faces rushing toward her, support crew for the dig, the production crew brandishing their cameras and equipment, but Professor was not among them.

Of course not. He's up on the ridge trying to save me. Nevertheless, his absence left her feeling hollow inside. She desperately wanted him with her.

She froze in mid-step as she recognized another face, not someone from the dig, but someone from the past, someone she had hoped never to see again.

Running toward her, or more accurately waddling, red-faced and panting from the exertion, was the corpulent form of Gerald Roche.

Her mind immediately flashed back to her first and only encounter with the rotund British conspiracy theorist and occult enthusiast. Eight months earlier, when she had been tracking down a lead involving the famed Elizabethan era astrologer John Dee. She had thought to consult with Roche, a Dee expert and collector, but the situation had spiraled out of control, with Roche accusing Jade of trying to steal an object from his collection—Dee's Shew Stone, a crystal ball used for divination—and subsequently trying to kill her. The fact that she actually had ended up stealing the Shew Stone probably didn't help matters.

Damn it! How did he find me?

All thoughts of helping Rafi or seeing Professor slipped from her mind. She turned on her heel, looking for an escape route. Surely he wouldn't try anything in front of a crowd, with cameras rolling.

But why else would he come here?

She was still debating the best escape route—seek refuge in the crowd or make a run for it—when Roche summoned up the breath to call out to her.

"Dr. Ihara! Please. It's urgent that I speak with you!"

THREE

Several hours would pass before Roche got the opportunity to further elaborate. Jade's first priority was ensuring that Rafi received medical attention which involved an ambulance ride to the nearby city of Pisco where the doctor credited her for saving the young man's life and indicated that he would make a full recovery with no attendant brain damage. The news was welcome though not completely unexpected since Rafi had been completely lucid by the time she returned to him on the beach. The only reason she had insisted on taking him to the hospital was to put a little space between herself and her unexpected visitor.

In all the confusion, she almost completely forgot about the strange crypt under the Cerro Colorado and what she had seen and felt there.

Had any of it been real?

Aside from declaring the dig site a hazard area, due to the possibility of further collapse, she had revealed nothing about what had transpired in the spherical chamber. It definitely was not something she wanted the camera crew or Jeremiah Stillman to know about, but she had hoped to get Professor's level-headed perspective on what had happened. Unfortunately, Roche's unexpected arrival had him preoccupied as well.

It was for the best. Professor would just laugh at her and dismiss it as a hallucination, and that was probably all it was.

"I don't think he's here looking for trouble," Professor announced as he joined her in the waiting room outside the hospital ward. He had spent the better part an hour working the phones, trying to trace Roche's movements and divine his intentions.

"Well, what does he want?" The question came out more harshly than she had intended.

Professor shrugged and spread his hands. "I think the only way you're going to figure that out is by talking to him."

"Should I?"

He stared at her for a long time before answering. "Regardless of whether or not you should, I think you probably will. You're too curious to just walk away."

"Am I that predictable?"

"'Predictable' isn't a word I would normally associate with you," he replied with a grin. "But in this case, yes."

"I really hate you sometimes."

"Only sometimes?" The grin slipped away. "He'll only meet with you at the Paracas Museum. He says it's the only place he feels safe."

"He feels safe?" She rolled her eyes.

"You don't need me to tell you that he's paranoid. There's no record of him arriving in the country, which means he either bribed someone or used a forged passport. Probably both. He's definitely trying to move under the radar."

"It didn't look to me like he was trying to be inconspicuous at the museum. There were cameras everywhere."

Professor shrugged. "He'll be long gone before any of the footage shot today airs. He might be paranoid, but he's still a celebrity. He thrives on attention."

Prior to the matter of the Shew Stone, Jade had never heard of Gerald Roche, but she had no difficulty learning all there was to know about the man. A former Minister of Parliament, Roche had achieved notoriety with his astonishing claim that all of reality was a holographic computer simulation, and that world leaders and celebrities were in fact inhuman creatures—he called them "Changelings"—manipulating global events and enslaving humanity. But for his already well-established wealth and influence, Roche would almost certainly have been institutionalized, but instead, he parlayed his bizarre worldview into a multi-media empire—with a radio talk-show and a series of books that delved deep into the changeling conspiracy.

In spite of the sheer lunacy of his ideas, he enjoyed widespread support from a cross-section of British society, even from some intellectuals who claimed that the Changelings were not meant to be taken literally, but were symbolic of the pervasive influence of banks and multi-national corporations in a climate of globalism. Some of his supporters cited recent discoveries in the field of physics as proof that Roche was not far off the mark in asserting that reality was deterministic in nature, playing out like an extraordinarily complex but utterly mathematical computer program.

Among people like Jeremiah Stillman and fans of the *Alien Explorers* television series, Gerald Roche was a true prophet—maybe even a god—so it was no surprise that he felt right at home surrounded by his acolytes at the museum. He was not, as far as Jade knew, an alien astronaut theorist—in his world, there were no aliens, just renegade computer programs—but the true believers tended to draw inspiration from all across the spectrum of possibilities, turning contradictions into connections with reckless abandon. The only constant in their world was the pervasive conspiracy to hide the truth and silence those who would reveal it.

"What about my safety?" she said, with more than a little sarcasm. Although Roche had surprised her by showing up without warning, she was not scared of him in the least.

"Like I said, I don't think he wants trouble. He obviously knew where to find you. If he wanted to hurt you, he could have hired someone."

"That's not his style." Jade recalled her first meeting with Roche, which had taken place in Roche's London flat. He had invited her in like a spider welcoming a fly into its web. "He likes to play games."

"You can always tell him to get lost."

She sighed. "No. You're right. I am curious. Besides, I beat him once. I can do it again."

"Like I said. Predictable."

There were no cameras waiting for them at the museum. In fact, there was only one car in the parking lot when they pulled up—a black Land Rover almost identical to the rented vehicle Jade and Professor were riding in—and no sign of the production company or anyone else outside the squat little concrete structure, save for a single burly man guarding the museum door. He wore a black suit, cut loose to accommodate his bulging biceps. Jade did not recognize the man, but it was safe to assume that he was Roche's bodyguard.

"Guy looks like Randy Couture," Professor observed as they strolled toward the entrance.

"Who?"

"Never mind."

The man took a step forward as if to block their passage. "Just her."

"Looks like Couture," Professor amended, "but sounds like Statham. You're like the whole cast of the Expendables all rolled into one."

Jade flashed him a quizzical look then turned to the bodyguard. "I'm not going in there without him."

The big man shook his head. "Mr. Roche's orders."

Jade stared up at him for a moment then shrugged and started to turn away, but Roche's voice issued from beyond the door. "Let them in, Jonathan."

"That's right, Jonathan," Professor taunted. "Let us in."

The surly bodyguard moved out of the way without comment. As Jade stepped toward the door, she leaned close to Professor. "What the hell was that about? You channeling Bones or something?"

"Bones"—Uriah Bonebrake—was one of Professor's former SEAL swim buddies, and had a terminal case of "no filter" syndrome. A hulking six-feet five-inches, Bones could say whatever he pleased—and frequently did. Professor may not have been as physically imposing as Bones, but he was no pushover. Generally speaking though, he kept a low profile. Testosterone-fueled posturing was definitely not his style.

"Just testing a hypothesis," Professor whispered, throwing a faint nod in the direction of the bodyguard. "I pushed and he didn't push back. The guy's a pro."

"Why does that matter?"

"I'm not sure yet, but if he's hiring former military for protection, maybe your old pal Roche isn't just paranoid after all."

Roche was waiting for them inside.

"Where'd everyone go?" Jade asked him.

"I sent them away," Roche said

"You sent them away? What, you just asked nicely?"

"I have a great deal of influence, both with the museum and the producers of *Alien Explorers*."

Roche sounded almost apologetic. Jade searched his face for some hint of treachery but saw none of the arrogance she recalled from their first meeting. Roche looked truly frightened. He stared at Professor warily for a moment before turning to Jade. "Do you trust him?"

It was an odd question, but then Roche was nothing if not odd. "Of course," she replied.

"How long have you known him?"

"A few years. Why?"

Roche scrutinized Professor's face again. "Ask him a question, something about your first meeting that no one else would know."

"Seriously?" Jade put her hands on her hips. "I don't have time for this. Get to the point or I'm out of here."

Roche made no effort to hide his irritation. "This *is* the point, Dr. Ihara. You have no idea what they are capable of. I need an assurance."

"They?"

"The Changelings. They're here. They're everywhere. Do you think what happened to you this morning was a coincidence?"

"No. I think it was an accident."

Roche laughed harshly. "There are no accidents, Dr. Ihara. No coincidences."

"It's okay, Jade" Professor said. "Now *I'm* curious. Ask

me something."

Jade shook her head. She was done playing Roche's game. "I said, I trust him. Now, what do you want?"

Roche's nostrils flared but then he made a dismissive gesture. "I suppose it doesn't matter. *They* already know what I'm about to tell you."

Instead of answering her question however, Roche turned and headed further into the museum, the tacit implication that she should follow. He made his way to a private office and settled wearily into the chair behind a desk cluttered with papers and a scattering of Paracas artifacts. An elongated skull rested on one corner, looking more like a cheap paperweight than the remains of a once-living human being. Roche drummed his fingers on the desktop as if trying to organize his thoughts, then looked up at Jade. "You found something today, didn't you?"

"If you call a sinkhole and an underground tidal cave 'something,' then yes."

"That's all you found?"

Jade managed, with an effort, to keep her face a neutral mask.

He knows about the ghosts. Somehow, he knows.

She glanced over at Professor, wondering how much to reveal. "Pretty much. I haven't had time to conduct a survey. There's no evidence that the Paracas used the sinkhole or even knew about it." She thought about the smooth walls of the chamber and the precision of the tunnel leading out into the bay, and knew that was not strictly true. "But even if they did, I would imagine that two thousand years of immersion in salt water would have destroyed anything they might have left." She paused a beat. "What's your interest? This doesn't seem like your usual thing."

"Everything is connected, Dr. Ihara. The Changelings have been among us longer than all of recorded history. However, I will confess to a particular interest in the Paracas and Nazca cultures."

"Ah. Let me guess. The skulls aren't aliens, they're Changelings."

Roche gave a patient smile. "I took the name 'Changeling' from faerie mythology. Are you familiar with it? According to the legend, the faeries would sometimes steal human infants from their cradle and leave a fae shape-shifter child behind in its place, like a sort of supernatural sleeper agent. How would you know if your child had been taken?"

He reached out and let his hand caress the oblong skull resting on the desk. "I believe the Paracas—and many other civilizations that practice extreme body modification techniques—did so as a way of ensuring the humanity of their children. The Changelings might be able to alter their appearance, but bone structure would be more of a challenge."

He raised his eyes to Jade. "That's my hypothesis in any case, but I'm no expert on American cultures. That's why I hired you."

"*You* hired me?"

"My foundation is sponsoring your work here."

Jade shot Professor an accusing glance. "Is that true?" It had been his job to vet any potential employers to ensure that a job offer was not some kind of trap to lure her into the open. "How did you miss that?"

"My involvement in the foundation is a closely guarded secret," Roche went on before Professor could respond. "For my own safety. If they knew…" He shook his head and left the ominous statement hanging. "I wanted you here, Dr. Ihara, because despite the unpleasantness of our previous encounter, I knew that you were the one person I could trust."

"You're not making any sense, though I suppose that's par for the course with you. Oh, by the way, I quit."

"Dr. Ihara, please hear me out." The fear she had noticed earlier in his eyes was back. "The noose is tightening. I may not…" He took a deep breath. "I may not survive this. I have to tell someone."

Professor laid a hand on her arm. "Jade, let's hear what he has to say. What could it hurt?"

A dozen rejoinders popped into her head but she knew

Professor was right. The curiosity that had brought her to this meeting remained unsatisfied. "Fine." She stabbed an emphatic finger at Roche. "But *I* don't trust *you*."

Roche gave her a relieved smile as if distrust was her most compelling personality trait. He sat up straighter. "Have you ever heard of Phantom Time?"

Jade almost groaned aloud. "Phantom time?"

"Actually," Professor said, almost before Jade had finished. "I have."

She threw him a sidelong glance. "Why am I not surprised?"

Long before finishing his first PhD, Professor had earned his nickname with his almost encyclopedic knowledge of trivia.

But still…phantom time?

"Is it as bad as it sounds?" she asked. "Because it sounds like the name of a really bad science fiction movie."

"Even worse," he replied. "The Phantom Time hypothesis is a conspiracy theory first advanced by Herbert Illig and Hans-Ulirch Niemitz, which—in very broad terms—posits that during the early Middle Ages, the Church added an extra three hundred years to the calendar."

Jade's forehead creased in a frown. "What do you mean by 'added'?"

"Four centuries after the conversion of Constantine to Christianity," Roche explained, "and about seven centuries after Christ was thought to have walked the earth, the Holy Roman Emperor Otto II, along with Pope Sylvester II and the Byzantine Emperor Constantine VII, made a pact to change the calendar system in such a way that their respective reigns would coincide with the end of the millennium."

"Like a kid tearing out pages in a calendar in the belief that he can make Christmas come sooner," Professor said.

"The deception endures to this day," Roche went on. "You see, it is not actually the 21st century AD, but rather the 18th."

Jade gaped at him. "People actually believe that?"

"Not nearly enough people," Roche said, gravely. "Most have been completely hoodwinked by the great hoax."

"Phantom Time is the hoax," Professor countered. "The entire hypothesis rests on an alleged error during the change from the Julian calendar to the Gregorian calendar in the year 1582."

"Oh," Jade said. "Well, that clears everything up."

"According to the Julian system," Professor continued, "the solar year was 365.25 days long."

"That's why we have a leap year every four years."

"Right, but the solar year is actually 365.2425 days long. I know it sounds like a meaningless difference, and practically speaking, it is. About ten minutes a year. But over the course of a few hundred years, it adds up."

"The Julian Calendar was introduced in the year 46 BC," Roche said. "The error was known even then, but it was thought too insignificant to correct. Ordinary people lived by the turning of the seasons, not some arbitrary system of time-keeping. The Church however was very concerned with dates since it was necessary for Easter to coincide with the vernal equinox, so Pope Gregory instituted the calendar system we use today, which corrects the problem by skipping a leap year at the turn of each century, except in years divisible by 400."

"Which is why we had a leap year in 2000," Professor supplied.

"Instead of twenty-five leap years per century, there would be ninety-seven leap years in every four hundred year period. However, to adjust for errors in the preceding years, it was necessary to delete the days that had been inadvertently added over the course of the centuries, so Thursday, October 4, 1582 was followed by Friday October 15, 1582."

"That part really happened," Professor said. "It's well documented in history. Unlike the so-called Phantom Time conspiracy."

"The Gregorian calendar adjustment accounted for ten extra days," Roche said, ignoring the barb as he closed in on the crux of his argument. "Counting forward from 46 BC, there should have been 394 leap years, but under the Julian calendar, there were 407. But if it was really the year 1582, the correction should have been thirteen days. Gregory knew this, and he knew what his predecessors had done. That's why he only moved the calendar forward ten days. He knew it was really the year 1183."

Roche delivered this pronouncement with such gravity that Jade almost felt guilty for not caring.

"See what I mean," Professor said. "It's pretty thin soup."

"Look, this is really interesting," Jade said, openly disingenuous. "But it seems like something that should be pretty easy to prove or disprove."

"There is surprisingly little physical evidence *against* the hypothesis," Roche said. "The Church was the accepted time-keeping authority in its day. The historical record relies heavily upon medieval chronicles, which were fabricated for the sole purpose of reinforcing the deception. Many of them, such as the so-called contemporary accounts of Charlemagne, are little more than romantic fiction, but scholars do not question their veracity. To do so would undermine everything we think we know."

Asserting that all evidence refuting a viewpoint was manufactured and proof of a conspiracy was a common defensive tactic among the true believers, but as Roche spoke, it finally occurred to Jade that the man actually believed what he was telling her.

"Hold on," she said. "You're saying that everything that happened between 600 and 900 was just made up?"

"That's what he's saying," Professor said. "Charlemagne, the beginning of the Holy Roman Empire, Muhammed and the rise of Islam, the Tang Dynasty in China—"

"Fiction," Roche insisted. "Every bit of it. Tug a loose string and the web of lies unravels."

Jade raised a hand. "Just for argument's sake, let's say you're right. What difference does it make?" *And why on earth,* she did not add, *do you think I would care?*

"Don't you see?" Roche stared at her as frustrated that she could not see something so obvious. "If those three hundred years never happened, then the foundation of our entire world is built on a lie."

"So? A lot of people believe things that have been scientifically disproven."

"And many of them are willing to kill to protect those beliefs," Roche insisted.

Jade realized he was not talking about wars fought over religion but rather a much more immediate threat. "You think people are after you because of this?"

"Phantom Time is a fringe theory," Professor added, "but it's hardly a secret. The 'truth' if you want to call it that, is already out there."

"There's more going on than anyone suspects," Roche insisted. "Illig may have uncovered the truth about the conspiracy, but he was wrong about the motive behind the Phantom Time adjustment. It wasn't just to fool the world into thinking the millennium was at hand. There was a much darker purpose at work. It was my intention to explain everything in my next book, but there are powerful forces working to keep the truth from being revealed. They murdered my publisher to prevent the book from being released."

"Murdered?" Jade asked. Paranoia was one thing, but if Roche's publisher had actually been the victim of foul play, it might confirm everything he had just said. On the other hand, even a mysterious or unexpected death might turn out to be a coincidence. True believers like Roche were adept at turning such coincidences into proof of a conspiracy. "By the Changelings?"

Roche ducked his head as if the question had been a physical assault. "Possibly. Ultimately, I'm sure they are the puppet masters, pulling the strings of their unwitting agents."

Professor leaned forward. "Why bring this to Jade? Are you looking for protection?"

"Protection?" Roche murmured. A sad smile touched his lips. "Truth is the only protection. But knowing the truth is not the same as proving it. That is where you can help."

Jade made no attempt to hide her skepticism. "You think I can find proof that Phantom Time is real?"

"No. You can find—" A loud bang from outside the room cut him off in mid-sentence. It might have been a car backfiring or a firecracker thrown by a prankster, but Jade knew it was neither.

"That was a gun." Professor instantly went on the defensive, seizing hold of Jade's arm and pulling her down. She needed no further urging, scrambling around the end of the desk, seeking cover behind it with Professor right behind her, but while her body knew what to do, her mind was reeling.

This can't be happening.

It was not the threat of danger that tripped her up. She had been shot at before. Rather, her denial stemmed from the fact that this apparent attack seemed to validate Roche's paranoia, and by extension, his insane theories, and that was a big pill to swallow.

Roche reacted as if he had been rehearsing for just such a scenario. He slid from his chair, dropping to his knees behind the desk, and lowered his bulk so that only his eyes and the top of his head were visible above it, a small semi-automatic pistol gripped in his pudgy hand.

The door to the office swung open and Jade's already overtaxed brain did a back-flip as she instantly recognized the man framed in the doorway.

"Rafi?"

Roche raised up just enough to stab his pistol in Rafi's direction but he pulled the trigger prematurely. The gun barked, the small room amplifying the noise of the report, but the bullet plowed harmlessly into the wall two feet to the right of the intended target. Jade's ears rang with the noise of the shot and her nostrils were filled with the sulfur smell of burnt gunpowder. Before Roche could correct his aim and loose another shot, Rafi raised the gun in his right hand, calmly took aim and fired.

FOUR

The bullet punched into Roche's chest, knocking him back. Jade gave an involuntary—and inaudible—yelp, but Professor pushed her aside and dove for the pistol that had fallen from Roche's grasp. Faster than Jade's eyes could follow, he crawled around the end of the desk and returned fire.

Jade's senses were assaulted by the roar of gunfire and the sound of bullets striking the wall behind her and the heavy wooden panels of the desk. Even though none of the shots found her, each impact reverberated through her like a punch to the gut. A haze of sulfur fumes and wood smoke curled in the air overhead, further obscuring her view of the gun battle, and a blizzard of splinters stung her face, forcing her to seek refuge behind Roche's body. In the instant that she did, the tumult ceased. She looked up just in time to see a crouching Professor disappear around the end of the desk, taking off in pursuit of—

Rafi?

—the gunman.

"Wait!" She started after Professor, but a hand gripped her forearm, restraining her. It was Roche.

He was still alive, but only just. The shadow of death, a gray pallor, was on him and in his wild eyes, Jade could see that he knew it. His lips moved, a torrent of blood spilling out as he tried to form words.

"Fuuuuhhhh…" She could not hear what he said through the ringing in her ears, but the way his teeth and lips came together, she could only assume he was wasting his final breath on a curse. "Eeewww."

His pupils, sharpened to pinpoints by pain, abruptly lost focus, and Jade knew he was gone.

Murdered.

Rafi, the young man she had saved from drowning earlier in the day, someone with whom she had broken bread and shared jokes, had just gunned down a man in cold blood, and tried to kill her as well.

Maybe I didn't know him as well as I thought.

She pulled free of Roche's deathgrip and scrambled after Professor. She caught up to him just as he was preparing to venture through the exit. His eyes met hers, just for a moment, but long enough for her to divine what he was thinking.

The killer had been in their midst, and Professor blamed himself. Despite all his precautions, a deadly assassin had insinuated himself into their circle, waiting for the moment to strike.

Yet, Rafi had killed Roche first, almost as if he had been lying in wait for the conspiracy theorist. But how could he have even known Roche would visit her? It didn't add up, which she assumed was why Professor was giving chase. Who was Rafi working for? The Dominion? The Changelings?

A body—Jonathan, Roche's hulking bodyguard—lay sprawled across the exit, blood leaking from the precise hole drilled into his forehead. Just beyond, a car—a silver sedan that had not been there when they had arrived—peeled out of the parking area in a cloud of dust,

"Stay here," Professor growled, and then leapt over the corpse and sprinted toward their parked Land Rover.

"Like hell," Jade muttered and bounded after him.

Professor shot her an irritated glance but knew better than to argue. As he opened the driver's side door, Jade was right behind him. "Let me drive. You shoot."

"Shoot what?" he retorted, displaying the pistol he had taken from Roche. The slide was locked back, an indication that Professor had already fired out every round in the magazine. He tossed it onto the passenger seat and then slid behind the wheel and slotted the key into the ignition.

Jade hastened around the front of the vehicle, more than a little worried that Professor would try to leave her behind. She climbed inside as the engine turned over, and barely had time to close the door before the Rover began to move. Professor stomped the gas pedal and the tires threw up a shower of sand and gravel. Though the fleeing car had a lead of only a few hundred yards, it had reached the paved highway and was pulling away. The Rover jounced down the dirt access road, but once the wheels reached pavement, it took off like a rocket. Jade stole a look at the speedometer and saw the needle creeping toward 150 Km/h—almost a hundred miles per hour.

She shifted to the side and wriggled the spent pistol out from under her. The metal was hot to the touch. "So what are we going to do if we catch him?"

"Bluff." Without taking his eyes off the road, Professor reached over and worked the pistol's slide release one-handed. The gun shuddered in Jade's grip as the spring-loaded mechanism shot forward, giving the appearance that the weapon was ready to fire. "Judging by how many rounds he fired, he's probably out, too."

"And if he has more bullets?"

Professor shrugged. "He ran. If he had the ammo, he would have stayed to finish us."

"You're betting our lives on that."

"I told you to stay behind."

Jade could not argue with that so she changed the subject. "Rafi. Damn. Why do you think he did it?"

"First thing I'm going to ask him."

Jade had questions of her own, and felt a burning need to ask them, if only to make sense of the insanity she had just witnessed, but before she could articulate her thoughts, the Rover began to shudder as Professor pegged the speedometer. She decided to let him focus all his attention of the task of driving. The town of Paracas was only two miles away along a lightly traveled road that curved gently as it followed the shoreline, but at their current speed, every bump in the pavement was amplified, every mistake potentially fatal. Jade was glad that Professor had refused to let her drive; his military experience had included training in tactical driving, and those lessons were paying off. They were starting to close the gap. Unfortunately, they were also approaching a populated area.

The fleeing car abruptly vanished into a smudge of brown as Rafi, without any warning and seemingly without reason veered off the highway and out onto the open sand.

"What the hell is he doing?" Professor let his foot off the accelerator, allowing engine compression to slow them down. Even so, they were still pushing ninety Km/h when they reached the edge of the dust cloud. Jade felt herself thrown forward as Professor applied the brakes, further reducing their speed, as he steered to the left in pursuit of the barely discernible dot trailing a plume of dust. Rafi seemed to be heading straight for the bay.

The pillar of dust seemed to stall at the water's edge, momentarily eclipsing Jade's view of their quarry, but she knew what had happened. Rafi had stopped the car. Professor put on the brakes and steered to the right, coming to a full stop fifty yards away.

There was a loud crack as something slammed into one of the Rover's fenders. Jade did not have to hear the gun's report to know that it had been a bullet.

"Down!" Professor shouted, leaning over the center console and forcing Jade's head down below the dashboard. The noise sounded again and the driver's side window went opaque as a round struck the safety glass, fracturing it into a thousand tiny beads.

"Out of ammo, yeah?" Jade said. She grimaced, as much a response to having unconsciously slipped into Pidgin, which made her sound remarkably like her mother, as to their current situation.

Professor ignored the accusation and reached past her, working the lever to open Jade's door. "Stay here," he said as he started to crawl over her. "I'm going to try to flank him."

"Are you serious?" Jade pushed him back. "Just drive away."

"We might not get another chance."

"Another chance to what? Get killed?"

"I'd like to know who he's—"

Before Professor could finish the sentence, something

like the fist of God slammed into the Rover and Jade's world dissolved into darkness.

FIVE

In the instant that he jolted back to consciousness, Professor knew what had happened. He had been in close proximity to enough explosions to recognize the signs even without raising his head. The overpressure wave had pulverized the Land Rover's windows and sucked the air out of the interior, which more than anything had probably contributed to the black out.

"Jade?" He knew he was shouting, but all he could hear was a persistent ringing sound inside his head.

He could feel her beneath him, still breathing but not moving. Unconscious. Possibly concussed, but more than likely just stunned. He lifted up a little, brushing away particles of safety glass that looked like a shower of diamonds, and stared out at the still burning wreckage of the car they had been chasing. The sedan looked like it had been turned inside out.

Professor did a quick check in every direction to make sure that no one was creeping up from behind, and then turned his attention back to Jade. He shook her gently. "Jade. Wake up!"

She stirred and then came awake with a start. Her lips moved, a question. *What just happened?*

He faced her squarely so she would be able to read his lips. "Gas tank explosion."

Her forehead creased in confusion. *Rafi?*

"Don't know." He laid a hand on her shoulder. "Stay here."

He doubted that she would heed his admonition, but at least this way, if something happened, she would have only herself to blame. It was the kind of lesson that only experience could teach.

He twisted around and worked the door lever, but the door did not budge. He tried shouldering it open, but the explosion had mangled the door and the surrounding frame and nothing less than the Jaws of Life would get it open.

Professor abandoned the effort and instead squirmed through the hole where the window had been.

Heat from the burning car buffeted his face, prompting him to raise a shielding hand to his eyes. There was little chance of a secondary explosion; as he had surmised, the gas tank had been the source of the explosion, though what had triggered the detonation was anyone's guess. He had not fired a single round outside the museum which strongly suggested that Rafi himself had caused the explosion, probably by shooting into the tank. That explained the what, but not the why.

His first thought was that the killer might have been trying to use the exploding car as a diversion to cover his escape or possibly some kind of flanking attack, but if that had been Rafi's plan, it had ended disastrously. A smoldering body lay twenty feet beyond the wreckage. His clothing had been almost completely burned away, and his skin had not fared much better, but there was enough left for Professor to recognize the corpse as the young intern that had worked alongside him only a few hours before.

He felt Jade's hand on his arm, felt her shudder in horror as she glimpsed the burned remains. Whether by accident or intentionally, Rafi had killed himself with the explosion, and any answers that he might have given had gone with him into the afterlife.

"I have to know," Jade insisted.

Professor smiled patiently. He had seen this confrontation coming almost from the moment the attack had occurred. "I understand that. And I agree with you. It's imperative that we learn what's really going on. But that doesn't mean you can go off half-cocked. Let me do some digging."

"Fine. You dig. I'm going to London."

He sighed. Although they had been taken by ambulance to the hospital in Pisco—the same place Rafi had been treated after his near-drowning—the doctor had elected not to admit them for observation. Professor felt certain part of the reason for the clean bill of health was the fact that the hospital was now under intense scrutiny from the police who wanted to know how Rafi had slipped away from the hospital without anyone raising an alarm. That was fine with Professor. The hospital was too public, too exposed. Their current accommodations, a cabana at a resort in Paracas, were marginally safer, but Professor would not breathe easy until they were well away from Peru.

He and Jade had also been the focus of police scrutiny, initially at least, since there were no witnesses to corroborate their version of what had happened. Several members of the television crew confirmed that Roche had requested a private meeting with Jade but that did little to exonerate them, particularly when those same individuals reported that Jade's reaction to Roche's arrival had been "tense." An investigation into Rafi's background however had soon shifted the suspicion away from Jade and Professor.

A cursory examination of Rafi Massoud's social media presence revealed a connection to the "Crescent Defense League," a coalition of journalists and Muslim social activists dedicated to fighting Islamophobia. Given the level of anti-Islamic sentiment in the United States and Western Europe, which often took the form of outright racism, the mission of the CDL was laudable, but their tactics, more often than not, only added fuel to the fire. Overly generous application of terms like "Islamaphobe," "racist" and "Nazi" had stifled meaningful discussion of what many believed was valid criticism of a religious belief system that seemed inextricably, and all too often unapologetically, linked to acts of violence, while inflaming extremists on the opposite side of the political equation who were only too happy to wear such titles as a badge of honor.

Some of their crusades had a polarizing effect on people who would otherwise have been sympathetic to the cause, such as the call to boycott a summer blockbuster film because one of the characters used the term "pachys," an abbreviation of the polysyllabic name of a particular dinosaur species appearing in the movie, which to the ear of

CDL social justice warriors sounded suspiciously like "Pakis," a slur sometimes used in the United Kingdom to refer to citizens of Pakistani descent. What most regarded as a completely innocuous homophone instead became yet another subtle racially-charged attack. The resulting blowback, predictably, was further antipathy toward the so-called "politically correct" movement and an increase in anti-Muslim sentiment, which was, Professor suspected, what the CDL had intended all along.

There was nothing on the CDL's carefully worded website that could be construed as advocating violent solutions, but the rhetoric was rife with subtext and dog-whistles, particularly in the section listing "Enemies of Islam."

Gerald Roche had been on that list.

Rafi Massoud seemed to have merely been a passive supporter of the group—a Facebook follower, one of several hundred thousand worldwide—and not an activist, but it was a connection the Peruvian national police had no trouble making. Their working hypothesis was that the young archaeology student, seeing an opportunity to strike a blow against a hated enemy of his faith, had slipped away from the hospital, procured a rental car and a gun, and then gone after Roche, subsequently immolating himself in an explosion intended to take the lives of the only witnesses to his crime.

There was no denying that the narrative fit the facts of the situation, and Professor had seen Rafi pull the trigger on Roche with his own eyes. Nevertheless, something felt off about what had now become the official version of events. He knew Jade felt it, too.

For one thing, although the Crescent Defense League had put Roche on their hit list, there was very little in his conspiracy-theory fueled world-view that could be described as anti-Muslim. In fact, he was on record as being a supporter of Palestine and a vocal critic of the Israeli government, which on balance ought to have made him a hero to the CDL. His inclusion on the list seemed to derive solely from a chapter in one of his books where he described in great detail how religions—not just Islam, but all the world's major faiths—were being used to advance the "Changeling hegemony." Professor suspected that Roche, who was almost universally regarded as delusional, had been included to make the other people on the list seem equally deranged—insane by association.

Of greater concern to Professor however was the fact that Roche had specifically sought Jade out, and now he was dead. If the official version was correct, then the attack had been an impulsive action brought on by a coincidental encounter. But if the official version was wrong, there were a lot of missing pieces in the puzzle, and Professor needed to know what they were.

Jade wanted to know as well, and she had every right to feel that way, but in typical fashion, her response was to leap before looking, which in this instance meant traveling to London in order to figure out what Roche had been trying to tell her.

"Roche is the key," she said, almost shouting, though whether this was because of lingering temporary deafness from the explosion or simply unrestrained ardor, it was impossible to say. "Rafi targeted him. Almost like he wanted to silence him. Roche was onto something."

"You may be right," Professor said, not for the first time. "All I'm saying is, take it slow. Before we do anything, we have to figure out who was behind this."

Jade regarded him warily, as if sensing that he was trying to catch her in a logic trap. "So you agree that this whole Muslim extremist thing is a load of crap."

"I don't know what to believe. Something about it seems a little fishy. But what's the alternative? Changelings? Aliens?" He waggled his hands like Jeremiah Stillman which had the desired effect of getting Jade to crack a smile. "Roche said he was being targeted because of what he had discovered about Phantom Time. I've got to say, that makes even *less* sense than the idea that Rafi was some kind of terrorist assassin, but that's about the only lead we've got."

Jade folded her arms. "Which is why I want to go to London. Roche said he wrote a book explaining everything. We need to see what's in that book."

"Roche also said that his publisher was murdered to keep the book from being released. That's something we can verify with a phone call."

"Fine. Make the call."

"I will," he replied, a little more sharply than intended. She stared back at him for several seconds and then they both burst into laughter.

With the tension finally broken, Professor set about making good on that statement. He took out his smart phone and entered the string "Gerald Roche publisher" into Google. The top result directed to Chameleon Press International, a British firm with a catalogue primarily composed of books written by Roche, but the search also returned an unusual news item.

The story, dating back three weeks, was actually quite familiar, though Professor did not immediately grasp the connection until he looked at the section of the article which had caught the attention of the automated search engine. "Oh, this is interesting."

"What?" Jade moved closer so she could read over his shoulder.

"Roche was technically wrong when he said his publisher had been killed. Officially speaking at least, Ian Parrott, president and editor-in-chief of Chameleon Press International, is not dead. He's missing, along with everyone else on Flight 815."

"Wait, *the* Flight 815?"

Professor nodded. There was no need for further elaboration. Three weeks after the fact, the disappearance of Flight 815, Sydney to Los Angeles, was still the subject of water-cooler discussions across the globe.

The plane, a Boeing 777, had been proceeding along its designated trans-Pacific flight plan, the pilots making routine checks with international air traffic controllers, with no hint of trouble, until three hours into the flight, all communication ceased. The plane's GPS locator and radar transponder failed to return any signals and an exhaustive—and still ongoing—search for the plane had not yielded even a scrap of physical evidence as to its fate. The only thing that could be said with any certainty was that Flight 815 had not crashed anywhere along its intended course.

The loss of the aircraft was eerily reminiscent of Malaysian Air Flight 370, which had gone missing more than a year earlier, which invariably led to the as yet impossible to refute belief that the two events were connected. The fact that some debris from Flight 370 had recently been discovered did little to silence the speculation. Were the disappearances the work of international terrorists who were hijacking planes in mid-flight in order to build a fleet of jets for a 9-11 style suicide raid? Or was the explanation something even more diabolical? Theories ranged from the improbably mundane to the unthinkably impossible.

"Roche's publisher was on *the* Flight 815," Jade said again. "Do you realize what that means?"

"It doesn't *mean* anything,." Professor said, a little more forcefully than he intended. "It's a coincidence. The kind of thing men like Roche and Stillman use to spin their conspiracy webs. Nothing more."

"Except now Roche is dead," Jade countered.

Professor lowered his voice an octave, as if afraid that someone might overhear. "Jade, you don't seriously think that some shadow conspiracy killed hundreds of people just to keep a crazy man from publishing his book. The world doesn't work that way."

Even as he said it, he knew better. The world *did* work that way, all the time.

"You know I don't believe in Changelings or aliens or any crap like that," Jade said, "but we both know that conspiracies and secret societies *do* exist. Maybe Roche stumbled on something in his research, something that they don't want anyone knowing. Probably something that doesn't have anything to do with Phantom Time. The answer will be in Roche's book. There's got to be a copy of the manuscript. Either at his place in London, or with the publisher. If you're right, and this is all just a bizarre coincidence, then we won't be in any more danger in London than we are right here. But if Roche was killed to keep this a secret, then whoever did it is going to come after us eventually. We need to know."

"Even if you're right, and there is some kind of conspiracy at work, why go to the trouble of taking out a whole plane just to kill one guy? They could have just popped him on a street corner, made it look like a mugging. Or simply walked up and shot him, like Rafi did. And for that matter, how did our intern get mixed up in this?"

"Maybe this Parrott guy wasn't the only target on that plane. As for Rafi, I have no idea, but you're right. It doesn't make any sense. That's why we have to go to London. We have to figure out what Roche's big secret is."

Professor sighed. "You're insufferable when you're right. You know that, don't you?"

Jade just grinned.

SIX

Atash Shah opened his front door before the visitor could knock. "Gabrielle. Thank you for coming so quickly."

"Of course. I was still at the office when I heard. I came straight away." Gabrielle Greene gripped Shah's hand, not shaking but clasping it in both of hers. Her dark eyes, framed by even darker hair, a stark contrast with her pale skin, probed the interior of the apartment.

"Raina is already in bed," Shah said, answering the unasked question.

He thought he saw something like a smile flicker across her face. It was probably his imagination.

Wishful thinking.

Even now, facing this unprecedented crisis, he could scarcely contain his longing for her. Just being around her was intoxicating. Working with her day in and day out at the Crescent Defense League home office was enough to make him perpetually giddy, but having her here, in his home, with his wife sleeping so close…that made the forbidden fruit of their unconsummated love seem all the sweeter.

Gabrielle's dark serious gaze fell squarely on him. "How bad is it?"

Shah allowed the fantasy to slip away, and looked around furtively. He had it on reliable authority that he was the subject of a secretly sworn and executed FISA warrant. His telephone calls and emails were being screened and he was certain that both his apartment and office were bugged.

Ordinarily, the watching eyes and listening ears did not concern him. He scrupulously avoided doing or saying anything that might even be faintly construed as illegal. As both a Muslim and a journalist who frequently exposed the government's illegal excesses and abuses of power, there were many—both in government circles and in the mainstream news media—who considered him far more dangerous than any terrorist, and rightly so. The old saying was true after all; the pen was mightier than the sword. Tonight however, was a different matter. Tonight, the distinction between pen and sword had become very blurry indeed. He touched a finger to his lips and stepped out of the apartment, closing the door behind him. He led Gabrielle to the stairwell and up to the roof where, hopefully, they would be able to converse without being overheard by federally sanctioned eavesdroppers.

Gabrielle understood the need for discretion. Thought she was not a Muslim, her hard-hitting investigative reporting, which often made use of highly-placed informants—men and women who were legally and technically committing treason by sharing what they knew with a journalist—had put her on the government's radar as well. The fact that she worked closely with Shah, co-founding the Crescent Defense League with him, as well as using him as a source for her freelance articles, surely had not improved her reputation, but that was the price both of them were willing to pay to see a world free from tyranny and intolerance.

It was their holy crusade. A *jihad*, not for Islam—Shah's faith was a complicated thing, informed more by science than the words of the Prophet—but for the truth.

With more than 1.6 billion adherents—twenty-three percent of the global population—the world's fastest growing religion was also arguably the world's dominant religious belief system, regaining a status it had once held for more than four hundred years, from the 8th to 13th centuries. That time, still remembered as the Golden Age of Islam, had been a period of unparalleled scientific, intellectual and cultural achievements, made possible by the unifying power of the Prophet's writings. Shah, like many modern thinkers who shared his culture and faith, was skeptical when it came to matters of divine revelation, but he was a believer in the power of a united purpose. A second Golden Age of Islam *was* possible, but only if Muslims everywhere recognized and lived up to their potential for greatness.

Shah's mission in life was to make sure that happened. He would be the Mahdi, the last imam, who would reunite Sunni and Shia, and all the fractured sects of the faith and lead them to a greatness surpassing even the days of the Prophet. Truth was his weapon, a fire that burned through the endless storm of lies and prejudices. The articles he posted on the Crescent Defense League website not only exposed the agenda of Islam's enemies, who sought always to characterize Islam as a violent faith, filled with radicals and terrorists, but dug deeper, revealing more subtle forms of intolerance, such as unflattering portrayals of Muslims in movies and television shows, which all too often conflated "Muslim" with "terrorists."

Unfortunately, like fire, the truth was sometimes difficult to control, and letting it loose could have unpredictable consequences.

"Roche is dead," Shah said.

Something like relief or satisfaction spread across Gabrielle's countenance. "How?"

"That's the problem." He briefly related what his sources had told him about Rafi Massoud and the brutal murder the young student had committed. "They're going to try to put this on us," he continued. "They'll say that I incited this young man to commit murder."

Gabrielle made a cutting gesture with her hand. "Let them."

Shah swallowed nervously. Gabrielle may have shared Shah's mission, but her motives were more complex.

"This is what we do, Atash," Gabrielle went on. "Turn their attacks against them. If you distance yourself from this, you'll appear weak. Apologize and they win. You have to own this."

"I don't think that will work this time. They want to paint us as a religion of violent extremists and terrorists. You would have me admit they're right?"

Gabrielle reached out and took his hand again. Shah felt an electric tingle at the touch. "This is how the world works now, Atash. A lunatic shoots a school full of children. What does the gun lobby do? Do they apologize for the behavior of one crazy person and admit that maybe some common sense regulations might be a good idea? Not a chance. They double down and turn the tables, blame the victims for not having guns of their own and paint everyone who says otherwise as the real extremists."

Shah stared back dumbfounded. "You can't be serious. We created the CDL to fight that kind of echo chamber mentality."

"We created the CDL to defend Islam. Our enemies will try to use this against this. We have to make it work to our advantage."

Her passion radiated through her hand into his, burning through his reflexive opposition. "How exactly do we do that? Do we say it's Roche's fault for not being Muslim?"

He said it half-jokingly but to his astonishment, Gabrielle nodded. "Just like we did after the Charlie Hebdo shootings. We'll release a statement saying that, while we do not condone what happened, we strongly condemn the sort of blasphemy that prompted a young man to martyr himself."

Shah's forehead creased in a frown. "The cable news outlets will make hay out of rhetoric like that."

"It doesn't matter what they do with it." She squeezed his hand again. "All that matters is that your people—our people—will recognize your strong and decisive leadership."

Shah felt his resistance crumbling. "You're very persuasive."

"Only because I'm right about this. Trust me. And don't worry. We'll run the statement past legal to make sure it's airtight." She paused a beat. "You said this happened in Peru? What was Roche doing down there?"

"I have no idea. He's been hiding out ever since…that thing with his publisher."

"The shooter, he was a student, right?" Gabrielle pressed. "An archaeologist? We need to know how he came to cross paths with Roche. The old crank might be dead, but he can still hurt us if he told someone what he knows or gave them his book."

"I'm not sure there's much we could do about it if he did."

Gabrielle's expression hardened abruptly, her dark eyes boring into him. "Atash, I don't think you fully appreciate just how serious this situation is."

Shah gaped at her. "How can you say that? I've been in damage control mode ever since I heard about the shooting."

"I'm not talking about Roche's death. I'm talking about his secret. It must stay buried. At all costs. If he's shared this knowledge with anyone we have to find out. And we have to silence them."

"Silence them?" The question came out much louder than Shah intended. He imagined the government surveillance team hastily sweeping his building with parabolic microphones, trying to reacquire him. In a more subdued voice, he continued. "We're journalists, Gabrielle, not killers."

Gabrielle regarded him with a cool gaze. "You're right, Atash. We're not killers. But this is a war and whether you intended to or not, you have built an army. There are a lot of young men like this Rafi Massoud out there just waiting for someone to tell them what to do. The only question is whether you have to courage to be their leader."

Shah swallowed. He did not feel very courageous, but he knew he would never be able to say 'no' to her.

PART TWO
FACES

SEVEN

London

As Jade stared at the queue of black TX4 Hackney cabs lined up outside the arrivals gate at London's Heathrow Airport—all facing the wrong direction, or so it seemed to her—she could not help but think back to her last visit to the city and her first meeting with Gerald Roche. Although that trip had been a net success, it had not gone smoothly and she had left believing that she had made an enemy in Roche. Now, Roche was dead and she was back in London, hoping to solve the mystery behind his murder and possibly fulfill his last request.

"Truth is the only protection," Roche had said just before his death. "But knowing the truth is not the same as proving it."

Proving Roche's pet theory was not her objective. The only truth that she cared about right now was the truth about why Roche had been killed, and why Rafi, without any apparent provocation, had pulled the trigger and subsequently immolated himself. She did not know if there was a connection to Phantom Time, or one of Roche's other wild conspiracy theories—her instincts told her there was—but it was a starting point.

Professor selected the third taxi in the line and waved for Jade to join him. She shouldered her backpack, the only piece of luggage she had brought along and crossed to the waiting cab where he was holding the door open for her. It was early afternoon but the gray sky seemed unusually dark and depressing after the sunny equatorial clime of Peru. Nevertheless, despite the fact that she was exhausted from the trip—long flights and even longer layovers—Jade was eager to get started, and couldn't resist tapping her foot and shifting in her seat throughout the forty-five minute ride from the airport to Bedford Square in the Borough of Camden, where Chameleon Press International's offices were located.

The idyllic setting, nestled amid garden squares and elegant historical buildings that dated back as early as the 17th century, seemed wholly inappropriate for a publisher who dealt primarily with sensational speculative topics, but like its namesake, Chameleon seemed to blend right in, occupying a small corner of the Bloomsbury district, a place synonymous with London's historic literary culture.

The office was little more than a room with two cluttered desks and a handful of chairs, occupied solely by a handsome if a bit harried-looking man, about her age, with light brown hair and blue eyes that peered out through tortoiseshell framed spectacles.

As Professor opened the door and stepped aside to allow Jade to enter, the man at the desk looked up from his computer screen, then jumped to his feet and rushed over the greet his visitors. "Hello. You must be Dr. Ihara."

Though she had never seen him before, Jade recognized the friendly voice and understated accent from their earlier phone conversation. She put on her most winning smile and extended her hand. "And you must be Mr. Kellogg."

"Please, it's just Jordan." After introducing himself to Professor, he gestured toward the chairs positioned in front of his desk. "I am sorry that I wasn't more help over the telephone. Things have been a bit chaotic of late. Recent events…" He shrugged. "I'm the…well, I used to be the assistant editor and vice-president, but that's not as impressive as it must sound. There was only ever just Mr. Parrott and myself, and since his disappearance, it's essentially a one-man show, and I'm the one man."

Jade heard no trace of lingering grief in Kellogg's tone at the mention of Parrott's fate. Maybe three weeks had taken the edge off the tragedy. She decided to probe a little deeper. "How will Roche's death affect the business?"

"Well this may sound a bit ghoulish, but business has never been better. As soon as word of his death hit the news, the booksellers started calling. I've emptied the warehouse and I'm going to have to order print runs of several backlisted titles. Tricky business, that. It's impossible to predict how long we'll be able to capitalize on public interest. If the buzz fades away too quickly, I'll be stuck with a warehouse full of unsold books."

"Must be tough," Professor muttered, and Jade had to bite her lip to keep from laughing. Kellogg however seemed immune to sarcasm.

"You have no idea. Thank goodness for e-books. That's where most of our money is made anyway. Instant gratification." He tapped the side of his nose in a gesture that meant absolutely nothing to Jade.

"Roche told me that he was working on a new book," she said. "Will you be able to release that?"

"Sadly, no. I know that's what you've come here for, but Mr. Roche shared the manuscript with Mr. Parrott in electronic format and I haven't been able to locate the file just yet. As I said, things have been chaotic."

"Even so," Professor said, "I would think you'd want to strike while the iron was hot, so to speak."

Kellogg spread his hands in a gesture of helplessness. "As soon as it turns up, I'll publish it."

Jade decided to push a little harder. "Roche believed that Parrott was murdered to keep the book from being published. What do you think about that?" The man's eyes widened in dismay, but Jade pressed ahead. "And now Roche is dead too. Do you think he was right?"

Kellogg spent several seconds shaping his answer. "I don't wish to speak ill of the dead, but…Mr. Roche was right bloody-minded about these theories"

"So you don't believe any of it?" Professor said. "It's all just grist for the mill, right?"

The other man answered with a guilty shrug.

"Could the manuscript be at Roche's home?" Jade asked.

Kellogg raised an eyebrow as if he found the possibility intriguing. "Why, I don't know. I would have to get permission to search the premises."

"Mr. Roche gave me permission," Jade said quickly.

"Not in so many words of course, but he told me about the book and wanted me to look for more supporting evidence. I think finding the manuscript is the obvious first step, don't you? Here's an idea. Why don't you come with us to Roche's place? Once we've had a look at the manuscript, you can take it and do with it what Roche intended."

She almost said "cash in," but decided not to push that particular button too hard.

"Can't argue with that," Professor added quickly before the other man could reply.

Kellogg frowned as if the logic of the statement troubled him. "How would we get in?"

"Don't worry about that," Professor said. "We have a key."

An avaricious gleam appeared in Kellogg's eyes. "Well, what are we waiting for?"

Professor's "key" was a set of lock-picking tools which, in his expert hands, would be able to defeat the lock securing the door of Roche's Mortlake townhouse almost as quickly as if he possessed an actual key. Breaking into Roche's home had been their plan all along, but enlisting Kellogg's assistance was necessary to give their illicit intrusion a veneer of authenticity. A pair of foreigners lurking about the dead man's front door might arouse the suspicion of locals. This way, if the police did come to investigate, Kellogg would be able to explain that they were there on official business.

It was a fragile illusion, and as it turned out, an unnecessary one. When they arrived at Roche's residence on the south bank of the River Thames, they found the door standing slightly ajar.

Jade's breath caught in her throat. *We're too late. Someone beat us to the punch.*

Someone wants that book.

It was an enormous leap of logic, but Jade knew it was true. And when taken with what had happened in Paracas, and the disappearance of Ian Parrott, the conclusion was inescapable.

Roche had been right about everything.

Professor raised a hand, warning them to freeze, and then touched a finger to his lips. Jade dragged Kellogg a few steps back, while Professor crept forward and pushed the door open a little more.

"What's going on?" Kellogg whispered the question, but it sounded as loud as a shout to Jade, who immediately shushed him. She tensed, half-expecting the intruder to burst through the doorway like a homicidal jack-in-the-box, but nothing happened. Professor moved inside and then, after a full two minutes, came out and signaled for them to join him. She could tell by the look on his face that her earlier assumption was spot-on, and as soon as she stepped inside, she got final confirmation.

The tastefully decorated sitting room—where just eight months earlier, Jade had sipped tea with Roche, blissfully unaware of the trap he had laid for her—was a shambles. Every stick of furniture had been overturned, every seat cushion slashed with a razor. The content of drawers and cabinets lay strewn haphazardly on the floor amid piles of furniture stuffing. The intruder had even knocked holes in the wall plaster in an evidently futile search for a wall safe or some other secret compartment.

"The whole place is trashed," Professor said, breaking the ominous silence. "But if it's any consolation, I don't think they found what they were looking for."

"How can you know that?" asked an aghast Kellogg.

Professor waved his hand in an expansive gesture. "Look at this place. This kind of overkill is the result of frustration."

Jade did not find this the least bit consoling. "Roche kept his collection of Dee memorabilia in a basement room. Maybe there's something down there. Something the burglar missed."

"I saw the room you're talking about. It's been completely ransacked, but I guess since we're here, we might as well take another look."

Kellogg found his voice again. "I say, shouldn't we call

the police before tramping around and destroying the evidence?"

Jade ignored him and headed for the stairs, descending the familiar route to the basement. She had last trod these steps eight month earlier, racing up them with a gun-wielding Roche chasing after her. The memory haunted her until she reached the bottom step, whereupon the scope of the damage wrought to the collection of unique artifacts and books snapped her back to the present.

The room was unrecognizable. All of the bookshelves that had once lined the walls had been toppled, and now lay atop their scattered contents. The glass display cases which had held remarkable clockwork devices from the Elizabethan era, as well as exotic occult items of dubious provenance, were smashed apart, their contents scattered. Jade stared in disbelief at the ruined collection, feeling both angry and helpless. "Looks like we're back to square one."

"This was always a long shot, Jade," Professor said from behind her. "It's the 21st century. The manuscript, if it even exists, is probably a computer file stored on a secure Cloud server."

Jade knew he was right but that didn't make the pill any easier to swallow.

"There's a line from an old James Bond novel," Professor went on. "'Once is happenstance. Twice is coincidence. The third time, it's enemy action.'"

Jade tore her gaze from the wreckage and stared at him. "What the hell is that supposed to mean?"

"Rafi didn't do this. And I doubt very much that he was involved in the disappearance of Flight 815. I could almost believe that Roche's death and Parrott's disappearance on that plane were coincidences, but this…" He waved to the room. "Strike three. Enemy action."

"But who? Who's the enemy?"

"That's what I intend to find out." He took out his phone and began tapping the screen, scrolling through his contacts list. "The disappearance of the plane is the piece that doesn't fit. Roche's murder and this break-in both could be the work of disorganized Muslim extremists, but making a plane vanish completely requires planning and sophistication on a different order of magnitude."

He held the phone to his ear and was silent for a moment until the connection was established. "Tam, it's me."

Jade returned her attention to the wreckage while Professor updated Tamara Broderick on what had happened and what he intended to do about it. Broderick was the director of a special CIA cell—code-named "Myrmidons"—primarily tasked with battling the Dominion. She was, technically speaking, Professor's boss, though the arrangement was a little more complicated than employee-employer. Professor had a great deal of latitude when it came to operations, as long as he kept Jade safe and occasionally saved the world. Jade had briefly worked with the Myrmidons as a contractor, which was how she and Professor had initially became acquainted, though at the time, he had been working directly for her as a researcher, and international intrigue had been the last thing on either of their minds.

She knelt over a pile of books, scanning the titles. Some were leather-bound gilt-edged tomes—collectible books, not meant to be read, but one overturned shelf had contained a number of perfect-bound trade paperbacks, ranging in subject from geography and history to political science to UFO encounters. Most of the titles on the more speculative end of the spectrum sported amateurish and often lurid cover art. She opened one and idly thumbed through it, noting pages that had been marked with sticky notes and entire paragraphs highlighted in fluorescent yellow.

She realized that she was looking at Roche's research library, the garden where he had gathered the raw ingredients to brew up his outrageous conspiracy concoctions. It was an apt metaphor. The pieces to Roche's Phantom Time theory were lying scattered before her, but the exact recipe—the specific ingredients and proportions—had died with the man.

"I really don't think you should be touching anything," Kellogg said from the relative shelter of the stairwell. "This is a crime scene. We should step away and summon the police."

Professor threw him a withering glance, and cupped a hand over his phone and continued speaking in a subdued voice.

Jade set the book aside and turned to face Kellogg. "What exactly do you think the police will do?"

"Well..."

"The police will write this off as a simple break-in," She continued. "Vandalism. Nothing more. But they will probably seal this place off so that we can't conduct our own investigation. Is that what you want? Is that what you think Mr. Roche would want?"

"I see your point." Kellogg's eyebrows drew together in a frown, then he brightened. "Do you think there's something here that will help us crack the case?"

Crack the case? Jade thought. *This guy has read too many Sherlock Holmes stories.* "I doubt the people who did this will have left any evidence behind, but that's not what we're looking for."

"What then?"

"Just before he died, Roche told me he wanted me to find something. Proof that this latest theory was right. I don't really know exactly how to do that, but maybe if I can retrace his steps, so to speak, I can figure out what sort of proof he wanted me to find."

"You want to rewrite his missing book, is that it?"

"Well, I wouldn't have put it that way, but yeah. And the first thing we have to do is put this place back together."

Judging by his expression, Kellogg found that prospect about as exciting as root canal surgery, but before he could reply, Professor ended his call and rejoined the conversation.

"I have to go to Sydney," he said with the abruptness of pulling off a Band-Aid. "Tam has given me the green light to join the search for Flight 815."

"Join the search? How is that going to help?"

"There are a lot of wild rumors about what happened, but I'm guessing the authorities have kept a lot of information about the disappearance out of the news. Maybe if I can get inside, I can get someone to open up and tell me what they really think is going on, and that will give us an idea of who's behind it."

The full import of his words finally hit home. "You're leaving?" Jade was surprised by her reaction to the prospect.

"Just for a few days." He cocked his head sideways, brows furrowed in consternation. "I figured you'd be happy for the breathing room. You're always telling me that you don't need a babysitter. I think you'll be safe here, but you're welcome to come with me."

Jade tried to affect a mask of indifference. "Tagging along really isn't my style. Besides, I've got my own leads to run down."

"You sure?"

Jade was anything but sure. Although she would never tell him to his face, Jade liked having Professor around for a lot of reasons, and she was dismayed at the prospect of being separated from him for an indefinite length of time. But "tagging along" was exactly what she would be doing. She had nothing whatsoever to contribute to the search effort. The idea of sifting through the disaster zone that was Roche's library was not particularly appealing, but it was something she could do, and truth be told, she wanted to know the secret that had evidently cost Roche his life.

She looked away, hoping that he would not see the hesitancy in her eyes, afraid that if he asked again, she might not be able to refuse. As she did, she glimpsed another book title. Like the others, it was a slapdash production; the cover featured a sepia-tinted black and white photograph, emblazoned with bold red letters in a Comic Sans typeface. It was the letters that had caught her eye, or rather the words they formed:

Fogou: Doors to the Underworld

She picked the book up and murmured the title, or at least a phonetic approximation of it. "Foh-goo."

She flipped it over and glanced at the back matter. Fogou, she learned, was a term for ancient Iron Age subterranean vaults scattered throughout Cornwall and Scotland. The brief description of the dugout chambers reminded her of the *kivas* used by Native Americans in the southwestern United States, but that was not what had initially aroused her interest. Rather it was that word.

Fogou.

It was what Gerald Roche had said with his dying breath.

She raised her eyes to Professor and managed a smile. "I'm sure. Be sure to send me a postcard from Down Under."

EIGHT

Kilmaurs, Scotland

The gray drizzle permeating London intensified to an almost constant downpour the further north Jade traveled, but as she left the urban and suburban environs of the metropolitan area behind, Jade's mood steadily improved.

Part of the reason for this change was the almost magical contrast between the stormy sky and the green pastures and fields of rural Great Britain and the Scottish Lowlands. Although it was a lot colder and darker than she ordinarily preferred, she could understand how people could easily romanticize the moorlands and heath.

Mostly however, the reason for her elevated spirits lay with the fact that every mile brought her closer to a tangible objective.

She arrived in Kilmaurs, a picturesque settlement in East Ayrshire, Scotland, on the afternoon of her third day in the United Kingdom. It had taken her that long to make sense of the clue she had discovered in Roche's library, though in truth, it was not much of a clue.

She had not shared her discovery with Professor, who probably would have told her that she had misheard Roche, nor had she discussed it with Kellogg, who probably wouldn't have known what to make of it. Because it was such a slim lead, she decided the best course of action was to continue with the plan to conduct a methodical search of Roche's home. After seeing Professor off, she and Kellogg returned to Mortlake and started sifting through the mess. The clean-up was not that much different than what she did everyday on a dig site.

That first evening, after several ultimately fruitless hours of reconstructing Roche's research library and sweeping up shards of broken glass, Jade yielded to her nagging curiosity and read the book about fogous. It was a short read, long on folklore and quick to jump to the kind of sensational conclusions that would have thrilled fans of the *Alien Explorers* television series.

She learned that there were only fifteen confirmed fogous in the United Kingdom, but similar structures—called *erdstall* tunnels—could be found all over western Europe. Although there was no uniformity in structure, both fogous and erdstalls were dry stone chambers, about six feet deep and five feet wide, usually found near the center of ancient settlements. There was no clear consensus on their function. Food storage and shelter were obvious explanations, but the discovery of what appeared to be religious artifacts had led some scholars to believe that the fogous served a ritualistic purpose. The author of the book had gone a step further, proposing that the fogous were doorways between the human world and the world inhabited by faerie creatures, which reminded Jade of Roche's comments about Changelings having their roots in faerie lore. What was not so apparent however was why Roche had chosen to expend his last breath to point her in this direction. There was nothing in the book that leapt out at her.

The next morning, she and Kellogg went back to work at Roche's home, and while she found nothing more in the dead man's personal effects to help make sense of the clue, she was able to make a few casual inquiries of Kellogg, and learned that Roche owned a hunting lodge near Kilmaurs, west of Glasgow. Kilmaurs, which took its name from the Gaelic *Cil Mor Ais*, which meant "Great Cairn", was the site of a fogou that had yielded several artifacts including a knobby orb of carved stone, the purpose of which, like the chamber in which it had been discovered, remained a mystery. It was, as Professor might say, pretty thin soup, and she had no idea what it was she was supposed to be looking for, but Jade felt certain that Roche had been trying to direct her to the fogou at Kilmaurs. If she was wrong, there were still fourteen other possibilities.

As she left the motorway behind and began navigating the narrow backroads through farm country, her excitement began to wane a little. There would be no concealing the fact that she was an outsider and there was no telling how the local residents would react to her presence. Without their help there would be little chance of finding Roche's hunting lodge, to say nothing of the fogou site. Dealing with the natives, whether it was a primitive tribe in Central America or a rancher in middle America, was one of the most challenging aspects of archaeology, but through trial and error, Jade had developed a knack for charming even the most suspicious locals.

After booking a room for the night at a roadside inn, Jade asked the clerk about the fogou, and after some confusion stemming from her pronunciation—"D'ya mean the fuggy hole at Jocksthorn Farm?"—she was given a hand-drawn map that would, if the clerk was not having a bit of fun at her expense, take her right to the "fuggy hole." Jade thanked the clerk and then asked for a dinner recommendation.

"You'll want to visit the Weston Tavern," the clerk told her. "Try the haggis, neeps and tatties, if only to say you did."

"I'll do that," Jade lied. For the first time since his departure, Jade was actually glad for Professor's absence, as he would have almost certainly double-dog dared her to eat the traditional Scottish meal of sheep's stomach stuffed with organ meats and oatmeal, and served with turnips and mashed potatoes. As it was, she had no intention of stopping for dinner, not with the goal finally within reach.

Armed only with a flashlight, she braved the chilly rain and set out on foot from the hotel for the two mile walk to Jocksthorn Farm, a forested parcel of land that jutted up out of the rolling fields like an island in a sea of green. After a quick look around to make sure that no one was around to observe her, Jade, hopped over the low stone guardrail and ventured into the woods.

The map was of little use since there were no landmarks to speak of, but twenty minutes of methodical searching finally brought her to a fenced area surrounding a hole in the ground that, if the hotel clerk was to be believed, was the entrance to the fogou. Jade climbed the fence, switched on her light and dropped into the opening.

The ground at the bottom of the hole was covered with loose soil and moss, but just a few steps into the covered passage brought Jade to a tunnel with gently sloping walls of carefully fitted stones—a technique called "battering"— reinforced every few feet with buttresses and corbels, and roofed with large stone slabs that easily held the weight of the earth above. The floor was damp but mostly clean and free of debris. Jade proceeded slowly down the passage, playing the beam of her light on every crack and crevice, looking for anything that might reveal the reason for Roche's interest, but aside from the obvious craftsmanship required to construct the subterranean vault, there was nothing remarkable about the tunnel leading into fogou. After about twenty-five feet however, the passage opened into the central chamber and Jade was obligated to revise that opinion.

The heart of the fogou was a broad circular chamber. The battered stone walls sloped outward gently up to a point higher than Jade's waist, then reversed, with each successive layer of rock overhanging the layer beneath it to create an inward slope that continued all the way up to form a domed ceiling. It took Jade a moment to realize that she was standing in a roughly spherical room, remarkably similar to the cavern she and Rafi had fallen into in Peru.

Jade glimpsed something out of the corner of her eye, a man standing beside her, lurking in the gloom. She spun toward the shape, aiming the light where she thought his eyes would be, but the flashlight beam revealed nothing but stacked rock.

She took a deep breath, trying to calm her racing heart. Her eyes had tricked her. The similarity to the Paracas chamber had triggered a subconscious memory of the strange "ghost" hallucinations, and her imagination had taken care of the rest. That was the most plausible explanation, but she could not shake the feeling that she was missing something.

She took another breath. She had not thought about the ghosts since leaving Peru. That particular mystery had taken a back seat, yet she recalled now that Roche had asked about her discovery. Almost as if he knew, she thought. As if he had seen something like it.

Jade shone the light around, searching for more ghosts, but instead of the elusive and ephemeral shapes, her beam picked out something almost as fleeting. A shadow, sliver thin, cast by a rock protruding ever so slightly from the thousands just like it, stacked up to form the curving walls of the fogou. She took out her pocket knife, a Victorinox Swiss Army Tinker model. Professor had laughingly called her "MacGyver" when she'd purchased the slim red folding knife, but it was a lot easier to keep in a pocket than the bulky Leatherman multi-tool he favored. She opened one of the smaller blades and worked it into the crack between the stones. The protruding rock shifted enough for her to grab one end with thumb and forefinger, allowing her to wriggle it loose, revealing a small cavity the width of her thumb.

Her light glinted off a polished surface inside the hollow and a probing finger teased out a rectangle of plastic that she immediately recognized as a USB compatible thumb drive. Jade closed her fist around in and allowed herself a smile off satisfaction. Without a computer, it was impossible to say what the external storage device contained, but her instincts told her that she had found Roche's missing manuscript.

She turned to leave but then froze as her light revealed something else, a human shape standing in the mouth of the tunnel, and this time, it was no ghost.

NINE

If there was one thing Professor had learned during his time in uniform, it was that, no matter the location, branch of service or flag they flew, military bases were all pretty much the same. It wasn't a physical similarity, though block construction and grim utilitarian uniformity were a constant, but rather something less tangible. He couldn't quite put his finger on what it was, but Royal Australian Air Force Base Richmond on the outskirts of Sydney was no exception.

Even before getting past the main gate, as he waited beside his rental car for his bona fides to be checked and his visitor's pass to be issued, Professor felt like he had been transported back in time twenty years to when he was a freshly scrubbed swabbie arriving at Coronado to begin Basic Underwater Demolitions/SEAL training. He found himself automatically checking the rank of every Aussie airmen that passed by, separating officers from enlisted like he used to do in the old days, just in case a salute was required. He had to fight the urge to stand at parade rest.

The airmen manning the gate handed him a clip-on pass and supplied instructions on how to find the ad hoc command center where the ongoing search for Flight 815 was being coordinated. Although the Australian Transportation Safety Bureau was the lead agency, there were more than a dozen different organizations—military, civilian, and private—and hundreds of aircraft looking for the plane, which made the RAAF base the ideal hub from which to oversee the effort.

Professor was posing as an FBI counter-terrorism consultant, on loan to the Australian government. The cover was vaguely defined, just official enough to allow him to hang out at the fringes of the search, ask a lot of questions, and get a feel for what had really happened. He did not expect to do any actual consulting, but if there was information being withheld from the public, something that provided a more concrete link to Roche's murder, he had to find it. He had opted for casual attire—chinos and a navy blue polo shirt—but thought his Explorer fedora might set the wrong tone. It stayed in the rental car.

He decided to begin his search by introducing himself to ATSB operations manager Steven Sousa, the man in charge, notionally at least, but despite the fact that he had both emailed ahead to make an appointment and called to confirm, Sousa was nowhere to be found. The ATSB office was all but deserted. The lone agent manning the phones answered Professor's inquiries about Sousa's whereabouts with a shrug, which left him little choice but to park himself in a chair outside the office and wait.

Sousa arrived two hours later, a stout balding man with a haggard expression but a determined carriage. He brushed past Professor and went straight into the office where he immediately began making a phone call. Professor slipped in behind him and took a seat in front of the desk. Sousa acknowledged his presence with an irritated frown, but continued with his phone call—which mostly consisted of "No, sir. Not yet, sir" delivered with an almost stereotypically thick Aussie accent—as if Professor were not even there.

Finally, after a promise of "right away, sir," Sousa hung up and leaned across his desk. "Let's hear it."

Professor offered a cordial smile and proffered his bogus credential pack. "I'm Chapman. FBI counter-terrorism."

"Great. Another seppo."

It did not sound like a question so Professor let it go. "I've got some questions I need answered and then I'll be out of your ha... errr, your way."

Sousa let out a noncommittal grunt. "Fine. Ask your questions. Hope you don't mind if I keep working." He reached for a stack of papers and began leafing through them.

The man's recalcitrant attitude was the main reason

Professor had not simply conducted this interview by phone. Getting anything useful out Sousa was going to be like pulling teeth. He decided to push back a little. "We're on the same team, Sousa. I'm not here to piss on your hubcaps. As soon as I get what I came for, I'm gone. How long that will take is up to you."

Sousa glared at him for a moment then tossed the papers down and folded his arms across his chest. "Go on."

Professor took out a notepad and pen. "For starters, why don't you tell me exactly what happened. I've heard what the news media are saying, and just about every crazy conspiracy theory imaginable. Now I want to hear it from you. What really happened to that plane?"

"What happened is that the plane bloody vanished."

Professor's pen remained poised above the page, but he said nothing.

Sousa sighed. "The aircraft took off from SYD at 0958. It's a daily flight, originating here, not a turnaround, so the plane received a thorough maintenance evaluation before departure. Not so much as a loose nut anywhere on that bird. The flight left on time, and everything was fine until it wasn't."

Professor had just started writing, but stopped at the cryptic comment. "What does that mean?"

Sousa gave him a hard look. "You know anything about how airplanes work?"

"I understand principles of lift and aerodynamics, if that's what you mean."

"It's not." Another sigh. "I'm talking about the air traffic control system. People watch movies and they get this idea that ATC is like some kind of computer game, with a great big screen and little lights that show the exact location of every aircraft in the sky."

"It's not?"

"At any given moment, there are close to seven thousand commercial flights in the sky worldwide. There are more than a thousand different air carriers, and a lot of them are flying old birds that haven't been fully upgraded with the latest bells and whistles. Air traffic control has to manage all of them, and the only way to do that is with radar and radio navigation. Both of those rely on line of sight, which isn't terribly useful a thousand miles out over the Pacific Ocean. There are a lot of gaps in radar coverage. Planes aren't tracked in real time. Sometimes, we don't know there's a problem until a plane fails to show up, or misses a scheduled check-in. What we know about this plane is that they reported in right on schedule for the first three hours or so, and then...nothing."

"So the crew did not report any problems."

"Not a peep. The odds are that this was a mechanical failure, not a deliberate act, but we won't know what happened on that aircraft until we find it. So while I understand that you have a job to do, Agent Chapman, you're just pissing into the wind."

Professor didn't back down. "And why haven't you found it?"

"Didn't you hear what I said? We don't track these planes in real time so we don't know where it went down."

"But that particular plane was equipped with both a radio transponder and a GPS locator, right? I heard those systems were shut down by someone on the plane."

Sousa sighed again as if weary of answering these particular questions. "If the aircraft experienced a major failure, like a fire in the electrical bay, those systems would have been disabled along with the radio. That doesn't mean someone aboard intentionally shut them off."

"Okay what about the black box? That's supposed to be indestructible, right?"

"The cockpit voice recorder and flight data recorder are designed to survive a crash, and yes, they do broadcast a 37.5 kilohertz locator ping, at least until the batteries die. Right now, search vessels are deployed in the projected crash area listening for that signal, but in case you haven't looked at a map lately, it's a big bloody ocean."

"If the plane's disappearance was a deliberate act," Professor said, "say, an act of terrorism, it might have deviated from its course. A difference of even a few degrees would put it thousands of miles from where you're looking. That would explain why you haven't found it, right? I'd say that's a pretty compelling reason to at least investigate the possibility that this was an act of terrorism."

Sousa rolled his eyes. "I thought you wanted to know what really happened."

"What makes you so sure this wasn't a deliberate act?"

"Occam's Razor. Look, if the aircraft broke up suddenly in mid-flight, whether because of a bomb or a system failure, we probably would have found the wreckage by now. That means that the plane continued to fly after the communications system went down. Here's my theory. A fire in the E and E bay—that's Electronics and Equipment—takes out the radios and the cockpit fills with smoke. Captain Norris is unable to send a distress call, so he immediately changes course, looking for the nearest place to set down, but the flight crew, and probably everyone else aboard, is overcome by the smoke and the plane keeps flying with no one at the stick until it runs out of fuel and crashes into the ocean. It's happened before."

Sousa's expertise was eroding the foundation of the assumption that had brought Professor to the opposite side of the world, but there was something he knew that Sousa did not. "What if I told you there was credible intelligence indicating that one or more of the passengers on that plane had been specifically targeted for assassination?"

Sousa remained unmoved. "You aren't hearing me, Agent Chapman. The plane was not destroyed along its flight path, which means that someone manually changed course. Only the flight crew could have done that."

"The 9-11 hijackers took flying lessons."

"If anyone had attempted to take over that plane, the captain would have immediately sent a distress call. The same goes for a passenger trying to sabotage the plane."

"What about the crew? Maybe one of them was the perpetrator. It wouldn't be the first time."

"We've already looked into that. Captain Norris and

First Officer Carrera had impeccable records and no ties whatsoever to extremist groups. We've even done voice stress analysis of the recorded radio transmissions. There's nothing at all to indicate that either one of them was suicidal or under coercion. No, I'm sorry. The simplest solution is almost certainly the correct one. All the evidence points to this being an accident. A tragedy to be sure, but not a crime."

Professor's certitude began to crack apart like thin ice. He had made the same mistake as Roche and Jeremiah Stillman and all the other kooks who saw conspiracies in every coincidence. Maybe Sousa was right.

"Can I ask you a question, Agent Chapman?"

It took Professor a moment to process Sousa's request. He met the other man's gaze and nodded.

"Who?"

Professor blinked. "I'm sorry?"

"You said you had credible intelligence." An odd gleam, more than mere curiosity, had entered Sousa's dark eyes. Professor thought he looked like a cat contemplating a goldfish in a bowl. "I've become intimately familiar with ever name on the manifest of that aircraft. There were no red flags. Who was being targeted?"

"It's not something I can talk about just yet," Professor said with a tight smile. "Besides, you're probably right. It's most likely a dead end."

Sousa regarded him a moment longer, then laid his palms flat on his desk. "You got what you need here?"

A low buzzing in Professor's pocket signaled an incoming text message. He resisted the urge to check it immediately. "I'd like to talk to a few more people. Get a broader perspective. Like I said, I don't want to be in the way. I just want my report to reflect that I did my job. Can you point me in the right direction?"

"I'll make a list," Sousa said. His tone was indifferent but the glimmer had not faded from his eyes. "You know, if you really want to understand what's going on here, you should get your hands dirty."

"Meaning what exactly?"

"There's an Orion leaving in about an hour. A search plane."

Professor knew what an Orion was. The venerable Lockheed P-3 Orion was a four-engine turboprop anti-submarine/surveillance aircraft, developed in 1959 but still in service throughout the world.

"You should ride along," Sousa continued. "Talk to the men who are actually out there looking. Besides, I can't think of a better way to get a broader perspective than looking down from a search aircraft over a hundred thousand square miles of open water."

Before Professor could respond, his phone buzzed again, another message or perhaps a reminder for the first. He dug it out and glanced at the notification, a single message from Tam Broderick: "Did you see this???" followed by a truncated Internet URL.

It was not Tam Broderick's style to forward funny cat videos.

He rose from his chair. "I'll get back to you on that, Mr. Sousa. Right now, I need to take this."

Sousa rose as well and moved toward the door while Professor tapped his screen to see what Tam had sent him. The URL directed him to a familiar website, the Crescent Defense League's "Enemies of Islam" page. The page had been updated since his last visit. There was a new name on the CDL hit list.

Frigid adrenaline surged through Professor's veins.

Jade.

The picture of her was a recent one, taken in Peru, probably a production still from the *Alien Explorers* website. Underneath, a short article outlined the reason Jade Ihara was considered an enemy to the faith, which mostly boiled down to her alleged collusion with Gerald Roche, in the pursuit of spurious evidence to support the "lie" that the Prophet Muhammad never existed.

While the article did not explicitly call for violence against Jade, the implicit message was hard to miss. Enemies of Islam like Roche and Jade needed to be silenced.

It was the last sentence that made Professor's blood run cold.

Ihara is believed to be in Scotland, near Glasgow.

He jumped to his feet but before he could turn toward the door, he felt a sharp stinging at the back of his neck. He jerked away reflexively, spinning on his heel even as the sting transformed into a spike of cold, like an enormous icicle stabbing through his upper torso. He whirled around to face his assailant, but whatever Sousa had injected was already robbing him of motor control. Professor's legs collapsed under his weight and he crashed into the wall.

He clung desperately to consciousness but knew that it was a losing battle. The last thing he heard before the fog closed over him was the distant sound of someone speaking. It was Sousa's voice, but without any trace of an Australian accent.

"I need a replacement… No. Take him to the facility. We'll get what we need from him there."

TEN

Kilmaurs, Scotland

As her flashlight beam illuminated the face of the man standing in the passage, Jade managed to stifle her shriek of alarm. The noise that issued from her sounded more like a burp of displeasure.

"Kellogg! Damn it! What are you doing here?" She paused a beat, though not nearly long enough to allow him to respond. "Wait, did you…follow me here? You did, didn't you?"

A guilty look flickered over his face, but it was replaced almost immediately by an expression of triumph. He pointed a finger at the object peeking from Jade's clenched fist. "You found it. Roche's book. I knew you would."

She jammed the thumb drive into a pocket and took a step toward him, hands on her hips. "You followed me," she repeated. "What the hell?"

"I didn't follow you. But when you kept asking about Mr. Roche's hunting lodge, it wasn't hard to figure out that you would come here. And I realized that it was the obvious place to look for his manuscript." His eyes narrowed in suspicion. "I do hope you weren't trying to cut me out of the picture."

"I didn't keep asking and I never told you about the fogous, so how did you find me *here*?"

"The innkeeper said I'd find you here or at the tavern. You weren't at the tavern."

"He just told you where I was?" Jade stopped herself, realizing there was nothing to be gained by hammering at the issue. "Never mind. I wasn't trying to cut you out of anything, Kellogg. Roche wanted me to find this. That's what I'm doing. As soon as I figure it out, the book is yours."

Kellogg spread his hands as if genuflecting. "That's all I wanted. That, and for you to start calling me Jordan."

"Quit while you're ahead." She shone the light up the length of the tunnel. "Come on let's get out of—"

She broke off abruptly as she spied movement directly ahead. Something—an animal perhaps, or possibly a person—had drawn back into the shadows at the first touch of light, like a sea anemone shrinking from contact. She turned to Kellogg. "You saw that, yeah?"

"I didn't...I wasn't really looking."

Jade frowned. Another ghost? She didn't think so. Whatever she had spotted had seemed more substantial. More *real*. "You bring a date, Kellogg?"

Kellogg's only answer was a bewildered stare.

Jade was pretty sure no one had seen her enter the fogou, but she doubted Kellogg had been as discreet. Maybe a local farmer or shepherd had spotted him tramping through the woods and followed. She waggled the light back and forth, creating a stroboscopic effect. "Hey you," she called. "Don't be shy. Come and say hi!"

Several seconds ticked by. After half a minute, Jade was starting to believe that she had imagined it but then a man stepped fully into view. At least, she assumed it was a man. The build looked decidedly masculine, average height and weight, not overly muscular, but definitely not dainty. The facial features would probably have resolved any remaining doubt about the gender of the new arrival, but those remained mostly hidden behind a black ski mask. That, and the two-foot length of steel pipe in the man's hand, told her this was no mere curious passerby.

Jade kept her light pointed at the man's face. The flashlight was an older, low intensity affair, bright enough to irritate but not blind the would-be attacker, but in its glare, Jade could see the man's eyes, and read the fear written there. This man was no killer, had probably never even been in a serious fight.

Why'd you pick today to start something? Jade thought.

Another figure, similarly attired and equipped, stepped into view behind the first. The second man's eyes were harder than his companions but only a little. Of the pair, the second man was clearly the instigator, pushing his timid friend forward to ensure that he would not run away.

Jade took a deep breath. "Okay, boys. I'm not sure what this is about…"

She trailed off when she realized that the first man was muttering something. She could just make out the outline of his lips moving under the fabric of his mask, but the words were nonsense. "La-la-la…"

The man abruptly lurched forward, raising his cudgel even though he was still a good ten steps away. Jade took an instinctive step back and bumped into Kellogg who was also retreating. She didn't need to look behind her to know that there was nowhere to go.

Okay. Fight, then, but with what? It wasn't like she could just pull a weapon out of thin air.

She straightened her back and widened her stance, trying to remember all the self-defense courses she had taken, all the martial arts instruction Professor and her ex-boyfriend Dane Maddock had tried to impart to her.

Maddock's new girl was some kind of professional cage fighter.

She'd know what to do, Jade thought mordantly.

The man seemed to be moving in slow motion, as if every step, every action, was being stretched out deliberately to accentuate the dread Jade now felt. She saw his muscles tensing like a clockwork spring being wound tight, and then the subtle shift in his balance as he reversed direction and swung the cudgel at her.

Jade easily side-stepped the attack and thrust outward with both hands, planting the heels of her palms in the man's chest. A hard shove sent the man stumbling back, his cudgel swiping empty air, yet even as he went reeling, the second man moved in, aiming his pipe at Jade's head. She tried to duck away, but inertia conspired against her. She had invested too much momentum in repelling the first attacker to change course now. The bludgeoning instrument swung toward her cranium with the precise angle and timing required to deliver a crushing blow, and there was nothing she could do to avoid it.

Something clamped onto Jade's wrist, pulling her arm taut with such ferocity that Jade thought her shoulder would be dislocated. The violence of the unexpected seizure caused her head to snap sideways. The sound of cracking vertebrae was so loud, she didn't ever hear the length of pipe whooshing through the space where her head had been only a moment before.

It took her a moment longer to realize what had just happened. Kellogg had yanked her out of the way of the crushing blow. Unfortunately, in so doing, he had also whipped her around and sent her careening into the wall of the fogou.

The impact shuddered through her, rattling her teeth, but it wasn't as bad as hitting solid stone. The battered rocks shifted like a pile of gravel, and then something broke under her and she spilled forward into a cavity that had been concealed behind the wall. Kellogg, his hand still locked around her wrist, was pulled along with her into the newly opened hole. The flashlight tumbled from her grasp and hit the ground with sufficient force to snuff out the light, plunging the cave and all its newly revealed secrets into darkness.

The darkness offered only a brief respite. A light, probably from a smart phone, flared to life in the circular main chamber, revealing the irregular break in the wall through which Jade and Kellogg had crashed. The light shifted, filling the opening with blinding radiance, forcing Jade to look away, but as she did, Jade realized that the space beyond the wall kept going.

"A tunnel," Jade gasped. She hoped it was a tunnel at least, and not just a dead end passage. "Come on!"

Jade thought about digging her own phone out for light, but doing so would have served only to give the club-wielding men something to focus on. As long as she and Kellogg could avoid being illuminated, they would be safe.

She started forward, one hand stretched out before her in order avoid colliding with another wall, the other gripping

Kellogg's hand and pulling him along. After a dozen steps, her groping hand encountered something. A wall, but not the dead end she feared. Instead, it was merely the oblique angle of a bend in the tunnel. She shifted direction and continued forward, following the turn. For a few seconds, the darkness was absolute, but then a faint glow from behind signaled that the two attackers were still in pursuit.

The retreat, fumbling along one cautious step at a time, gave Jade time to process what was happening. If the third time was enemy action, then this could only be construed as a declaration of war, yet something about that explanation didn't ring true. She did not doubt that the disparate events were somehow connected, but each successive link in the chain seemed weaker, as if the enemy was intentionally deescalating the conflict.

The enemy.

Who the hell was the enemy? Islamic extremists? Changelings? Neither felt plausible, but regardless, it was hard to believe that all of the incidents were being carried out by the same group. After disappearing an entire jet full of people, a couple of thugs with crude clubs was almost embarrassingly unsophisticated.

Jade came to an abrupt stop.

"What is it?" Kellogg hissed.

"This doesn't make any sense."

"What?"

Jade turned, pushed past him and started back up the tunnel, toward the diffuse glow of her attackers' light. "Hey! Who the hell are you, huh? What do you want?"

She knew she was shouting but could barely hear herself over the sound of blood rushing in her ears. Every step forward brought her closer to what might very well be a fatal encounter, but instead of fear, she felt only anger. She had faced life or death situations plenty of times before. She could handle the threat, but she absolutely hated not knowing why.

"What do you want?" she repeated.

The light bobbed uncertainly, shifted away as if the man

holding it was thinking about turning to flee.

"Answer me, damn it."

She thought she heard him say something, not words, but the same nonsense chant she had heard before. "La-la-la-la…" Then the light shifted toward her again and she knew that the man was about to make a move. Jade threw an arm up to ward off the expected blow and charged toward the light.

The impact wasn't as bad as she expected. Her shoulder caught a glancing blow to something relatively soft—probably the guy's gut—and then she rebounded away like a pinball, striking the second man solidly.

The darkness concealed most of what happened, but the grunts of pain and sounds of bodies hitting the ground painted a vivid enough picture. There was a loud clank as one of the men dropped his pipe, and then a scuffling noise. The light bobbed and then went dim as the man holding it turned away and shone it back up the tunnel. Jade scrambled back to her feet, fists raised, but the light was moving away.

The men were fleeing.

Jade stared at the receding glow, too astounded at the unlikely victory to even think about what would happen next.

Another light flashed behind her. She whirled, fists still up but it was only Kellogg holding up his own mobile phone. "You…" He swallowed. "That was incredible."

"Uh, thanks."

Kellogg brought the phone close to his face. "No signal. We need to get out of here."

"Right," Jade's answer was automatic but then she realized what Kellogg was trying to do. "Are you calling someone?"

"I should say so. I'm calling the police."

She extended her hand, palm out. "No. No police."

"In case you weren't paying attention, we were just assaulted."

"Yes, and in case you weren't paying attention, I sent them packing. But until we know who's behind it, we don't trust anyone. Got it?"

Kellogg snorted. "Oh, it's obvious who's behind it."

The only obvious thing about the attack, as far as Jade could tell, was that the perpetrators would eventually figure out that they had left the job unfinished. "No police," she repeated. "Now come on. Let's get out of here before they realize they just got their asses kicked by a girl."

As she started forward, her toe struck the discarded metal pipe and sent it rolling down the tunnel. She scooped it up and hefted it in her right hand. "That's more like it." She half-expected Kellogg to lecture her about destroying fingerprint evidence but he thankfully remained silent.

With the cudgel held in both hands like a baseball bat, Jade moved back up the passage to the break in the wall of the fogou. There was no sign of the two men. She turned back to Kellogg. "Turn off your phone," she whispered. "No light, and not a sound. But stay close."

He nodded and then vanished along with the rest of the fogou when the screen went dark. Jade picked her way slowly through the breach, and then began walking stealthily, rolling her feet forward heel-to-toe with exaggerated slowness so as not to betray their presence. She strained her ears, listening for any noise that might indicate the two attackers were returning or lying in wait at the entrance to the chamber, but all she could hear was the sound of falling rain, growing louder with each step forward.

When she could just distinguish the outline of the tunnel mouth, the stormy night sky a faintly lighter shade of darkness than the subterranean depths, she stopped and listened for a full thirty seconds. It was the perfect place for an ambush. She leaned back until she felt Kellogg's chest against her head. "Stay here," she whispered.

Before he could reply, she leaped into motion, sprinting to the far end of the stone-lined trench and scrambling up the slick stone surface. If the men were waiting to attack, her best chance at surviving was a dynamic exit. She heaved herself onto the damp earth above ground, and rolled forward in a somersault twist that brought her up in a crouch facing back toward the fogou, the pipe held up and ready to parry any attack.

None came. The two men were long gone.

Jade took a few calming breaths before calling out to Kellogg. "All clear. Come on up."

Kellogg emerged tentatively, then clambered out of the hole to join her. "Now will you let me call the police?"

"What did you mean when you said you knew who they were?"

Kellogg's face was unreadable in the gloom. "Are you serious? Didn't you hear what they were saying?"

"I was kind of preoccupied."

"'*La ilaha illa'lla.*' It's Arabic. 'There is no god but God.'"

As he said it, Jade's memory of the muttered words became crystal clear, and she knew he was correct. Their attackers had been reciting the *shahadah*, a statement of faith considered one of the pillars of Islam. Not only was the *shahadah* part of the five-times daily Muslim prayer ritual, but it was also reputedly the last words spoken by suicide bombers as a way of ensuring that their self-inflicted death would be counted as an act of martyrdom and not suicide, which was a damnable sin according to the Quran.

"Those men were Arabs," Kellogg continued. "Just like the man that killed Mr. Roche. So, may I please call the police now?"

Jade felt an inexplicable confusion, as if knowing the truth about the motive behind the attack was somehow worse than ignorance or uncertainty. She had not wanted to believe the official version of Roche's death because accepting it would mean admitting that she had badly misjudged Rafi's character. Obviously, she had done exactly that.

"They're going to ask what we were doing here," she finally said. "They might even take the thumb drive with Roche's book."

She thought she saw him sag visibly in defeat, but in the darkness it was impossible to say. "I suppose you're right."

For some reason, postponing a conversation with the local constabulary elevated Jade's mood by a few degrees. "I say we go somewhere safe, change clothes and get something to eat. I hear the haggis and titties at the Weston Tavern are simply to die for."

Kellogg made a futile attempt to stifle his laughter.

"Then we'll find a computer and plug this thing in," Jade said, "and see if we can figure out what Roche discovered that's worth killing over."

ELEVEN

Professor drifted on the edge of consciousness, sometimes rising to the surface just long enough to wonder where he was and what had happened, before sliding back down into the darkness. He caught disjointed bits of conversation, but none of it made any sense. He was not sure that the words being spoken were in English, though he had a vague sense of comprehending what was being said even as it slipped out of his memory. Each time it happened, he knew that it would not last. Brief moments of lucidity were a common occurrence when under the influence of anesthesia. When he was able to keep his eyes open for more than a few seconds, he knew he was finally coming up for good. The drug, whatever it was, had worn off.

Sousa dosed me. Why the hell did he do that?

The obvious answer, namely that there was a conspiracy to hide the truth about Flight 815's fate and that Sousa was part of it would have made perfect sense if not for the fact that, up until the moment he felt the needle prick his skin, Professor had been prepared to accept the ATSB investigator's explanation for the disappearance of Flight 815.

"What the hell…?" He sat up, winced as a wave of nausea rolled over him, and then looked around for something to help orient himself. There was nothing familiar at all about his surroundings.

He was in a windowless cube that might have been either a low-rent no-tell motel room or a jail cell—odds favored the latter. His head cleared after a few seconds and he took a chance on standing up. He steadied himself with one hand outstretched to the wall, and when he was sure that his legs would hold him up, he began walking toward the door. He expected the door to be locked, but to his surprise, the doorknob turned and the door swung open without any resistance. He winced as bright sunlight flooded into the dim room, stinging his eyes for a moment. The world was a blur of green, which eventually resolved into a stand of evergreen trees.

Pine trees, but despite his comprehensive knowledge of minutia which included being able to recognize most plants on site, he couldn't place the exact species. The air, which was cool and dry, offered no clue whatsoever as to where on earth he might be. He took a step through the door and turned a slow circle.

He was standing in front of a small plywood structure that reminded him of the backyard shed where his father had kept his tools. The structure appeared to have been built on the ground, without any sort of foundation. The cabin was not especially remarkable. What was remarkable however, was the fact that it was not the only one of its kind. In every direction, stretching all the way to the trees, lined up like soldiers in a formation, were dozens more just like it.

"Toto, I don't think we're in Oz anymore," he muttered.

"Good morning, neighbor."

Professor whirled in the direction of the voice, which brought on another attack of vertigo that sent him reeling. He leaned against the plywood wall of the cabin, closing his eyes to keep the world from spinning.

"Hey, take it easy." It was the same voice, a woman's, speaking English with a faint Australian accent, but closer than before.

He opened his eyes and saw her approaching from the cabin to his right. She was tall and slim, with an olive complexion and straight black hair pulled back in a pragmatic pony tail. But for her accent, Professor would have guessed that she was Hispanic. She wore dark blue trousers and a white shirt with black epaulets crossed by three gold lines.

"That stuff they give you packs a fair wallop," the woman said as she reached him. She allowed her hand to rest lightly on his shoulder. "I chundered for an hour straight when I woke up."

"Woke up?" He gave her another look. "They drugged you, too?"

Her eyebrow shot up. "You're a yank?'

"That's right." He stared back at her for a moment. "Who are you? And where am I?"

She returned the searching look for several long seconds, as if trying to decide whether to trust him with those answers. "Where, as near as I can reckon, is forty degrees north, and somewhere between one-twenty and one-thirty degrees east. It's a lot harder to judge longitude without instruments."

Professor blinked at her, too surprised by the fact that the woman had answered him with navigational coordinates to even think about the location those coordinates represented. Things stared clicking together. The uniform…navigation by dead-reckoning… mention of instruments….

"You're a pilot." Another click. "You're from Flight 815. First officer…" He searched his memory. "Carrera? Oh my God. You're alive."

Despite everything else that had happened, Professor felt emotion welling up into his throat. He looked past the woman and saw that a small knot of people had gathered to watch the exchange.

"What happened to you?" He straightened, pushing off the wall, ignoring the resulting head rush. "You said you were drugged. Did someone hijack your plane?"

Click.

"Forty north… A hundred and twenty…" His breath caught in his throat. He glanced up at the midday sun but without any other way to orient himself, it was impossible to immediately confirm what she had just said. "North Korea?"

"Take it down a peg, friend." The woman threw a nervous glance in the direction of the growing crowd, "That lot doesn't know the map as well as you. I haven't told them where we are… or where I think we are, anyway."

"But you are First Officer Carrera? And those are the

passengers?"

Carrera nodded. "Some of them. There's forty-seven of us here. I don't know about the rest."

"What happened? Were you forced to fly here?" Professor's mind was whirring like a computer hard drive. There was no way the plane could have made it all the way to North Korea without someone picking it up on radar or catching a transponder ping. That was why the conspiracy needed a highly placed asset like Sousa, to hide or falsify any data that might reveal what had really happened. He wondered how many others were involved in the cover-up.

Carrera shook her head. "No. I was drugged. Just like you. Woke up here. I don't know where the plane is."

"And you've been here the whole time? Three weeks?"

She let out a heavy sigh. "Three bloody weeks. I take it everyone thinks we're dead?"

Her despondent tone finally dampened Professor's excitement over the discovery. Not only had he learned the fate of the aircraft, but it seemed he would share it. "Who's behind all this?" he asked in a more subdued tone. "Is it the North Koreans?"

Carrera pursed her lips for a moment. "Don't think I caught your name, friend."

"Pete. But everyone calls me 'Professor.'"

"Seriously?" She shook her head, then pointed to the cabin adjoining the one he had awakened in. "Let's talk in there. These people are still my responsibility and I'd rather not start a panic."

The exterior of Carrera's cabin was almost identical to his own, but in the short time she had occupied it, the flight officer had managed to personalize her space with cardboard boxes serving as makeshift tables, and soft drink cans repurposed as flower vases and drinking cups.

"Sorry," she said as she caught him checking out the décor. "Haven't figured out how to make furniture yet. Robinson Crusoe I'm not." She motioned to an open box beside the bed which contained several parcels wrapped in brown plastic that Professor immediately recognized as military rations—MREs—though not the same brand used by the United States military. "Hungry?"

He picked up one of the prepackaged meals just long enough to verify that the label was printed in English. "Maybe later. This is what they're feeding you?"

"Whatever else they've got planned for us, they aren't going to let us starve." She folded her arms across her chest. "So what's your story, Pete? Why are you here?"

"I could ask you the same thing." He realized that a confrontational tone was not going to win him any points, so he quickly added. "I came down here…to Sydney, I mean… to help with the search."

He had no difficulty at all recounting the conversation with Sousa. It seemed like it had happened only a few minutes before, but as he replayed it in his head, he struggled to find some precursor to Sousa's attack. Even with the benefit of hindsight, he could see no hint of treachery.

Carrera stared back appraisingly. "That's it? You must have said something to make him suspicious."

Professor shook his head. "I don't think so. He had me convinced it was just a mechanical failure."

"Maybe he thought you would keep looking. Ask the wrong person the right question and blow the whole thing wide open." She blinked. "You weren't part of the original search, then? What made you decide to look into it?"

"We got some intel indicating that your plane's disappearance might have been aimed at a specific passenger. It was shaky, but I had to follow up on it."

Carrera was incredulous. "You're saying someone took my aircraft and everyone on it, just to get one guy? Who?"

"A Brit named Parrott. Ian Parrott."

"Name doesn't ring any bells. He's not part of the group here. What's so special about him?"

"He's the publisher for a guy named Gerald Roche." Carrera's blank look indicated that she had not heard of him either. "Honestly, I can't say for certain that Parrott is the reason for all this, but the coincidences are piling up."

Professor paused a beat. "Your turn. What happened up there? And who's behind it?"

"I don't know. We were flying, no problems, and then Seth put a needle in my neck."

"Seth? That would be Seth Norris, the pilot?"

"The captain," she corrected. "Only…"

Professor waited several seconds for her to elaborate, and when she did not, he prompted. "Only what?"

"Well, it's going to sound crazy but… He was different."

"Like he was being coerced?"

"No, not at all. He was cool as ice. But he just didn't seem like the Seth Norris I know."

Professor turned this revelation over in his head but could not immediately see how it fit with everything else. "What happened then?"

"Woke up right here. Been here ever since."

"No one told you why?"

"No one told us anything. Haven't seen the buggers. One guy talks to us on the public address. We call him 'Boss.' Don't recognize the voice, but he doesn't sound Korean if you know what I mean."

"Talks to you? What does he say?"

"Mostly just reminds us not to make trouble. This morning he told us all to go inside and stay put. That's what happens when they bring in a food delivery, but we weren't due. When I came out, I saw you."

Professor mulled this over as well. "Is there a perimeter? A fence or wall around this place?"

"Don't know. I haven't gone looking. That would be the kind of trouble Boss told us not to make." She squinted at him. "I hope you're not thinking about making any trouble."

"I'm not going to sit here and do nothing."

"The safety of the people here is my responsibility. I won't let you put them in danger."

"They're already in danger. They aren't holding you as hostages. The world thinks you're all dead, and they're obviously content to leave it that way. If the North Koreans or some other government is behind this, then they're damn sure not going to want anyone outside to know."

Carrera's nostrils flared angrily. "You'll get us all killed."

"I don't think so. They want something from you all. That's the only reason you're still alive, but as soon as they get it, they won't have any further use for you. Ergo, we need to make our move sooner rather than later."

"Make our move? And go where? We can't escape from North Korea."

"Actually, we can. I've done it before."

"You?" Carrera gaped at him. "You're serious, aren't you? What, you James Bond or something?"

"Something." He turned for the door.

"Hey." She grabbed his arm. "I'm serious. Why should I believe that you can do this? Who are you?"

Professor pursed his lips. Like most former operators, he did not like to parade his military service in front of others, but it wasn't like he was trying to pick Carrera up at a bar. "I was in the SEALs," he said. "US Naval Special Warfare Group. That's really all I can tell you."

"Let me guess," she said, arching an eyebrow. "If you told me anything more, you'd have to kill me."

"No," he answered with a chuckle. "But it's need to know, and all you need to know is that I can get us out."

"You were really in the SEALs?"

He raised three fingers. "Scouts honor."

Carrera pursed her lips. "There's forty-seven of us. I don't care how Rambo you are, there's no way we'll all make it out. But you might be able to make it out on your own. Let the world know we're here. It's the best chance any of us have."

As reluctant as he was to accept half-measures, he could not argue with her logic. Even with his knowledge of escape and evasion tactics, the odds of such a large group successfully running the gauntlet of North Korean security forces were slim to none. If he escaped on his own, there was a very good chance that his mysterious captors would punish those he left behind, but what he had told Carrera was the absolute truth. They were all living on borrowed time.

"I won't be able to do anything until nightfall. Let's take a look around. You can give me the nickel tour."

Her expression remained apprehensive but she nodded and gestured to the door. Even before he was outside, Professor started running through possible escape scenarios, compiling checklists of items he would need to acquire, like water, food, weapons, and things he would need to watch for like hostile observation posts, surveillance cameras, minefields, and most importantly, places where he might be able to take refuge. He took note of the layout of the camp, the spacing of the cabins and the distance to the tree line. The location of the sun....

He stopped abruptly and stared at the sky in disbelief. "Damn it," he muttered.

"What's the matter?" Carrera asked.

Her voice snapped him back to the moment. He raised his wrist in an almost reflexive action to check the time, though he already knew that he would find only bare skin where his Omega Seamaster chronograph ought to have been. "They took my watch."

Carrera shrugged. "Mine, too."

"What time is it?"

"I'm not really even sure what time zone we're in, but my best guess is a little after noon."

"Guess I'll have to make do," he said with a rueful smile. "I really liked that watch."

His dismay was sincere but it had nothing to do with his missing timepiece. He was mad at himself, and not just for almost letting his poker face to slip. He was mad because he had made a rookie mistake by trusting someone he didn't know.

He surreptitiously glanced up at the sky again, confirming what he already knew. It was indeed midday, but from the angle of the shadows and the subtle change in their position, he was able to orient himself, and while it would have taken him at least half an hour of careful observation to make a precise determination, it was patently obvious that the sun was in the northern sky. The location of the secret prison camp was more likely at forty degrees south latitude, rather than north.

Which meant that woman claiming to be Jeanne Carrera was lying about being a professional aviator, or intentionally deceiving him about their location. Either way, he had already told her far too much.

TWELVE

New York City

Gabrielle Greene swept into Shah's office with all the subtlety of a thunderstorm. "Have you heard?"

"Heard what?"

"Two of your jihadists attacked Jade Ihara in Scotland."

Shah sat bolt upright in alarm. "Gabrielle! It's not safe to talk here."

She waved a dismissive hand. "That's the least of our problems right now."

"What do you mean? Is Ihara....?" He left the question unfinished. Gabrielle might be unconcerned about electronic surveillance, but watching what he said to avoid self-incrimination had become a deeply ingrained habit for Shah, one he could not easily break.

"Oh, she's fine. She sent them packing."

"Oh. Well, then I don't understand why you're so upset."

Gabrielle leaned over his desk. "She's fine, Atash. They didn't kill her. That's the problem. It was a ham-fisted amateurish attempt, and they completely blew it."

Shah stood up and took Gabrielle's elbow. "Not here," he repeated, steering her toward the door.

If there was still active surveillance, then she had probably said too much already, but Shah needed a moment to think, and his office, where he labored day in and day out to conduct a strictly legal defense of the Islamic faith and its adherents, was not a place where he felt comfortable talking about orchestrating a murder attempt. Thankfully, Gabrielle waited until they were out of the office and in the elevator to resume the conversation.

"Things are spinning out of control, Atash."

Shah glanced nervously up at the security camera mounted in the corner, wondering if the FBI had tapped into it. "I don't understand why you're so upset," he said through clenched teeth. "This is what you wanted, isn't it? Put her on the list and let the faithful take care of the rest. Nothing to directly implicate us. That was the plan, wasn't it?"

"The plan failed. Ihara found something in Scotland. And now she knows that we're coming after her. We can't afford any more screw-ups."

"What did she find? Roche's book?"

"I don't know. Does it matter? She needs to be silenced."

Shah felt overwhelmed by the intensity of Gabrielle's demand, but he could not disagree with the last point. Thankfully, the elevator doors opened on the lobby, giving him another brief respite in which to process the rush of information. Gabrielle had been absolutely right about one thing: the situation was spiraling into chaos.

She had come to him only the night before with a reliable tip that Jade Ihara, the archaeologist Gerald Roche had visited just before his death, was in the United Kingdom, trying to pick up the pieces of Roche's investigation. The last report was that she was on her way to Scotland so, at Gabrielle's urging, he had put the word out on the CDL website. He had also circulated more explicit information anonymously on a number of Internet bulletin boards frequented by disenfranchised Muslims living abroad, mostly young men, who fulminated endlessly over the persecution of the faithful by Zionist puppets and were desperate to strike a blow in the ongoing Holy War.

Evidently, someone had heeded his call, but subsequently failed to deliver, and now Jade Ihara was one step closer to making a discovery that would shatter everything Shah and billions of faithful Muslims across the ages had fought to build.

Gabrielle was right about that, too. Jade Ihara had to be stopped.

He strode purposefully through the lobby, with Gabrielle matching him step for step, and emerged onto a chilly but nevertheless bustling Manhattan sidewalk. Out here, despite being surrounded by hundreds of people, they could speak with greater freedom.

"Where is Ihara now?"

"Still in Scotland," Gabrielle said, her earlier zeal only somewhat diminished. Shah did not need to ask how she came by her information. In the twenty-first century, tracking someone in real-time was the easiest thing in the world.

Shah glanced at his watch. "It's late evening there, but if we hurry, we should be able to arrange something."

Gabrielle grabbed his elbow. "You need to take charge of this personally, Atash."

"What do you think I've been doing?"

"Personally," she repeated. "We can't entrust this to a bunch of hopped-up students who will turn and run at the first sign of trouble."

He blinked at her. "You mean... Me?"

"I'm not saying you need to pull the trigger. In fact, we don't have to kill anyone."

"I don't understand."

"We take Ihara alive. At least until we know what proof she has. Then we can let someone else..." She paused as if searching for an appropriately benign euphemism. "Finish. But you need to take charge in person to ensure that there are no more screw-ups."

Her grip on his arm tightened. "This is important, Atash. They're looking for a leader. A real leader, not just some religious demagogue who will tell them to go blow themselves up. Someone who sees their real potential. Show them that you can be that leader."

"You want me to drop everything here and fly to Scotland?" It seemed like an impossible request, but Shah knew he would not be able to refuse.

"It has to be done, Atash."

He stared at her, marveling at the power she had over him. "Will you come with me?"

She smiled and the last of his resistance evaporated. "Of course. I wouldn't miss it for the world."

THIRTEEN

Scotland

Despite her playful suggestion that they sample some traditional Scottish fare, Jade had no intention of remaining in Kilmaurs. Their attackers were still at large, and aside from Kellogg's assertion that the men were Arabs, they had no idea who the men were or what they looked like. Even the assumption that they were Middle Eastern was a guess. Arabic was the language of the Quran, but that did not mean all Muslims were Arabs. Over the centuries, Islam had spread far and wide, from Eastern Europe to Africa to Indonesia, and their descendants had brought their faith to enclaves in nearly every corner of the globe. It was not inconceivable that the two men might be locals. The safest course was to keep moving.

Jade called the car rental agency to arrange the recovery of her rental, then she and Kellogg struck out for London in his car. While he drove, she plugged the flash drive into his laptop and began scrolling through the directory. Her eye was immediately drawn to the label on one of the file icons.

"'*The Three Hundred Year Lie.*'"

"That's it," Kellogg said. "That's the name of Mr. Roche's book."

Jade clicked on the icon and opened a list of document files, several of which were marked with chapter numbers. She clicked on the first and began reading silently.

Her initial impression, after reading the first few chapters, was that Roche had somehow contrived a way to stretch the essence of their conversation at the Paracas museum into a forty thousand word screed. He relied on cherry-picked and often irrelevant data, logical fallacies, *ad hominem* attacks against the men allegedly responsible for the deception, and constant repetition of his core premise. There was nothing particularly persuasive in his argument, and if not for the fact that someone had killed Roche, evidently to keep the information from being released, she would have dismissed it as foolishness.

She turned to Kellogg. "You know what this book's about, right?"

"I read a synopsis. It all sounded a bit daft to me."

"Yeah, I was thinking that, too. So what about this has Muslims so upset?"

"You really don't know?" Kellogg gave her a sidelong glance then returned his focus to the road ahead. "If the Phantom Time hypothesis is correct, then everything the history books say happened between 700 and 1000 AD is a complete fraud. That would include the life of the Prophet Muhammad and the accepted history of the rise of Islam. If Roche is right, then none of it really happened."

"So what? I mean, he probably isn't right, but what difference does it make? A lot of people don't think Jesus was real. Or Moses. That doesn't seem to bother the people who do believe."

He shrugged. "You and I both know that, but Muslims take perceived insults to their faith very seriously. Do you recall what happened with *The Satanic Verses?*"

"Vaguely. I was a kid."

"In 1988, Salman Rushdie released a novel which included a fictional account of the revelation to the Prophet Muhammad, and Muslims everywhere were outraged. The Ayatollah Khomeini issued a *fatwa*, calling for Rushdie to be killed. Rushdie spent ten years in hiding, and several of his translators were attacked. Some of them were killed. That same year, Martin Scorsese released his movie *The Last Temptation of Christ*, which included a fictional account of the crucifixion. There was controversy, and outraged Christians picketed theaters showing the film, but that was it. No one died."

"That was almost thirty years ago," Jade said.

Kellogg arched an eyebrow. "You think the Islamic world is more tolerant now than they were then?"

"Okay, point taken. But this Phantom Time stuff is…" She smiled as she recalled Professor's opinion on the topic.

"Thin soup. Getting all spun up about it…killing Roche for God's sake, just legitimizes it."

"I never said it would make sense. But you did ask." Kellogg paused a beat. "Anti-Muslim sentiment is also on the rise, thanks to 9/11 and 7/7. There are politicians in your country and mine who wouldn't hesitate to seize on the possibility that Islam is all a sham, just to score political points."

Jade pondered this for a moment. Was it possible that Rafi and the two men who had attacked them at the fogou had seen Roche and his book as an existential threat to their way of life? "He's wrong though, isn't he? Roche, I mean."

Kellogg shrugged. "I haven't read the book yet, but it probably doesn't matter. People believe what they want to believe. Mr. Roche was always preaching to the converted. This won't change anything."

"You just sell books, right?" Jade shook her head. "You shouldn't publish this."

Kellogg's head snapped toward her. "Why on earth not?"

"It's irresponsible. You would be pouring gasoline on a fire that's already out of control."

"People have a right to make an informed decision."

"Informed decision?" Jade replied. "Seriously? This is a crank theory, and you know it. And people are getting killed because of it."

"That's exactly why it must be published. Once it's out in the open, they'll have no reason to come after you."

The argument took the wind out of Jade's sails. Kellogg was right about that. "Damn Roche," she muttered. "If he wasn't already dead, I'd kill him myself."

Kellogg chuckled mirthlessly. "So it's settled then. I'll take the file and set the book up. You can wash your hands of it."

"I hope it's as easy as that," Jade replied. She glanced down at the computer screen again. "Why did he come to me? That's the part that doesn't make any sense."

"I should say many of the things Mr. Roche did made

little sense."

"He thought I could prove something for him," Jade said, more to herself than Kellogg. She reread the words on the screen, the last few lines of the fourth chapter of Roche's book.

All of which begs the question: Why? Why go to such extraordinary lengths to alter the calendar and then cover up the change?

Illig proposes that Otto II was motivated by a desire to be the reigning autarch of the Holy Roman Empire at the coming of the millennium, but does this answer suffice? As we will see in the next chapter, the real purpose behind The Three Hundred Year Lie was to prevent humankind from opening the Archimedes Vault.

Jade sat up a little straighter. "Archimedes Vault?"

She scrolled back up to see if she had missed something, but there were no previous mentions of Archimedes or any other vaults. The reference was a complete non sequitur. She clicked on the next file, curious to see where Roche would go with it.

The next chapter began with an exhaustive biography of the legendary mathematician and inventor, Archimedes of Syracuse. Some of the information was familiar to Jade, but much of it seemed sensationalized, like the claim that Archimedes had created a solar-powered death ray and an elaborate crane device to destroy the ships of Roman invaders in Syracuse harbor. Jade found herself wishing that Professor was around to fact-check the information, or at the very least, give her an abbreviated version.

"Do you know about this Archimedes Vault?"

Kellogg gave her another sidelong glance. "No. I don't recall that from the synopsis. Do tell."

"Here's what it says. 'Although some of his inventions were weaponized for use in the defense of his home, Archimedes held back many of his discoveries, fearing that the men of his time were not sufficiently evolved to use such technology wisely. Like the Robert Oppenheimer of his day,

Archimedes recognized that, once this knowledge was revealed, there would be no going back. To preserve these discoveries for future generations, Archimedes constructed a secret impenetrable vault, secured with a lock that would only open once every thousand years."'

"Is that true?" Kellogg asked.

Jade shook her head. "It's not really my field, but I've never heard of anything like that. You would think if something like that really existed, we'd have heard about it."

"A lock that can't be opened for a thousand years? Is that even possible? I'm sure it would be easy enough to accomplish today, but two thousand years ago?"

Jade shrugged. "The way Roche tells it, if anyone could pull it off, Archimedes would be that guy."

She kept reading, curious to see if there was any evidence to support the statement. According to Roche, the plans for a fantastic timelock mechanism had been found on a palimpsest—a parchment skin which had been erased and written over by medieval scholars. Jade knew this was a common practice. Parchment was expensive and rare, and recycling it was a common practice. While it was possible, in some cases, to restore the original document, historians were faced with the dilemma of choosing which document to preserve. Advances in imagery techniques and electron microscopy however, had made it possible to produce digital versions of documents long thought unrecoverable. Several treatises by Archimedes had been recovered in this fashion, including, or so Roche posited, the ingenious plans for the vault and timelock, which had been leaked—briefly—to the Internet. Unfortunately, or so Roche claimed, that particular palimpsest was not regarded as authentic, and all digital copies of it had subsequently disappeared—if they had in fact existed at all. According to the conspiracy theorist, this was evidence of a Changeling plot to suppress the discovery. Even the original erasure played into this narrative.

We should not be surprised at the lengths to which the Changelings will go to prevent the world from learning about the vault.

Archimedes was no doubt aware of the Changeling conspiracy, even in ancient times. He almost certainly intended his Vault as a way to equip future generations with the weapons to unmask and defeat this insidious threat. The location of the vault was entrusted to his loyal acolytes, the Society of Syracuse.

To be sure, the Changelings knew about the vault and feared what lay concealed within. The Roman siege of Syracuse was orchestrated by the Changelings for the sole purpose of killing Archimedes and wiping out all mention of the existence of the vault. Indeed, Archimedes was murdered despite the explicit orders of the Roman general leading the attack that he be taken alive.

As the time-lock ticked inexorably toward the day when the vault would be unlocked, the Changelings took bold action to ensure that the secrets within would never see the light of day. Since they could not enter the vault or destroy its contents, they contrived a bold plan to confuse Archimedes' successors, so that they would fail to recognize when the thousand year time limit elapsed.

Archimedes sealed his Vault sometime before his death in 212 BC. Counting forward one thousand years, we arrive at AD 787. In AD 614, more than eight hundred years after the murder of Archimedes, Emperor Otto II and Pope Sylvester II, at the direction of Changeling agents, added approximately three hundred years to the calendar. The deception was so successful that, a century later, the scattered and persecuted remnants of the Society of Syracuse thought the opportunity to enter the vault had already passed them by.

How does this knowledge affect us today?

Based on the correction to the Gregorian calendar, we can surmise that about two hundred and ninety-seven years were added to the calendar, which means that instead of 2015, it is actually 1718, or 1,931 years since the death of Archimedes. While we do not know exactly when the thousand year cycle will be complete, we do know that the Vault of Archimedes will open sometime in the next sixty-seven years.

Jade stopped reading. "I think I know why Roche came to me," she said. "He wanted me to find the Archimedes Vault."

Kellogg looked at her again, longer than was perhaps

safe given the road conditions. "You think it really exists?"

"Roche certainly did."

There was a long pause before Kellogg finally said, "You're going to do it, aren't you?"

Jade smiled in spite of herself. "Professor was right. I am predictable. Speaking of which…" She dug out her phone and started composing a text message. "I should probably let him know where I'm headed." She hit the "send" button.

"Where exactly is that?"

"Syracuse. That's in Italy, I think. It's the logical place to start looking."

"Sicily," Kellogg murmured.

"Yeah?" The phone buzzed in her hand, signaling Professor's reply to her text. *That was quick,* she thought.

Just about done here. Will meet you there in a few days. Be careful.

"Huh. That's weird. I thought he'd freak out." The brevity of his reply was surprising, but there was probably a good reason for it. Maybe he was driving. She wanted to inquire about the results of his investigation, but decided to let that wait until they were face-to-face again. The fact that he was wrapping up meant that he had either found something conclusive, or more likely, nothing at all.

"You do realize," Kellogg said, "if the vault is real, it would be pretty compelling proof that Mr. Roche was right. About Phantom Time and everything else."

She looked up from her phone. "Your point?"

"You were the one who thought we should just let it go. Remember? Don't pour petrol on the fire?"

"The existence of the Archimedes Vault—if it exists— wouldn't prove Phantom Time any more than the existence of the pyramids or the Nazca lines proves that UFOs are real."

"And if there is some kind of thousand year timelock?"

"Look, the whole thing is probably a wild goose chase,

but I'll never forgive myself if I don't at least look for it."

Kellogg pondered this for a moment. "Mind if I come along?"

"Really? I figured you would be busy trying to get Roche's book out."

Kellogg smiled. "Unless I'm very much mistaken, the book's not finished. There's still one more chapter left to write."

FOURTEEN

"'**The woods are** lovely, dark and deep. But I have promises to keep.'" Professor muttered.

"What's that?"

Professor turned away from the edge of the all but impenetrable tree line and offered Carrera a smile. "You haven't gone past this point?"

"No. Boss made it very clear that there would be consequences if anyone did that."

There was no obvious sign of a security presence, which only confirmed Professor's earlier suspicion. If this had been a North Korean prison camp, the perimeter would have been well defined, with guard towers, dogs, guns, land mines… The DPRK did not believe in subtlety. This was something else.

While he and Carrera—or rather the woman claiming to be the First Officer of Flight 815—roamed the camp and strolled along the tree line, Professor surreptitiously worked out a rough estimate of the latitude—forty-five degrees, south. Most of the earth's landmass was in the Northern Hemisphere. The Southern Hemisphere was mostly ocean, and below forty-five degrees, there was a dearth of real estate. There were really only two places they could be: South America—Chile or Argentina—or New Zealand. The latter made the most sense. If the stubble on his chin was any indication, he had only been unconscious for a few hours, certainly not long enough to make the trans-oceanic flight to South America. What made absolutely no sense at all was why Carrera had lied about their location.

She's testing me, he decided. *But is she working with the people who abducted me, or does she suspect I'm one of them?*

"Can you arrange some kind of diversion back at the camp?"

Carrera stared back at him. "I can't put the passengers

in any danger."

"Just make some noise. Bang some stuff around. All I need is a few minutes to get from my cabin to the trees."

Carrera's expression remained uncertain. An act? If so, she was an Academy Award caliber actor. He just hoped his own performance was as convincing.

"Let's get back," he said, not waiting for a reply. "I should eat something and grab some shut-eye. I'll make my move two hours after sunset."

"Not midnight?"

"Everyone goes at midnight. It's cliché." He said nothing more on the subject as they made their way back to the cabins. He asked a few more perfunctory questions, paying more attention to how she answered than to what she actually said. The woman had no tells that he could discern, which he decided almost certainly meant that she was willingly working with his captors.

Her story about the takeover of the airplane was probably the truth, only she had probably been the one drugging Norris, instead of the other way around. That part was easy enough to figure out, but it brought him no closer to solving the real mystery.

Why?

Why take an aircraft full of people just to eliminate one man? Why go to the trouble of constructing this elaborate ruse—Carrera, the bogus North Korean prison camp, the other survivors, if in fact that was what they were? And why had they brought him here?

The scenario reminded him a little of a British television series from the 1960s, about a secret agent who had been abducted and taken to a bizarre village where no one was what they seemed. The villain of the story, the mysterious "Number Two," played by a different actor in every episode, never revealed exactly what it was he wanted from the hero, just "information." The program had been heavy with symbolism—a metaphorical struggle of the individual against society's demand for conformity and homogeneity—and psychedelic to the point of self-parody, but the tactics employed by the nameless antagonist were right out of the Cold War spy handbook. Gaslighting 101. Professor had a sneaking suspicion his captors had either read that book or watched the show. Probably both.

On the return trip, Carrera took him to one of several cabins that served as supply depot and restroom facilities. He collected a box of MREs and a flat of bottled water, and carried them back to his own cabin, where he bade Carrera good-bye. He picked a meal at random and ate, though he barely tasted the unappetizing fare, and then settled onto the mattress for a nap. He had not been lying to Carrera about his intention to eat and sleep before making his escape attempt, but he had misled her about the timing of his attempt. He would not be waiting until two hours after sundown.

Forty-five minutes later, and—judging by its position in the sky—a good hour before nightfall, Professor rose and left his cabin. He walked at a languid pace, casual but purposeful, strolling through the camp in the direction of the restroom cabin. As he went, he nodded to the handful of people he saw, all of them ostensibly passengers from Flight 815. Some waved back, others regarded him uncertainly, but no one spoke to him or made any move to stop him. When he got within sight of his destination however, he shifted course, moving away at the same pace, toward the tree line.

He thought he saw, out of the corner of his eye, some of the passengers taking note, perhaps even following him, but he did not look back. He kept his eyes forward, his pace quickening ever so slightly, as if he had somewhere important to be. When he got within fifty yards of the woods, he broke into a run.

At the edge of the woods, he risked a quick glance over his shoulder. No one was giving chase, which was not necessarily a good sign. He wondered if he had misjudged the allegiances of the people purporting to be his fellow prisoners. His strategy was predicated on the belief that some or all of them were actually working with his captors, and that security beyond the camp would be minimal. If he was wrong....

I'm not wrong, he told himself, returning his focus to what lay ahead. *Not completely, anyway.*

He scanned the woods in front of him, looking for tripwires or areas of disturbed ground that might hide pitfalls or even mines, checked the branches of trees for surveillance cameras. The most important thing was to establish short-range waypoints in order to stay oriented. Beneath the forest canopy, with so many trees clustered together forcing him to weave back and forth, and no direct view of the sun, he could easily wind up running in circles. Keeping a true course while maintaining a running pace required intense concentration. He did not dare look back again.

He counted his steps, and was able to estimate both the distance he had traveled and the time that had elapsed since fleeing the camp. Five minutes out—give or take a minute—he figured he had gone about a quarter of a mile, with no sign of human activity and no indication that the woods would ever end.

A quarter of a mile. Probably a lot less given the zig-zagging course he was obliged to take.

Miles to go before I sleep.

He strained to catch some noise of pursuit—shouts, alarms, the barking of bloodhounds—but the only sounds he heard were the crunch of his footsteps on the litter of conifer needles and dry seed cones covering the ground and the occasional snap of a low hanging branch breaking against his shoulder.

Two or three minutes more passed by and then, without warning, the woods ahead grew brighter. Professor froze in mid-stride and remained that way while his heart hammered out a hundred beats. The light seemed to be natural, probably the result of a clearing that was allowing more sunlight to penetrate the canopy overhead, but it might also signal the end of the wooded area or worse, a secured perimeter. He crept forward, staying behind tree boughs until his field of view cleared.

It was a clearing, of sorts, but not a naturally occurring one. A swath of bare dirt, at least two hundred feet wide, cut through the midst of the forest. The ground was uniformly flat, obviously packed down and graded with road building equipment, but Professor saw immediately that it wasn't a road.

It was a runway.

A Boeing 777 sat idle more than a hundred yards away. Radar-scattering camouflage nets hung on poles all around the aircraft formed a shroud that would effectively hide the plane from satellites and search aircraft. The markings and registration number on the tail confirmed what was already plainly obvious. He had found Flight 815.

He studied the aircraft for a full minute but saw no sign of activity, no guards posted, no workmen disassembling or modifying the evidently derelict plane. He fleetingly contemplated trying to fly the aircraft out—how hard could it be after all?—but shelved the idea. Even if he was able to figure out the controls, getting the plane moving would take time, time which he doubted his captors would allow.

Still, there were other ways the aircraft could be useful to what he had planned.

He moved laterally down the length of the runway, keeping to the woods and pausing often to check for signs of pursuit. The fact that there had been none was disconcerting. He felt conspicuously like a mouse being toyed with by a stealthy cat who felt secure enough in its ability to pounce long before the prey escaped.

Tom and Jerry, the dueling cartoon characters, ran through his head, and the thought brought a smile to his face. Jerry always outsmarted Tom.

He stopped a stone's throw from the plane. The front hatch, where passengers normally boarded and debarked, was open and a makeshift staircase had been erected to facilitate access from the ground. The doorway was dark, the window blinds open to reveal no lights inside. It was almost certainly a trap, but Professor knew something that his captors did not. He was not trying to escape.

He stepped from the trees and crossed to the steps, ascended and cautiously entered the plane. Although some light was getting in through the portholes, it did little to illuminate the interior. The atmosphere was surreal, like being inside the corpse of some immense cyclopean beast. Professor turned toward the front of the plane and found the door to the cockpit. It was open, revealing empty seats and a dark instrument panel.

He sat down in the left hand seat and stared out the front windshield. The nose of the plane was facing west, giving him a view of the darkening sky. There were more trees at the end of the runway, another hundred yards or so distant, but beyond that, only sky.

He folded his hands in his lap and waited. He did not think he would have to wait very long.

FIFTEEN

Syracuse, Sicily

On the map, the island of Sicily looked like an enormous triangular rock poised on the end of the toe of the boot that was Italy, but Sicily was no footnote. The largest island in the Mediterranean, sloping away from the flanks of the majestic 11,000-foot high Mount Etna, the largest volcano in Europe and one of the most active volcanoes in the world, had been inhabited by humans for more than 12,000 years. Greek culture had taken hold in 750 BCE, and for 500 years thereafter, the island had been part of *Magna Graecia*— Greater Greece—until, in the time of Archimedes, it had been claimed by Rome. Its fertile soil had fed the Roman legions, fueling the rise of the Roman Empire and conquest of the entire region. In more recent times, the campaign to capture Sicily, spearheaded by the flamboyant American general George Patton, had been pivotal to breaking the Axis powers in World War II.

Though her specialty was pre-Columbian America, Jade was not unfamiliar with the Classical period, and like any archaeologist worth her salt, could not help but be awed by standing in the presence of so much history. She only wished Professor could have been there to share the experience, but his last text message had indicated he was still in Australia and that it might be another day or two before he could get a flight out. Jade did not dare to hope that she would find the Archimedes Vault in that short a time, but she was not about to postpone the search to wait for him.

Shortly after returning to London, Jade and Kellogg had caught an early train to Paris, and then transferred to a Eurostar train bound for Rom, followed by a third train ride and a trip on a ferry. The total journey lasted about thirty-six hours, including short layovers at the transfer points, putting them in Syracuse, Sicily shortly before midnight of the second day since the escape from the Kilmaurs fogou. Flying would have reduced the actual travel time, but trains offered a sort of anonymity that, given the ongoing threat from Islamic extremists—or whomever it was targeting her—seemed the most prudent method of getting to their destination.

The late arrival necessitated finding lodgings for the night. Citing security concerns, Jade insisted on a five star hotel. It would have been too easy for an assassin to slip into a hostel or budget hotel and dispatch her in the dead of night—but after days on the road and weeks of camp life in Peru, a long soak in a hot tub and eight hours—*okay, maybe more like nine and half*—sleeping on 400 thread count sateen weave Egyptian cotton sheets were just what the doctor ordered. Kellogg grumbled at the rate, but Jade suggested he write it off as business expense. She awoke feeling refreshed and ready to dive into the search. It didn't hurt one bit that Sicily was warm and sunny, and not nearly as humid as her native Oahu.

From his research notes, it was clear that Roche believed the vault would be found somewhere on the island of Sicily, but he had little evidence to back this supposition up. Ever the conspiracy theorist, he claimed that there had been a systematic effort, either by the Changelings, or by the acolytes of the Society of Syracuse—or perhaps both, though for very different reasons—to erase any mention of the vault's location from the historical record. Jade would be starting her search from square one, but she was counting on her lack of preconceived notions to give her a fresh perspective. Maybe Roche, in looking too hard for what he expected to find, had overlooked some important clue.

She began looking, as she almost always did, at a museum—specifically the Paolo Orsi Regional Archaeological Museum. Given the rich history of Sicily, and specifically Syracuse, it was not surprising that the city hosted one of the premiere archaeological institutions in Europe. The museum complex—situated on the edge of the historic Villa Londolina, where ongoing excavations continued to provide new insights into the Greek and Roman period—was unusual and a bit anachronistic. A top down view revealed a geometric design of conjoined hexagonal cells, a decidedly modern design for a repository of history. Archimedes would probably have approved, but despite his status as Syracuse's favorite son, there was very little information about him in the Orsi. After two hours of touring the facility, Jade headed to the next museum on the list, which in hindsight, should have been at the top: the Arkimedeion.

The reason the Arkimedeion had not been her first stop was that it was not a history museum, but rather a science museum, showcasing the mathematical discoveries and inventions of Archimedes. According to a tourist guide website, the Arkimedeion had only been open a few years and the reviews described an ambitious tourist attraction that fell short of its promise. Jade's hopes were not high as she and Kellogg made the trip by taxi to Ortigia, the small island district where the Arkimedeion was located. The museum occupied an elegant stone building on the edge of a cobblestone piazza, at the center of which was a marvelous fountain with a sculpted mermaid—possibly meant to represent the Roman goddess Diana—and a child riding on the back of a large fish. The setting would have been more impressive if not for the fact that stone buildings were ubiquitous in the Old World, and you couldn't throw a Frisbee in Italy without it splashing down in a fountain. With appropriately low expectations, Jade headed toward the front entrance while Kellogg paid their taxi driver.

A smiling middle-aged man at the ticket counter greeted her in Italian. He was handsome enough, but like elegant buildings and fountains, that was nothing remarkable. Jade peered at his named badge and then addressed him in English. "Sorry, Paolo. I don't speak Italian."

"Ah, *scusi*. Fortunately, I speak your language well enough. And you are also fortunate that the *museo* is having free entry to beautiful ladies today."

"How lucky for me."

"*Sì.*" He extended a hand like a game show host. Jade noticed a glint of gold on his pinky finger, a signet ring with an emblem she couldn't quite make out. "And we are very slow today, so it will my pleasure to give you a tour."

The door opened and Kellogg strolled in. Jade turned to him. "Good news, honey. Free admission today. And a guided tour."

Paolo's smile fell but he nodded gamely and gestured to the entrance. "Please, this way."

Atash Shah watched Jade and Kellogg make their way into the museum from the shelter of a black Volkswagen van, parked on the far side of the fountain. Despite the dark tinted window, which ably concealed the six men in the passenger seats behind him from outside scrutiny, Shah felt exposed. Conspicuous. But if their quarry had noticed the vehicle tailing them through the city, they gave no outward sign.

"We can take them here," Gabrielle said.

"In broad daylight?" Shah shook his head. "It's too public."

"Look around. There's no one in there. We won't get a better chance." Her eyes flitted ever so slightly, looking over her shoulder at the men seated behind them, the implicit message: *Send them in.*

He understood why she wanted him to give the order. The men behind them, young Muslim immigrants who had answered Shah's call to arms, needed to hear it from him, their leader, not from a woman and an infidel at that.

He had issued his summons in one of the Internet chatrooms where would-be jihadists flirted endlessly with the prospect of joining al Quaeda or ISIL. Most were poseurs, unwilling to make good on their boasts. Some were probably undercover policeman—FBI or Interpol—though they were pretty easy to unmask. But there were always a few who were willing, eager even, to embrace martyrdom. The trick was in separating the wheat from the chaff.

These six had come from Paris, carrying their own

illegally obtained weapons, ready to do whatever he asked of them.

And Shah had to be the one to ask it of them.

He drove the van around the fountain and pulled up in front of the entrance, close enough that no one looking out from the surrounding buildings would see them bring their hostages out the front. Then, he turned to face his holy warriors. "Cover all the exits so they can't slip away. And remember. We need them alive."

Shah wondered if they heard the fear in his voice. Would they see through him? See how weak he was? Did they know that the real reason he wanted them to take hostages was that he was afraid to give the order to kill?

If they doubted him, they did not show. One by one, they filed out of the van and headed toward the entrance to the Arkimedeion.

Gabrielle's hand close over his in a reassuring squeeze, and Shah felt some of the fear slip away.

"How about this one," Jade said, gesturing to an exhibit that, if the poster was to be believed, was a reconstruction of Archimedes' "heat ray." One of his more famous—and probably apocryphal—inventions, the heat ray was an array of parabolic mirrors that the inventor had supposedly used to set enemy ships on fire in Syracuse harbor.

"So sorry," Paolo said. "Is not working right now."

"What a surprise," Jade muttered, sharing a knowing glance with Kellogg. It was not the first time their guide had said those words.

The heat ray simulations, like several other displays and dioramas in the supposedly interactive museum, was currently closed for repairs. Jade now understood the reason for the negative reviews on the travel guide website. It wasn't that the museum was run down. In fact, the space was bright and welcoming, with vibrant colors utterly unlike the subdued earth tones of the Archaeology Museum. It wasn't really even that so many exhibits were out-of-order. Rather, the most disappointing thing about the Arkimedeion was how it failed to live up to its potential. An entire museum dedicated to one of the greatest minds in scientific history, and nothing worked. It was hard to believe in the legend of Archimedes when the reproductions of his most famous inventions were non-functional.

"No matter," Paolo said, waving a dismissive hand at the broken exhibit. "You will like the stomachion."

"With a name like that, I'm sure I'll love it."

Paolo led them up the stairs to another bright room with more vivid primary colors, and not much else. He gestured to the table in the center, which displayed a rectangular mosaic composed of differently colored triangles.

"That's the... um...stomachatron?"

"Stomachion," Paolo repeated. He went to the table and began picking up the individual triangles and rearranging them. "Is an ancient Greek game. You create different shapes. Animals. Houses. Anything the mind imagines."

Jade now saw that the almost psychedelic wallpaper in the room was actually made up of hundreds of different variations on the arrangement of the geometric tiles. "It's like a tangram puzzle."

"*Sì, sì.* Archimedes, he uses it to test complex mathematical ideas. He wrote book, all about how he uses stomachion, but..." He shrugged. "We have only part. The rest is lost."

"Speaking of lost books, can you tell us anything about the Vault of Archimedes?"

Jade thought she saw surprise flicker across the museum guide's face. "Vault?"

"With a timelock that only opens once every thousand years."

Paolo's smile returned. "Ah, a new story. I have never heard this one before."

"I think we can take that as a 'no,' then," Kellogg said.

Paolo opened his mouth to reply, but then looked away suddenly. "Ah, more guests. Please, enjoy the stomachion. Perhaps, you can tell me more about this Vault before you go."

"Actually," Jade said, "I think we've seen enough."

She followed Paolo out onto the balcony overlooking the guest lobby, but stopped short when she caught a glimpse of the two men who were just starting up the stairs. Her instincts screamed an alarm.

It was not merely that the two men with dark complexions and full beards seemed to fit perfectly the stereotype of what she imagined their attackers in Scotland must have looked like under their ski mask. Looks could certainly be deceiving. Rather, it was the none-too subtle aura of menace that radiated from them. They both looked ready to explode into violence.

Paolo called out to them in his typically friendly manner but before he could finish his greeting, they reached him and brushed past him like he wasn't even there.

Jade shrank back into the stomachion room. "Company's here. We need to find a back door."

Kellogg stared back, dumbfounded, so Jade grabbed his arm and dragged him toward the exit. His reflex to resist slowed her down just enough to allow the two bearded men to reach the landing at almost the same instant she and Kellogg stepped out. The reaction was instantaneous. The gazes of the two men fixed on Jade like a missile-lock.

"Run!" she shouted, and then without waiting to see if Kellogg would follow suit, she spun on her heel and sprinted away, heading deeper into the exhibits. After a few seconds of searching on the run, she spied a red exit sign on the ceiling. Unlike several of the other signs she had passed, this one did not point to the stairs behind them, but to a destination somewhere further inside the museum. Fire stairs, or perhaps an exterior fire escape in the rear of the building. Jade swerved toward the sign and then glanced over her shoulder to see how close the pursuit was.

Too close.

Although Jade was a good ten yards ahead of the closest assailant, Kellogg's earlier hesitation had put him within their reach. In the instant she looked back, Jade saw the lead pursuer reaching out to snag hold of Kellogg's collar.

Without stopping, Jade snatched up a gold-colored sphere—about the size and weight of a bowling ball—and spun it around, heaving it like an over-sized Olympic shot put. As she released it, she shouted, "Duck!"

The warning was not only unnecessary but overly optimistic. The sphere arced through the air with agonizing slowness, and then, as gravity overcame what little inertia Jade had been able to give it, dropped suddenly, almost straight down, to strike the ground a few feet to Kellogg's left with a resounding thump. After releasing the sphere, Jade's own momentum carried her completely around, and for a moment, it was all she could do to stay on her feet and not go careening into the rest of the geometric display.

Nevertheless, the attempt was not entirely futile. The two men hesitated, prepared to take evasive action if needed, giving Kellogg a few precious seconds' lead. Jade got back on an even keel, and with Kellogg now beside her, sprinted in the direction indicated by the exit sign. They rounded a corner and Jade saw, about fifty feet away, a metal door marked with the words "Fire Exit" in both English and Italian.

Jade's flickering glimmer of hope was extinguished as the door suddenly swung open to reveal two more bearded men.

Great, Jade thought. *Reinforcements.*

The surprise of the two men at discovering the fleeing figures charging headlong toward them barely gave Jade enough time to avoid a collision. She veered to the right, and then using the wall like a swimmer making the turn at the end of a lap, rebounded back the way they had come, snaring Kellogg's arm in the process and whipping him around.

The abrupt reversal caught the two pursuing men completely off guard. One of them made a half-hearted attempt to tackle Jade as she shot by, but Jade just lowered her head and plowed through like a football player charging the scrimmage line. She made glancing contact and felt a sharp pain in her scalp as the man's hands snagged a few strands of her hair, and then she was past them both, running at full speed back toward the distant landing. Kellogg likewise made it past the two men, slipping between them with unexpected gracefulness.

Jade's dismay at realizing that the odds against them had doubled since the confrontation in Scotland was at least partially offset by the fact that, unlike the cramped tunnels in the fogou, their assailants were behind them and there was plenty of room to maneuver. But as she reached the landing, the balance tilted against her once more. Two more men stood in the reception lobby, temporarily waylaid by an extremely agitated Paolo. One of them looked up, spotted her, and cried out in alarm.

Jade looked around frantically for some other avenue of escape. Kellogg skidded to a stop beside her, likewise searching for an alternate exit but there was nowhere else to go. Then Jade spotted the golden sphere she had thrown earlier, rolling aimlessly toward them.

"I hope second time's the charm," she muttered as she reached down and gave it a shove toward the stairwell. The orb cracked loudly on the first step, bounced slightly, cracked again on the next tread, picking up speed and energy as it descended one step at a time. "Go!"

The rolling orb did not appear especially menacing but the two men coming up the stairs balked like it was the rolling boulder from an Indiana Jones movie. Paolo still shouting angrily at the intrusion as he gave chase, broke into a smile at the strange sight. He raised his fist in the air and shook it. "*Sì!* Archimedes would be proud."

The cascading sphere was just enough of a distraction to allow Jade and Kellogg to close with the men on the stairs at the midpoint. Jade worked all the angles and didn't care for her chances of bulldozing past the two, so instead, she planted a hand on the rail and vaulted over the side of the stairs. It was an impulsive decision, and as she arced up and over the bannister, and realized just how much space there was between her and the first floor, she instantly regretted it, but there was no turning back. The floor rushed up at her, and then before she was completely ready, she landed.

The impact sent jolts of pain up her legs, but she managed to stay loose, letting her bent knees absorb some of the shock. A vague memory of someone—probably Maddock—explaining parachute jumping techniques prompted her to lean sideways and curl into a ball. It must have been the right thing to do because the landing was not nearly as bad as she thought it would be, and a moment later, she was back on her feet and staring up at the astounded men on the stairs, which included Kellogg.

"You staying?"

Her shout snapped Kellogg out of his amazed stupor and he plowed forward, slamming into his closest assailant and sending him tumbling backward in a flail of arms and legs. Jade whirled around looking for the exit. Between her and it stood Paolo and an array of strange-looking devices—scale models of Archimedes' siege engines and other inventions.

The sharp report of a pistol startled Jade. She ducked reflexively behind one of the contraptions and looked up, trying to see which of the men had taken the shot. It was impossible to tell since all of them, except for the one Kellogg had knocked down, were now on the stairs and brandishing guns.

It might have been just a warning shot, but it was a message Jade couldn't ignore. She could outrun the men, but reaching the exit would require her to outrun bullets. A lot of them. Kellogg was even closer to the shooters. If they unleashed a fusillade, he would be cut down instantly.

A memory of what had happened in the fogou returned to her. When retreat had not worked, she had gone on the offensive. Attacked and won.

But those men hadn't been carrying guns.

A nearby replica—a full-scale model of a scorpion ballista, a giant crossbow artillery piece on wooden wheels, which the ancient Greeks and Romans had used to hurl three foot long iron bolts across long distances—gave her an idea. It was a crazy idea, but maybe just crazy enough to work.

She wheeled the scorpion around so that the business end was facing the foot of the stairs, and raised a hand above the release lever. She knew the men were watching her, hoped they realized what she was attempting. Her insane plan depended on that.

Kellogg reached the foot of the stairs and headed her way. She waited a moment longer for the gunmen to get there.

"Down!" Even as she shouted the warning, her hand striking the release trigger, Jade spun around, ready to dash past Paolo and sprint for the exit.

There was a loud crack, like a giant mousetrap snapping shut, and Jade felt the air shudder as the scorpion's torsion springs released their pent up energy and propelled the payload across the exhibit hall. An instant later, there was another sharp cracking noise as the bolt penetrated the wall plaster.

The discharge shocked Jade into momentary paralysis. Her intent had been to bluff the gunmen with the ancient weapon, get them to dive for cover in order to buy Kellogg and her the precious seconds they needed to reach the door. She was counting on their instinct for self-preservation to override the obvious knowledge that there was no way on earth a museum replica would be fully functional.

It was impossible to know if the bluff would have worked, but the actual scorpion bolt striking the wall was considerably more persuasive. The gunmen all vanished, ducking behind the balustrade.

She turned to Paolo. "*That* works?"

He gave a guilty shrug then waved urgently. "Come. This way. Follow me."

Shah jolted at the loud report. The heavy stone walls of the Arkimedeion building muffled the sound, but there was no doubt in his mind about what he had just heard.

"That was a shot," Gabrielle said, dismayed. Her

reaction was further confirmation that something had gone wrong inside the museum. "They wasn't supposed to be any shooting. We need her alive."

Before Shah could respond, Gabrielle threw open her door and charged up the front steps of the museum.

"Gabrielle, wait!" Shah fumbled with the door lever, finally succeeded in getting it open, and raced around the front end of the van in pursuit. Some part of him knew this was a mistake. He was not one of them, not a man of violence, not a warrior ready to kill for his faith. Would they heed his exhortation against killing, especially when he had been the one to declare Jade Ihara an enemy?

He reached the entrance before the doors closed behind Gabrielle and wormed his way through just in time to see her leave the reception lobby to enter the exhibit area. Past her, he could see some of his men shouting and brandishing their guns, but there was no sign of Jade. Gabrielle was crossing in front of the gunmen, waving her hands and shouting for them to put the guns away, but if their wild-eyed looks were any indication, they were having none of it. For the first time, it occurred to Shah that perhaps Jade had been the one doing the shooting.

He continued forward, still not completely certain what he would do to regain control of the situation, and glimpsed movement, someone disappearing behind a partition. "There!"

Gabrielle's eyes followed his pointing finger and then she was moving again, charging through the entrance to the exhibit. Shah saw the rest of the six jihadists moving to follow her, and raced on, rounding the partition just a few steps ahead of them and right behind Gabrielle.

The temporary walls enclosing the exhibit blocked nearly all outside light, and it took a moment for his eyes to adjust. He saw Gabrielle, momentarily stalled by the darkness, searching the room for some sign of their elusive prey. The room seemed bigger than it was due to the enormous mirrored wall that ran along one side. On the other side, behind a low wall, stood a mock-up of a Roman war galley, replete with armored soldiers posed as if ready for battle. In the low light, the life-sized diorama offered countless places to hide in plain sight, a fact which evidently had not escaped Gabrielle's notice. She hopped over the low parapet that separated the model from the viewing area and began shoving each of the mannequins in turn, knocking them to the floor and sending helmets and weapons flying. None of them offered the least bit of resistance.

"Not here," she growled. "There must be another way out of here."

Shah nodded dully and turned around to search the mirrored wall. His eyes had adjusted enough to realize that it was not a single flat mirror, but rather several smaller mirrors, each tilted slightly to form an gently concave surface, curved inward like the inside of a spoon.

At that instant, a voice resonated through the little room like the voice of the angel speaking to the Prophet, though the speaker did not sound particularly angelic and the words were not Arabic, but rather a familiar Latin phrase.

"Fiat lux!"

And then Shah's world became nothing but light and fire.

SIXTEEN

Jade looked away, shutting her eyes tight, but she could not blink faster than the speed of light. The flash as the high-powered spotlight, designed to simulate the sun's rays, shone from the ceiling of the heat ray exhibit, to be subsequently reflected and focused by the parabolic mirror array, was so bright that, in the instant of the flash, Jade thought she had seen the skeletons of the men pursuing them, visible through their skin. Even the smoked glass window of the observation booth, situated above the mock-up of the Roman war galley, was not dark enough to keep the light, indirect though it was, from being painfully bright.

"My God," Kellogg gasped. "You just incinerated them."

"No, no," Paolo said, his expression equally horrified at the prospect. "Is simulation."

"I thought you said this thing wasn't working," Jade said. Green blobs floated in front of her eyes. "Looks like it worked pretty well to me."

Paolo shook his head. "Blinding guests, no good for business."

"Good for us though."

"*Sì.*" Paolo rose and moved to the door. "But their eyes will recover and they still have guns. We must go. I take you somewhere safe."

Jade was having trouble reading the Italian's face through the retinal fireworks caused by the flash, but his willingness to help set alarm bells ringing in her head.

"Maybe we should call the police," Kellogg suggested. Although it had become something of a signature comment for him, in this instance Jade was inclined to agree.

Paolo seemed to be scrutinizing them. "And will you tell the *carabinieri* about the Vault of Archimedes?"

Jade's internal alarm bells got even louder, but before she could figure out an appropriate response, Paolo waved urgently. "I have the answers you seek, but right now we must go. Quickly."

The promise of answers was enough to help Jade overcome her wariness. Paolo was clearly more than just a humble museum guide, but the mere fact that he had a secret life did not automatically make him an enemy. She nodded and followed.

Paolo led them back down a short flight of stairs and past the hidden door behind the galley model, to a long access corridor. He stopped at the door leading to the fire stairs, opened it a sliver and peeked through. After a moment, he threw it wide open. "Come."

He crossed to a door on the opposite side of the stairwell and again checked that the coast was clear before venturing outside. The fire exit let out into a narrow alley between the museum and a neighboring building. Paolo hurried them to the far end, away from the piazza, to a back street crowded with parked cars. He stopped in front of one, a boxy red two-door Fiat hatchback. Jade wasn't much of a car person, but Jade guessed it was probably as old as she. As Paolo slotted his key into the lock, she realized that this was their escape vehicle.

"Shotgun!" Both Paolo and Kellogg began looking around in alarm, so she clarified. "Dibs on the front seat."

"*Sì*, of course," Paolo said, opening his door and working the lever to tilt the seat forward. He turned gestured for Kellogg to get in.

Kellogg turned to Jade. "Maybe we should talk about this first?"

"What's there to talk about? Paolo here just saved our bacon. And he can tell us about the vault." She opened the passenger door and glanced at their new benefactor. "You can tell us about the vault, right Paolo?"

"*Sì*. But not here. Not where they can find us."

She turned back to Kellogg. "See? Let's go."

Her cavalier attitude was a put-on. The age-old wisdom of countless generations of parents—don't get in cars with strangers—was echoing in her head. Her gut told her that Paolo was harmless, yet there was clearly more to him than met the eye, and that unknown quantity concerned her. But if he did know something about the vault, then it was worth the risk.

He navigated the back streets with easy familiarity, eventually merging into the chaos of the main thoroughfares. Jade knew she ought to be paying attention to where they were, but her gaze kept drifting to the faces of the people around them, pedestrians at sidewalk cafes, the drivers of the vehicles they passed. Every attack she had survived had come seemingly from out of the blue. Whether they were Muslim extremists or something else, the enemy stalking her seemed to have the ability to blend into the woodwork. Were they, even now, watching her every move? Tracking her somehow?

The thought sent an electric shock through her. They *were* tracking her. She would have to do a head-to-toe search for tracking chips...Kellogg, too, but the most obvious way for them to keep tabs on her was by pinging the GPS in her smart phone. She dug the device from her pocket and stared at it as she might a ticking time bomb.

The phone was her lifeline, her only means of staying in contact with Professor. She could write down his number, but if she threw her phone away, he would have no way of reaching her.

And what if I'm wrong?

If she was wrong, then it wouldn't matter what she did. They would find her again.

She tapped out a quick text message to Professor, letting him know that she was about to go dark then shut the phone off. "I need a paper clip. Or a safety pin."

Paolo glanced over at her, then pointed to the glove compartment.

"Why?" Kellogg asked, leaning over the seat.

"I'm going to pull the SIM card on my phone." The glove box contained a sheaf of paper held together by a paper clip. She removed it and unbent a section, which she then used to depress the release on the side of her phone. Removing the SIM card would make it impossible for anyone to track the phone remotely but still give her the option of using it again if the need arose. "They might be tracking me that way."

Kellogg's eyes went wide. "Should I do that too?"

"Might be a good idea." She handed him the paper clip, and then shoved both her phone and the SIM card into a pocket. She saw Paolo nod in approval. "That should keep them off our backs for a while," she said, meeting the Italian's stare. "Now, how about those answers?"

"I will tell you what I know, but first, tell me please, how did you learn of the vault?"

Jade cocked her head sideways. "Answering a question with a question. That's not a great way to start a conversation. Do you actually know something, or are you just stringing us along?"

"Ah, pardon me. I meant no offense. I am wondering because, you see, I thought that all knowledge of the vault had been lost forever."

"Obviously not. You know something about it."

"*Si, si.* But is a very closely guarded secret. Those who know would never share it with…" He smiled. "The uninitiated."

Jade stared at him for a moment. "Uninitiated? Oh, wonderful. You're part of a secret society, aren't you? I really hate secret societies."

Paolo just laughed.

"Let me guess," Jade went on. "You are modern descendants of the Society of Syracuse, entrusted with preserving Archimedes' secrets. I guess it makes sense that you would be the one running the Arkimedeion. Though frankly, I would have expected it to be in a little better shape."

"Better shape?" The Italian seemed amused by her assessment. He waved a hand. "Everything in the Arkimedeion works exactly as it was meant to. Some people, they see a broken thing and want to throw it away. Others see the same thing, and want to fix it."

"Oh, so it's a test. To see who's worthy to join your

little club."

"A test. A game. It is not so hard to join." He turned the Fiat off the road and drove down a side street until he found a parking spot.

"Really? You guys have a website or something? Society of Syracuse dot com?"

"I do not know this Society of Syracuse you speak of."

He gestured through the windshield toward their destination, a modest office building with dark windows and no signage, save for a small brass plaque affixed to the front. The words on the sign were in Italian, but a translation was unnecessary. The symbol at the center of the plaque—a drafting compass and a carpenter's square, arranged to form what looked almost like six-pointed star—was known universally. It was the same symbol, Jade now realized, that appeared on Paolo's signet ring.

"But to join the brotherhood," Paolo continued, "a man has only to ask."

Because he was not standing at the focal point, where the rays of the spotlight were focused by the mirrors into a searing pin-point, Shah's blindness was only temporary. At first he saw the world as if through a red fog. His companions were indistinct silhouettes. He couldn't even tell them apart. The loss of vision however was not the worst of it. Shah's eyes felt like someone had driven shards of broken glass into them.

Some of the jihadists, who had not been looking directly at the mirror array, recovered even more quickly, though not quickly enough to prevent Jade Ihara from escaping. The blind followed the partly-blind back to the van, and one of the latter drove away from the piazza just as the police sirens became audible in the distance.

The red fog in Shah's vision continued to diminish, though the relentless pain in his eyes made him want to claw them out with his fingertips. Gritting his teeth through the agony, he found the dark shape that he thought was Gabrielle. "Are you all right?"

"I can't see," she replied, her voice strangely calm.

"It will pass," he said. "My vision is returning. Slowly."

"Mine isn't."

"What?" He peered at the place where he knew her face was, as if by sheer willpower he might accelerate the restoration of his sight.

"I was looking right at it. I'm not sure this is going to go away."

Shah turned to the driver. "We need to find a hospital."

"No!" Gabrielle said. "No hospital. They may be looking for us now."

"If this isn't treated, you might lose your sight permanently."

She shook her head. "That doesn't matter now. All that matters is stopping Jade Ihara before she finds the vault."

"I don't know how to do that. You were the one who told us where to find her."

Gabrielle contemplated this problem silently for several seconds. "It doesn't matter. I know where she will go next."

"How do you know, Gabrielle? Don't keep secrets from me. How do you know that?"

Gabrielle reached out a hand and groped for him. "You must believe me when I say that we want the same thing. I cannot tell you more. You will have to trust me."

"Look where trusting you has brought us." A volcano of rage built in Shah's chest. His arms trembled with the effort of holding back the eruption. Though his vision was still dim, he saw everything clearly now. He had willingly permitted Gabrielle to enslave him with her seductive wiles and her empty promises of love, and she had in turn perverted his faith and twisted his mission to safeguard Islam into some agenda that, even now, she refused to share with him.

"Keep your secrets then. I no longer care. I will find Jade Ihara and I will kill her. And then, I never want to see you again."

As angry as he was, some part of him hoped that she would beg his forgiveness and, at long last, confess her love for him and share her secret, but she did not. Instead, she merely nodded, and then told him their next destination.

"Freemasons," Kellogg muttered as they followed Paolo into the Lodge. Jade shushed him, but he paid no heed. "It makes perfect sense when you think about it. They're the puppet-masters orchestrating everything from behind the scenes."

"Right," Jade said. "And those little cars they drive around at parades are frigging terrifying."

Jade's antipathy toward secret fraternities did not extend to organizations like the Masons. She was merely indifferent toward them. While she did not doubt that the friendships and alliances forged in Masonic Lodges over the centuries had been pivotal in shaping the political landscape— particularly in the United State where, if certain popular authors were to be believed, many of the founding fathers of the country had been senior Masons—Jade suspected this was more a matter of ambitious men also being Masons, and not the other way around. Their reputation for secrecy, more than anything else, had made them a target for persecution by the Church and harassment by conspiracy nuts like Roche, but the truth of the matter was that, despite their reputation as the diabolical architects of the Illuminati's New World Order, in the modern era, Masons were about as secretive as the Boy Scouts. The members of actual secret societies did not, as a rule, advertise their membership with signet rings and bumper stickers.

"Mock if you want. Mr. Roche warned about this. The Freemasons are the public face of the Changeling conspiracy."

Jade jerked a thumb in Paolo's direction. "He can hear us, you know. And do I need to remind you that he just saved our lives from the people who were actually trying to kill us?"

Kellogg gave a dismissive snort.

"Besides, I didn't think you actually believed all that stuff Roche wrote."

"Not in a literal sense. But he wasn't wrong about the world being ruled by an invisible power elite."

Jade shook her head and followed Paolo through the door and into a lobby that was about as sinister as a doctor's waiting room. "Please. Make yourselves comfortable. You will be safe here." He flashed a wry smile at Kellogg. "Our secret plan to rule the world does not include harming the two of you."

Kellogg glowered.

"Did I hear correctly? You are associates of Signore Roche?"

"Not really," Jade said, at almost the same instant that Kellogg said: "I'm his publisher." Jade had to fight the urge to stomp on Kellogg's toes.

"His publisher?" Paolo's smile darkened a little. "Well, *signore*, I am not a hot-tempered man, though we Sicilians have a reputation for it, eh? But you are publishing lies." He hissed the last word and Kellogg flinched.

Jade moved between the men. "Let's just all take a step back, okay? I'm not fan of Roche either, but someone killed him a few days ago."

The news seemed to genuinely surprise Paolo. "Killed?"

"The same people who attacked us at the museum. Not the Freemasons." She threw a quick look over her shoulder to Kellogg before going on. "They're trying to stop us from finding the Archimedes Vault. You said you could help us find it, right?"

"I said no such thing," Paolo replied. "But I did promise you answers, and I will tell you what I can, but please, I must know. How did you learn of it?"

Jade saw no further reason to withhold that information. "Roche wrote about it an unpublished manuscript. He said that it was mentioned in the Archimedes Palimpsest."

"Ah, yes. I know of the codex, but it is a book on mathematical philosophy. There is nothing in it about the vault."

"But the vault is real?" Jade pressed.

"Real?" Paolo spread his hands. "Who can say? I know only stories that are passed down in our tradition. Stories that are to be kept secret. That is why I was surprised to hear you speak of it. Is there a real Vault? I do not know. But I can tell you this. If it is real, Archimedes did not build it."

Jade raised an eyebrow. "Then who?"

"Do you know the story of Hiram Abiff, the widow's son?" Paolo did not wait for an answer. "It is a very important part of our tradition. Hiram Abiff was the chief architect of King Solomon. He possessed all the secrets of the building craft, and was the grandmaster of the craftsmen's guild of his day.

"One night, three hooligans attack him and threaten to kill him if he does not reveal to them the secret passwords of the guild. With these passwords, they can demand more money from the guild. Hiram refuses and the men stab him to death."

Emotion glistened in Paolo's eyes and he paused momentarily. "It is a story we tell to remember the importance of keeping faith, even unto death. Death comes to all men of course and the brave man does not fear it, but when we come face to face with death, even the bravest man may try to explain to God why it should not be his time. Hiram Abiff was the keeper of the secrets of stone craft. Some say he was not merely a craftsman, but the king of Egypt, and keeper of the secret knowledge of the builders of the pyramids. Who can say if this is true? If he died, much knowledge would be lost forever. He could have said, 'I am too important to die,' but he did not. He kept faith, and was struck down. The traditions of our fraternity honor the sacrifice of Hiram Abiff, and cherish his secrets."

Jade wondered if Professor would have been able to make sense of the story. She certainly could not. "Paolo, I don't understand. Even if that story is true, it would have taken place hundreds of years before Archimedes lived. What does this have to do with the vault?"

"I told you. Archimedes did not build the vault."

"You're saying this Hiram built it? Centuries before Archimedes?"

Paolo's cryptic smile told Jade that he was not about to give her a straight answer. "Archimedes was a genius, *si*, but even a genius must learn from a master. Sir Isaac Newton, another of our great heroes, he say, 'If I have seen further, it is by standing on the shoulders of giants.' Archimedes traveled to Alexandria to study mathematics and philosophy from the giants of the ancient world. Alexandria," he repeated. "In Egypt."

"And Hiram was the king of Egypt."

Paolo nodded. "*Si*. Just so."

Jade turned this over in her head, trying to find the connection. "Are you saying that…" *No, he couldn't be saying that.* "Archimedes was a Freemason?"

She expected Paolo to shake his head, but instead he seemed almost gleeful. "The Masonic lodges as we know them today were created only three hundred years ago, but the Masonic tradition goes back much further. We trace our ancestry back thousands of years. The Knights of Malta and the Templars. The Library of Alexandria. Archimedes."

"Hiram and Solomon's Temple."

"*Si*, but even Hiram was not the first."

Jade stared at him for a moment. "The pyramids?"

"And before that, the Tower."

"The Tower…you mean the Tower of Babel?"

"These are just stories. Allegories. Most do not believe them, even among the brotherhood." He paused then leaned forward and lowered his voice to a conspiratorial whisper. "Everything that I have told you is known outside the brotherhood. There are many things I cannot tell you. I have sworn an oath. But, you already know more than most, and if you keep looking, you will find what you seek."

Jade let out a growl of frustration. "Damn it, Paolo. You said you had answers."

"And I have told you much. The rest, you will find for yourself." He rose from his chair. "I can hire a car to take you to Pozzallo. You can catch a ferry there to Malta."

"Malta? Why should we go there?"

Paolo smiled. "If you keep looking, you will find what you seek."

SEVENTEEN

Malta

Even before making landfall on the tiny windswept island, a mere half-hour ferry ride from the Sicilian port city of Pozzallo, Jade grasped that Paolo's hint was not nearly as obtuse as it had first seemed. She needed only to see the place as Archimedes might have seen it 2,200 years before. Or if Roche was correct, 1,900 years.

Malta, despite its size, had a remarkable history that stretched back well beyond the time of the Greeks or Romans. The megalithic Ggjantija temple—the word literally translated to "Giant's Tower"—which dated back to 3,600 BCE, was just one of several scattered all over Malta and the neighboring island, Gozo. The Stone Age temples, built to honor an unnamed Mother goddess, were some of the oldest man-made structures on earth, older even than the pyramids of Egypt, a fact which had not escaped Jade's notice. Only the ruins of Gobekli Tepe in Turkey were believed to pre-date the temples of Malta, and those had been buried and lost to history thousands of years before the emergence of the Neolithic culture that had settled Malta. The temples to the Mother goddess on the other hand, had still been extant in the time of Archimedes. One of these, Jade felt certain, concealed the entrance of the vault. By the time they debarked, she had a list of sites to visit, but one site in particular stood apart from the others.

"This place," she told Kellogg, showing him the entry in the local tourist guidebook. "The Hypogeum of Hal Saflieni."

"What makes it so special?"

"For starters, it's underground. Exactly where you would expect to find a hidden Vault. It was discovered in 1902 by workmen digging cisterns for a housing development. An entire temple complex carved into the limestone at least five thousand years ago. Three levels have been discovered, though there could be more. They haven't explored all the rooms on the third level yet. But that's just the tip of the iceberg.

"The complex was used as a burial chamber later on, but it was originally a temple to the Mother goddess— Astarte, or the local variation on that. The upper levels are decorated with the usual symbols of fertility you would expect, but there are also dozens of strange spirals and other geometric shapes."

"Just the sort of thing that Archimedes would have noticed."

"Yup. And there's a room on the second level called the Oracle Room, which has unique and not completely understood acoustic properties. Supposedly, if you stand in it, you can feel an unusual vibration. People report feeling energized, more creative. Some claim to have visions, which might explain the name."

She paused, thinking about her experience in the spherical chamber in Peru. Was it possible that a similar effect had been at work there? She made a mental note to look into that.

"And some people," she went on, "believe the Hypogeum is a doorway to another dimension."

"Just like the fogous," Kellogg said.

"Maybe. But maybe that 'other dimension' is the vault. Maybe if you go to the Oracle Room on the right day, when the timelock expires, the vault opens and you can go in."

Kellogg frowned. "That doesn't help us much."

"Archimedes figured out a way to get in," was Jade's confident reply. "We will, too."

"Maybe he timed his visit better. No matter how you do the math, we're at least several decades away from the next chance to get inside. Maybe several centuries."

"There are other ways into a locked room."

Jade was less confident about that statement however, but there was no actual proof that Roche was actually correct about the existence of a timelock. He had wrongly attributed the vault's creation to Archimedes; maybe he was wrong about the thousand year waiting limit, too. She did not share this information with Kellogg. That conversation could wait until after they found the vault door.

As interesting as the Oracle Room was, there were other features of the Hypogeum that made it, if not a likely candidate for concealing the entrance to the vault, then at least worth further exploration.

The remains of more than 7,000 individuals had been discovered in the Hypogeum, which was not in itself that unusual. Many religions, even in modern times, placed great importance on inhuming the dead on sacred ground. What was unusual about the skeletons found in the Hypogeum was that many of them showed evidence of artificial cranial deformation, just like the Paracas skulls.

Whether or not Roche's theory about skull binding being a defense against the Changelings was true, there was some kind of connective tissue, stretching around the world to cultures separated by time and distance. Maybe there was a reason for subterranean vaults and skull deformation that no one had ever considered. Not even Roche.

This too, she kept to herself.

"There is a wrinkle though," she said. "Another locked door that might be an even bigger problem. The Hypogeum is a UNESCO World Heritage site, and access is limited to no more than ten people per hour—sixty visitors per day—and you have to purchase your tickets months in advance."

"You want to break in?" Kellogg's tone was apprehensive but not surprised.

"It wouldn't be the first time."

"Maybe there's another way. Let me try to get us permission. Money talks, and whether or not you put any stock in what he wrote, Roche's books made a lot of it. Maybe we can unlock that door without doing anything that might get us arrested."

Jade weighed the offer. Breaking and entering, while risky, would keep their interest in the Hypogeum a secret. If Kellogg tried and failed to bribe their way in, it would alert the authorities to their intention, making it that much harder to sneak in. Even if he was successful, they would be on the radar of a corruptible public official. Still, Jade was no cat burglar. "Okay, give it your best shot, but be discreet."

"Fear not. Negotiations are what I do."

While Kellogg conducted his "negotiations," Jade took the opportunity to visit an Internet café in Valletta—evidently the advent of smart phones had not completely eliminated the need for such establishments—and dug deeper into the mysteries of the Hypogeum.

There was, as she had expected, a great deal of misinformation, ranging from unsubstantiated stories to wild speculation to outright fabrication—the kind of stuff Roche had built his fortune on—but there was a surprising amount of reliable science as well.

One article detailed the most recent research into the acoustics of the Oracle Room, which was shaped like a bell, amplifying sound so that the voice of a priest speaking from the center of the room would be magnified to thunderous and no doubt terrifying proportions, and vibrating not only the air in the room, but the very bones and tissue of the people in it.

Sound in the Oracle Room resonated at 110 Hertz, a design feature found in many other ancient chambers and temples in the world, and a frequency believed to induce altered states of consciousness. That this technology was understood and exploited by a Neolithic culture centuries before the pyramids, and millennia before Archimedes, was nothing short of astounding, but as she delved deeper into the physical effects of acoustic resonance waves, Jade discovered something even more amazing.

Because acoustic waves could partially cancel each other out, it was possible to combine two or more moderately high frequency waves to produce a low frequency wave—called infrasound—in underground spaces like the Hypogeum and, Jade now realized, the chamber in Paracas.

There were many ways to produce such sounds. Musical instruments and chanting. The movement of wind and wave action, both of which were abundant in Malta. The rotation of the earth and friction with the atmosphere produced a resonance frequency of approximately 7.83 Hertz, well below the audible range for humans, but even an inaudible sound could have a profound effect on the human body and brain. Frequencies of about 10 Hz could induce a state of awe or fear. A 17 Hz waveform could produce extreme anxiety, revulsion, and even tightness in the chest and chills down the spine. At 19 Hz, visual hallucinations were reported. Researchers were increasingly convinced that infrasound might be the cause of ghost sightings and other supernatural encounters. It was believed that the frequency disturbed regions in the brain or perhaps in the ocular fluid of the eyeball, producing indistinct figures glimpsed in the peripheral vision, exactly like the ghosts she had seen in Paracas.

"One mystery solved," Jade mused, "And I didn't even need Professor to explain it to me."

The thought made her feel his absence all the more acutely, but assigning a rational explanation to her experiences in Peru not only greatly improved her disposition, it also provided the basis for a hypothesis that might explain how the Hypogeum had become conflated with the Archimedes Vault.

Kellogg returned a few moments later with good news. "We're in." he declared. "I've arranged special permission from Mr. Eco, a local official of some sort, for us to visit the site this evening. Now it's up to you to figure out how to open the vault door. If it's really there, that is."

"On that subject, I think I may have this figured out." She recounted her findings about the Oracle Room and infrasound. "So picture this. You're Archimedes, on your way back from Alexandria, head full of information. You stop off at Malta, visit this crazy temple, and suddenly your head is bursting with new ideas and connections."

"So the 'Vault'…" Kellogg made air quotes with his fingers, "is the place where Archimedes was inspired to become a genius, and not some a repository of secret knowledge."

"That's what I think."

"If that's all it is, then what about Phantom Time?"

"It's not real," Jade said. "Never was. Roche was trying to connect dots that just don't exist."

"It was real enough to the people that killed him. And who are, I might add, trying to kill us."

She shrugged. "I can't help what they believe. But if we can prove there's no Vault, it should get them off our backs."

Kellogg did not appear completely convinced. "People have been visiting the Hypogeum for almost a century. Why have there been no similar reports of such…divine inspiration."

"The natural state of the Hypogeum has changed from what it once was. It's covered over, surrounded by concrete walls. Maybe those block the production of natural infrasound. If we could get down there and experiment with different frequencies, maybe we could produce a similar effect."

"You can prove this with a visit to the Hypogeum?"

"I think so. The real question is, are you willing to publish our findings?" She held his stare. "Even if it means debunking Roche's pet theory?"

"Ah, I see your point." He managed a tight smile. "Well, let's see what we find first, shall we?"

The entrance to the legendary Hypogeum of Hal Saflieni was a depressingly prosaic yellow cinder block building occupying almost half a city block in the middle of a neighborhood in the small southeastern town of Paola. There were no windows on the wind1scoured exterior, no ornamentation to speak of. Raised metal letters reading simply "HYPOGEUM" marked the recessed entrance. Because of the limited numbers of visitors allowed into the site, there was little need for additional publicity. The door was closed, blocked by a sandwich board displaying the message "SOLD OUT" in English which was, Jade had learned, one of the two official languages of the former British Commonwealth state. Kellogg stepped to the intercom mounted beside the entrance and pushed the button to announce their arrival. A few minutes later, an older man wearing a rumpled, sweat-stained linen suit appeared to greet them.

"Ah, Dr. Ihara, the renowned archaeologist. Welcome, welcome. I am Roberto Eco."

Jade accepted the proffered hand and did not resist when Eco pressed it to his lips. She had no idea that she was "renowned" but if Eco believed it, who was she to disabuse him of the notion? Kellogg had greased the wheels, the last thing she wanted to do was derail things on the doorstep. Almost as an afterthought, she checked to see if he was wearing a Masonic signet ring; he was not. "A pleasure, Mr. Eco. I can't thank you enough for allowing us to visit the Hypogeum after hours."

"Certainly. Just leave everything as you found it, and be sure to lock up when you go. We are…how should I put it…bending the rules a bit tonight."

"You won't even know we were here," Jade promised.

Eco brought them inside, revealing an interior that was far more promising than the modest exterior suggested. After passing through a museum gallery featuring artifacts recovered from the Hypogeum and other Neolithic sites across Malta and Gozo, they reached the literal centerpiece, a glass enclosure that looked down on the entrance to the subterranean temple.

Before descending the metal staircase into the first level, Jade and Kellogg donned LED head lamps. The sections of the Hypogeum on the tour route were equipped with electric lights, but Jade preferred to see what she might discover on her own, peering with fresh eyes into the unlit corners of the site.

Weather and the passage of millennia had softened the edges of the Hypogeum's upper reaches, blurring the handiwork of ancient craftsmen who had carved it. At first glance, it looked more like a naturally occurring cave, and indeed, many of the chambers in the complex had been created from existing hollows in the natural limestone. Below the entrance however, sheltered from the wind, she saw the temple as its creators intended, and perhaps as Archimedes might have seen it two thousand years before, with rectangular niches and doorways, and trilithons— monumental arrangements of laboriously carved stones, two vertical and one laid across the top like a lintel, strikingly reminiscent of the interior ring of Stonehenge in England.

Jade's light picked out the geometric shapes and spirals etched upon the walls and ceilings and painted with red ochre, which would no doubt have been of great interest to the mathematician Archimedes, but reminded Jade more of petroglyphs she had seen in the American Southwest. Spirals, she knew, were a symbol of fertility, but also harmony with the natural order of the universe.

The first level was both shallow and relatively small, but the second level, nearly twenty feet below the surface, was where the Hypogeum earned its magnificent reputation. After passing through several spacious chambers, they entered a vast hall, decorated with what had been dubbed "the Monumental Facade." The room, with its decorative entrance to the "Holy of Holies," had become the public face of the Hypogeum, its image adorning posters and postcards. The half-domed chamber had been hewn out with astonishing precision to produce an effect not unlike the Pantheon in Rome, a feat all the more remarkable considering that its craftsman had used primitive flint tools.

The marked route took them next into a room known as "the Snake Pit" surrounding a six-foot deep well believed to have been used for the keeping of snakes, an ancient totem of fertility in cultures around the globe. Thankfully, it had been many thousands of years since a snake had slithered there.

Their destination, the Oracle Room, lay just beyond the Snake Pit. As she entered, Jade immediately sensed the strange acoustic properties of the chamber. The sound of her own footsteps were muted—the closest analogy she could come up with was the sense of being inside a glass jar—but she could hear Kellogg moving with astonishing clarity. Even the creak of his leather shoes was amplified.

She turned a slow circle, playing the light on the ceiling with its vivid red spirals. They almost seemed to be moving whenever she looked away from them. "Turn off your light," she said, her voice whisper-quiet in her ears. There was no echo.

"Why?" Kellogg's voice boomed in the enclosure and Jade could feel it vibrating in her bones.

"Just do it."

He complied, and a moment later, Jade switched hers off as well, plunging them into funereal darkness. She stood motionless, eyes open, waiting to glimpse an infrasound induced hallucination.

Nothing.

"That's enough of that," she said, clicking the light back on. She took out her phone and turned it on. Even without the SIM card, this far underground it was useless for communicating with the outside world, but it was still a functional audio playback device. Jade opened a frequency generator app she had downloaded earlier and set it to 110 Hz, the same frequency as the Oracle Room itself, then pressed the play button.

There was no sound, but that was not completely unexpected. When she had played the tone earlier, even at maximum volume, it was barely audible when she put her ear next to the speaker. Although the theoretical low end of the human auditory range was 20 Hertz, many people could not differentiate the very low tones. It was also possible that the room's unique acoustic design was cancelling out the frequency waves, creating a dampening effect. She moved the setting down to zero, and then began advancing it slowly, adjusting the frequency about ten Hertz every few seconds. It was a frustratingly tedious process and Jade had to fight the urge to simply crank the tone generator up to produce some kind of audible result.

Finally, at about 120 Hz, she heard something, a low

hum like the sound of a refrigerator compressor with a discernible pulsing at each wave peak. The sound quickly grew in intensity until, even with the phone held at arm's length, it was almost painfully loud. A queasy feeling settled in her gut, the sensation almost identical to what she had felt in Peru.

She looked over at Kellogg, saw the discomfort on his face. She managed a smile and mouthed, "It's working," then adjusted the tone generator again.

In the corner of her eye, she saw someone moving into the Oracle Room. Her first thought was that their enemies had tracked them down, but when she whipped her head in that direction, there was no one there.

Despite the nausea churning in her gut, Jade broke into a triumphant grin. She advanced the tone again, and the room began to spin.

She glimpsed movement overhead, not another ghost figure, but something else. The red spirals on the ceiling appeared to be spinning like whirlpools draining out of one reality and into another. Suddenly, she felt lighter, as if the swirling vortices were sucking her out of the Oracle Room. She reached down to change the frequency…or perhaps to stop the tone generator altogether…but her hand refused to move and before she could do anything else, the world around her dissolved into darkness and she was swept away.

EIGHTEEN

As a journalist, Shah was especially appreciative of irony. Gabrielle had cajoled and goaded him relentlessly, appealed to his heritage and his faith, teased him with the promise of her affections—a promise he now realized she never intended to keep—all to transform him into a leader, a new Mahdi to unite the factions of the Islamic world and lead them to greatness. Her scheming had cost her dearly, not just her eyesight but ultimately the respect—the love—Shah had once felt for her. And yet, it had at last borne fruit. Shah was now the leader she had pushed him to become.

A leader of only four perhaps, but great things often arose from small beginnings. Gabrielle was not the only person to suffer lasting, perhaps even permanent damage from the strange light-burst in the Syracuse museum. But four men—five counting him—would suffice. They would put an end to Jade Ihara's plot to destroy the faith, and when it was finished, these four would tell the rest of the world how he had led them into battle.

The door to the Hypogeum was unlocked, just as Gabrielle had said it would be. He did not know how she knew this, and she refused to explain, just as she refused to explain how she knew that Jade would be there. Her obstinacy had been the final straw.

She had asked to accompany them into the Hypogeum and he had refused—what choice did he have? Her blindness was a liability, but it was her refusal to accede to his leadership—the very thing she had labored to establish—that had really been the deciding factor.

"Atash! Just don't kill them. Not yet."

He did not ask her to explain. He knew she would not, and besides, he had no intention of complying. Jade Ihara had to die. Yet, he could not help but wonder why she was so insistent about this matter. In Syracuse, she had argued in favor of keeping Jade alive so that they might interrogate her about her next destination, but clearly, Gabrielle already knew where Jade would go next, which meant Jade had no information that Gabrielle did not already possess.

Perhaps I should be interrogating her, Shah thought, and did not immediately dismiss the idea. She was nothing to him now.

Her refusal to tell him what was really going on was unacceptable. Nor would he tolerate her making demands of him in front of his chosen warriors. He had left her behind, blind and helpless, unable to follow, unable to do anything.

Shah motioned for the others to put their guns away. He could feel the outline of his own pistol, a gift from one of his men, pressing against the small of his back. He had almost refused the offer. He knew nothing about guns aside from what he had seen in movies, most of which was probably wrong. In fact, he despised guns. As far as he was concerned, the obsession with firearms was one of America's greatest cultural failures, second only to rampant ethnocentrism. But since he could not very well lead men into battle without a weapon of his own, he had accepted the weapon, and after making sure that it would not accidentally discharge, he had tucked it in his belt where he intended to let it remain. The others were better suited to violence, eager for it even. He would merely direct and observe, as was proper for a general.

He pushed through the door and into the dark interior beyond. "Hello? Anyone here?"

He had only Gabrielle's assurance that Jade was there, in the Hypogeum, and if that information was wrong, the last thing he needed was to be involved in a random shootout that failed to accomplish its sole objective. Better to risk giving up the element of surprise than unnecessary bloodshed.

There no response however. The building appeared to be deserted. He waved the men inside and turned on the flashlight built into his phone, cupping his hand over it so that only a dim glow was visible.

"Spread out," he whispered. "Search the area but do not shoot unless you absolutely have to."

Their grunts of acknowledgement were not reassuring, but it was too late to call the attack off now. He only hoped the building was as empty as it looked. With luck, they had arrived ahead of their target and would be able to lie in wait.

If she's even coming, Shah thought, and wondered again where Gabrielle had gotten her information.

He found the entrance to the subterranean complex and waited there for the men to finish their sweep. One by one, they joined him to confirm that they were alone in the museum. He directed one man to stand watch at the front door, and then led the way into the ancient temple.

Despite his best efforts at stealth, the sound of his footfalls on the metal steps sounded like the ringing of an enormous gong. Gabrielle would have told him he was imagining it. For all his anger, he felt her absence acutely. He needed her.

Why was she being so obstinate? What secret was so important that she refused to trust him, after everything they had been through?

He stopped, turned off his light and searched the darkness for several seconds, then resumed moving. He continued in this fashion until, at the threshold of the second level, he heard something, a strange hum that, when he stood perfectly still, made him feel like he was sliding across the floor. Intuitively, he grasped that Jade was connected to whatever was causing this effect.

Stealth was unnecessary now. The hum was almost painfully loud, an assault on the senses that left him feeling nauseated. The urge to turn away, to run and never look back, was nearly overwhelming.

This is a trap. Gabrielle sent us here to die.

He knew it wasn't true, but the random thought took root like a dandelion seed.

The bitch. I'll kill her myself.

"Keep going," he rasped, not looking back to see if the others were still with him. As he pushed deeper into the Hypogeum, the feeling began to abate, transforming from panic to something more like euphoria, but his resolve remained unchanged.

"I'll kill her myself," he whispered gleefully, squeezing the grip of the pistol that had somehow found its way into his hand. He didn't know if he was referring to Jade Ihara or Gabrielle Greene. Maybe both.

Yes. Definitely both.

He spied light emanating from one of the carved doorways, rushed toward it with his gun arm extended.

He saw two figures standing in the chamber beyond. The light was behind them, revealing only silhouettes, a man and a woman, but he knew that the pair could only be Jade and her companion, the man she had been with at the Arkimedeion. Gabrielle never mentioned him, and only now did he wonder at that omission. Did she know who he was?

It did not matter. Whomever he was, he would be dead in a few seconds.

Just like Jade Ihara.

Shah stretched his gun arm out and stared down the length of the barrel, lined the iron sights up on Jade's head, and pulled the trigger.

The vortex drew Jade up into the darkness, and then suddenly she was...somewhere else.

Forget ghost hallucinations, she thought. This was a full-on out-of-body experience.

In an instant, she was transported from the Hypogeum and flying through the night sky above Malta, rising...rising...higher and higher into the sky.

It felt like a dream. In fact, she was certain that was exactly what it was. A waking dream. The infrasound frequency had somehow thrown her into REM sleep.

She wondered if Archimedes had experienced something like this. With his genius, the vision had probably been even more fantastic—an Alice in Wonderland-like journey through the landscape of mathematics. Maybe he had seen the true value of pi or the square root of two.

Strangely however, there was nothing familiar about the imagery in this dream. Despite her best efforts to take control, she continued rising skyward, as if strapped to a rocket. Malta was just a dark spot in a darker sea. She could make out the outline of Sicily and the toe of the Italian peninsula. She wondered at how high she was, in both respects. Ten miles up? A hundred?

Am I in outer space?

She tried to look up, into the emptiness of the sky, but even this small measure of control was denied her. This was not so much a dream as a mind movie, but where was it coming from?

All of the Mediterranean was visible to her now, Europe and North Africa, the curvature of the earth falling away in every direction, and then something changed. She was no longer rising, but moving laterally above the globe as it rolled relentlessly beneath her. It was nothing she had not seen before on television or in computer generated images of the earth as seen from orbit, but the detail of the landscape was astonishing. Jade had never really paid close attention, but evidently her subconscious had recorded every minor knob of rock jutting from the sea, every fjord and mountain summit.

The Iberian Peninsula passed beneath her, and then the Strait of Gibraltar. The great gray expanse of the Atlantic crawled beneath her and then something like a great fiery phoenix rose into view above the Western horizon.

She was chasing the sun.

The Atlantic crossing seemed to take forever, though the same journey that she was making in minutes would take hours by jet airplane. She wondered how much time had passed in the Hypogeum, and to what destination Kellogg's dreams had taken him.

Land masses came into view, nothing recognizable, but she knew enough about geography to assume that she was seeing the islands of the Caribbean. They too passed beneath her as she continued west, toward the blazing orb of the sun. More land now, and no ocean beyond. North America, Mexico perhaps? No, that great brown smudge had to be the Mississippi River pouring into the Gulf.

The landscape began to make a little more sense now. The sea of brown earth flatter even than the Atlantic Ocean had to be Texas. The southern extremity of the Continental Divide and a patch of white gypsum sand, like snow in the middle of the black desert—New Mexico. She knew this country well, had flown over it dozens of times. There was the Mogollon Rim, the great chasm of the Grand Canyon....

Now she was descending, falling from the sky. Falling towards....

Why am I seeing this?

For the first time since the journey began, it occurred to her that she might have been wrong about everything. This was not a dream, not the product of infrasound and her fevered imagination.

The Hypogeum was showing her the route to a destination, just as it had shown Archimedes two thousand years before. A specific place, and there, a door with a fantastic mechanical lock that could only be opened....

Roche had been wrong. Paolo and his Freemason brethren, too. The Hypogeum was not the vault. It was the map that showed the way to the vault.

The very idea was so preposterous that, if she had not been experiencing it for herself, she would have dismissed it out of hand. The Oracle Room had been created in such a way as to stimulate specific regions of the human brain to produce exactly this result. Yet, what was so strange about that? Audio and video recordings were nothing more than specific frequencies of electromagnetic energy, easily rendered into digital patterns, and then reconstituted into light and sound. Couldn't the same thing be done to the human brain?

It really is a mind movie.

The door to the vault appeared, a circular chamber ringed by circles that turned this way and that, sometimes appearing to be linked like the Olympic rings, but somehow never crossing.

I know where this is, Jade thought.

Suddenly the image before her fractured, as if someone

had thrown an enormous rock through the television screen in her mind, and Jade was wrenched out of the sublime vision and into the chaos of reality.

Shah's bullet missed Jade by a country mile, which was not a completely unexpected outcome given his inexperience. He had thought of it as more a signal for his men to open fire than an actual attack. In the final accounting, it would not matter whose bullet actually killed Jade; only that he had fired first.

But no other shots were fired.

Just as the mirror array in the Archimedes museum had focused the spotlight into a searing ray of heat, the unique shape of the Oracle Room had focused the report of the pistol into a deafening sonic assault that brought everyone in the chamber to their knees. He dropped the pistol, clapped his hands to his head as if he might squeeze the noise out of his skull. He thought his head might actually come apart if he let go.

The effect reached its agonizing climax almost immediately and then died away as quickly as the echoes of the shot itself, but recovering from the staggering decibel levels took considerably longer. As a still-grimacing Shah groped for both his light and his gun, he glimpsed a pair of figures—Jade and the other man—making a mad dash past the gunmen.

"No!" Shah rasped. "Not again."

His fumbling fingers found the gun. He whirled around, trying to line up another shot, but immediately realized the foolishness of such an action. "Hold your—"

One of his men fired at the moving targets and another freight train of agony slammed through Shah's head.

"Damn it!"

Yet, somehow, the second episode wasn't quite as bad as the first. Maybe the damage to his hearing had inoculated him against further pain. He endured the pain with a grimace and kept his eyes open long enough to see Jade go down.

Although the first shot had disrupted the tone from the frequency generator, shattering the infrasound spell and snapping Jade out of the vision, she had not actually heard the report. Her abrupt return—figuratively speaking—had left her disoriented but she was in far better shape than the wriggling figures on the floor at the entrance. Though she could barely see them, she had little doubt that these were the same men who had attacked them at the Arkimedeion. She did not immediately grasp what had caused their debilitation, but the tang of sulfur in the air revealed that someone had fired a pistol. She had not heard it because the same acoustical trick that gave the Oracle Room its power had caused the sound waves to almost perfectly cancel each other out at the center of the room where she had been standing. The shot itself had sounded muffled and distant to her ears.

She was not so sheltered when the second shot rang out.

The bullet creased the air next to her ear, but the amplified report blasted her off her feet and sent her reeling through the doorway to the Oracle Room.

Kellogg, who had been stunned by the noise of the first shot, managed to stay on his feet and dragged her onward, out of the line of fire.

More shots sounded, accompanied by the noise of bullets slamming into the limestone walls. Dust and rock chips filled the air but none of the rounds found their target, and as soon as the pair was out of the bell-shaped chamber, the decibel level dropped like a stone.

Jade stumbled along behind Kellogg, her wits still jumbled, part of her brain still trying to process what she had seen during her out-of-body excursion. Was it just something that had arisen randomly from her unconscious mind? A dream? All she knew for certain was that she had woken up to a nightmare.

How did they find us here? I didn't tell anyone….

A sliver of doubt wormed into the fractured jigsaw

puzzle of her awareness. She had made a critical mistake.

The realization brought her fully back to the moment. Her quest for the vault, whatever it really was, would have to wait until she wasn't being chased by a gang of killers. She pulled free of Kellogg's grasp and sprinted out ahead of him, following the metal floor back to the stairs, bounding up them three at a time. A few seconds later, she was threading her way through the museum building, following the dim glow of overhead exit signs.

It was déjà vu all over again. Her enemies had tracked her down—again—trapped her underground—again—and now she was running for her life. Again. The only consolation was that the men trying to kill her seemed incapable of learning from their failures.

The thought had barely formed when a man stepped out of the shadows, directly between her and the doorway. Jade's eyes were drawn, not to his face, but to the dark and all too familiar shape of the pistol braced in his outstretched hands and aimed right at her.

Because her gaze was fixed on the gun, she did not see a third arm appear above the gunman's right shoulder and snake around his neck. It was only when his head tilted back sharply and then twisted halfway around with a sickening crack, the unfired gun falling from nerveless fingers, that she realized there was someone else there.

As the gunman crumpled into a heap, the face of her savior was revealed. Though still cloaked in shadow, Jade immediately recognized the person standing there. Her surprise at the appearance of the gunman was nothing to what she now experienced.

"Professor?"

His grim expression transformed into a smile as he briskly advanced, arms thrown wide invitingly. Jade ran forward, not interested in escape as much as she was in being in his arms. The same arms that had just broken a man's neck enfolded her in a tight embrace which she returned with matching vigor. Then his lips found hers.

The kiss was so unexpected that, for a moment, she

didn't know how to respond. Not until this moment did she realize how long she had been waiting for him to do this, how much she wanted it.

Kellogg's voice intruded on the moment. "There are more of them behind us. We have to go."

Professor pulled away, taking Jade's hand and pulling her, gently but urgently, along behind him. They emerged onto the warm but still breezy streets and Professor headed toward an SUV parked across the street. There were no other cars, but Jade remained wary. There had been at least half-a-dozen attackers at the museum in Syracuse which meant several were unaccounted for.

A tumult arose from behind them as the gunmen from the Oracle Room spilled out of the entrance to the Hypogeum. Their shouts were not a warning to the escaping prey but rather an internal communication between the pursuers. A moment later, the shots started.

Jade ducked involuntarily as the bullets began hammering into the fenders of the vehicle to which they ran. Professor however whirled around, drawing a semi-automatic pistol from his waistband, and squeezed off several shots. His return fire shattered the attack and sent the men—all but one of them who now lay sprawled out on the sidewalk, clutching a bloody chest wound—scrambling back into the museum.

Without putting the gun away, Professor wrenched the SUV's door open. "Inside. Hurry."

Jade didn't need to be told twice. She and Kellogg piled into the vehicle—she took the passenger seat, Kellogg got in back—while Professor slid behind the steering wheel. A few seconds later, they were racing away down the quiet backstreets of Paola.

Jade's heart rate and breathing gradually returned to normal, but her mind refused to slow down. Part of her was still out in the cosmos, racing above the earth like a guided missile, homing in on the vault, even though she now felt she knew less about it than she had half an hour before. Part of her was still reliving this latest attack, which had come closer than any of the others to ending her search forever.

Part of her could not stop thinking about the kiss. About his lips pressing against hers, firm, assertive but not overly intrusive. It was almost everything she could have hoped for.

Which made it so much harder for her to admit what she knew to be true.

The man that had just saved her… just kissed her… was not Professor.

He looked like Professor, sounded like him…even smelled like him. But something about him was wrong. The kiss and the emotion behind were so out of character that there could be no doubt.

Professor had been replaced by a Changeling.

NINETEEN

As the hours stretched into days, it became increasingly harder for Professor not to second guess his decision to allow himself to be recaptured. His reasons were still valid. His escape had been a carefully orchestrated fiction, a test to see what he would do if given the chance. He was certain of that, just as he was certain that First Officer Carrera, or the woman claiming to be her, was working with his captors.

A true escape under those circumstances was impossible for the simple reason that he had no idea who or what he was escaping from. He did not know who was really behind his abduction, or the hijacking of the airliner. He did not even know for certain where he was. Sitting in the cockpit of the derelict aircraft, he had decided that learning the answers to those questions took higher priority than trying to get away.

The "escape" had been a fiction in more ways than one.

They had come for him in force, a force of eight men... scratch that, eight persons. Their genders had been concealed, along with their faces and any easily identifiable features, behind shapeless gray coveralls and mesh head coverings. They carried Taser X26C stun guns, which was interesting but not particularly illuminating. Their movement through the plane had been orderly but not exactly tactical. His sense was that they were not trained operators, not even soldiers, or if they had received formal training, it was from a playbook of their own devising. Without uttering a single word, they closed on him, tased him senseless, and then tranquilized him with another injection.

When he came to again, he was back in the squalid little cabin, no closer to answers than he had been before making his run into the woods.

He remained there for what felt like several hours, silently daring his captors to send Carrera or someone else in to check on him, but no one came knocking. Finally, he cleared his throat and addressed the ceiling. "I'm sure you guys are watching… listening at least, so why don't we cut to the chase. If you want something from me, just ask."

No reply.

He counted his heartbeats, trying to gauge the passage of time. After what felt like about half an hour, he tried again. "If you don't tell me what you want, I can't very well give it to you."

Silence.

It was an answer though.

His thoughts kept drifting back to that old television series. He remembered the intro word for word, could still hear the defiant voice of the captive secret agent.

What do you want?

And the reply, a different voice each week, but always the same words.

Information.

Information about what? Ongoing espionage missions? The names of highly placed NOC agents? Moles in the politburo?

It didn't matter. Information was just a MacGuffin, a symbol of the man's defiance in the face of Byzantine plots to break his spirit.

You won't get it, the secret agent had replied, week after week, and always the reply was the same.

By hook or by crook, we will.

Information.

He swung his legs onto the floor, stood up and went outside. The sun was overhead, which meant he'd been under for a full day. A few minutes later, he spotted Carrera walking toward him. There was something different about her. Her bearing had changed, her posture and gait were more assertive. She was the same person, but no longer playing the same role.

"Okay," he muttered. "Now we're getting somewhere."

"I thought you were going to wait until after sundown," she remarked, undisguisedly sardonic.

He shrugged. "That's what I told you. It was never my plan."

She got within a few yards of him, stopped and put her hands on her hips. "When did you know?"

"Know what?"

She gazed back at him as if trying to judge his sincerity. "I know you're not stupid," she said after a long pause.

"Flattery now?"

"Look, just answer the question. When did you know?"

Interesting, he thought. *She repeated the question, but didn't specify. Didn't give anything away. She's fishing. Two can play that game.* "I was a Boy Scout. One look at the sun told me that we weren't in the Northern Hemisphere. So I knew you were lying. Either about where we were, or about being a pilot."

She nodded slowly. "I didn't know if I could trust you. I thought it might be some kind of test."

"A test?"

"You know, to see if I'd go along with you or turn you in. They like to play games like that."

"Who? Obviously not the North Koreans."

She shook her head. "Obviously. But I wasn't lying when I told you that they never show themselves."

As before, she spoke without any noticeable tells. Either she was the most convincing liar on earth, or she was actually telling the truth. He shook his head, trying to resist the seductive urge to believe her.

She's trying to play me, trying to get me to reveal something. What?

Information.

There was something his captors wanted and if they wouldn't tell him what, wouldn't even ask the question, then it could only mean that they expected to learn it simply by observing him.

He had been wrong about this being a cat and mouse game. There was no cat. Just a maze through which he was being forced to run so that his captors could learn... what?

Information.

The only way to beat them, to figure out who they really were and what they really wanted, was to change the game. Instead of information, he would give them disinformation. He would have to become someone that he was not.

"Well, if you're satisfied that I'm not a plant, maybe we can put our heads together and come up with a better plan for getting out of here."

"Seriously? After what happened last night?"

"I'm not going to stay here," he said, and that wasn't a lie. "I will get out of here, or die trying." He took a breath. "I have to get back to Jade."

"Jade?"

"Jade Ihara. My girlfriend."

Her response was almost too perfect. "We've all got people waiting for us back home."

"Jade needs me. I need her. I'd go through hell itself to be with her again." He tried to inject the appropriate amount of emotion into his voice so that they would believe this, the first of many lies he planned to tell. He was a little surprised by his own sincerity.

That had been two days ago, and he felt no closer to understanding what was really going on. He was beginning to question his underlying premise; had he given his enemy too much credit for cleverness?

I should have kept going that first night.

But no, he knew better. He was right about everything. It was all a game, a test. He had confused them at the plane. They had been waiting for him to try something… to reveal the extent of his knowledge and abilities. Would he try to fly the plane out? Call someone on the radio?

But why? That was the question that still nagged at him. *Why? What did they want?*

Information.

Okay, Professor. You've always prided yourself on being the smartest guy in the room. Figure this one out. Start back at the beginning.

The plane. Flight 815. Why had they taken the plane?

It occurred to him only then that he had lost track of

that particular thread. He had only gotten mixed up in the investigation because Roche's publisher had been on the missing plane. And it had only been after he had tipped his hand, in a very roundabout way, that Sousa had hit him with the tranquilizer and then arranged his abduction.

Hypothesis: Roche was close to exposing their operation. His obsession with Changelings had unwittingly uncovered something else. An ongoing intelligence operation. A highly placed mole in a government agency. A changeling of a different sort....

He shot to his feet, ran outside the little cabin, but stopped after only a few steps, looking around at the other huts, the handful of people roaming between the rows, idling away the days of their captivity.

Carrera's voice reached out to him. "Pete? Everything okay?"

He stared at her for a moment, but then he started forward again without answering.

"Pete!" He heard her footsteps pounding the earth as she raced to catch up, then quieting as she fell in beside him. "Pete... Sorry, *Professor*, what's up?" She lowered her voice to a whisper. "Oh, my God, you're going for it aren't you?"

He continued to ignore her, striding purposefully past the huts, passing into the woods without hesitation. Carrera did not repeat the question, but maintained a curious silence as she kept pace with him.

He reached the runway a few minutes later but instead of following it to the idle plane as he had before, he crossed to the other side and kept going, pushing deep into the crowded evergreens. Though he tried not to show it, he was wary now. He was being unpredictable—that was his intent at least—and the response to his actions would be equally hard to anticipate. They might continue watching as they had before, or they might send out the goon squad and zap him into submission again. His gut told him they were more interested in seeing what he would do, but he was going to be ready if and when the guys with tasers showed up again.

Halfway down the far side of a wooded hill, the forest

opened up to reveal more signs of human habitation—not an ad hoc containment area like the camp where he had been held, but an actual neighborhood with houses and paved streets that branched and looped, and sometimes dead-ended in cul de sacs. It looked exactly like a suburban housing development, with at least two hundred separate homes, perhaps more. There were small parks, a few large buildings that might have been auditoriums or churches, though strangely, there were no cars on the streets, and no roads leading away from the community. Like the camp of huts, the neighborhood was an island in the middle of a sea of trees.

He risked a glance over at Carrera and found her staring, not at the suburb, but at him. He pointed down the hill. "You don't look very surprised to see that?"

She said nothing.

"Should I keep going?" he asked.

She spread her hands in a noncommittal gesture. "You seem to have it all figured out."

"Vinnytsia."

Her brow furrowed in confusion.

"Early in the Cold War, the Soviets built a mock American town in Vinnytsia, Ukraine to train deep cover agents in how to behave like Americans. They spoke only English—American dialect. Drove American cars, ate American food, listened to American music and read American magazines. All so that their sleeper agents would be able to blend in seamlessly with the American population."

"You think the Soviets are behind all this?"

"Why don't you tell me who's behind it? You took that plane. God only knows how many other people you've taken over the years. Brought them here to populate this little farce so that your agents would be able to insert themselves into the real world. Who will I find down there? The real Jeanne Carrera? Maybe the people who were really on that plane?"

"You think I'm—"

"Don't bother denying it. We're way past that. Gerald Roche got too close with his Changeling conspiracy. If enough people believed him, started questioning whether their elected leaders had been replaced by doubles, there was a chance—remote, but there all the same—that something would come out, and then the dominoes would start to fall.

"I'll admit. I'm still not clear on why you took that plane. If all you wanted was to shut Roche up, it seems like there were easier ways to accomplish that with less risk and a lot less collateral damage. Did you just need live bodies? Shanghaied extras to make the training scenario more believable? Or is there something else you needed? Someone else on that plane? Something you needed Parrott to tell you?"

He took her silence for a tacit admission of guilt. "So, let's see if I've got this right. You've been doubling people, probably for a while now. You start with someone who's a close physical match, do the rest with stage make-up. *Mission Impossible* stuff. Maybe even cosmetic surgery if there's time for it. But looks aren't everything. Your imposter wouldn't last ten seconds in a conversation with someone the subject actually know—close friends, relatives, lovers. You could learn a lot about someone from discreet surveillance, but what you really need is an immersive environment. A place to both train your agents and observe your subjects. Your own little Vinnytsia.

"You kidnap them, bring them here and then watch what they do. Learn everything about them. Mannerisms. Tastes. Am I in the ballpark? You doubled me, right? When I showed up asking the wrong questions, you were worried that it might all start to unravel, so you brought me here to pump me for information, while you got my double ready to head back to the real world and make sure the investigation goes nowhere. Is that about right?" He turned and scanned the woods at their back. "Is he out there? The guy you got to double me? Hey. Come on out. Let's talk."

"You are a remarkable man, Professor Chapman," Carrera said, without a trace of sarcasm. "Mimicking your intellect may be the most challenging part of replacing you."

She smiled and Professor was shocked to see that she no longer looked like the First Officer of Flight 815. It was as if voicing his revelation had triggered a sympathetic physical reaction in her, stripping away the veil of illusion. She still bore a passing resemblance to Carrera, but there were discernible differences. She reached up with her left hand and peeled back her right eyelid. A finger sweep removed an opaque contact lens, revealing her natural, jet black iris.

"I'm afraid you've already missed your replacement. He left twelve hours ago to rejoin your girlfriend, Jade Ihara." She removed the lens from the other eye, and flicked it away like a nuisance insect. "You see, we knew who you really were before you came looking for Flight 815."

Professor snapped his fingers. "Rafi. You doubled him, used him to kill Roche so that it would look like Muslim extremists. You had the real Rafi in that car. The double triggered that explosion to cover his tracks and make it look like Rafi killed himself."

"An opportune scapegoat. The replacement was a hasty affair, but then it was never meant to stand up to close scrutiny."

He narrowed his gaze at her. "So who are you really working for? The Russians? Chinese? No, this is something else." He snapped his fingers. "Some kind of international crime syndicate, right? That's why you wanted to pin this on Muslims. You get rid of that nuisance Roche, and stir up a little profitable international unrest in the bargain. Win-win."

"Unfortunately, you and Dr. Ihara refused to just let it alone."

It was the second time Carrera had mentioned Jade by name. A chill ran down Professor's spine. "Jade isn't going to find anything. Roche was barking up the wrong tree. You know it as well as I do. Leave her alone. She's no threat to you."

Carrera smiled again, but there was no humor in her cold black eyes. She waved to someone in the woods.

Professor's *doppleganger* might not have been lurking there, but several figures wearing mesh head coverings and gray fatigues emerged and began closing in around him.

"You are intelligent," she said, "but believe me when I say that you have no idea what's really going on."

TWENTY

Malta

Jade's first impulse was to deny. It was a crazy idea. There weren't any Changelings except in Roche's delusional brain...*and he's dead now, isn't he...* so Professor couldn't possibly be one. That this perfectly rational argument, which she so desperately wanted to believe, was an even less convincing possibility, went way beyond unsettling. It terrified her.

If that's not really Professor, then where is he? Is he... No, I won't even think that.

But her refusal to frame the thought did not keep her dread at bay. This impostor was wearing Professor's clothes, his watch, even his ridiculous fedora.

He's a hostage. That's what happened. He figured out what they were up to, but they caught him, and sent this guy in his place.

They who? The Changelings? She glanced over at the startlingly familiar visage. *Who else?*

"Find anything down there?" she asked. Her voice caught in her throat, so the words came out like a coughing fit.

"You okay, babe?"

"Yeah," she croaked. She didn't need any more proof than that. Professor—the real Professor—would never, ever call her 'babe.' "You know how I get around dust."

He threw her a sidelong glance as if trying to decide if she was testing him, then returned his attention to the road in front of them. "It was a dead-end. Looks like you've been busy though."

Jade barely heard him. She could barely hear herself think, a condition that had nothing to do with the jet engine loud blast of sound she'd experienced in the Oracle Room.

Changelings are real. The Vault is real. Professor is...not here. What the hell am I supposed to do?

Kellogg, perhaps sensing the awkward silence, jumped

in. "Good thing you showed up when you did. Those Arabs nearly had our guts for garters."

"Not Arabs," Professor—

Not Professor!

—corrected. "At least not all of them. The guy leading them is Atash Shah, co-founder of the Crescent Defense League. He's actually Iranian." His eyes found Jade again. "That's the group Rafi was working with."

She blinked at him, fighting the urge to ask how he had known to go to the Hypogeum. She had pulled her SIM card in Syracuse, before Paolo ever mentioned Malta, and had not tried to contact him since. As if sensing her anxiety over this discrepancy, Not-Professor added, "That's how I found you actually. I followed him and he went right to you."

"Makes sense," she murmured. Except it did not explain how Shah had tracked her in the first place. Paolo? No, that couldn't be right.

Kellogg?

She bit her lip to keep from letting out a gasp of dismay. Kellogg was working with Shah… or he was a Changeling, too. Were the two factions working together?

She pressed her fingertips to the bridge of her nose, as if to squeeze the paranoia out of her brain. There was a conspiracy at work, but if she let her imagination run wild, she would be virtually paralyzed, unable to defend herself or stop them.

"From what I can gather," Not-Professor went on, "he thinks that Roche put you on the trail of some historical evidence to prove that the Prophet Muhammad was fictional."

Kellogg leaned through the space between the car seats and gave her a playful slug in the arm. "What did I tell you? Mr. Roche was right about Phantom Time."

"Well, I don't know if I'd go that far," the impostor said. Then after a pause, he added, "Unless you found something you haven't told me about. Did you?"

Kellogg drew back suddenly as if realizing he had spoken out of turn. "I'll…aah, let Jade tell you. I'm not actually quite sure what to make of it."

The Changelings are using Shah as a stalking horse. That has to be it. They sicced him on Roche...

Suddenly she understood where it had begun. Rafi, the real Rafi, had been replaced by a Changeling, in order to pin the blame for Roche's murder on the Crescent Defense League, and by extension, the Islamic religion. No doubt, a similar fate had been planned for her.

But Kellogg has been helping me. Do the Changelings want me to find the vault for them? Or am I wrong about him?

"Me either," Jade said. "I'll tell you when we get wherever it is we're going. Where are we going?"

"That's up to you, babe."

"Ummm, how 'bout we find a hotel, yeah?"

Not-Professor threw her a lascivious grin. "Exactly what I was thinking."

She managed a half-hearted nod. "Yeah. I need a shower. And a drink."

Kellogg piped up again. "Should we be worried about those Arabs...or Iranians or whatever?"

"I doubt we'll see them again. This is a small island, and they've got nowhere to hide. The shooting will bring out the police."

The police, Jade thought. Maybe it was time to finally take Kellogg's suggestion seriously and seek help from law enforcement. *And tell them what, exactly? That there are Changelings running around?*

Okay, not the police. But who else could she ask for help? "Good," she said finally, doing her level best to sound confident and calm. "It's settled then. Let's find a hotel and worry about all this in the morning."

"Got a preference? Or should we just see what comes up on Google?"

An idea started to take shape in Jade's head. "Give me your phone for a sec. We got rid of ours, remember?"

Not-Professor did not challenge the request or question the conspicuously guilty-sounding elaboration, but simply handed his phone—*Professor's phone*, Jade thought—over to her.

Her fingers were jittery on the touch-screen controls as she scrolled through the icons and finally tapped the Settings button. Her heart was hammering in her chest. Did he suspect what she was doing?

Privacy...Location Services...System Services....

There it was. An inconspicuous item in the menu marked "Frequently Visited Locations." She tapped it and a list of locations appeared—every city he had visited on the journey through Malta, a stop in Rome. Sydney. Some place called Rosebery TAS. Sydney, again.

Rosebery. Where on earth is that, and why the hell did he go there?

She exited out and hastily typed the words "hotels Paola Malta" into the search bar. There were no lodging results, but one of the hits for "Things to Do in Malta" gave her another idea. She clicked on it, read the short paragraph, then went back to the search and refined it to "hotels close to Paola Malta."

She glanced over and caught Not-Professor staring back. He smiled, and she tried to smile back. *Crap. I'm taking too long. He knows.*

No. He doesn't. Stay cool.

"Looks like we'll have to go to Valletta," she said.

He shrugged. "Great thing about islands. They're small. I guess I don't have to tell you that."

"Right. How does the Hotel Phoenicia Malta sound?"

"It sounds expensive," the imposter said with a grin. "Who's picking up the tab?"

Jade tried again to smile but it felt more like a grimace. She glanced back at Kellogg who made a show of rolling his eyes. "I'm not a bottomless pit of money, you know."

"Yeah, but that next book is going to be a best-seller."

"You're not wrong about that."

Not-Professor chuckled. "Tell me where to turn."

Jade relayed the driving directions—the hotel was only a few minutes away—while she surreptitiously studied the road map. Getting away from Professor and Kellogg would

192 | WOOD AND ELLIS

be relatively easy, provided she had not already aroused their suspicions, but getting away from Malta might be a lot trickier, especially since anyone she encountered might be working with the Changelings.

For the first time since the nightmare began, she understood how Roche had become so paranoid. There was only one person she could trust. Just as Roche had turned to her for assistance, she would have to go to her sworn enemy.

She spent the rest of the drive in silence, speaking only when it was necessary to convey the directions to the hotel. The Phoenicia-Malta was a sprawling palatial resort—a blend of Old World colonial and 1930's art deco, with just a hint of Moorish influence—situated just outside the City Gate of old Valletta, with a spectacular view of the harbor. Jade felt a slight pang knowing that she would not have the opportunity to indulge in the available creature comforts. She did not know where, much less if, she would sleep tonight, but it would not be here.

In the elegant hotel lobby, Jade stood by patiently while Not-Professor booked their rooms. She kept her reaction completely neutral when he asked for a double room for them to share, but her mental gears were spinning. From the moment he'd appeared, this impostor had acted as if a romantic involvement between them was well-established—the kiss, the pet names, and now the assumption that they would be sharing a bed. Where had the Changeling gotten such a ludicrous idea?

Is it ludicrous? Doesn't part of you wish that it was true?

She shook her head to banish the idle thoughts. It didn't matter that the Changelings had tapped into that particular fantasy; they had gotten reality completely wrong, which meant maybe they weren't omniscient after all.

Or maybe Not-Professor had a different reason for wanting to share a room with her. What better way to keep an eye on her.

Go! Now! You won't get a better chance.

"Hey, hon," she said, trying to sound light and airy, and

hearing instead a faint quaver. "I'm gonna find the ladies room."

"I'm almost done here. We'll be in the room in five minutes."

She pressed her thighs together and danced from foot to foot. "When you gotta go…"

He nodded and turned back to the reception desk. Jade made a show of searching for the restroom as she wandered through the lobby and then angled toward the hotel lounge, where presumably there would not only be restroom facilities, but also an exit from the building. As she was about to pass out of view of the lobby however, she hesitated.

What if I'm wrong? She glanced back at them—Kellogg, fidgeting a few steps behind…*Professor? Not-Professor?*—and wondered again if her imagination had run away from her. Maybe the infrasound had messed with her mind. Maybe this was some kind of neurotransmitter-overload-induced delusion?

As much as she wanted to, Jade couldn't make herself believe it.

If I'm wrong, he'll forgive me.

She found a door that opened onto the pool deck, where she broke into a jog, darting past rows of chaise lounges and scantily clad tourists, toward the low wrought iron fence that separated the pool from the landscaped garden beyond. She vaulted the fence and kept going, heading toward the noise of traffic.

Her destination was less than three miles away, walking distance, but she needed to get there before her protracted absence was noticed. She figured she had only a few minutes—five, tops—before Not-Professor got suspicious. Time enough for a taxi to get her across Valletta and back to Paola. When she told the driver where she wanted to go, he looked askance at her, but then shrugged and started the meter.

She saw her destination from several blocks away, a tall illuminated spire—like a king's scepter—jutting up out of the surrounding cityscape. Beside it, and only slightly less obtrusive, was an enormous dome. The surrounding area, several acres, was undeveloped, a rare thing in one of the most densely populated countries in Europe, and formed a wooded buffer zone for the campus of buildings surrounding the tower. The occupants of the religious compound evidently valued their privacy.

She handed the driver a stack of Euro notes, then leaned in close. "Listen, there's this guy. My ex-boyfriend. He doesn't agree with…" She nodded at the building. "Some of the decisions I've made. It's probably nothing to worry about, but I'd appreciate if you could forget you ever saw me."

"I don't think I could ever forget you, miss," the man said with a wink. "But fear not. Chivalry is not dead in Malta. Good luck."

Jade breathed a sigh of relief as the cab drove away, but her sense of satisfaction at having made it this far was dulled by the realization that her next task was going to be far more challenging. Not to mention dangerous. She took a deep breath to muster her courage, and then marched up to the arched gate. She stood there for a few moments until a young man wearing what she assumed to be clerical garments came out to investigate.

His bearded visage was pinched, as if he was mildly constipated, though it was more likely that his discomfort arose from having to deal with this after-hours visitor. "Are you lost, ma'am?"

He spoke with a British accent, which sounded strange coming from someone dressed as he was, standing where he was.

"Is this the Mariam al-Batool Mosque?"

"It is."

"Then I'm exactly where I want to be."

"I don't think—"

She interrupted before he could finish the brush-off. "I don't need you to think. I need you to go get Atash Shah. I know he's in there somewhere. He'll want to talk to me. Tell him it's Jade Ihara."

Jade did not actually know for a certainty that Shah would retreat to Malta's only mosque, but she figured the odds were good that, following the deadly encounter at the Hypogeum, he would seek the protection of fellow Muslims. Even if he wasn't actually there, she figured someone inside would know where he was hiding out.

She was not wrong however.

The young man's constipated frown deepened, but he reluctantly opened the gate and allowed her to step inside. "It is not appropriate for you to be here without your husband," he said.

The scolding was half-hearted, as if he realized that her business with Shah was more important than this violation of protocol. "I say this for your own protection," he added. "As well as to safeguard others from temptation."

She bit back a scathing rejoinder, and simply said. "Thanks for your concern. I'm sorry, I don't have a…scarf or anything to cover my head."

"I will see that you are provided with one. Please wait here and do not speak to anyone."

"Where else would I go?"

Shah's first impulse was to run to the gate, gun in hand, and take revenge for the blood that had been spilled.

Two of the men that had accompanied him into the Hypogeum were dead. Another had been seriously wounded, and without adequate medical attention, would probably not survive the night. Whether he could get that at the Islamic Cultural Centre's clinic facilities was anyone's guess, but Shah dared not take the man to a hospital.

But killing Jade on the front steps of the mosque was not an option, and once his initial rage cooled a bit, his curiosity got the better of him. He could not decide if she was bold or arrogant or something else. Desperate, perhaps? Was she here to plead for her life?

Doubtful, but he was curious despite himself. He set aside his anger, along with his weapon, and headed out to

196 | WOOD AND ELLIS

meet her at the entrance. Although her hijab, provided for her by the gate attendant, framed her face and completely covered her hair, it was the first time Shah had been able to get a good look at her. He stopped and met her stare.

She did not appear to be desperate.

"I thought you'd look…" She paused, searching for the right word. "More radical."

"That's a hell of an icebreaker."

She shrugged. "I meant it as a compliment."

Shah turned to the attendant. "Give us some space."

The young man gave a perturbed frown but moved away. Shah looked back at Jade. "Why are you here?"

"The truth? I need your help."

Shah tried to conceal his surprise. "Help? Why would I help you?"

She folded her arms. "Why wouldn't you? Do you even know why you've been trying to kill me?"

Her directness was disconcerting. "I…ah—"

"That's what I thought. Someone handed you a BS story about how I was trying to destroy Islam, and you swallowed it whole. Did you even stop and think, just for a second?"

A red flush bloomed on Shah's cheeks, not anger, but embarrassment. Jade had cut to the heart of it. He had let Gabrielle push him into a course of action that was so far beyond anything he had ever contemplated. He did not even recognize what he had become, what Gabrielle had turned him into.

"It wasn't supposed to be like this. No one was supposed to get hurt." The response sounded so pathetic that he couldn't help but be defensive. "But you kept pushing. You brought this down on yourself."

"Do you even hear what you're saying? You have a hit list on your website. A hit list! What did you think was going to happen?" Before he could reply, she shook her head. "Look, I'm not here to fight this out. The truth is, you've been played. Roche wasn't killed by one of your followers. You were set up."

The statement left Shah stunned and speechless.

"My intern, Rafi…They killed him and then made it look like he killed Roche. Not only to distract everyone from what they were really doing, but to get leverage over you. Manipulate you into doing their dirty work for them. And you bought it. You chased me across half of Europe, and never even stopped to ask why." Jade stared at him, narrowing her gaze to laser-like intensity. "You know I'm right, don't you?"

Shah ground his teeth together. "Who? Who is doing this?"

Jade offered a tight smile. "Now we're getting somewhere."

Shah listened without comment as Jade related everything she knew or thought she knew about the conspiracy that had claimed Roche's life and given Shah's jihad the nudge it needed to become an actual terror campaign. She had expected incredulity, but Shah regarded her with a journalist's inscrutability even as she fumbled for the right words to express something that was still hard for her to grasp. It was only when she started talking about Professor's replacement that his demeanor changed.

His eyebrows came together in a frown. "How can you be sure it's not really him?"

It was a valid question, and something Jade had not considered, but what struck her most about it was Shah's tone. Some part of him had already recognized that she was telling him the truth.

"I…" She hesitated. Despite the fact that she had come to him for help, Shah was still the man who had effectively put a bounty on her. She needed his trust, but that did not mean she was ready to share intimate details of her life with him. "I just knew. There was something off about his behavior…I can't really explain it. I just knew that it wasn't the same man."

"Could your friend have been brainwashed? Reprogrammed somehow?"

She shook her head. "It isn't him."

He let out a long sigh. "I think that…my partner…might be working with your Changelings. Maybe she's even…even one of them."

Jade could not help but notice his halting manner and the way he said the word "partner," but she said nothing, silently prompting him to continue.

"Now that you've told me, it's like the scales have fallen from my eyes. She kept pushing me to do more, to be more of an activist. I guess now I know why."

"Is she here?"

He shook his head. "I sent her away already. I knew she was working with someone else, but she wouldn't tell me who."

Jade sensed that a chance to move things forward had arrived. "Well, we know who, sort of, but I don't think we know why."

Shah blinked at her. "It seems pretty clear to me. They're trying to set the stage for a new religious crusade. Islam versus the rest of the world. Everyone loves a good war, and Muslims are such an easy target. Ratchet up the fear factor and give people an enemy, and they'll trip over each other in the rush to give up their civil liberties. Meanwhile, the military industrial complex cashes in, the Israelis get more political capital to support their apartheid regime in Palestine, and the one percent takes another slice off the pathetic crumbs the rest of us are squabbling over."

Jade cleared her throat to end the rant. "I'm not saying you're wrong, but if that's all this is about, then they're going to way too much trouble. I think there's something else going on here. It all comes back to Roche."

"Two birds with one stone. His conspiracy theories got too close to the truth."

"Right, but what truth? He been talking about his Changeling conspiracy for years. Why did they wait until…" She trailed off, searching her memories for the answer to her own question. "His new book."

Shah stiffened a little. "The one where he claims that the Prophet never existed?"

Jade put her hands on her hips. "Really? You can't see past that? He barely even mentioned that. Besides, the Phantom Time hypothesis wasn't even Roche's idea. No, it's something to do with the vault."

"At the Hypogeum."

She looked back at him. "I forgot you were there. Did you...see anything strange?"

"Like what?"

"I guess not. The Hypogeum isn't the vault. The Vault is..." She stopped herself. No sense in showing all her cards. "It's somewhere else. The Hypogeum showed me where, sort of like a primitive magical Google Maps."

Shah accepted this without question. "You think these...Changelings want to get to the vault first?"

Jade felt a little like she had finished the border on a 1,500 piece jigsaw puzzle. Good so far, but there was still a great big hole in the middle. "If the Changelings wanted the vault for themselves, it would have been smarter to let me find it for them." She shook her head. "I think they already know where it is. They just don't want us finding it. They knew I would keep looking, so they arranged for you to come after me."

"After Scotland..." Shah started. "That wasn't me. I mean, I put you on the Enemies list, but those men were acting on their own. After that, Gab...my partner kept insisting that we take you alive, so we could get you to reveal how much you knew."

"Maybe she was also trying to protect Kellogg. I think he's one too, too. He's been keeping tabs on me since London. Probably waiting to see how far I would take this. Maybe the left hand didn't know what the right was doing. Once your partner figured out that Kellogg was tagging along with me, she had to do something to keep your people from killing him."

"My people?"

"You know what I mean. She couldn't just come out and tell you though. And she couldn't very well just call it all off. Not when she had worked so hard to make you the fall guy." Shah's expression darkened and Jade sensed that she might be losing him. "Hey, the good news is, you didn't actually hurt anyone. Other than a little property damage, you haven't done anything wrong."

Shah blinked at her. "Is that supposed to make me feel better?"

"It should." She allowed that to sink in for a moment. "So, will you help me?"

"What exactly is it that you want me to do?"

"Help me get Professor back. And help me stop them."

Shah frowned. "Stop them? If even half the stuff you've just told me is true, then these Changelings are everywhere. They've already won."

Jade shook her head defiantly. "If that were true, they wouldn't be trying to stop me from finding the vault. We can beat them."

"If we find the vault?"

"I already know where it is." She did not add that, that there was a very good chance that it would be impossible to get into the vault, at least for a few more decades. Or centuries. "That's the easy part. Getting Professor back is the real challenge."

"About that," Shah began. "What do you…"

"I have a lead on where they might he keeping him. I managed to get a look at the location history on his phone. He spent the better part of two days in a place called Rosebery."

"Doesn't ring any bells. Where is it?"

"Australia. I think so anyway. My guess is that they captured him in Sydney and took him there. The impostor took his stuff after watching him for a while. I'm sure he's still there. It would be too risky to move him." She said the last part quickly, hoping Shah would take her word for it. "We go there. We find him. We rescue him."

"Simple as that," Shah retorted, sarcastically.

"You managed to track me down. You've got international resources. And an army at your disposal."

Shah did not challenge this. "Why should I help you?"

"Well, for starters, it would be your way of saying: 'I'm sorry I tried to kill you.' Then there's a little thing called payback. I thought you might be interested in that."

"I'll help you. I think this is a long shot, but I will do what I can. However, if we somehow get through this alive, I want you to take me with you to this Vault."

"Done."

"I'm not finished. If we find anything in that Vault that might be...let's say confusing regarding the life of the Prophet or the origins of Islam, I want you to promise me that we'll destroy it."

Jade stared at him, incredulous. "Whatever happened to journalistic integrity?"

"You don't yell fire in a crowded room, even if the curtains are smoking. There are a billion and a half Muslims in the world. It's a very crowded room."

Jade blew out her breath. Agreeing to Shah's request was easy enough under the current circumstances. Her interest in the vault had nothing to do with proving or disproving the origins of the Islamic belief system.

But what if the proof is there? Do I just ignore it? Go along with the lie?

If it meant saving Professor, absolutely.

"Deal."

TWENTY-ONE

Unknown Location

The noise roused Professor from his drug-induced slumber. He opened his eyes but resisted the urge to rise and investigate. His brain was still mired in the soporific chemical, and he had no doubt that his body would be even more sluggish. He lay still for several minutes, listening to increasingly strident noise which his addled brain finally recognized as the howl of jet engines some distance away.

They're moving the plane, he thought.

His last clear memory was of the masked guards closing in on him. He had raised his hands to indicate that he would offer no resistance, but they had knocked him out anyway. Judging by his physical condition, that had been only a short time ago, perhaps just a few hours, but evidently something had happened in that brief period of time to prompt his captors to alter the status quo.

He lay motionless, breathing deeply to oxygenate his blood and hopefully purge some of the drug from his system, while he mulled over the significance of this development.

Why are they moving the plane? Has this location been compromised? Or is this some new phase of the plan?

Carrera—or the woman impersonating her—had not confirmed his speculations about the camp or the motive for capturing the plane, but her response made him think he hit pretty close to the mark.

He had been captured by Changelings. Not aliens or supernatural creatures out of mythology, but ordinary humans with an extraordinary talent for impersonating real people. They were method actors, immersing themselves in their roles, not merely imitating their targets, but becoming them to such an extent that even close friends and family members would not notice the substitution.

The town he'd spied from the hillside was a prison

where the passengers would live out their days, unaware of the fact that they were being used to train Changeling infiltrators. It was a rehearsal stage, where the Changeling pretenders could hone their abilities, learn real world skills and practice the art of deception and manipulation.

The noise of the jet engines continued building to a climax but was suddenly punctuated by a much more immediate sound, his door bursting open. He rolled his head sideways in the direction of the disturbance and saw a pair of barely visible silhouettes framed in the doorway.

"It wasn't locked," he mumbled, wondering why his captors had felt the need to make such a dynamic entrance.

One of the figures stepped forward and then the room was filled with light. Professor winced, squeezing his eyes shut against the brightness, but in the afterimage, he saw a face that he had despaired of ever seeing again.

Jade?

"It's him!"

It's her. But how...?

He felt her arms enfolding him, smelled her hair, oddly counterpointed by sulfur tang of recently burnt gunpowder, heard her voice, trembling with emotion as she whispered in his ear. "Oh, God, I didn't think I'd ever see you again."

"Jade? How?"

Another voice, low and insistent sounded from behind her. "We gotta go! This place is about to get hot."

"I'll explain everything," Jade said, speaking quickly. "But we have to get to that plane. Can you walk?"

Walk? "I don't know. How did you find me?"

She insinuated an arm under his shoulder and eased him to a sitting position. "I think they drugged him," she said, looking back to the other commando. "Have we got any antidote?"

His eyes were getting used to the harsh light, which he now saw came from the small tactical flashlights mounted to the rails of the H&K MP5S pistols that Jade and her companion carried. The gunpowder residue he had smelled issued from the sound suppressor fitted to the machine pistol. They were both dressed in woodland camouflage fatigues—faces painted to match—with black watch caps covering their hair and tactical vests brimming with spare magazines and grenades. The man reached into a pouch and took out an atropine auto-injector device—standard US military issue to counteract the effects of nerve agents. The atropine would probably counter the effects of the drug in his bloodstream too, but the side-effects would be a lot worse.

American military. The guy's an operator. The thought was a far more powerful stimulant.

"No," Professor mumbled, gripping Jade's arm. "I'll be okay. Just help me up."

She gave his arm a reassuring squeeze and then turned him on the bed until his feet touched the floor. He was back in his cabin, right where his captors had left him.

He stiffened, pulling free of her grip. "How did you find me?"

"We don't have time for this," the other man said, but Jade held up a hand.

"We'll make time. I told you what these people can do. He deserves an explanation." She knelt in front of him and stared up into his eyes. "They sent someone to impersonate you, but I wasn't fooled for a second."

He laughed. Of course she wasn't. He had spent two days behaving erratically, spinning falsehoods about his life so that his captors wouldn't know which buttons to push to get him to cooperate. Later, when he'd realized the true reason for their scrutiny, he had taken every opportunity to sell the notion of a fictional romance with Jade. He had purposely fed them bad data, with predictable results. Garbage in, garbage out. Jade had seen right through the pretense.

"I realized they must have taken you hostage," she continued, "so I called some of your old SEAL buddies."

He raised his head and scrutinized the camouflaged face. The man didn't look familiar, but that didn't mean anything. Almost everyone he had served with was either retired or had been promoted out of the Teams, but those people still had the connections to launch a rescue operation.

"But how did you know where I was? I don't even know where I am."

"The impostor. He was…" She raised a knowing eyebrow. "Very cooperative."

Something about that explanation nagged at him. *One cabin out of dozens,* he thought. *A needle in a haystack, but they found me.*

"We have to go," the commando insisted again. "That bird is taking off in five minutes, with or without us."

Jade glanced at him for a moment then returned her gaze to Professor. "You heard the man. I'll tell you the rest on the plane."

The plane… "The passengers. We have to get them, too."

"That's being taken care of. We'll get as many as we can."

"You don't understand. Some of them are… Might be…" The word caught in his throat. *Changelings.*

Jade nodded in understanding. "We'll keep them quarantined until we can sort out who's who."

But how will you know for sure? He thought it, but didn't say it out loud. How would he know for sure? His head was still addled from the drugs. His instincts were screaming for him to slow things down but the urgency of the situation was pushing him to make a snap decision.

He struggled to stand, leaning heavily on Jade, but as soon as he was up, he turned to her, pulled her close and kissed her, unleashing months of pent-up longing, all of the passion and desire that he had never dared reveal to her.

He felt her body instantly go taut, defensive, and for a moment, he thought he had made a grave misjudgment, but then she was returning the kiss with equal fervor.

It lasted less than two seconds before she pulled away. "Okay, lover boy. I'm happy to see you too, but we'll have to save the rest of it for when we get back home."

He nodded but did not let go. "You know I love you, right?"

She grinned. "Pete, please. We've got an audience."

"Yes, we do." He dropped one of his hands to her machine pistol, which dangled from the sling over her shoulder. In the same motion, he spun her around, grabbed a handful of her collar, and leveled the gun over her shoulder. "Drop it or she dies!"

The commando jerked involuntarily and then went for his weapon. Professor had expected something like this, and despite the chemicals clogging up his central nervous system, he was reacting even as the man started moving. He flicked the fire selector toggle to full automatic and pulled the trigger. The compact weapon shuddered faintly in his grasp, the suppressor and the distant jet engine roar masking the sound of the multiple discharges, but the commando went down twitching. Professor released the trigger and thrust the pistol against the woman's neck. There was a faint sizzle as the hot metal branded her flesh.

"Who are you? Your real name. It's not Carrera and it sure as hell isn't Jade."

The woman started to struggle in his grasp, and given his physical condition, he doubted he would be able to restrain her much longer, so he screwed the suppressor in tighter. "That was me asking nicely," he growled. "Who are you?"

She grunted and lifted her hands in a show of surrender. "You win."

"Name."

She was silent for a moment, then finally said: "Eve."

"Sure it is. That's two strikes. You don't want a third."

"We don't use names, okay?" Her tone, both frantic and exasperated, made him think she might be telling the truth. A name—any name—would have helped him establish her nationality, and perhaps reveal the true origins of the Changeling conspiracy, but he had more important questions. "Fine. Eve it is. But you've still got two strikes. *Do not*—" He jammed the MP5S against her again for emphasis. "—lie to me again."

She nodded.

"That's more like it," he said. "First question. Why this charade? What's changed?"

"Just like I told you. We sent your replacement. Your woman didn't buy it. She ran. We lost track of her. We need to know what she's going to do next."

"How does this phony rescue help you with that?"

"You know her better than anyone."

Professor laughed despite himself. Evidently his performance had been very convincing, but even he couldn't predict what Jade might do in such a situation. "You thought she might pull off a stunt like this. Organize a rescue mission."

A slight nod. "It was a possibility we couldn't ignore."

"And my double? Did she really capture him?"

Eve shook her head. "She gave him the slip."

"Then how would she know where to look for me?"

Eve shrugged. "She's resourceful. We can't take any chances."

The noise of the jet engines seemed to reach a climax, and then settled into a low rumble. "You really are bugging out, aren't you?"

"Like I said. We can't take any chances."

"You're going to ditch the plane."

Eve said nothing.

"That was always the plan. Ditch the plane somewhere in the middle of the ocean, where nobody's looking. Then in a few months, or a few years, some debris will wash up on a beach somewhere and everyone will say 'mystery solved.'" He shook her. "And the passengers? Are they aboard?"

No answer.

He pulled her head close, shouted in her ear. "You're going to murder them all?"

The distant aircraft engines abruptly grew louder again. The noise built to a fever pitch and then the tone changed, dopplering away to nothing. The aircraft had just taken off.

"Looks like you missed your flight," Eve remarked.

Professor gave her a tooth-rattling shake and pushed the machine pistol into her neck so hard that her knees buckled.

"Call them back."

"Can't. Couldn't even if I wanted to. Radios are disabled."

"Find a way," he shouted. "Call them back or I swear to God, I will execute you."

For a moment, Eve was silent. Then she said, "You think he'll really do it?"

"Who are you—?"

The dead commando abruptly sat up. "I actually think he might."

Professor's reaction was immediate, outpacing the part of his brain that struggled to process this unexpected twist. He pulled the trigger.

The pistol clicked and shuddered just as it had before. There was even a whiff of burnt gunpowder in the air, but he knew that Eve was uninjured. The weapon was loaded with blanks. The suppressor, which was already designed to absorb most of the gas and energy from a gunpowder explosion, had been further modified to ensure that even a close-range discharge would produce no harmful effects.

Another deception.

Even as he processed this, he felt the woman twisting out of his grip. He swiped the machine pistol at the place where her head had been, but she ducked away, and then lashed out with her fist, striking him in the solar plexus. Professor dropped to his knees, his breath gone, his grasp on consciousness slipping.

"No!"

The denial was like a war cry. He threw himself at her, flailing, and somehow succeeded in knocking her off her feet. The ferocity of his attack took not only Eve by surprise but the ersatz commando as well. The man brought his machine pistol up, either an act of desperation or yet another attempt to bluff Professor into submission, but Professor paid it no heed. He hurled himself across the room, swinging his captured MP5 like an axe, driving it straight down at the man's head. There was a sickening crunch as the gun's solid metal frame made contact. The gun was torn from Professor's hands by the severity of the impact, but he made no effort to retrieve it. Instead, he pushed away from the unmoving man and rushed the still disoriented Eve a second time.

She was on hands and knees, crawling away from him, but there was nowhere for her to go. He caught up to her and grabbed hold of her collar again, heaving her to her feet. She fought, but he was ready this time. He lashed out with one foot, jamming it into the side of her knee. Cartilage and tendons popped and her leg buckled, leaving her without the leverage to resist. She howled in agony, and this time it was no act. He slammed her to the floor and planted one knee in her back, silencing her cries.

"Enough!" he shouted.

In the silence that followed, he could hear blood rushing though his veins, pounding in his head. The bottle of primal fury he had uncorked for this burst of energy was spent, a shot of nitrous oxide that had redlined his engine and left him dangerously overheated. If Eve's confederates were lurking outside, he would be helpless to resist. No one came in though, and as the seconds ticked away and the head rush gradually subsided, he realized that no one would.

He took a deep breath, then another. When he was able to speak in a steady voice, he leaned close to Eve. "I suppose you would rather die than tell me anything, right?"

A low groan was the only reply.

"That's what I thought. Happy to oblige you."

"You won't," she rasped. "I know you. You're not a killer."

Professor did not miss the note of desperation in her tone. "You don't know anything about me." He put his hands around her neck.

"Wait—"

The rest of her plea was choked off, but after a couple seconds, he relented. "Something else you wanted to say?"

She managed a hoarse laugh. "See. I knew it. As long as there's a chance that I can help you save the people on that plane, you won't do it."

There was a measure of truth in what she said, but he did not miss the subtext. "They're already dead though, aren't they?"

"You can threaten all you want, but it's too late to save them. If you kill me, it's cold-blooded—"

He tightened his grip again, held it until she started thrashing. Her arms curled back, fingers clawing at the floor.

"I can live with that," he whispered in her ear. "It's not like your face will haunt me. I don't even know what you really look like."

Her struggles continued, growing more frantic with each passing second and then she abruptly went limp. Professor waited a moment longer then let go and flipped her onto her side, into the recovery position. He massaged her neck for a moment to stimulate the flow of blood in the arteries and then felt for a pulse. Her heart was still beating out a rabbit-fast rhythm. He shook her until she drew a single gasping breath, then rolled her over, face down again. Before she could even begin to recover her wits, he drew her tactical vest down halfway, pulling her elbows together behind her back, and then cinched the straps to form a makeshift restraint system.

While it had never been his intention to actually kill her, his rationale had nothing to do with pity, weakness or even an antiquated notion of chivalry. He did not doubt that it was already too late for the passengers of Flight 815. Even if they were still alive aboard the plane—something he seriously doubted—he was out of options for calling the aircraft back. The only thing he could hope to accomplish now was to expose the Changelings, find out just how deep their conspiracy went, and maybe prevent a similar catastrophe. To do that, he needed a live prisoner, not a corpse.

He did a quick pat down, searching Eve's pockets for useful gear or anything she might be able to use as a weapon if she got free. The magazines held only blanks but he removed them from their pouches and tossed them aside, along with the grenades which were almost certainly duds but had enough heft to be dangerous if thrown or used as a bludgeon. There was a capped syringe in one of her pockets, probably containing a dose of the tranquilizer the Changelings were so fond of using. He slipped it into his own pocket and then moved over to check on the commando. The man was truly dead this time; there was no way to fake a crushed skull. Professor did not bother with the phony combat load, but searched the man's pockets for anything that might shed light on his identity. There was nothing, save for another syringe which Professor added to his inventory.

Eve was semi-conscious, staring at him through heavily lidded eyes, but she neither moved nor spoke as he scooped her into his arms and then heaved her onto one of his shoulders. The effects of the narcotic seemed to be easing, which meant that either it was nearly out of his system or his body was developing a tolerance for it, but he moved cautiously, as wary of a relapse as he was running into more Changelings. As he approached the door however, he was filled with a new sense of urgency. Waves of heat were radiating off the door, and the smell of wood smoke was creeping into the cabin.

Eve's accomplice had not been speaking figuratively when he had warned her that things were about to heat up. *They're burning it all down.*

TWENTY-TWO

Professor pushed the door open, careful to avoid the blast of super-heated air that rushed in, and was met by a wall of fire. The entire north end of the camp was in flames, the orange radiance so bright that he was unsure whether it was day or night. The conflagration had already reached the row of cabins directly in front of him. Nevertheless, he edged out and skirted along the front of his cabin and rounded the corner. There were a few isolated fires to the south, but for the most part the route was clear. He surmised that the Changelings had set the fire as soon as the plane was in the air, or more probably, just before taking off. Eve's accomplice hadn't been exaggerating about the need to hurry.

He wondered if they had actually intended to put him on the aircraft at all. That seemed unlikely since it had not waited around, but it also meant that they had arranged some other means of escaping the fires, which had probably been set to erase all traces of the Changeling camp. Judging by the height of the towering flames, the fire was not merely consuming the ramshackle cabins, but also the forest beyond, and maybe even the town on the far side of the hill—a literal scorched earth retreat.

He quickened his step to a steady jog, running down the narrow alley between the cabins and away from the approaching firestorm, until he reached the southern edge of the camp. There, just fifty yards from where he emerged, he saw something that had not been there during his earlier explorations. A parked SUV.

With some distance between himself and the fire, he saw that it was nighttime, and while the orange glow of the flames provided more than enough light by which to see, the cabins cast nearly impenetrable shadows over the vehicle. He observed it for a few seconds to make sure there was no one lurking nearby and then crossed to it. It was unlocked and the key was in the ignition, so he dumped Eve into the passenger seat, checking to make sure that her bonds were still tight, then turned the key.

The headlights revealed a pattern of parallel grooves in the earth, the tire imprints from a small convoy of off-road vehicles, which converged into a trail that led away to the south. The tire tracks were fresh. Trace evidence of a recent evacuation. He followed the tracks, keeping the SUV moving at a crawl through the rough unfamiliar terrain.

He glanced over at Eve and was surprised to find her staring back at him with eyes full of hate. There was something that looked like a flap of skin—still streaked with camouflage paint—hanging from her face, and under it, another layer of smooth unmarked skin. He considered tearing away the latex simulacrum of Jade's face to reveal Eve's true countenance, but decided the unmasking could wait until they were in a more secure environment. Besides, the Changeling's true face was the least of her secrets that he wanted to know.

"Feeling talkative yet?"

She continued glowering.

"That's okay. I've figured some of this out for myself already. You know how you observe your targets, learning all the little details in order to create a perfect duplicate?" He laughed. "Well, maybe not perfect. But it's a little like being an FBI profiler. Studying behavior, reading the clues, and putting it all together. While you were observing me, I was observing you. Here's what I came up with.

"You've been at this for a while. Decades. Maybe longer." He noticed a slight eye-twitch. *Okay, definitely longer*, he thought. *I'll come back to that.* "You're skilled at the art of illusion. Not just masks and imitating people, but creating elaborate scenarios to manipulate us. Like that fake rescue scene. You could have doped me up with truth serum and asked me anything, but instead you tried to con me into giving up the information. Playacting is like a compulsion for you. A pathological need."

Eve maintained her stony silence. Professor looked away, allowing the accusation to sink in for a few seconds while he negotiated the narrow trail that wound through the trees.

"I guess it only makes sense. If you've got a particular talent or ability, naturally you'd see everything as a problem to be solved in those terms. Like that old saying, when you're a hammer, every problem looks like a nail. That's how I can tell that you aren't working for a national intelligence service."

She looked up suddenly, evincing surprise at the statement, and inadvertently confirming his statement.

Professor grinned. "A trained spy uses the best methods available to complete a mission. A confidence artist only knows how to run a scam. Now, you're probably wondering why I'm going on about this. Here's the thing. Spies are also trained in how to resist interrogation methods. And they know that, no matter how tough they are, if captured, they will eventually break. I'm telling you this so that you know what's in store for you. You've probably heard about 'enhanced interrogation' techniques? Those are fun, though they aren't much good against trained assets. You on the other hand…" He shook his head gravely.

Eve sneered. "It doesn't matter. Even if I told you everything, you would not live long enough to share it. We are everywhere. We don't work for some pitiful government agency. We *are* the governments. We are everywhere. You think we've been doing this for a few years? Try a few millennia. We're everywhere. We've always been everywhere."

Professor listened carefully to her rant and decided that she was telling the truth, or at least what she believed to be the truth, but he shook his head. "Nice try. I hope you can come up with something better than that when I'm pouring a gallon of water down your throat."

She gave a disdainful snort and turned her head to avoid his gaze. "You wanted the truth. The truth is that there is not a soul on this earth you can trust."

"Then indulge me. Answer my questions. Why take the plane? Why kill Roche? If you're as powerful as all that, what difference does one crazy guy make?" When she did not respond, he asked one more question. "Why go after Jade?"

Even as he uttered the words, he realized that he had been looking at everything wrong. He thought back to the meeting with Roche, moments before his life had been snuffed out. He had asked the conspiracy theorist a similar question.

Why bring this to Jade?

And Jade had said, *You think I can find proof that Phantom Time is real?*

Roche had died before answering the question.

"You think Jade is going to find something." He watched for a reaction, but this time, the Changeling woman maintained a steady poker face. "What? Something to do with Phantom Time?"

He thought he saw a faint glimmer of amusement in her eyes. *Okay, not Phantom Time. What then?* "Well, you're right to be worried. Jade can be a regular bulldog when she puts her mind to something, but I guess you're already figuring that out."

"It's not for you."

Eve spoke so softly that it took him a moment to comprehend what she had said.

"What? What's not for me?"

She did not answer and he had to turn his full attention back to the matter of driving as the trees thinned and the trail dipped down into a drainage ditch before rising back up to a dirt road. He down-shifted and engaged the four-wheel drive low range, then eased down the embankment. The vehicle nosed down so steeply that he had to make a conscious effort not to take his foot off the accelerator and brace himself to keep from falling. The SUV's front bumper scraped the bottom of the ditch for a moment, then the vehicle tilted up and it was all he could do to keep his foot on the gas pedal.

When the vehicle was finally level again he turned to Eve. "Will you at least tell me which way to go?"

"That depends on where you're going."

"How about we go join the rest of your friends? I'm game if you are."

She looked forward again, refusing to answer.

Professor shook his head and stared out the windshield at the deeply rutted road. From what he could tell, it ran north-south, leaving him with a fifty-fifty chance of getting it right on the first try. He could always backtrack if he hit a dead-end, but such a mistake might cost valuable time, or possibly exhaust his fuel supply, leaving him stranded. The ruddy glow of the distant fire was brightest to the north. Depending on how the road meandered, it might take them right into the heart of the blaze.

"Two roads diverged in a wood," he muttered. "So I flipped a coin."

He cranked the wheel to the right, turning the SUV away from the fire, but Eve stopped him. "Go the other way."

He corrected immediately, veering to the left and, as soon as the wheels were all pointing forward, shifted the four-wheel drive back into high-range. "Why the change of heart?"

"Because I don't know how far that road goes, but I do know that if you run out of gas out in the middle of nowhere, I'm screwed. Since you dislocated my knee, I won't be walking out, and I doubt you'll be able to carry me very far. It's pretty simple math, really. Oh, and I don't think that's how the poem goes."

"Poem?"

"Robert Frost. *The Road Not Taken.* 'Two roads diverged in a wood and I, I took the one less traveled by, and that has made all the difference.'"

"Ah. I didn't think you were familiar with Frost."

"You're thinking of Jeanne Carrera."

He looked at her again, wondering about the woman under the mask. "Is it worth it?"

"What?"

"Whatever it is you get from playing this game. Wearing a mask all the time. Living other people's lives instead of your own."

She turned away and looked straight ahead. "You don't know anything about me."

He shrugged and did the same, pushing the SUV as fast as conditions would permit. The headlight beams picked up the smoke in the air, but after about two miles, the road began to veer away from the fire. Not long after that, the road came to a T-junction with a paved highway.

"Left," Eve said without looking.

He followed this guidance, but remained wary. Her pragmatic explanation for helping him earlier did not carry as much weight now that they had reached a road more traveled. "So where are we anyway? New Zealand?"

She gave a short, humorless laugh. "I figured you would have worked that out already."

"I'm in the ballpark, right?"

"Tasmania."

"Ah, of course." The island of Tasmania, located a hundred and fifty miles off the south-eastern tip of Australia, shared the same latitude as parts of New Zealand, but was about eight hundred miles further west. "Well that's a little embarrassing."

Tasmania was fairly large for an island, about the same size as Ireland, but with only one-eighth the population, half of which was concentrated in the capital city of Hobart, with the rest mostly occupying settlements on the coast. Nearly half of the island had been set aside for parks or nature preserves, most of which were not easily accessible by vehicle, making it the perfect place to hide from the rest of the world.

"I take it that wasn't your permanent headquarters."

"We don't have 'headquarters.' I told you. We are everywhere."

"Well, it won't be too hard to root you out." He reached over and tugged the dangling flap of latex, revealing a little more of her true face.

She looked away again, staring absently out the side window. "Not everyone wears a mask."

That thought was chilling. If the Changelings had truly been infiltrating the halls of power for several generations, then there would be no need for them to replace world leaders. They could simply leverage their preferred candidates into the limelight, and let democracy take care of the rest.

"I don't believe you," he lied. "But it doesn't matter. You're afraid. Afraid that Jade will find something that will utterly destroy you, and that tells me that you're a lot weaker than you want me to believe."

She continued giving him the silent treatment, which seemed proof enough that he was right. *I have to contact Jade,* he thought. *Let her know that she's on the right track. But how?*

How indeed, if even the omniscient Changelings could not find her?

A light appeared further down the road, the headlights of an approaching car, the first he had seen. *Probably someone coming to investigate the fire,* he thought. *But what if it's not? What if it's more Changelings coming to see why Eve was taking so long?*

There was something strange about the lights too, but with them shining directly in his eyes, he couldn't quite put his finger on what was bothering him. When the lights were only about a hundred yards away, Eve broke her silence, speaking in a calm detached manner. "They drive on the left here."

Professor hauled the steering wheel to the side, veering into the left lane, even as the sound of the oncoming car's horn reached his ears. The SUV shuddered as he fought to regain control, and for a moment, he thought it might go tumbling down the highway. Instead, the vehicle spun around sideways, the rear end clipping a white guard post, and then rebounded away, spinning across both lanes, just missing the passing car, and hit another guard post on the right side of the road.

Something exploded in Professor's face, showering him with a spray of hot vapor and debris, and then his face slammed into the airbag that had deployed from the center of the steering wheel. The collision combined with the unexpected punch from the safety system left him momentarily dazed, but even before his wits returned, he started groping for the door handle. It took him a few seconds to realize that the door was already open, sprung out of its frame by the crash, and that the only thing holding him a prisoner of the wrecked SUV was his seat belt.

As he wrestled with the buckle, a bright red glow from outside the vehicle caught his attention. It was the brake lights of the car he had narrowly missed. The back-up lights came on, and the car began rolling backwards down the road.

He breathed a curse and then looked over to see how Eve had fared. To his dismay, the passenger's seat was empty. "Damn it!" He squirmed out of the seat belt and pitched forward onto the pavement, feeling acutely every bruise sustained in the crash and in his earlier struggle with Eve. Nevertheless, he got his feet under him and sprinted around to the other side of the vehicle.

There was no sign of Eve.

He searched the woods, certain that he would see her limping or crawling away. With her injured knee, she could not possibly have gotten very far... Unless she wasn't heading for the woods.

He ducked down behind the end of the SUV and sneaked a look at the car which had come to a full stop about thirty yards away. The doors opened and four figures—all men, judging by their physique—emerged.

"Help me!" The shriek, a woman's voice liberally accented with the local brogue, was accompanied by a flurry of movement near the crumpled front end of the wrecked vehicle. A woman shambled into the open, waving her arms. "He tried to kill me! Help!"

It was Eve, and yet it was not her, or rather not the woman he had captured in the Changeling camp. Her mask was gone, revealing smooth white skin and a cascade of blonde hair. She had also shed her commando attire, stripping down to her underwear.

"Damn it!" The men in the car evidently weren't

Changelings, just Good Samaritans, but she would turn them against him all the same.

"Help!" she cried again, falling into the arms of the closest man. "Save me!"

While the one man was occupied with comforting the damsel-in-distress, the other three began advancing. Professor pulled back into the shadows. He would never be able to convince the men that she was not the victim she purported to be. He did not think he could outrun them, which left only one option. He would have to fight his way out of this.

He dug the syringes from his pocket. The fast-acting drug might be enough to even the odds, but he would have to let the men get very close in order to inject them. He backed away from the SUV, staying in a low fighting stance, and waited for Eve's hapless saviors to close to within striking distance. As the first man stepped into view, Professor realized he had made a grievous miscalculation. The men were armed with pistols, all of which were trained on him.

He raised his hands. "Guys, it's not what you think."

The plea sounded utterly ridiculous. These men were not going to take his word over that of a beautiful, half-naked blonde with bruises all over her body, and he doubted very much that Eve would implore them to simply take him prisoner until the police arrived.

"You're American?" one of the men asked, seemingly apropos of nothing. There was something odd about his manner of speech. He did not sound like an Aussie. The man who had raised the question did not wait for an answer, but instead holstered his gun and took out his phone. He held it up as if to take Professor's picture then turned to the others. "It's him!"

Professor watched incredulously as the other men put their guns away and rushed forward, repeating the message in a low murmur.

It's him.

What the hell?

"We were sent to find you," explained the first man.

"What are you doing?" Eve screamed. "Shoot him!"

The man looked back to where his comrade was still hugging the woman protectively. "Hold her. Do not let her escape."

Professor ignored Eve's cries and continued to regard the other man warily. "Sent by whom?"

"Mr. Atash Shah."

Professor now recognized the odd lilt to the man's voice. Indian, or more likely, Pakistani. His swarthy features, along with a long but well-groomed beard, suggested the latter.

He also recognized the name. Shah. The founder of the Crescent Defense League. The man who had put Jade on his hit list. *Wonderful*, he thought, miserably. *And I didn't think things could get worse.*

"And Dr. Jade Ihara," the man continued.

"Jade?" He felt a glimmer of hope, but then just as quickly grew wary again. *It's another trick.* Eve's dire pronouncement still rang in his ears. *There is not a soul on this earth you can trust.*

Except Shah had no reason to work with the Changelings, much less with Jade. And how would Jade even know to approach Shah, someone who was actively targeting her? If this was another Changeling ploy, it was positively Byzantine.

"Jade sent you?" he repeated. "I want to talk to her."

The man looked at his phone again. "The reception is a bit spotty out here, but I'll try."

A moment later, he brought it to his ear and began speaking in English. "It's Ahmad. We found him...Yes...Yes... He wants to speak to Dr. Ihara." His face broke into a broad grin as he held the phone out.

Professor regarded the mobile device cautiously—

Not a soul on this earth you can trust.

—then accepted it and held it to his ear. "Jade?"

"Prof?"

The sound of her voice, the palpable concern and relief

in her tone, brought tears to his eyes, yet he could not forget that Eve had perfectly mimicked Jade's voice. "How do I——?"

"Know it's really you?" she finished the question before he could get the words out. She thought for a few seconds, then said: "Where did you get that ridiculous hat?"

"I don't own a 'ridiculous hat,'" he said quickly. "But I do have a very dashing and stylish fedora that I picked up in Costa Rica last year. My turn." He searched his memory for some trivial bit of shared information that no Changeling would ever guess at. Finally, he said. "Jade. I love you."

There was a long silence at the other end. "Knock it off, Professor. And get your ass back here. I need you."

It's really her.

"Jade, I…" A short triple-beep signaled the termination of the call. He sighed and finished the sentence. "I don't know where you are."

PART THREE
CIRCLES

TWENTY-THREE

Edwards Air Force Base, California USA

The first thing Jade did when Professor stepped off the loading ramp of the United States Air Force C-130 Globemaster cargo plane was run up to him and tug his cheek to make sure that it was really him and not someone wearing a mask.

The second thing she did was kiss him.

He did not resist. Jade was pretty sure that he was enjoying the display of affection, but she also knew he would never let her live it down, so as she pulled away she said, "Just needed to do that for future reference."

"I missed you, too," he said. "Future reference?"

"There are some things a Changeling can't duplicate."

"Eww. Don't tell me you kissed… You know what, I don't want to know." He threw his arms around her and hugged her. "God, what a nightmare that was."

"You can tell me about it on the way." She took a step back and gestured to the man standing a few steps behind her. "Professor, meet Atash Shah."

Professor regarded Shah suspiciously then extended his hand. Shah accepted the hand clasp, then went rigid, the blood draining from his face, as Professor squeezed.

"I appreciate what you did for Jade," Professor said in a low voice, "but let me be clear. I think you are a terrorist—"

Jade put a hand on Professor's chest and gave him a hard shove. "Knock it off. You would probably be dead if it wasn't for him and his *terrorists*, so give it a rest."

Shah however seemed oddly pleased by Professor's display. "That's okay. I'm rather used to that sort of ignorant prejudice."

"Ignorant?" There was strange gleam in Professor's eyes. "I guess I have more experience with your so-called 'religion of peace' than you realize. Not as much as the friends I've buried, mind you—"

"Hey!" Jade said sharply. "Enough!"

Professor offered a tight smile then let go of Shah's hand. "Looking forward to working with you."

"So much for the happy reunion," Jade growled under her breath. "I hope you got that out of your system. We've got work to do."

"Something I have to take care of first." He looked past her, settling his gaze on a convoy of black vans rolling toward the flight line.

Jade's forehead drew into a crease. "You told someone you were coming here?"

Professor's travel arrangements—hers and Shah's too— had been shrouded in secrecy. With no way of knowing who could be trusted, it had been necessary to create several different itineraries and modes of travel, with multiple decoy destinations, and even then, there was no way of knowing if they had covered all their bases.

"Tam sent them. Of course I told her. Who do you think set everything up?"

"Well what are they doing here?"

"I brought Tam a souvenir." He waved to someone in the interior of the aircraft, and two people emerged, moving slowly down the metal deck. One was a tall, muscly guy, wearing jeans, a Harley Davidson T-shirt and cowboy boots. Jade thought the second person might be a woman, but it was hard to tell for certain since she wore a shapeless orange prison jumpsuit with a high-collared bullet-proof vest and a burlap sack over her head.

"Whoa. You caught a live one?" Although they had spoken several times over the phone to coordinate this rendezvous, there had not been time to catch up on the details of their respective misadventures. Jade knew only that Professor had been imprisoned by the Changelings and had eventually escaped on his own.

"The big guy there is Billy Sievers, one of Tam's new hires. He rode with me from Sydney. I guess as the low man on the totem pole, he got stuck with escort duty."

"I do have some experience with it," Sievers said in a

deep Texas drawl.

"Used to work for an escort service, yeah?" Jade asked with a mischievous smile.

Seivers winked. "Wouldn't you like to know?"

Jade turned her grin on Professor. "He's cute. Let's keep him."

"Sorry, ma'am. I've already got a date." Seivers gestured to the prisoner. "Not sure where I'm takin' her yet, but it's bound to be a good time. For one of us anyway."

There was a hint of menace in his tone, and Jade decided that maybe Seivers wasn't so cute after all.

The vans rolled up close to the cargo doors, forming a tight horseshoe with no gaps through which an observer might be able to see what was happening inside. Each of the vehicles opened, disgorging a contingent of men in army uniforms—the combat variety, replete with body armor, helmets, and assault rifles. They took up defensive positions all around the inner perimeter, as if anticipating an immediate attack.

Seivers turned to the prisoner. "Our ride's here, honey."

The woman did not respond to the sound of his voice but at a none-too-gentle nudge from Seivers, she began walking straight ahead. He guided her toward the second van in the line and then helped her step up into the vehicle. When she was back inside, he raised a hand to his forehead as if tipping the brim of an imaginary hat to Jade. "See you round, darlin'."

Jade smiled, but muttered under her breath. "Not if I see you first."

The soldiers broke formation and piled back into the vans. When they were gone, Jade gestured to the waiting rental car that would bear the three of them away. Once inside, with Jade behind the wheel, Professor riding shotgun and an eerily quiet Shah in the back seat, she asked, "Where will they take her?"

"A black site. A secret detention facility for enemies of the state too dangerous to be put into the criminal justice system."

"Isn't that illegal? Especially on American soil."

"She's one of them," Professor said. "A Changeling. Leaving aside the fact that she deserves anything we could do to her, she's part of a conspiracy that runs so deep, there's no way of knowing who in our government is already compromised. Tam is going to play this very close to the vest. It's the only way to root out the Changeling infiltrators."

As Jade drove off the tarmac and navigated roads leading out of the base, Professor launched into a quick recap of everything that had happened, beginning with his capture in Sydney and ending with the crash on the Murchison Highway, a few miles outside of a remote Tasmanian mining town called Rosebery. When he told her about the uncertain but almost certainly terrible fate of the passengers on Flight 815, Jade was a little less inclined to worry about the prisoner's civil liberties. If even half of what the woman—Eve—had revealed was true, then she and her Changeling brethren were beyond the reach of ordinary justice.

Jade almost interrupted Professor when he recounted his conversation with Eve regarding the Changelings' true objective, but managed to contain herself until he finished his story, just as Jade turned east onto California state highway 58.

"There's no trace of them now?" she asked.

"None. The fire is being investigated as a possible arson but it will be weeks before anyone can get in there to sift through the ashes. They covered their tracks pretty well. The investigator I met in Sydney, Sousa, supposedly went missing when the search plane he was riding in went down in the Pacific. According to the news reports, I was on that plane, too."

"Wow. So you're officially dead?"

"Officially missing," he corrected, then added in a somber tone. "Like Flight 815." He looked away, staring out at the barren landscape outside the car. "Where are we going?"

230 | WOOD AND ELLIS

"The Vault," she announced triumphantly, grateful for a chance to change to topic and share her discoveries. "It's not what Roche thought it was."

He returned a blank look.

"I sent you a text about this."

"Somebody stole my phone, remember?"

"Oh, right." She launched into her own account of recent doings, carefully glossing over the repeated attacks by Shah and his minions, focusing instead on what they had discovered with each successive stop along the way. When she mentioned infrasound, and related what had happened in the underground chamber in Peru, Professor sat up straighter. "You should have told me about that."

She frowned. "You were supposed to tell me how clever I was for figuring it out on my own."

"Well, obviously. But you shouldn't keep things like that to yourself. I could have helped you figure it out."

"At the time, I didn't know what was happening. I only put it all together when we went to the Hypogeum."

Professor rubbed his chin thoughtfully. "The chamber in Paracas and the Hypogeum have two things in common. Unusual acoustic properties and deformed skulls."

"You think there's a connection?"

"Let's just say I don't buy into Roche's theory about artificial cranial deformation as a defense against the Changelings. But it would be interesting to compare the frequency shifts in a regular round human skull versus a flattened one."

"Flat skulls can pick up more channels?"

"Actually, I was thinking the opposite. A lifetime in close proximity to those resonance chambers would probably drive an ordinary person insane."

Jade grinned at him. "I'm so glad you're back."

He looked askance at her. "I'll just pretend you really mean that."

"Of course I meant it."

"And still not convinced. So, what did you find at the Hypogeum?"

"God, it was incredible. Way more than just seeing ghosts. I had an out-of-body experience. I flew up into space, went halfway around the world, and then landed at the vault. I actually saw the lock mechanism that Archimedes described."

"And was it a timelock like Roche said?"

Jade shrugged. "It was like looking at an electrical schematic. I can tell what it is, but I have no idea what it means or how it works."

"Could you draw it from memory?"

"Possibly. There's one thing I remember vividly. It was the last thing I saw before…" Her eye found Shah in the rear view mirror. "Before the vision ended. Three circles. They looked like they were linked, sort of like the Olympic rings, but they weren't really. It was just an optical illusion."

"Sounds like Borromean Rings."

"Is that a Tolkien thing?"

Professor laughed. "Not quite. It's a math problem. Complex geometry. It would be easier to show it than try to explain it. Got any paper?"

Jade took a notepad and the stub of a pencil from her shirt pocket, and passed it over. Professor flipped through page after page of sketches and field notes until he found a blank page. He spent a few minutes drawing a figure, then held it up to show her.

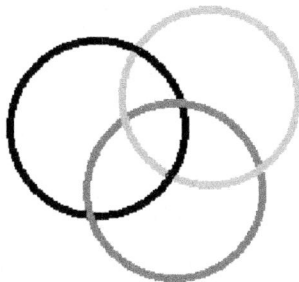

"That's it," she confirmed.

"Borromean Rings," he confirmed. "They appear to be linked at the center, but when you follow the individual circles, you see that they're actually sitting on top of each other, which is physically impossible. Well, with true circles anyway. You've never seen anything like this before?"

"Don't think so. Archimedes was a math guy, yeah? Would he have known about them?"

"They don't show up in the historical record until the 6th century, almost eight hundred years after Archimedes, but he was a genius. Way ahead of his time. And most of his writings have been lost. I wouldn't be at all surprised if he at least toyed with the idea." He stared at his sketch for a moment. "You know, according to most accounts, Archimedes was working on a problem right before he died. Supposedly, his last words were, 'Don't disturb my circles.' Something to that effect. Maybe he was trying to solve the riddle of Borromean Rings."

"Well, that was the last thing I saw. I think it's important. Maybe the key to opening the vault."

He nodded, then looked at her with the same suspicious glance. "Wait a second. You said we were going to the vault. But we're driving toward Death Valley. Don't tell me…"

"I saw where it is. In my vision."

"And it's in California?"

"Arizona, actually."

He shook his head. "No. This is crazy. You had a bad trip, Jade. Infrasound stimulates different parts of the brain, but it can't put ideas in your head that aren't already there."

"Why not? When you hear a song on the radio, it's just a bunch of high frequency radio waves assembled a certain way. Maybe the ancients who built the Hypogeum built it so that it would play a specific pattern of resonance waves, to produce a specific effect."

"Jade, think about it. You've done most of your work in the Southwest. Of course that's what you would see. It's just your brain trying to make sense of it."

"If you had been there, you'd know that it wasn't a hallucination. But it doesn't matter. We'll be there in a few hours. If we find it right where I saw it in my vision, then we'll know I'm right. If it's not there, I'll admit I was wrong. Does that work for you?"

"If I may," Shah said, breaking his long silence. "The Hypogeum is important. My partner knew that Jade would go there, and I think she knew what you would find."

Professor craned his head around and stared at Shah. "Why is he here, again?"

"That was part of the deal for saving your ass," Jade said. "I made the call. Get over it."

He frowned but did not push the issue. "I'm still pretty skeptical about the role of infrasound in this, but I'll allow for the possibility. We've seen too much crazy stuff to dismiss it out of hand. And like you said, if it's not there, we'll know. But has it occurred to you that, if it really is there, the Changelings know about it and will probably be waiting for you?"

"Which is why I'm glad that you're back. One of the reasons, anyway."

"So where is it? Exactly, I mean."

Jade glanced at Shah again. She had not revealed the exact location to him or anyone else yet. But Professor was right. The Changelings weren't looking for the vault. They almost certainly knew where it was. They were only interested in keeping anyone else from finding it. She was keeping the secret only to keep Shah from trying to double-cross her. Even a few hours' advance notice would be enough for him to set up an ambush. But if that was his plan, then he would not make his move until the door to the vault was open, if it could be opened. She would only know his true intentions then.

"The Vault," she said, "is in Sedona."

TWENTY-FOUR

Village of Oak Creek, Arizona

Although he initially greeted Jade's declaration much the same way that he might have reacted to Jeremiah Stillman or someone of his ilk going on about extraterrestrial astronauts—for very nearly the same reason—he had to admit that it made a lot of sense.

The area surrounding the northern Arizona town—equal parts artists' colony and tourist trap—situated about halfway between the city of Phoenix and the Grand Canyon, was renowned for a wide range of paranormal activities ranging from frequent UFO sightings to energy vortices capable of transporting people to parallel dimensions. The sheer volume of anecdotal evidence suggested that something might actually be happening at Sedona. There were simply too many stories to discount them all as cynical hoaxes or delusions brought on by too much time in the hot desert sun and unrealistic expectations.

The actual scientific evidence for such phenomena was sketchy. Pictures purporting to show auras and other ghostly images were easily dismissed as lens flares, or more often than not, were the result of hucksters using techniques like Kirlian photography to produce visually stunning, but definitely not supernatural images of electromagnetic fields. Terrestrial electromagnetic energy was widely cited as the source of Sedona's strange phenomena. The area was reputed to be a major junction of electromagnetic meridians, often called "ley lines"—similar effects were often reported at the Pyramids of Egypt, Stonehenge, Easter Island, or anywhere that New Age gurus might be able to convince the gullible to part with their money—but EM effects could be measured, and there was no observable difference in the earth's magnetic field at Sedona to back up this pseudo-scientific explanation.

Nevertheless, Jade's experiences in Paracas and the

Hypogeum had convinced him to give those stories a second look. In almost every case, the effects described by visitors to Sedona and the surrounding area mirrored the effects described in infrasound experiments, ranging from altered mood to hallucinations to temporary loss of consciousness and lapses of memory, which could be mistaken for teleportation—another commonly reported phenomena associated with the Sedona vortices. A resonance chamber in the hills of Sedona, either naturally occurring or constructed by one of the civilizations that had inhabited the area over the preceding nine thousand years, was a perfectly plausible explanation.

It did not of course explain how Jade was able to "see" an elaborate Vault from the other side of the world, *but*, Professor thought, *one impossible thing at a time.*

It took a little over seven hours to make the drive from Edwards AFB to Sedona and then a little further south to the place Jade revealed to be the *actual* location of the vault, a 547-foot high red limestone butte shaped like a bell—thus the name, Bell Rock—though to Professor, it looked more like a medieval castle perched atop a huge domed mountain.

According to the tourist pamphlets Jade had collected, Bell Rock was one of the four prominent vortex sites in the Sedona area, and rumor had it the mountain concealed an enormous crystal that produced harmonic energy waves—more New Age-y nonsense, as far as Professor was concerned—or possibly a hidden alien city, which now didn't seem quite as preposterous as it once had. Bell Rock had achieved near-global notoriety in 2012 when a Sedona retiree, obsessed with the belief that all of human existence was actually an elaborate computer simulation—probably after reading one of Roche's books—claimed that a portal to another dimension would open up during the winter solstice, which not-coincidentally corresponded to the arrival of the overhyped end of the Mayan calendar, and that by taking a literal leap of faith from the promontory, he would be hurled through space and time to the center of the galaxy. Professor could not recall hearing the man's eventual fate, but he could not ignore the similarities to what Jade had described. Perhaps there was some kind of doorway at Bell Rock, and a resonance chamber that could, figuratively at least, send a person on a cosmic journey.

Was that a secret worth killing for? Evidently both the Changelings and Atash Shah thought so, though for very different reasons. Shah's faith-based concerns he could understand, even if they were wholly irrational, but what did the Changelings hope to gain from protecting what was essentially a great big hallucination machine?

Jade pulled the car off in a parking area at the trailhead near the highway. It was late afternoon but there were still several other cars in the lot, most of them bearing Arizona license plates, though there were a few from other states. All of the cars had an innocuous well-traveled look about them, but that was exactly the sort of attention to detail he would expect from the Changelings.

Jade got out and went to the trunk. Inside was a small backpack along with an ample supply of bottled water. "Load up," she said. "The entrance is in a cave about fifty feet up the cliff. We'll have to do some climbing."

"That's a pretty precise estimate," Professor remarked. "I wonder if you were seeing it as it is now, or as it was when the Hypogeum was first built. Did the vision account for erosion and weathering?"

"Don't be such a spoilsport. I know exactly where to go. When we get there, you'll either see that I'm right, or get to crow about me being delusional."

"I didn't say you were... You know what, you're right. Let's go."

Jade stuffed several bottles into the pack and then handed one each to Professor and Shah. "It's not far, but we should probably get moving if we want to get there before dark."

"Lead the way." He fixed Shah with a pointed stare. "I'll bring up the rear."

A frown flickered across Shah's face but he did not reply. Instead, he fell into step behind Jade and did not look

back. Professor allowed them to get a lead of about fifty
yards before heading out. He walked with his hands on his
hips, his right hand just a few inches from the Beretta nine-
millimeter pistol tucked into his belt at the small of his back
and covered by the tail of his shirt. Sievers had brought him
the weapon in Australia, and though he only had one spare
fifteen-round magazine, he was not as worried about being
outgunned by the Changelings as he was being outfoxed by
them. A frontal assault wasn't their style, but that did not
make them any less formidable.

The well-maintained trail headed north toward the
towering formation, paralleling the highway for the first mile
or so. They passed several day hikers and mountain bikers
returning to the trailhead, presumably after completing the
nearly four mile long loop that encompassed both Bell Rock
and the considerably more massive but not quite as
photogenic Courthouse Butte to the east. None of the
tourists gave them more than a second glance, but Professor
varied his stride, sometimes falling back as much as a
hundred yards to see if anyone was paying closer than usual
attention to them.

When they reached the Y-junction and the beginning of
the loop, Jade paused as if taking a rest break. When she
sure there was nobody in their line of sight, she left the trail
behind and headed due north toward the base of the rock.
Professor lingered a few minutes to make sure they were not
being observed, and then headed out at a jog.

Jade moved toward the butte as if guided by a homing
beacon. Despite his skepticism concerning her supposed
out-of-body experience, he marveled at the certainty with
which she sped toward her goal, but that was easily enough
explained by the fact that this was probably not her first visit
to Bell Rock. The Sedona area had been inhabited for
thousands of years, and there were ongoing archaeological
excavations all over the region. He knew for a fact that Jade
had done extensive field work in the Southwest as part of
her search for the legendary Seven Cities of Cibola. In the
great Venn diagram of life, that had been the moment where

Jade's circle and his had first intersected; Jade had been working with Professor's former SEAL commander, Dane Maddock.

Even so, a prior visit did not fully account for her laser-like focus. Jade was moving with a purpose, scrambling onto the slope as if following a GPS device in her head, forcing him, reluctantly, to revise his hypothesis. Dreams—and that was the most rational explanation for the out-of-body-experience phenomenon—were rarely a perfect representation of reality. The brain had a way of mixing things up, combining memories and filling in the gaps with subconscious expectations. If Jade's vision were nothing more than a mental rerun of a previous visit, then he would have expected her to begin exhibiting confusion, searching the terrain for familiar markers to reorient herself. She was most certainly not doing that.

"Up there," she said, pointing to a weathered draw that ran up to the foot of the sheer vertical slope.

The draw, which channeled rainwater away in the path of least resistance, had been millions of years in the making, just like everything else in the landscape. Caves, like the one Jade had described, were like the bubbles in a block of Swiss cheese, disappearing as the passage of time scoured away the surrounding rock. It would be nothing short of miraculous if the cave Jade sought was actually the opening to an ancient Vault—

"There," Jade said, pointing up to a shadowy divot about fifty feet above the top of the draw. "That's the one."

She opened her backpack and took out a bundle of kernmantle climbing rope, along with three nylon safety harnesses. "I'll lead and set protection," she said, as she donned the harness. "We'll top rope Atash since he's the least experienced climber here."

"And you're the second least," Professor said. "I'll lead and top rope both of you."

She shook her head. "I know the route. It's a piece of cake."

"Let me guess. You saw that, too?"

"I saw what I saw," she retorted. "And I've been right so far. Why is it so hard for you to just trust me?"

He decided not to answer that, but gamely slipped his legs into the hoops of the harness and then helped Shah do the same. Jade did not wait for them to finish, but threaded the belay rope through the carabiner attached to the front of her harness and started up the wall.

She climbed quickly, as sure-footed as a spider, setting her first piece of protection—a spring-loaded cam that she slipped into a two-inch wide vertical crack—about twenty feet up. Limestone, formed from the calcium carbonate shells of ancient sea creatures, was sort of like nature's concrete, but even the hardest rock could crumble under stress. If Jade fell, the camming device was just as likely to be yanked out of the wall as it was to arrest her fall. Jade however seemed unconcerned, as if setting the anchors was merely a formality. Beyond that point, she was less frugal about the gear, putting a piece in place every five feet or so, but she moved with the same purposefulness that had brought her this far. Less than ten minutes after beginning the climb, she pulled herself into the cave opening and set a final anchor.

"I'm up," she called out.

Professor turned to Shah again. "You think you can do what she just did?"

Shah nodded but without enthusiasm. "If I must."

Jade's plan had been for Professor to top rope Shah—maintaining tension of the belaying line so that if Shah slipped, the rope going up to the last anchor Jade had set would keep him from falling. It was the way most beginning climbers got their start, but Professor was having second thoughts about the plan. For one thing, Shah's safety would depend on whether or not Jade's anchor held fast. Climbing protection was generally reliable, but if Shah repeatedly lost his grip, the anchor could conceivably come loose.

Of course, the real reason he didn't like the plan was that it would put Shah and Jade alone together in the cave.

"That's what I thought. I'm going to go up first. That

way, I can pull you up if I have to." He did not bother giving Shah a crash-course in climbing techniques or how to belay from below, which meant that he would be climbing more or less without anyone to arrest him in the event of a fall, but he trusted his own abilities a lot more than he trusted Shah.

Shah's hesitancy turned into something more like suspicion, but he nodded again. "Whatever you think best."

Professor cinched the rope to Shah's harness with a figure-eight knot. "When I give you the signal, start climbing. I'll be pulling in the slack from up there, so you won't be in any danger. Just pay attention to where I put my hands and feet and do the same. Got it?"

Another nod.

"Good." Professor turned away and, using the anchored rope Jade had set like a thread to guide him through a maze, made the ascent in half the time it had taken her.

"You were right," he said to her, grinning. "Piece of cake.

The recess was larger than it had looked from below, though it still looked more like a scalloped depression in the limestone than an actual cave. What might once have been the front porch of the mythical Vault now seemed more like a second story exit door with no attending staircase.

Jade shone a flashlight up into the darkest reaches of the niche, revealing a shadowy hole, like the opening to a chimney. It appeared to be just barely large enough to accommodate a person. "That passage leads to the entrance to the vault," she said, grinning triumphantly. "Believe me now?"

Shah watched from below as Professor disappeared into the shadowy niche. His eyes followed the rope that dangled from the cave entrance, zigzagged through the anchors, and then reached out, like the tentacles of some mythical sea creature to snag hold of the carabiner attached to the front of his climbing harness. His heart was racing but this had nothing at all to do with the impending climb.

This was the moment he'd been waiting for. He hastened forward, standing as close to the wall as he could to remove himself from Professor's line of sight, and took out his phone. He knew he had only a few seconds, but that was all he needed.

Although Jade had been very secretive about their ultimate location, she had revealed enough for him to set a plan in motion. He had assembled a new team of jihadists, college students from the Arab states and Pakistan, disgruntled immigrants from the Horn of Africa, even a young convert from Beverly Hills—the son of a geologist employed by an oil company, who had learned the Prophet's wisdom during an extended stay in Yemen. Shah had been able to make all the preparations surreptitiously, sending text messages and posting to the chatrooms whenever an opportunity presented itself. Now, his team was ready. Only one thing was lacking.

He opened the text message app and hit the menu button marked: "Send my current location."

He returned the phone to his pocket and took a step back from the wall, looking up expectantly, awaiting the signal to begin climbing.

Despite the unpleasantness at the airport, he bore no ill-will toward Jade Ihara or her friend—she called him Professor, but he seemed more like some kind of government agent, maybe a Special Forces soldier assigned to safeguard her. All Shah cared about was preserving the status quo. He genuinely hoped no one would be hurt, not even Jade's antagonistic companion, but he would do whatever had to be done to make sure that no one ever had cause to question the legitimacy of Islam.

After a few minutes of waiting, he heard Professor call out to him. He waved back and then put his hands on the wall. Up close, it didn't look so daunting. There were protuberances he could hang onto and cracks he could jam his fingers into. It was not that different than climbing a ladder, albeit a ladder where the rungs were randomly spaced and no bigger than a peanut. Or at least it seemed that way until he could no longer touch the ground with an outstretched foot. Then his heart began pounding again, and this time it had everything to do with the climb. He clutched at the wall, pressing himself flat against it, afraid to move, and almost immediately felt the rock slipping away beneath his fingertips.

A terrified but incoherent cry escaped his lips. Some part of him knew that it wouldn't be a fatal fall, but it would hurt. He might even break a bone or—

He did not fall. The rope cinched to his harness pulled taut, arresting his downward plunge, and he banged against the wall, though not with enough force to cause injury.

"Find your holds," Professor advised from above. "Three points of contact. It's not that hard."

"I can't," Shah gasped. "Let me down."

"If that's what you want."

Shah thought he heard a note of mockery in the other man's tone. The perceived insult, coupled with the knowledge that, if he did not make this climb, he would never know what lay inside the vault, was enough to help him regain his composure. "No!" he shouted. "No. I can do it."

"That's the spirit," replied Professor. "Loosen up. If you keep hugging the wall like that, you'll wear yourself out."

Heeding that advice was easier said than done. A primal fear of falling kept him gripping every hold so tightly that the tendons in his forearms felt like they were about to snap. Nevertheless, the further he went up the wall, the more confident he felt. The earlier mishap had taught him to trust the rope, trust that even if he lost his grip again, he would not fall. When he reached the top, Professor extended a hand to him and pulled him the rest of the way up.

"Congratulations," he said. "You're a rock climber now."

Shah was drenched in perspiration and it took him a moment to catch his breath, but he was smiling so broadly that his jaws hurt. "That was amazing. I wouldn't mind trying that again sometime."

"You'll like rappelling down even more."

Shah looked past him. "Where's Jade?"

"Scouting ahead." He pointed to the impenetrable darkness at the back of the cave.

As if on cue, a faint glow appeared there, growing brighter by the second as the light source moved closer and eventually filled the mouth of the passage that led deeper into the mountain. A moment later, Jade's face appeared in the opening. She did not look happy.

"I know that look," Professor said, his tone grim. "What's wrong?"

"The entrance chamber. It's completely flooded. And I'll save you the trouble of asking." She sagged in defeat. "I didn't see that."

TWENTY-FIVE

Shah was incredulous. "Flooded? In Arizona? How is that possible?"

Jade squeezed her eyes shut, recalling the vision from the Hypogeum. She had seen a round chamber at the end of the passage, and the three circles that appeared to be linked but really weren't. There had not been any water. She related exactly what she had seen to Professor.

"I think…" She hesitated. "Could this be how the timelock mechanism works?"

Professor nodded in understanding. "That makes sense. Water clocks have been around a long time. The Chinese may have created water clocks as far back as six thousand years ago. Water flows at a constant rate. Even though this is the desert, there's plenty of rainfall in the monsoon season. Rainfall on the top of the rock seeps down and recharges the reservoir. Throw in a sufficiently complex clockwork mechanism, and you could make a water clock that keeps time over very long periods."

"So we have to wait until it drains?" Shah said. "We just come back in… Ha! We don't even know how long to wait. Wonderful."

"We could probably pump the water out," Professor said, though his tone suggested that he considered this a measure of last resort rather than the best way forward. "I doubt very much we could pull that off without attracting a lot of attention."

"If the chamber was dry, we'd be able to unlock the vault," Jade said, thinking aloud. "Those rings are the key. They're like a… a pass code or the combination to a safe. Maybe we don't have to actually drain the chamber to open it."

Professor's eyebrows drew together. "SCUBA?"

"Why not?"

"Well, for starters, we don't have any gear. We'd probably have to drive to Phoenix to find a dive shop, which we wouldn't be able to do until tomorrow. And someone is bound to ask why we're hauling gas cylinders and wetsuits up the trail. But aside from that, the biggest problem I see is hydraulic pressure. Water is heavy. About eight pounds to the gallon. I don't know how big this chamber is, but let's say it's about the same size as a backyard swimming pool—roughly ten thousand gallons. That's eighty thousand pounds. Forty tons, pressing against that locked door. I'm not sure you'd even be able to open it, but if you could, the results could be…well, unpredictable to say the least."

Jade managed a wan smile. "We can handle unpredictable."

Professor threw her a withering glance.

"How about this," Jade went on. "I'll swim into the chamber and try to get a better look at it. Maybe then we'll have a better idea of how to get it open."

"You want to free dive in a cave? You want to swim into a dark cave, have a looksee, and then find your way back out, all on one breath? Cave diving is insanely dangerous under the best of circumstances. Without gear? No. It's suicide."

"I can hold my breath for two minutes. That passage drops right into the cave, so I could spend a whole minute looking around, and have plenty of time to get back out. We can pull the rope up and I'll tie off. That way I can't get lost and if anything goes wrong, you can pull me back."

Professor started to say something, but Jade cut him off. "I know, you think you're the stronger swimmer, so you should go. But I've seen that chamber in my vision. I know I can figure out how to open it."

Professor shook his head. "I wasn't going to say that. What would be the point? Once you get an idea in your head, there's no reasoning with you. I was going to say that maybe we can make some field expedient swim goggles so you can at least see what you're doing."

He took a half-filled water bottle from his back pocket, drained the contents in a long swig, and then held the empty plastic container up. "Should be able to do something with his."

"Oh. Why didn't you just say so?"

"Get the rope," he said. "And give me your knife. I lost mine in Australia. Once more thing that trip cost me."

Jade passed over her Swiss Army knife and then went to the edge of the cave mouth to gather up the belaying line. She knotted the end to her climbing harness and then threw the rest of the coil onto her shoulder. Professor, meanwhile sliced out two oval shaped pieces from the bottoms of two plastic bottles. He pressed them to his eyes and scrunched up his face to hold them in place.

"They'll be leaky," he said, removing them and handing them to her, "but they should be good for thirty seconds or so."

Jade tried the makeshift lenses. The edges were sharp, digging into her skin, but the discomfort was a small price to pay for being able to see clearly underwater.

Professor wasn't finished however. He took out the sketch of the circles and began drawing something new beneath them. "Borromean Rings are an impossibility using true circles. An optical illusion like something from Escher. But if you use slightly elliptical circles positioned at angles in three dimensions, the perspective changes make them look like circles when viewed top down. Sort of like this."

He held up the new sketch.

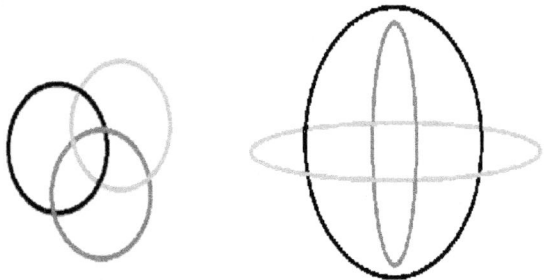

"Look for something like this. Then you'll know you're on the right track."

"You're kidding. Those are the same?"

He nodded. "More or less. This is only one possible solution of course. But keep your eyes open for it."

She squinted through the eye cups. "If I open my eyes too wide, these things will fall out, but I'll do my best." She handed him the climbing rope. "I tug on this as soon as I'm in the chamber. After that, if I give two sharp tugs, pull me back."

"And if you aren't out in sixty seconds, I'll drag you out anyway."

"Make it ninety. I want to be able to take my time in there."

"Fine, but not a second longer."

"Wish me luck." With that, Jade turned and headed back up the narrow passage. It was cramped. Professor would probably be able to scrape through, but barely. During her earlier exploration, she had been forced to crawl backward since there was no room to turn around at the far end; merely an opening about a foot above the water's surface.

She reached the opening and thrust her flashlight into the submerged chamber. The waterproof light revealed an enormous murky void and not much else. The water was chilly on her skin and immersion in it would be bracing, but not enough to cause hypothermia in the minute and a half she would be in it. She looked over her shoulder, back down the length of the passage but was unable to see Professor or Shah. She took several quick breaths, hyperventilating to oxygenate her blood, and then, with one hand holding the eye cups in place, she plunged forward, headfirst into the water.

The slap of cold was about what she expected and she had to fight the urge to let all her air out in a howl of dismay. Her natural buoyancy immediately tried to bring her back to the surface, and water began infiltrating the makeshift goggles, but in that first moment, she got her first real look at the entrance to the vault.

Being in the chamber was, Jade thought, like swimming in a municipal water tank. It was about twenty feet across and perfectly spherical, save for the strange and seemingly haphazard gaps and protrusions that ruined the otherwise perfect symmetry. As she studied the relief, looking for some kind of recognizable pattern, Jade felt something tugging at her waist.

Crap. I forgot. She found the safety line with the hand that held the flashlight and gave it a single hard pull, hoping that Professor would not misinterpret the signal and drag her out. She had already been in the water for a good fifteen seconds, and something told her she had overestimated her ability to hold her breath in the chilly conditions. When the rope did not go taut again, she assumed the message had been correctly received, and returned her attention to the walls of the chamber.

The momentary distraction gave her a fresh perspective, though the water seeping into the eye cups left her vision blurry. She realized now that, despite differences in depth, the grooves and protrusions still reflected the curvature of the surrounding chamber. It was almost as if large square sections of the wall had been excised to reveal another sphere underneath, and then another beyond that, like the layers of an onion.

A sphere inside a sphere inside a sphere. Almost like Professor's second drawing.

Inspired, she swam closer to the wall and pressed against one protruding square, about two feet on each side. When that yielded no results, she moved her fingers to the edge and tried pushing it sideways, like sliding a window open.

The stone moved laterally, but as it moved, it caused other sections to move as well.

It's a puzzle, Jade realized. *Like an enormous inside out Rubik's Cube. Move one piece and the whole puzzle changes. But what's the solution?*

The answer was so obvious, she felt stupid for not

realizing it immediately. The key to the puzzle, and the combination that would unlock the door to the vault, was embodied in the riddle of the Borromean Rings.

She swam sideways, trying to take in as much of the inside out orb as she could. Now that she understood what she was supposed to do, she had no difficulty visualizing the finished product.

There were four layers in all. The deepest was a perfect sphere. The squares of varying thickness would have to be moved around to form concentric circular bands that corresponded to the arrangement in the drawing Professor had shown her. None of the square sections was perfectly flat, nor were any two the same, even those that were of the same layer. Some of the edges met perfectly, while others differed by as much as an inch.

The longer she studied it, the more obvious the solution became.

I can do this. But I need time.

The burning in her lungs and the involuntary spasms in her chest told her that she was already out of time. She needed to breathe, needed to be out of the cold water. She followed the safety rope up through the murk to the top of the spherical chamber. There was a small air pocket there, supplied by the opening through which she had entered, and she floated there for a moment, greedily sucking in fresh air. The rope hung down a few feet away, marking the location off the exit. She could just pull herself up, back into the passage, crawl back and tell Professor what she had discovered. They could come back with SCUBA gear, wetsuits and high-powered lanterns...maybe sneak them in after nightfall. The Vault wasn't going anywhere, after all. What was another twenty-four hours?

I can do this, she thought again. *Right now. I can open the vault.*

She stared at the opening. *I should tell him.*

And if he says no?

He probably would, but in their particular working relationship, she was the boss, not him.

"Hey!" She directed her shout up into the opening. "Can you hear me?"

She heard Professor's voice a moment later, hollow sounding, like someone speaking into a tube. "Jade?"

"I found something. Give me a few more minutes."

There was a long silence, so she called out again. "Did you hear me? I found something."

There was something different about the way her voice echoed down the passage, and a few seconds later, she realized why when Professor's face appeared in the opening above. "What did you find?" he asked.

"I know how to open it," she said, through chattering teeth.

"Jade, this wasn't the plan."

"Trust me. This will only take a minute."

"That's what you said a minute ago. Your lips are turning blue. Come out. Now."

"No, they aren't." She dumped the water from the eye cups and jammed them back into place. "Be right back."

Before he could protest further, she ducked under and went back to work. She darted back and forth inside of the spherical chamber, moving one section left, then another down, then another left.

This time, there was no uncertainty in her actions. She went immediately to the wall and began pushing the square sections this way and that, connecting matching layers to form bands that would encompass the chamber. The stone sections moved easily, with only minimal resistance, hardly what she would have expected from a limestone cave submerged in water, but then this was no mere cave. It was a Vault for the Ages, built to withstand the passage of thousands of years.

The comparison to a Rubik's Cube was apt, since each time she moved one of the stone sections horizontally or vertically, it would affect everything else on the same plane, but she quickly figured out how to use this to her advantage. Fortunately, this puzzle was a lot simpler than the multicolored-cube. In thirty seconds time, she completed one of the bands, and saw in her mind's eye the sequence of moves she would have to complete to finish the other two.

Breathe!

She swam back up to the air pocket, breaking through the surface with a splash and a gasp. "Professor?"

She tried to shout it, but her teeth were chattering uncontrollably and she could barely get the word out.

No answer. She searched the top of the air pocket, trying to find the opening or at the very least, the dangling safety line, but found neither.

A cold fist of dread slammed into Jade's gut. She reached for the rope knotted to her climbing harness and began frantically pulling in the line, even though she knew what she would find. Sure enough, after pulling in twenty feet of sodden rope, she reached the end, which had been severed neatly, as if by a pair of scissors.

"Damn it!"

As she had maneuvered the pieces of the three-dimensional puzzle, reorganizing the stone squares into the ring-like bands, she had inadvertently covered the opening overhead and in so doing, sliced through the safety line. She was cut off from Professor and Shah. Worse, she was trapped inside the sphere, with only one way out.

That wasn't strictly true. If she moved the stones in the right sequence, she might be able to uncover the opening again and get out, but that would mean trial and error, a time-consuming process, and time was not something she had in abundance—and when it was done, she would have to start the puzzle all again.

No, practically speaking, the only way out was to align the rings, solve the puzzle and open the vault.

She tried to inhale deeply to fill her lungs again, but the cold had left her muscles rigid, and she was only able to take a shallow stuttering breath. It would have to suffice.

She swam back down, attacking the puzzle with frenetic urgency. Shift right. Slide down. Shift right. Slide up.

Breathe!

No. Almost done.

Shift. Slide. Shift.

Breathe.

A spasm racked her chest. She blew air into her cheeks then breathed it in, trying to fool her autonomic nervous system. It didn't really work, but the attempt dislodge the plastic bottle lens over her left eye, and as it drifted away, a rush of frigid water pressed against her eyeball.

Keep going. Almost done.

Slide, shift, push… And then, she saw that only one more move remained. When she pushed the stone into place, the puzzle would be solved and the pattern of interwoven rings would be formed. What happened after that would be, as Professor had indicated, unpredictable.

In a perfect world, the chamber would drain slowly and a concealed door would open, but Jade doubted her luck would be that good. It was far more likely that the door had been designed to be opened only when the chamber was dry, something that might happen only every thousand years, which mean that either the door would not budge, and she would still be trapped, or the rush of water through the newly opened portal would create a vortex with enough hydraulic pressure to suck her down and conceivably rip her limb from limb or smash her to a pulp against the walls of the vault.

She left the last stone as it was and kicked back up to the air pocket, hoping against hope that she would find Professor staring down at her, irritated but overjoyed to see her, but there was only the smooth wall of the sphere, with two bands of stone, one seemingly passing over the top of the other.

There was only one thing left to do.

She swam down, following the carefully organized bands of stone that now circumscribed the inside of the sphere, until she found the one piece that was still out of place. Without any further hesitation, she swam to it and gave it a final push. She did not wait to see the results, but immediately began kicking her legs for the surface. The sudden maneuver cost her the remaining eye cup, throwing everything into blurry indistinctness, but she kept kicking, racing toward the top of the chamber. Even though she could no longer see the smooth walls of the chamber, she could feel vibrations in the water around her. Something was happening. The interior of the sphere was moving.

She broke the surface with a gasp. The water was rippling all around her, and when she trained her flashlight straight up at the exposed section of the chamber, she saw why. The stone bands representing the Borromean rings were moving, rolling on three axes like a gimbal.

Suddenly, the entire chamber started coming apart. The square sections seemed to drop out of the ceiling, collapsing toward her. She threw up her hands to cover her head, but in that moment, she realized she was no longer floating, but falling. The water around her had disappeared as abruptly as if the entire bottom of the sphere had broken open, creating a whirlpool. Jade barely had time to gasp for air before she was caught in the frothing deluge and flushed away.

TWENTY-SIX

"Jade!" Professor hammered his fist against the smooth stone that had unexpectedly slid over the entrance to the underground chamber, blocking his access to Jade and slicing through the rope that was her only lifeline. His shout was as ineffectual as his pounding. Jade was cut off, beyond his reach.

"Damn it!" he raged, punching the stone again. "I told her this would happen."

"What's wrong?" Shah's voice drifted up the short but cramped passage.

"I don't know," Professor replied, and that wasn't a total lie. "Jade was trying to open the door, but now we can't get through."

"What does that mean? Is it some kind of booby trap?"

"I don't know what it means," he snapped. Then he took a calming breath. "We'll just have to wait and see. Jade said she knew how to open it. She's headstrong, but she's pretty good with stuff like this."

"So I've noticed." Shah's murmured comment was barely audible, and not just because he was speaking from the far end of the passage.

A strange hissing sound, like stone rasping against stone, filled the air, along with a faint but persistent vibration that seemed to be rising up through the rock.

Cave-in?

Professor's first impulse was to scramble back down the passage, and maybe even take his chances sliding down the sheer limestone face they had climbed, in order to avoid being entombed beneath tons off falling rock, but he fought this urge, and focused his attention instead on identifying the source of the disturbance. A moment later, he realized that the smooth rock blocking the entrance to the submerged chamber was moving. He reached out to it, touching it lightly with a fingertip, and felt it rolling in place like an enormous ball bearing.

What did you do, Jade?

The tremor intensified, but the sensation of movement against his fingertip vanished, along with the stone that had been blocking the passage. Professor could now feel cold musty air rushing up through the opening. The breeze lasted only a moment, like the last exhalation of a dying man, but it was strong enough to tousle his hair. A few seconds later, the vibrations ceased and all was still.

Professor reached his hand a little further into the gap, felt nothing, and then shone his flashlight into the void. Instead of reflecting off the water that had been there only a few minutes before, the beam revealed what looked like stone steps disappearing down into the earth.

"Jade!" His shout echoed back but there was no answer from the depths.

He felt his pulse quicken, his body leaping to the obvious conclusion even before the thought could fully form in his brain. Jade was gone. Swept away.

"No. She's alive." He said it aloud, as if doing so might convince the universe to change its mind.

"What's happening?" asked Shah.

Professor paid him no heed. He lowered himself through the hole and placed his feet on the steps. Once inside, he could see that the steps were formed of stone blocks, each about twenty-four inches to a side, stacked up to form a descending spiral staircase. There was a wall of tightly joined cut stone blocks to his left, and a yawning chasm, sixteen feet across, to his right, around which the steps coiled like the threads of a screw hole. The walls and steps were damp, but that was the only remaining trace of the water that had earlier filled the chamber.

"Jade!" Professor started down the steps, moving faster than was probably advisable given the unfamiliar environment, calling out to Jade over and over again, always with the same results. The stairs circled once, twice. His best rough guess put him thirty feet below the entrance with no end yet in sight, and no sign of Jade. He completed another orbit, screwing deeper into the earth, then another, and then the descent ended at a flat landing that curled once more around the open pit. At the end of the landing was an opening that led through the wall.

Professor stopped in front of the doorway and shone his light through. The landing was damp like everything else, but the stone floor on the other side of the opening appeared to be bone dry. About ten feet past the opening, a smooth stone wall—all the surfaces looked like burnished concrete rather than natural stone—curved away in either direction.

The absence of any footprints in the dry passage beyond told him Jade had not left by that route. He crossed back to the edge of the landing and leaned over, shining his light into the depths.

"Jade!"

Shah came down the steps. "This place is incredible. No one knows about it?"

Professor continued ignoring the other man. Short of taking a leap of faith into the unknown, there seemed no way to reach the depths below, but someone had gone to the trouble of excavating the chasm, and if he was not wrong, lining it with cement, and that strongly indicated a purpose and possibly another means of accessing the lower reaches. He turned back to the doorway and went through, with Shah just a few steps behind. He decided to go left, but ultimately the choice was irrelevant. The wall and the passage beside it curved around, forming a rotunda that probably would have brought him back to the staircase passage, only he never got that far. Halfway around the ring-shape walk, he spotted the glow of artificial light.

"Jade!"

He sprinted toward the light, and as he came around the bend, he saw a woman standing there. It was not Jade, and she was not alone.

The woman was very attractive, with pale skin and raven black hair, and an almost palpable air of haughtiness. Curiously, despite the fact that the light from the portable electric lamp on the floor behind her could hardly be considered brilliant, she wore dark wraparound sunglasses.

Professor only gave her a passing glance. His attention was on the two men standing to either side of her. He recognized both of them. One was Jordan Kellogg, the man who had introduced himself as the assistant editor of Chameleon International publishing house.

The other man's face was as familiar to Professor as his own. In fact, it was his own. He wore Professor's clothes, even had his Omega Seamaster wristwatch and his Explorer fedora.

The two men—the two Changelings—had pistols leveled at him.

"I assume you are armed," Kellogg said. "Let me assure you, it makes no difference to us whether you live or die, but if it matters to you, I suggest you place your weapon on the ground. Slowly."

Professor raised his hands. Two-to-one odds were manageable, and he wasn't afraid to get a little scuffed up, but there was a far more compelling reason for him to stand down. "Do you have Jade? Is she all right?"

Kellogg glanced at Professor's doppleganger. "I told you she'd figure out how to get in."

"Fat lot of good it did her," the other man replied in Professor's voice. "She got washed down into the waterworks. We'll probably never find her body."

While Professor did not grasp the context of the exchange, the implication was easily enough understood. The Changelings did not have Jade.

Which meant there was no reason to continue the conversation.

"What about Jade?" he said again. "Do you know where she is?"

He asked the question only to distract the two men. It was physically impossible to pull a trigger while talking, which meant that as soon as one of the men started to answer, he would draw his own weapon and start firing.

Before either Changeling could speak however, Shah stepped forward. "Gabrielle?"

The woman cocked her head in the direction of his voice. "Atash. I'm pleased that you're here. I had hoped that you would find your way, though we had expected you to pursue Jade Ihara, not join her. I'm very impressed."

Shah ignored the praise. "So it's true. You have been working for…them…all along."

"I am not working for anyone," she replied calmly. "They are my family."

"You used me!" Shah fairly screamed the accusation, stomping forward, heedless of the weapons pointed at him.

Professor caught Shah's biceps to stop his advance. "Get a grip," he said, speaking almost as loud as Shah had. "They've got guns. You'll just get yourself killed."

The woman's head tilted back and forth, bird-like, confirming what Professor had suspected from the moment he saw her sunglasses. She was blind. That fact seemed a lot less important than the matter of her prior relationship with Shah. He addressed the woman. "Gabrielle is it? What am I saying? That name is probably as fake as everything else about you. I take it you're the partner he's been talking about. The one who convinced him to go after Jade?"

The woman inclined her head in what might have been a nod.

"That was a real boneheaded thing to do," Professor went on. "Especially if you already had somebody on the inside."

"You're a military man," Kellogg said. "You know how lines of communication can sometimes get crossed."

"You could have gotten yourself killed Kellogg or whatever your real name is." He took a deep breath, surreptitiously lowering his hands an inch or two. "Let me see if I've got this straight. You three—and all the rest of the Changelings back at the nest—have known about this place…"

He gestured expansively. "This Vault, all along. You're the self-appointed protectors, making sure that nobody else finds it, right? If someone gets too close, you kill them. Or…" He nodded to Shah. "Trick someone else into doing the dirty work for you. Roche got too close to the truth, so you had to off him. And hey, while you're at it, set the Muslims up to be the bad guys. Hell, push the right buttons and they'll line up to deal some jihad on the infidels who insult the Prophet."

He sensed a subtle shift in Shah's ire—away from the blind woman and toward him—which given the circumstances wasn't such a bad thing. If Shah didn't take it down a notch, he might get them both killed.

"So what it is, exactly? What's the big deal about this Vault? What's so important that you murder people and disappear a whole plane full of people?"

The woman—Gabrielle—smiled. "It's not for you."

The words sent a chill through him. "Eve said that. What do you mean? What's not for me?"

Her statement must have been a signal to Kellogg and Professor's doppelganger. They started forward, pistols raised and gripped in both hands, bodies and arms positioned in a modified isosceles stance that Professor recognized immediately as the tactical shooting position he had learned in the Teams. For the first time since encountering the Changelings, it occurred to Professor that he might have misjudged their ability level. These men had been trained by experts. He could see it in every move they made.

Professor's duplicate stopped a mere ten feet away, nearly point blank range. Kellogg continued forward, careful to stay out of arm's reach, and circled alongside Professor. "Your weapon," he said. "Where is it?"

It was plain that any show of resistance would be suicidal. Professor raised his hands a little higher. "Under my shirttail."

Kellogg moved out of Professor's line of sight and then came in close enough to pluck the weapon from its holster. "Is that the only one?"

"Unfortunately," Professor replied. He felt a tap against his right ankle, then the left; Kellogg verifying that he did not have a backup weapon concealed there.

"Kneel," Kellogg said. "Hands laced behind your head."

Professor remained standing. "If you're going to kill me, just get it over with."

"I said—"

The woman cut him off. "It's all right. Let him stand." She tilted her head toward Professor. "Contrary to what you might thing, we do not shed blood with reckless abandon. And you may yet have some usefulness to us."

"This should be good."

She turned to Shah again. "Atash, are you armed?"

"No," Shah said, and then echoed Professor. "Unfortunately."

She reached out to him with an open hand. "Join me. I want to show you something."

Shah glanced uncertainly at Professor. "Show me what?"

"What you came here to see. The Vault. You do want to see it, don't you?"

"I…" He swallowed. "I don't know. What's in it?"

"Only the truth, Atash. Does that frighten you?" She smiled, which did not soften her arrogance in the slightest. "Gerald Roche was wrong. There was no conspiracy to alter the calendar. No fabrication of history to conceal this supposed 'Phantom Time.' That's the truth you want to hear, isn't it? You need not fear otherwise."

"The Prophet?"

"Peace be upon him," she said, sardonically. "Come with me and I will show you the truth about your Prophet."

"I don't understand. Is this another one of your tricks?"

"No tricks, Atash." She stretched her hand toward him again. "This is for you."

TWENTY-SEVEN

Somehow, Jade managed to hold on to her flashlight, though it offered little in the way of illumination as she was swept along in the torrent. Caught in the whirlpool, she was spun around so violently that, despite the light in her hands, all she could see for several long seconds was complete unrelenting dark. Her lungs burned and her chest convulsed with the need to breathe, but she could feel water moving against her face and had no way of knowing if she was submerged or not. She squeezed her fist tight around the flashlight, and fought the compulsion to draw in a liquid inhalation until she couldn't fight it anymore. Her mouth came open in a gasp that drew in neither water nor air but an aerosolized combination of the two. She gagged and coughed, all the while spinning around and around like a sock in the wash cycle.

Something struck her in the abdomen, turning her head over heels, and a blast of water swept across her, filling her mouth and nose once more. Then, the flood passed and she was able to breathe again.

It took a moment for her to realize that she was hanging in mid-air, suspended by the rope attached to her climbing harness. The blow she had felt was the line snagging on something, going taut and dragging her to an abrupt stop as the water rushed away. Even though she was caught fast, unmoving, she could still feel the vortex whirling around her.

When the sensation finally passed, she found the rope and pulled herself upright. The flashlight revealed the smooth wet walls of a cylindrical shaft about twenty feet in diameter. She was off center, dangling about five feet away from the wall. Though she could not make out the bottom of the well, she could see a ledge ringing the shaft about twenty feet above. The ledge was not a solid piece of stone, but composed of individual blocks jammed together tightly. Her trailing safety line was caught between two of the blocks like a string of floss between two molars. The improbability of this apparent reprieve did not escape Jade's notice, but she had more immediate concerns than wondering why fate had chosen to intercede on her behalf.

She stared at the rope for a few seconds, searching her memories of climbing lessons past for the best technique to make her way back up the rope. The nylon sheathed line was not thick enough to grip effectively. There were two perfectly good mechanical ascenders in her backpack, along with the rest of the climbing gear, but she had left the pack behind when she had gone into the water. She thought she might be able to use the carabiner on the front of her harness as a field-expedient ascender, but to do so would require unclipping the safety line, which would send her to the bottom in a hurry. The next best thing to a mechanical ascender was a Prusik, a friction hitch knot that could be fashioned out of a shoelace or a piece of paracord. When tied around a belay line and fashioned into handhold loops, a climber could slide the Prusik up a few inches at a time, and eventually regain her position after a fall. Jade stared at her boots, wondering how much effort it would take to remove the laces, and if there was a better option.

"Yo-yo," she murmured, and that was what she felt like; a child's yo-yo toy that had reached the end of the string and lost all its momentum.

Maybe she could rewind.

She reached up again, gripping the rope as hard as she could, and pulled. She managed to raise herself several inches, easing the tension on the rope a little, but knew that if she let go with either hand, she would immediately lose whatever progress she had made, unless she found a way to gather up the slack. When she was certain that she couldn't lift herself any higher and felt her arms starting to burn with the exertion, she whipped her upper body around the rope, coiling up the slack around her waist.

Her grip failed and the rope went taut again, constricting her mid-section, but she had gained almost twelve vertical inches.

"Okay. Just need to do that nineteen more times."

She reached up and pulled—

The rope slipped from between the stone blocks with a loud twang and then she was falling.

The first full second or two of the fall was weirdly distorted by the panic-induced rush of adrenaline that amped Jade's brain into hyper-drive. A single thought ricocheted around her brain: how far to the bottom?

But after three seconds of falling—*How far is that? How fast am I falling now?*—the question of distance became less important than the question of what she would encounter when she reached the end of the vertical journey. If it was solid rock, then she would either die on impact or wish she had. But if it was water….

If it was water, deep enough and not too much further down, she might survive.

She brought her hands together in front of her lower torso, the flashlight still squeezed in her fist. She kept her legs straight, toes pointed down and feet pressed together tightly. The flashlight illumed the darkness around her, but she was moving faster than her brain could process, so she simply closed her eyes and—

The impact shuddered up her feet all the way to her hips, but the chilly water was considerably more forgiving than solid limestone would have been. She arrowed deep, so deep that the pressure against her inner ear became uncomfortably intense—one more painful sensation reminding her that she was still alive. Too late to make a difference, she threw her arms and legs wide to slow her descent and immediately started kicking furiously back toward the surface. The pressure in her head relented slowly, but the spasms in her chest intensified as the surface remained maddeningly out of reach.

She felt like she was clawing her way out of Hell.

When she finally broke the surface, she was too spent to do anything more than lie on her back, floating motionless, trying not to think about the pain crackling along her shin bones.

The break did not last long. Professor was still up there, probably thinking the worst. And if she didn't find a way out of the pit, surviving the fall would mean a protracted death of hypothermia. She played the light in every direction, but saw only the same smooth walls she had seen from above. The rocks that had briefly snagged her rope were too distant to make out.

Damn.

But the walls of the shaft were too smooth, too perfectly round to be the work of nature. In some ways, the handiwork reminded her of ancient Roman structures, which despite the passage of thousands of years remained mostly intact. Some ancient craftsman had labored in the spot where she now trod water. Someone had carved out a cistern in the limestone to reclaim the water from the submerged chamber above, and that gave her hope. If the shaft had been cut for some purpose, then logically, there had to be a way to access it. If not above the water's surface, then perhaps below.

While the idea of another free dive did not exactly thrill her, the possibility…no, the certainty that she would find a way out compelled her. She filled her lungs and then plunged beneath the surface, diving in a corkscrew pattern around the perimeter of the well, shining the flashlight beam on the walls looking for an intersecting tunnel.

There it was, a dark opening about six feet across.

What if it goes nowhere at all? What if it feeds into a maze of pipes and I can't find my way back to the surface?

It was a choice between a slow death on the surface or a quick end from drowning. Neither fate was more appealing than the other, but not exploring the submerged passage was certain death.

She swam into the pipe, kicking and clawing her way forward. After more than half a minute of hard swimming, she spied the telltale flat shimmer of air above the water's surface, and kicked urgently toward it.

She came up in a large pool, surrounded by a gymnasium-sized chamber with cylindrical pillars rising up from the water to support the high ceiling overhead. She dog-paddled for a few seconds, playing the light in every direction, until she spotted a flat stone walkway that rose just a few inches above the water. She paddled over and hauled herself up onto it.

Solid ground had never felt quite so good.

But she was a long way from safe. When she was sure that her legs would support her weight, she gathered up the rope that was still attached to her climbing harness, coiling it and throwing it over one shoulder, then headed toward an arched passage that led away from the pool. She was about halfway to this intermediate goal when the ghosts began to appear.

The flash of movement in her peripheral vision startled her, as it always did, but once she realized what it was, she tried to ignore the infrasound induced hallucinations. This strategy worked for the length of time it took for her to reach the mouth of the passage. That was when the ghosts started talking to her.

She jumped in alarm, whirling around to face them, positive that this time, there would be a real person there…but the ephemeral phantoms had already retreated to a different threshold of perception.

The voices, like the ghost figures, gave the impression of being real, but lacked the necessary substance. It was not merely that the speech was incomprehensible. The words were not words at all, but tortured unnatural sounds, like someone playing a recording backwards. But then, from the midst of the aural chaos, a single word rang out.

"Jade!"

"Professor! I'm here!"

The stone consumed her shout, absorbing it completely, returning no echo.

The weird cacophony resumed.

"Screw it. There's got to be a way out of here." She started forward again, ignoring the figures flitting about in her peripheral vision, paying no heed to the noises that she knew were probably inside her head.

The passage led to a spiral staircase which she mounted without hesitation, charging up two steps at a time, pain and exhaustion as ephemeral now as the hallucinated phantoms.

More real words found their way into the mishmash of sound, as if moving up the staircase was akin to tweaking the tuner on an old analog radio. Garbled static one moment, the next, someone talking plain as day.

"They are my family." A woman's voice, but Jade did not recognize it.

"You used me!"

That was Shah. This realization was followed by another far more disconcerting one. *There's someone else in here.*

These voices were not auditory hallucinations. She was certain of that. They were real, filtering down through the levels of this strange citadel hidden under the mountain. That meant Shah and Professor had found their way in, but someone had come in after them.

Changelings.

What about Professor? Is he safe? She almost called out again, but realized that if she could hear them clearly, they might be able to hear her as well, and that would ruin any chance of taking them by surprise.

She kept going, consciously trying to lighten her step as she bounded up the stairs. The voices blurred back into random discharges of noise, though once or twice she thought she caught a recognizable word or a hint of the woman's voice.

The sight that greeted her at the top of the stairs was no hallucination, but that did not make it any more believable.

She had expected another chamber, or perhaps a cramped tunnel snaking through solid rock like wormholes in a sponge. Instead, she found herself surrounded by empty space… or very nearly empty.

She knew there must be cavern walls and a ceiling of stone high overhead, but these limits were beyond the reach of her light. The staircase she had just ascended appeared to rise up the middle of a cylindrical tower, and she now stood at its summit. There were several other towers of varying heights—one of them was probably the shaft she had fallen through after solving the puzzle at the entrance—all connected by stone bridges, but the network of towers was possibly the least amazing thing her eyes beheld.

Aqueducts curled around the towers, supplying water that turned stone wheels and gears, which in turn drove enormous vertical shafts and screw pumps that conveyed water up into the dark reaches overhead. Other structures, which resembled enclosed walkways or perhaps air ducts on a massive scale, wove through the midst of the waterworks, curling around the towers. The curves were reminiscent of a musical instrument. The water and air flowing around the cylindrical towers were creating a veritable storm of resonance frequencies combining in intricate but inaudible infrasound patterns to dizzying effect. In a leap of intuition, Jade realized that the Vault was not some hidden fortress or citadel where the knowledge of the ancients had been secreted away.

It was a machine.

More precisely, it was a sophisticated computer that employed mechanical logic systems, and utilized an infrasound interface.

This realization unlocked a memory, implanted during her experience in the Hypogeum, but incomprehensible without context. She had been here before, though only in a disembodied state. The recollections were not perfect and they did not come all at once, but she grasped, albeit in a very basic way, how the pumps and ducts, and the acoustic design of the towers and indeed the entire underground chamber, functioned. More importantly, she knew where she needed to go next.

She sprinted onto the bridge that led away from the tower and crossed to another. The visual and auditory phenomena chased after her, but it was just so much background noise now. From time to time, she caught a word—Shah or the woman she'd heard before—but never enough to make sense of what she was hearing.

The bridge connected to a larger cylindrical tower that

stretched from the cavern floor below to the unseeable reaches above. It might have been a massive support column, but Jade knew it served a far more important purpose. If the vault was a computer, then this was its central processing unit.

An arched opening led inside the cylinder, where she found herself immediately confronted by a choice. To the left, a flight of stairs curled upward, following the curve of the wall. To the right, the stairs went down.

Up felt like the correct decision, so she headed in that direction and bounded up the stairs. She ascended for at least a full minute, the stairs stretching up in the cramped confines of the passage like something from a surreal nightmare. Thankfully, the ghosts and whispers had not chased after her. Something about the composition of the stairwell walls evidently shielded her from the infrasound effects. When she caught a glimpse of a lurking figure, she knew the seemingly endless ascent was nearly at an end. She was not wrong.

The stairs brought her to a wide balcony overlooking a bowl-shaped pit that occupied the center of the cylindrical column. The pit was not deep, in fact it looked to be only about twenty feet from the top of the utilitarian stone guardrail to the bottom. The balcony ringed the pit, and on the opposite side, the stairs continued, disappearing into the space between the outer and inner walls. Overhead, the pit was mirrored by a domed ceiling which, Jade now realized, created yet another spherical chamber.

"If you're going to kill me, just get it over with."

The voice startled her, and not just because of its clarity. *Professor?*

It was definitely Professor, and what he had just said confirmed her worst fears. He was in trouble. Either Shah had betrayed them and somehow gotten word to his jihadist confederates, or the Changelings had caught up to them.

That question was answered a moment later when she heard Kellogg's voice, and then the woman she had heard earlier. The voices seemed to be coming from the pit, but

Jade knew this was just an acoustical trick. They were close, probably in a room or passage somewhere above this place.

She ignored the not-too-distant conversation and turned toward the rising stairs. She did not know what she would do when she found the others. Judging by Professor's statement, the Changelings were armed and she was not. Maybe she could distract them and give Professor a chance to gain the upper hand. She would think of something once—

She stopped suddenly as if a wall had suddenly appeared in her path. In a way, that was exactly what had happened, although the wall was not a tangible thing of limestone or concrete. Rather, it was a sensation, like a kind of magnetic repulsion pushing her back. She felt an overwhelming premonition, not of danger exactly, though that was certainly part of it, but of having missed something profoundly important.

She turned back, and it was as if the magnetic poles reversed. She staggered toward the balcony rail, throwing her arms around it for fear of being pulled over. The attraction was all in her head and she knew it, but that did not make the sensation any less real.

I need to go down there, she thought. *The answers are down there.*

Some part of her offered a weak protest. Professor needed her. Urgently. Whatever this was, it could wait.

But she knew it could not wait. A window of opportunity had opened. The Vault was offering her its secrets. If she turned away now, the window might close forever.

She had to know.

Jade shrugged the rope coil off her shoulder, wrapped the loose end around the rail, securing it with a bowline knot, and heaved the rest over the side. With a couple of quick adjustments, she reconfigured the carabiner on her climbing harness into a rudimentary rappelling brake and then eased herself over the railing.

She reached the end of the rope and hung there in

darkness, just a few feet above the floor. Her flashlight revealed a chamber that was remarkably like the Oracle Room in the Hypogeum, but with one significant difference. Scattered across the floor of the pit were dozens of smooth shapes that, from above, had looked like scattered stones. Now she saw that they were elongated skulls.

She dangled above the grisly tableau, turning slowly, playing her light in every direction, looking to see what other mysteries the pit concealed.

"Okay, you got me here. What am I supposed to—"

Before she could complete the question, the vortex opened and she was swept away again.

TWENTY-EIGHT

Professor had no idea why he was still alive, but he sensed his execution had merely been postponed.

Kellogg and the other Changeling—the man who still wore his face—walked a few steps behind him, their guns still trained on him, though not quite as aggressively as before. They kept a safe stand-off distance, close enough to maintain control but far enough away that Professor would never be able to get the jump on them. Further evidence of professional training. Shah and the woman walked ahead of them, continuing along the rotunda. Her hand was on his arm. It might have been a merely practical arrangement, a blind person and her guide, but Professor doubted the woman needed any assistance finding her way and there was something possessive in her manner. Shah seemed to be tolerating her touch, but only just.

"What is this place?" Shah asked. "Who made it?"

"Better that you see the answer for yourself," the woman replied. "Know this, however. It is old beyond imagining. A gift of knowledge sent from the heavens."

"Knowledge?"

"A revelation." The woman made an expansive gesture. "The prophets of old came to this place in secret to receive the Word. Now the gift of the revelation is given to you."

"The Prophet came here?" Shah shook his head. "No. The writings are clear on this. Muhammad was visited by the angel in a cave near Medina."

"Do you believe he could not have traveled, in secret, across the sea to this place? The cave where your Prophet prayed was a resonator, an echo of this place, just like the Hypogeum. He saw the way to the vault, just as Jade Ihara did. The revelation is not for everyone. It wasn't for her, but it was for him, just as it was for the prophets of old who came before. Jesus. Moses, Abraham. Adam. And now, it is for you."

Shah was incredulous. "They all came here?"

"All. A vision is given and a prophet goes forth. But with the passage of centuries, confusion sets in, the people lose their way, and it is necessary for another prophet to be called."

"And I'm supposed to be the new prophet?" Professor thought Shah sounded skeptical rather than awed. "The chosen one."

"You were meant for great things, Atash."

"Chosen by you," Shah said, insistently.

The woman stopped and turned her face toward Shah. "Who do you think we are, Atash? We have been safeguarding this secret, and watching over all of humankind, for ten thousand years. In the holy writings, we are called angels. Messengers of God."

"Angels with rubber faces," Professor muttered. "And contact lenses."

The woman's face turned toward him, but she ignored the remark. "Yes, we chose you. That is why I came to you, worked with you to lay the foundation. Roche's interference forced us to accelerate the timetable, but this was always your destiny."

"Don't believe it," Professor said. "It's a con. That's all they are. Con artists, selling whatever lie they think will get you to do what they want."

He had braced himself against an expected blow from behind, but none came. Instead, the blind woman continued to regard Shah with an intensity that might have been mistaken for worship. "When you have seen, you will be able to decide for yourself whether I am lying or not."

She pointed in the direction they had been traveling. "Up there, you will find a door. Go through. What you see is between you and God."

Shah hesitated. "You're saying the revelations of the Prophet, and all the prophets who came before...came from there?"

An impatient frown cracked Gabrielle's façade. "What difference does it make? Would you prefer a burning bush? An angel floating above you? You will see what you need to see. Trust me."

"Spoken like a true con artist," Professor said.

"Go, Atash. See for yourself."

Shah stared at her a moment longer, as if there was more he felt he needed to say, but then he turned away and headed off on his own. Professor waited until he disappeared around the curve of the rotunda before addressing his captors.

"Now that he's gone, would you care to tell me what's really going on?" He turned around to see if either of the men would give answer, but they were as stonily silent as the blind woman. "No? Then maybe we can talk about why I'm still alive."

"It's up to him to decide your fate," the woman said, not looking at him.

"Him? You mean Shah?" This was unexpected. He had made no secret of his antipathy toward the Iranian journalist, but they had reached an accord and Professor did not think the man would countenance further bloodshed, especially at the urging of the Changelings. Maybe they believed that sparing Professor's life would give them leverage over Shah, or perhaps they intended to continue using him as a hostage to assure Shah's further cooperation, but if either was the case, they had misjudged the nature of his relationship with Shah.

"When he has received the vision, he will face a choice. Spare your life and risk you telling the world about the vault, or kill you in order to preserve the secret."

"Ah, I see. So really, you just want him to be the one to do the dirty deed. Just like when you sicced him on Jade."

Her smile confirmed his accusation. "You've misjudged him," Professor said. "He hates you. Hates how you used and manipulated him."

"He will be a different man once he has received the vision," Gabrielle said, her tone a mockery of reverence. "He will understand that everything we have done was necessary."

"See that's what I really wanted to talk about. Maybe

you've convinced Shah with that nonsense about being angels, but you'll have to try a lot harder to convince me."

"And why would I waste my breath talking to a man who is already dead?"

Professor glanced at the two men but their expressions were as inscrutable as hers.

He had worked all the angles, counted the number of steps separating him from the gunman, rehearsed the moves in his head. In some of the scenarios, he succeeded in killing one of the men, but never both. No matter which of them he attacked first, the other would be able to shoot him dead. There was only one scenario where he did not die. Not right away at least.

"Okay," he said. "No more wasting our breath then."

He sprang forward, diving at Gabrielle like a baseball player trying to steal second. He could sense the men behind him tensing in response to the attack, fingers on the triggers of their pistols. He didn't think they would fire. Not if they were trained as well as he thought they were. Too much chance of a stray round hitting the woman. If he was wrong….

But he wasn't wrong. The two gunmen held their fire and Professor hit the unsuspecting woman and bowled her over. As they went down, he wrestled her body around, using her as a human shield. To keep them at bay, he wrapped one arm around her neck. "I'll kill her."

The threat stopped the two gunmen, but Professor knew the standoff would not last indefinitely. In fact, it would probably not last more than a few seconds. If he made good on his threat, he would be throwing away the only thing keeping him alive, ergo he dared not kill the woman. If the two Changeling gunmen had not figured that out already, they soon would. His only play was to double down.

"Drop the guns or I'll break her neck," he snarled. He shook her, hard. "Do it! Now!"

When the men did not comply immediately, Professor knew they had called his bluff. *Damn it. Can't kill her, can't let her go*. What did that leave?

He hauled her erect, lifted her off the ground so that his body was almost completely covered by hers, and started walking backward, in the direction Shah had gone. He had no idea whether he could count on Shah for assistance, but standing still was not an option. Unfortunately, his steady retreat was not much different than remaining where he was. The two gunmen matched him step for step, and he could see them growing bolder with each passing second. One of them would charge, or perhaps both at nearly the same instant, and then the loaded dice would be cast.

"Stop!"

The shout from behind startled Professor so much that he almost stumbled. The two gunmen were equally surprised, and whatever offensive action they had been contemplating was stillborn. The shout had come from Shah.

Professor twisted half-around, careful to keep Gabrielle between himself and the gunmen, and regarded Shah warily. Even a quick glance was enough to confirm that Shah seemed changed by whatever he had experienced in the vault. Though he had been gone for only a couple minutes, he appeared shaken, as if the foundations of his entire life had been hit by a magnitude eight earthquake.

"Atash?" Gabrielle's voice was barely audible. The pressure of Professor's arm across her throat made it difficult for her to breathe, much less speak.

"I'm here." His voice was flat, distant.

Shell-shocked, thought Professor.

He stared at Gabrielle for a moment, then met Professor's gaze. "Let her go." It was neither command nor plea, but more an indifferent suggestion.

Professor relaxed his hold enough to let the woman gasp in a hoarse breath, but did not release her. "Not until those guns are on the ground."

Shah turned to the men. "Do it."

The two Changelings exchanged a look with each other and with Gabrielle, and then by mutual accord, stooped over and placed their pistols on the cavern floor.

"And the one you took off me," Professor added.

Kellogg produced the Beretta and laid it beside the others.

"Now, take a great big step back."

The men conferred silently a second time, then complied.

"Shah, how about you collect those guns."

Shah knelt and picked up one of the pistols, then used his foot to send first one then the other skittering away down the passage he had earlier disappeared into. Professor frowned as he watched the guns vanish into the shadows, wondering if Shah was not thinking clearly or if he had intentionally deprived him of a weapon.

"Let her go," Shah said again without looking at Professor. "I need to speak with her."

Professor let his arm drop, allowing Gabrielle to stumble away. As she did, he tried to move nonchalantly in the direction of the cast-off pistols, but Shah immediately stopped him with a meaningful gesture from his gun hand.

"Damn," Professor muttered, looking up from the gun pointed at him to meet Shah's eyes. "Well, I can't say I didn't see that coming, but I was hopeful. So, I guess the con worked. You're buying into the Messianic malarkey?"

Shah ignored the jibe. "Gabrielle, what I saw… Tell me it's a trick. Special effects or something."

The blind woman shook her head. "No tricks."

Shah was not satisfied with the answer. "Jade Ihara said that sound frequencies can trigger hallucinations. Is that what happened?"

"Would you question the means by which God chooses to deliver his message? If he called you on your phone or spoke to you from a television set, would you consider that unseemly? The message is what it is, Atash. There is no god but God, and you are his Prophet."

Professor studied Shah's expression. The man did not seem particularly overjoyed by his calling. "The others came here? Muhammad? Jesus?"

"From Adam at the founding of the world, to Bahá'u'lláh."

Professor recognized the name taken by Mírzá Husayn`Alí Núrí, a Persian Muslim from the 19th Century, who claimed to have received a new revelation from God and subsequently founded the Baha'i religion.

"All came here?" Shah repeated. "Yet there is no mention of this place in any of the Holy writings."

Gabrielle was visibly displeased by Shah's refusal to simply embrace his new role in the divine plan. "You are the Prophet. It is for you to decide what you will share, but just as you have questioned the seemliness of the manner in which the revelation was given, know that there are others who would also do so. They might demand to see it for themselves. That is why the prophets of old did not reveal their journeys. And…" She gestured in Professor's direction. "It is why he can never leave this place."

"That's right," Professor said, sarcastically. "You can't have me telling the world that your religion is complete hogwash, and that the Wizard is really just a machine being run by a crazy old guy hiding behind a curtain."

Shah stared at Professor. "A cover up." It was a statement not a question, but there was nonetheless an undercurrent of disbelief.

Gabrielle's frown deepened and when she spoke, there was no hiding the disappointment in her tone. "You are the Prophet of God. Start acting like it. He is an unbeliever. His presence here is sacrilege. An affront to God. You know what must be done." She paused a beat. "It is not necessary for you to do the deed, Atash. Simply give the order and it will be done."

For several seconds, Shah just stared at the gun in his hand. "No," he said finally. "I'll take care of it."

Then he aimed the gun and fired.

TWENTY-NINE

The world opened, and Jade saw everything.

They came in vessels—spaceships, she supposed—that, to the primitive bands of hunter-gatherers who occupied the area, must have seemed like great monstrous beasts or spirits of the sky. With elongated skulls and unblinking black eyes, pale gray skin, long smooth sexless torsos, their appearance was remarkably like the images that would, in later years, inform descriptions of demons and much, much later, the entities known, to those who believed in such things, as "grays."

Extraterrestrial visitors. Aliens.

The grays paid little heed to their human neighbors. The nomadic people might have been insects, scurrying about, unnoticed by the alien workmen, whose attention was consumed with the task of hollowing out the great tower, which would one day be called Bell Rock. When they excavated a cavity using tools that were beyond even Jade's imagination, they used the overburden to fashion durable concrete with which to build structures and the machinery of the Vault. Jade had no sense of how many years passed while they labored. Decades. Perhaps centuries. When the machine was complete they turned their attention to the primitive humans, and Jade saw now that the grays had not been ignoring them after all, but merely making preparations. The Vault was, in fact, just the first phase of an experiment, and the humans would be, in scientific terms, the dependent variable. Lab rats.

To maintain the purity of the experiment, the grays took some of their subjects and modified them, imbuing them with enhanced intelligence and abilities with which to carry out the programming written into their DNA. Physically, they appeared no different, save for jet black eyes and smooth skin that seemed not quite fully formed—a blank canvas on which they might paint the faces of others whom they wished to impersonate as they went forth into the world to do their part of the great experiment. They, and all their scions through the ages, were the Changelings.

The experiment was a thing of simplicity. A man—a shaman or in later years, a priest—would be shown to a special place—the Hypogeum, or one of many such sites scattered across the world, whereupon they would be compelled to make a pilgrimage to this distant land, and there receive the vision. What exactly that vision would entail depended as much on the man and his preconceptions as it did on the machinery of the vault, for the great machine did not implant new ideas so much as stimulate connections between disparate memories and beliefs. That was, in fact, the whole point of the experiment, to see what wonders these men might accomplish with just a gentle nudge every thousand years or so.

Roche had not been far off the mark with his belief that all of reality was merely a holographic simulation being controlled by otherworldly entities.

It was not given to Jade to know if the grays continued to monitor their experiment, if the tales of demonic visitation and UFO sightings across the gap of history were actual encounters with the grays, or merely the product of random infrasound frequencies stimulating ancestral memories. She suspected the latter, just as she suspected that the experiment had gone awry over the millennia, the way a message handed verbally from one person to another and then to another got distorted with each telling. The Changelings, though bound to their purpose by genetic chains, continued to guard the vault, dissuading those whom they deemed unworthy of receiving the vision, men like Archimedes, who in their genius, might have envisioned a new way forward, a world built on logic and rationality, rather than superstition. Similarly, they used their chameleon-like abilities to infiltrate the halls of power, making subtle adjustments but when necessary, triggering upheavals and wars to reset the balance. Their signature was writ large across the tableau of history. Roche had seen it, though imperfectly, and it had ultimately cost him his life.

Jade's view was crystal clear. She wondered what that seeing would cost her.

As her awareness returned, she caught a glimpse of what was transpiring less than a hundred feet away. Shah had left the vault's interface, a room similar in design to the Hypogeum, situated right above the orb-shaped chamber where Jade now was. The spherical room served the same function as the lens in an eyeball, focusing the infrasound created by the machine and directing it into the interface. Shah had received a vision too, but of what, he alone knew. Now, he was with the others, the Changelings who had been waiting for him. Waiting for all of them.

They're going to kill Professor.

The thought snapped her back into herself. She needed only a fraction of a second to reorient herself, and another to find the wall with an outstretched foot in order to begin climbing back to the balcony. Urgency gave her a strength that had been lacking during her earlier mishap on the rope. A few moments later, she was able to reach the balcony rail and pull herself over.

She wrestled out of the harness and sprinted for the stairwell. She had no doubt of where it would lead. The vision had shown her the way forward and now she was intimately familiar with the stairwells and tunnels and passages of the vault. What was not as clear was what she would do when she arrived at her destination.

As she neared the top of the stairs, she slowed to a walk and flicked off her flashlight so as not to betray her approach. She could hear their voices clearly now, not a trick of acoustics but rather a matter of proximity. The woman Changeling was trying to convince Shah to kill Professor in order to hide the existence of the vault from the outside world, and from the sound of it, Shah was about to do it.

She saw shadows on the curving walls of the passage. A few more steps, and she would be able to see the bodies who cast them.

Her foot struck something. She froze, wincing at the clatter, but evidently no one in the passage beyond heard it.

She looked down and saw what she had kicked. A semi-automatic pistol. There was a second one, still tucked in a clip-on holster, a few feet from the first. She took both, clipped the second to her belt, then eased the slide back on the first to ensure that a round was chambered. She still wasn't sure how to save Professor, but at least now she was had some equipment to work with.

Before she could take another step however, the sound of a shot assaulted her ears. The close confines of the passage amplified the noise and set Jade's ears ringing deafening her even to her own cry of alarm. She ran forward, aiming the pistol ahead of her, ready to avenge Professor's death.

There was a second shot, the sound considerably muted after the first, and then a third as Jade rounded the bend. Her eyes went immediately to the man lying motionless on the floor.

"Professor!"

Blood was fountaining from his chest, soaking his shirt and staining the floor beneath him.

So much blood.

She did not let her gaze linger on him, but turned to look for the gunman and take her shot before he could think to shoot at her. Her attention fixed immediately on Shah who held the smoking gun. He was turned away from her, presenting his back as a target at point blank range. She could not miss.

But then another man dropped to his knees beside Professor. It was Jordan Kellogg. His hands were clutching his chest, trying in vain to stem the torrent of red flowing from a pair of wounds near his heart.

That was when Jade realized that the other dying man was not Professor, not her Professor, but the Changeling who had attempted to impersonate him. There was no uncertainty about this identification. The stricken man still wore the same clothes she had seen him in during their brief meeting in Malta. He even had Professor's watch and fedora, though the latter item had rolled away.

The real Professor was still standing, unhurt, a few steps away from both Shah and the two Changeling men. He saw Jade and his eyes went wide in a mixture of surprise, fear, and relief. He shouted to her, words that she could barely make out. "Jade! Look out!"

Jade was not sure exactly what he was warning her about. Shah appeared to have come through them, turning on the Changelings and sparing Professor. She swung the barrel of the pistol around, aiming it at the dark-haired woman in sunglasses who seemed completely oblivious to what had just occurred. That was when Shah finally noticed her. He spun around on his heel and aimed his pistol right at her.

Jade was caught off guard by the suddenness of this apparent reversal, but her nerves were already primed for action. Reflexively, she brought her own weapon to bear on him. In the brief instant that followed, she read his intention. His was not a reflex action brought on by her unexpected return. He meant to kill her.

He fired.

She fired… Or would have if Professor had not caught her in a low tackle that not only rushed her into the darkness behind them, but also removed her from Shah's field of fire. In the tumult that followed, Professor managed to relieve her of the unfired pistol, whereupon he rolled onto his back and pumped several rounds in Shah's direction. Jade wrestled the second pistol from it holster, but Shah was already gone, fleeing back down the rotunda. The woman was gone too, either having fled or in Shah's company.

Professor looked over at Jade, panting to catch his breath, just as she was. His lips moved but she couldn't make out what he said, so she answered simply, "Hey."

He flashed her a goofy grin then got to his feet, hands gripping the pistol, and started forward. "Shah!" he shouted.

She heard that just fine, but no answer was forthcoming. "What the hell is he doing?" she said.

Professor returned an uncertain headshake and kept moving. He said something, *stay behind me*, or *keep your head down.* The ringing in her ears was gradually subsiding, but he was turned away from her and whispering. She hefted the pistol, muzzle pointing up, and followed.

They crept along at first, but then quickened their pace when it became evident that Shah was not waiting to ambush them. When they reached the doorway connecting the rotunda to the landing outside, Jade glimpsed movement on the spiral staircase overhead; Shah and the woman ascending but making slow progress, probably because the latter was being dragged along unwillingly.

Professor shouted again. "Shah! Let's talk!"

Shah's answer was a fusillade of rounds fired down the center of the shaft. The angles were all wrong for him to hit them, but the resulting spray of stone chips and bullet fragments drove Jade and Professor back through the opening.

"Idiot," Professor rasped. He looked at Jade. "You okay?"

She laughed despite herself. "Stupid question." *At least I can hear again*, she thought. "You?"

"Better than my evil twin." He nodded in the direction of the stairwell. "What do you think got into Shah?"

Jade bit her lip guiltily. "You remember how I had to make a deal with him? Well, the deal was that if we found anything that might call the origins of Islam into question, I would let him destroy it."

Something like anger or disappointment flickered across Professor's face, but before he could voice his disapproval, Jade went on. "I didn't have much choice. There was literally no one else I could trust. At least with Shah, I knew where I stood. And he did help. I just didn't think we would actually find anything here that would fit the bill."

"You really blew that call." Professor's demeanor softened a little. "I suppose given the circumstances it was the right thing to do. And I am grateful that you were willing to do that for me. So what do you think pushed him over the edge?"

"This place. It's like a gigantic infrasound hallucination

machine." She decided now wasn't the time to go into detail about what she had seen in her own frequency-induced vision.

Professor nodded slowly. "The Changelings told him that Muhammad and all the other prophets revered by Muslims came here to receive visions from God. I suppose, from his point of view, something like that—an alternative version of events that doesn't agree with what the Quran teaches—could be construed as blasphemy."

"And since he can't destroy the vault, he decided the next best thing was to kill all the witnesses. The Changelings and us."

Professor nodded. "There's only one way out of here. If he's up there waiting for us, we'll have to shoot it out. But he's already fired eight rounds. I counted. That means he has seven more, eight max if those Changelings kept one in the chamber, which I doubt. He has no training, no fire discipline. All we have to do is make some noise and get him to shoot off the rest of that magazine. Then we'll leave on our own terms. Over his dead body if necessary."

"I'm remembering the last time you counted the bad guy's bullets. It didn't end well."

"Very funny. This time, I know he doesn't have any extra rounds. Besides, you're hardly in a position to be questioning my judgment."

Jade thought better of replying. She gestured to the doorway. "Lead the way."

He flashed a grim smile then stuck his head out. "Shah! We're coming for you!"

There was no answering fire, so he circled the landing and started up the steps. Jade stayed close on his heels. The stairs were familiar to her, the memory of traveling them implanted during her vision, but it wasn't until she was halfway up that she realized that she had been here before, actually as well as virtually. She had fallen through the central shaft after solving the ring puzzle and opening the door to the vault.

The memory nagged, a dire warning of a danger that she

couldn't quite wrap her thoughts around. *Not Shah… Something else.*

The stairs. Something about the stairs. Where did they come from?

One moment, she had been in the submerged chamber, sliding the pieces of the ring puzzle into place. The next she was falling, caught in the rush of water pouring down through the midst of the steps.

The steps….

In her mind's eye, she saw it happening, like a video playing in slow motion. The last piece of stone sliding into place, the rings completed, and then….

And then the sphere began to move. It had seemed random from her perspective, trapped in the flooded chamber, but it was anything but. The movement of the sphere was as precise as clockwork. As was what happened next.

The sphere had opened like the petals of a flower, the individual tiles shuffling and rearranging to form the stairs that led down to the vault itself. The unfurling had of course triggered the flood that washed Jade away, and that indeed had been somewhat more chaotic, but the unfolding of the sphere chamber had been exceedingly exact. When the puzzle was solved, the door opened. Simple as that.

And what happens when the door closes?

"We have to get off these stairs." She said it once, too softly to be heard. Then repeated it again, louder so that Professor could hear.

She saw the unasked question and knew that if she didn't at least try to explain, precious moments that might mean the difference between life and death might be lost.

"Once he reaches the top, the lock will reset. These steps will disappear."

Professor seemed to grasp the broader point. "And we'll be trapped in here."

Before Jade could respond to his hasty conclusion, Professor leaned into the stairs and poured on a burst of speed that she was hard-pressed to match. She heard him shout again, and then the noise of multiple reports filled the shaft. She threw herself flat as stone chips and dust filled the air. Jade tried to count the number of rounds fired, but it was difficult to distinguish one shot from the next, to say nothing of differentiating Professor's gun from Shah's.

After a few seconds, the shooting stopped. Something flashed through the air, hit the wall behind Professor and rebounded away, skittering across the steps and ultimately sailing out into the abyss. It was a gun. Shah's gun. *One less thing to worry about.*

She raised her head and caught a glimpse of Shah running, still dragging the dark haired woman behind him. He was on the far side of the shaft, nearly at the top of the stairs, and even though Professor was closing the gap, it seemed unlikely that he would be able to catch Shah in time to stop him from slipping through the exit passage. Nevertheless, Jade's sense of the place told her that close might be good enough. The ancient architects of the vault had designed the lock room to function like the automatic doors at a supermarket. As long as Professor was within reach of the exit, the mechanism would not reset.

Suddenly the stairwell erupted with another blizzard of gunfire. The incoming storm of bullets and debris was so intense, it forced Jade to retreat back down the spiraling steps until she was almost directly below the exit, out of the shooter's line of fire.

Professor scrambled back down to her position. "Son of bitch brought reinforcements," he growled. Before she could think to ask what Professor meant, he pointed at the pistol in her hand. "Let me have that. I'm out."

She passed it over. "How many?"

"Too many. But unless you know of a back door, the only way out of here is—"

Before he could finish, an ominous grinding sound filled the shaft as the steps on which they were standing, and all the others above and below, began moving.

THIRTY

Shah crawled down the cramped passage, one hand stretched awkwardly back to drag Gabrielle along. Though he had only been in the vault a short while, he was desperate to be in the open, breathing fresh air again. Perhaps having the sky above him again would help to purge his memory of the things that had been revealed to him, but somehow he doubted it. The truth would haunt him to the end of his days.

Gabrielle was sobbing behind him. That was something new. In all the time they had worked together, all the intimate moments they had shared—*all a lie*—he had never seen her cry. Her despair comforted him. She had brought his world crashing down; a little suffering was the least he could hope for.

He would put an end to her misery soon enough.

The jihadists' arrival could not have been more timely. Though he had only been able to give them vague directions in his text messages, the men had correctly divined the significance of the little cave in the sheer face of Bell Rock and rigged their own belay lines in order to transport the material he had requested and expedite his escape. Two were waiting in the niche at the end of the passage. The others were bringing up the rear, wriggling through the passage behind him. Shah did not know if Jade and Professor would attempt to follow, but if they tried, it would only hasten their inevitable appointment with fate. He could not allow them to leave the vault.

He emerged from the cramped passage and hauled Gabrielle forward. She went sprawling and would have tumbled out through the mouth the cave if the two jihadists, uncertain of his intentions toward her, had not caught her.

Shah did not actually know why he had brought her along. He should have left her behind, both as a practical matter and a moral one. She was the enemy, his enemy and the enemy of Islam, and she always had been. Every word she had uttered, and a thousand implicit promises never spoken, were false. Everything they shared, a deceit. And yet, here she was, still alive.

What power does she have over me?

Gabrielle raised her head. She had lost her sunglasses during their transit to the surface. Her tear streaked eyes staring at nothing. "Atash," she wailed. "What have you done?"

Shah choked on his disbelief. "What have I done? I?"

Her head turned toward the sound of his voice. "You have everything. You have *seen*. You are the Mahdi. The Prophet returned. I did this for you."

Rage in Shah's chest like steam in a geyser. She actually believed she had done him a favor. "I guess you never really understood me at all then."

He turned to the nearest jihadist and held out his hand. The man placed a pistol in his palm. "Did you bring what I asked you to?"

One of the others—the young man from California, the geologist's son—stepped forward. "Only about fifty pounds. All I could get my hands on."

"It's enough." He pointed up to the passage leading into the vault. "Place it there."

As the jihadists set about their task, he placed the muzzle of the pistol against the back of Gabrielle's head. Before he pulled the trigger, he leaned close and whispered in her ear. "I didn't see anything."

THIRTY-ONE

In a matter of seconds, the stairwell transformed into something else. The blocks that had arranged themselves in an orderly spiral began to shift and slide, changing position with mechanical precision. Some disappeared altogether, sliding into recesses in the wall, their purpose served, while others protruded further, tilting and rotating, rising or falling, reassembling the spherical chamber that was the entrance to the vault.

Professor grabbed Jade's arm and was about to start up the treacherous steps but Jade pulled free. "No! Down!"

"We'll be trapped in here!"

There was no time to explain to him that trapped was preferable to being dumped down the full length of the vertical shaft or crushed between blocks of stone, so she let her actions do the talking. She turned away from him and started down the stairs, or rather tried to. Negotiating the descent was part fun-house, part obstacle course. Every step took her from one moving surface to another and she wasted precious seconds with each move just to keep her balance. They were nearly clear of the blocks that were rising to form the sphere. Below, the steps were simply retreating into the walls, all the way down the landing. If they could not reach the passage back to the rotunda before the steps vanished, they would fall into the cistern below, as Jade had done earlier, but from more than twice the height.

"Shortcut!" Jade shouted. Instead of trying to corkscrew her way down the rapidly disappearing passage, she launched herself out across the chasm, landing on the lower steps on the opposite side. Her momentum, along with the movement of the block upon which she landed, carried her into the wall, but she pushed off and jumped again, arcing across the ever-widening gap to the next level. Professor had evidently decided to trust her judgment; he too was caroming back and forth from one side of the spiral to the other, but as the blocks slid back into the wall, the distance across the chasm increased while the potential landing zones continued to diminish.

Jade saw the landing, what little was left of it anyway, ten feet below. The wedge-shaped blocks, which had caught her climbing rope during her initial fall, were in full retreat—less than six inches remained, and even if by some stroke of luck she managed to make the nearly twenty-foot leap and stick the landing, the blocks would be gone completely before she could reach the opening to the rotunda, so she decided to skip a step and go straight for her goal. She turned forty-five degrees to aim herself at the passage, then jumped straight up, planting her feet against the wall and pushed off like an Olympic swimmer making a turn.

Yet, even as she straightened her legs, propelling herself out into space, she knew in her heart that she was going to fall short of her target. The difference would be miniscule, just a few inches, but those inches would make all the difference. She would slam into the wall just below the entrance, and then fall once more into the cistern below.

The open passage taunted her with its nearness. She knew she would never be able to reach, but she stretched her arms out anyway. A thought flashed through her head. *I might survive the fall if I don't get knocked out hitting the wall.*

Something moved, right above her. It was Professor, hurling himself across the gap, just as she had done. She felt his hand close around her arm and then….

The impact with the wall knocked the wind out of her. She thought she would fall then, but instead, there was a sharp pain in her shoulder as all her weight settled beneath the hyper-extended limb. Her mouth opened to issue an involuntary cry, but she had no breath to scream.

She hung there, pressed against the wall, hanging by one arm. Her immediate impulse was to claw her way back up the rock, but every time she tried to move, the pain in her shoulder spiked. If she didn't relieve the pressure, her arm was going to be ripped from its socket.

She glanced up and saw the hand that had saved her, Professor's hand, wrapped around her wrist. He lay flat in the opening to the passage, head and shoulders protruding, teeth clenched with the exertion of holding her.

He reached down with his free hand, and she reached up, stretching more than she would have believed possible, and somehow grasped his outstretched hand.

Suddenly she was moving again. The pain in her shoulder was nothing to the relief she felt as he lifted her to safety.

Her breath returned with a gasp and for nearly a full minute, all she could do was lie on the stone floor, enjoying the feel of something solid beneath her.

"Okay," Professor said, at length. "We're alive. I haven't decided if that's the good news or the bad news."

"The good news," Jade said, "is that we aren't trapped." She tried to sit up, winced at a fresh stab of pain in her shoulder.

"Don't tell me you saw a back door? That would have been nice to know."

"*I* didn't know," she retorted. "Not at first. But those Changelings that were waiting for us? They didn't come in the front door. And I got a look around when we were separated." She did not reveal that her look around had been mostly a virtual tour. "I know where to go."

"Well, why didn't you just say so?" He got to his feet then squatted beside her and began probing her shoulder. "Still attached," he declared. "Just a muscle strain. We'll get you some SEAL candy—you mere mortals would call it Motrin—and you'll be ready for the Olympic gymnastics team in no time."

She laughed despite herself. "That's good to know, because this archaeology thing is wrecking me."

He helped her to her feet and then gestured for her to lead the way. She backtracked into the rotunda, and soon happened upon a pair of bodies—Kellogg and the man Jade had called Not-Professor.

"I wonder who they really were," she murmured. "You think the real Jordan Kellogg is in a landfill somewhere?"

Professor's eye twitched. "If he's lucky."

His tone was enough to keep her from asking him to elaborate. She knelt to retrieve his fedora and placed it on his head. "There you go. Back in business."

That was enough to bring a sparkle of humor back to his eyes. He retrieved his watch from the dead imposter, and then riffled through man's pockets, reacquiring his passport, wallet and phone. "Now I'm back in business."

"Want to see what he really looks like?"

"Nope. I just want to find that back door and get the hell out of here."

Jade shone her light down the passage and moved toward the stairwell she had used to reach this level of the vault from the chamber where she had received her vision. The stairs did not ascend any further, but there was another opening on the inside wall of the rotunda, a passage that led to the chamber Jade thought of as "the interface."

She pointed to it. "We have to go through there. But I should warn you, you're going to see some things."

"Yeah? Like Biblical stuff?"

Jade shook her head. "It doesn't work like that. What you see kind of depends on what you take in with you."

He narrowed his gaze at her. "How do you know that?"

"That's how they built it."

"They?"

"The aliens," Jade said, feeling inexplicably foolish. "The grays. The extraterrestrial astronauts that Stillman was always going on about."

"You *saw* them?"

"Yes. And I also found a bunch of their skulls."

He nodded slowly.

"Don't patronize me," Jade snapped.

Professor raised his hands. "Sorry. Actually, I'm a little curious to see what this thing will show me."

Jade gave him a hard look, but his skepticism was already undermining her own certitude. What if everything she had seen was just the product of her own preconceptions? Was her vision of alien engineers any more reliable than the angels or devils that Shah and all the self-styled prophets before him had seen?

But in the Hypogeum, I saw this place. That wasn't a lie.

A tremor rippled through the floor and Jade felt a subtle change in the air pressure. Professor raised his head sharply, turning to look back down the passage. A moment later, a loud thump reached her ears.

"What the hell was that?" Jade asked.

He turned back to her, his expression now full of urgency. "That was an explosion. Shah's terrorist friends just blew the entrance."

Another violent shudder shook the passage, accompanied by a noise as loud as a gunshot, and Jade was thrown to the floor. Jagged cracks, like lightning bolts, appeared on the walls and ceilings, vomiting out a miasma of dust. Professor managed to stay on his feet. He seized Jade's arm, triggering a nauseating wave of pain in her injured shoulder, but she fought through it, got up and staggered through the doorway.

The floor heaved and then began to tilt crazily, like the deck of a ship climbing the face of a rogue wave. Pieces of stone and concrete tumbled down around them. Jade threw her good arm up as a shield and plunged forward as the vault began coming apart all around them.

The Interface looked nothing like her vision of it now. Although the initial blast yield had been relatively small, it had thrown a monkey wrench into the precisely engineered machinery of the vault. The infrasound amplifier had become nothing more than a roiling tangle of jagged stone, slumping down through the center of the cylindrical tower.

"There!" Professor's shout was barely audible in the tumult of grinding rock, but Jade heard and followed his pointing finger to their salvation, a rope ladder hanging down in the center of the chamber and rising up into the gloom overhead.

It seemed impossibly far away.

"We'll never—"

Professor let go of her arm and scooped her off her feet. Before she could protest, he heaved her out over the center of the stone vortex. Something—the rope!—slapped against her face and she threw her arms around it, hugging the woven fibers even as she started to fall. The friction burned her face and chest, but she squeezed tighter and managed to slip her arms between the rungs.

The rope jerked taut with a bone-shaking abruptness and then she was hanging again, dangling above the swirling whirlpool of debris.

The ladder shuddered again, as if trying to shake her loose, and she saw Professor above her.

"Climb!" he shouted, and then he was moving, scrambling up the rungs.

Jade kept hugging the ladder to her, certain that if she let go, even to get a better hold, she would lose her grip and fall into the meat grinder below. She tried to find the rungs with her feet, but felt only empty space.

Another thunderclap shook the mountain, and what little remained of the interface and the surrounding tower dropped away. For a fleeting instant, Jade saw the vast cavity inside Bell Rock—the towers and aqueducts and air channels crumbling like an elaborate house of cards.

Then the shockwave hit. The Vault breathed its last, a blast of heat that buffeted Jade, propelling her up even as it engulfed her in a cloud of scalding steam....

And then it was over.

She lay beneath a sky full of stars. The smell of crushed earth was still in her nostrils, but the air was clear.

Professor lay beside her, and between them was a heap of rope, the ladder that Jade was still clutching. Professor had made it to the top and then hauled up the ladder—and her—like a fisherman dragging in his net. He had saved her.

She made a mental note to thank him.

To her left, a narrow fissure marked the Changeling's secret entrance to the vault, or rather to the cavern where the vault had once stood. She did not need to look into it to know that the vault and all the answers it might have held—secrets or illusions—were gone forever.

Maybe it was better that way.

EPILOGUE

REVELATION

Sedona, Arizona—Two days later

The call came just after noon.

Jade had been lounging poolside, an activity, or more accurately a lack of activity that under normal circumstances, she would have found unbearably tedious. After the events of the past week however, lying out in the open with nothing buy sky above her, was just what the doctor ordered, literally as well as figuratively. The urgent care provider she'd seen the morning after her "climbing accident" had prescribed a regimen of rest and relaxation, along with ice, physical therapy and some heavy duty painkillers. She wasn't keen on the ice treatments, but she was developing a new appreciation for sunbathing

The spa resort where they had booked a suite was just a thirty minute drive from Bell Rock and the hidden ruins beneath. They had not gone back to the site, which had been closed by the Forest Service due to "seismic instability," and at last report, it would be several weeks before the popular tourist destination was open for business again.

Jade wondered if it would still be as much of a draw now that the source of all the paranormal activity associated with the place had been destroyed. She supposed it would. Stories of the Bell Rock Vortex, coupled with the human capacity to believe the unbelievable, would sustain the phenomena long after Jade was gone from the earth.

She had just returned to the room when Professor's phone rang. He muted the television, which was tuned to a cable news channel, and answered. "Hey, Tam." He glanced at Jade and then said, "I'm going to put you on speaker."

"Jade?" Tamara Broderick's strong voice crackled from

the device, but Jade couldn't tell if her tone was one of disapproval or awe. "You do have a knack for kicking the hornets' nest, girl."

Jade settled onto the couch beside Professor. "Hey, if it wasn't for me you'd have no idea the hornets were even there."

"Simmer down. It's a mess, but I'm not unappreciative. The problem is figuring out who I can trust with this. God da—" She stopped herself. Tam had a smoker's relationship with profanity—she was always trying to quit. "Frigging shapeshifters."

"Changelings," Jade corrected.

"They aren't able to change shape," Professor said. "It's all just theatrical makeup and method acting."

"I'm not stupid," Tam shot back. "I know what they are. That little package you sent us is the gift that keeps on giving."

It took Jade a moment to realize Tam was referring to Eve, the Changeling prisoner Professor had captured in Tasmania.

Tam was still talking. "We've got a list of probable infiltrators that includes at least two members of the President's cabinet. That's just in our country."

"Well that explains your good mood," Jade remarked.

"When does the roll-up start?" Professor asked.

"There's not going to be a roll-up," Tam said, wearily. "If we started arresting senior political figures and pulling their masks off, the world would come apart at the seams."

"You can't just leave them out there."

"Actually, we can." She paused as if trying to figure out how to deliver an unpleasant message. "There's going to be a negotiated phase-out."

Jade exchanged a worried glance with Professor, but neither of them interrupted Tam's explanation.

Tam explained that, in order to keep the secret of the Changeling conspiracy a secret, the infiltrators would be given the opportunity to voluntarily relinquish their positions of authority in exchange for a promise of amnesty and resettlement in the witness protection program.

"How do you know they'll go for it?" Professor asked.

"Why wouldn't they? They can't hide anymore, and you've utterly dismantled their *raison d'etre*." She paused a beat. "You have, right?"

"The Vault was completely destroyed," Jade said, letting Tam draw her own conclusions.

"These people are dangerous," Professor intoned. "They've held power for a long time. They aren't going to just roll over and give it all up."

"We had all better pray they do," was Tam's grave reply.

Jade wondered if it really mattered. Despite Roche's conspiracy theories, it seemed unlikely that the Changelings had ever wielded absolute control over the world's governments and economy. She wasn't sure that was even possible. In any case, if the Changelings were removed from power, someone just as unscrupulous would probably take their place.

Power corrupts and nature abhors a vacuum, Jade thought.

Tam was speaking again. "Do have any insights into what made the thing tick?"

"Infrasound frequencies can be used to induce a dream-like state," Professor said, authoritatively. "People in that state see what they expect to see."

"That doesn't explain how Jade knew the vault would be in Arizona."

Professor had no ready answer for that.

"It's not the first time we've found something we can't explain," Jade said with a shrug. She had no inclination to speculate further. "What about Shah?"

"Latest intel puts him in Tehran. He's gone back home."

"So we can't get to him?"

"Bigger fish to fry," Tam said. "He was never much of a threat, and from what you've told me, he has reason to hate the Changelings even more than we do. Whether he meant to or not, he did us all a huge favor by destroying the vault."

"Not sure how I feel about him," Jade said, thinking

aloud. "I don't think he even knew whose side he was on."

"Maybe we'll run into him someday," Professor said. "And you can ask him."

Jade shrugged. "Or not. I'm just glad it's all over."

When Professor did not respond, she looked over and saw him staring at the television. On the screen, a graphic banner announcing "Breaking News" was flashing over stock footage of naval vessels on the ocean. The crawl beneath the picture said, "Possible debris from Flight 815 found."

"Yeah," he said. "I guess it is."

Tehran, Iran

But for the mountains towering behind the city skyline and the signs on the shops—Farsi written in the elegant Nasta'liq script—Atash Shah might have believed he was back on Park Avenue. The affluent Zafaraniyeh neighborhood in northern Tehran was every bit as modern, and almost as cosmopolitan, as Manhattan. It even had a synagogue, which probably would have astonished most Westerners.

It had been a long time since Shah called this place home, but there was nowhere else to go.

He recalled a line from an old poem. *Home is the place where, when you go there, they have to take you in.*

The reunion with his family, and particularly his father who had never approved of his son's travels—both literal and philosophical—had been a little strained, and Shah sensed there would be many more tense conversations in the days to come, but for the moment, things appeared calm.

Deceptively so.

His entire world had foundered. He was in exile. Everything he owned was gone, his possessions abandoned along with his New York apartment. He did not know if the authorities in the United States would seize his assets or pursue criminal charges against him, and it seemed prudent not to find out. He still had a controlling interest in the

Crescent Defense League, though whether it could or even should continue remained in doubt.

After what he had learned under Bell Rock, he wasn't sure of anything.

The dream of a second Golden Age of Islam—an era of spiritual and secular prosperity, an end to the destructive schism between Sunni and Shiite—was dead for him. He believed it was possible, probably even inevitable, but he would have no part in bringing that dream to fruition. He would never be the promised Mahdi.

How could he, knowing what he now knew?

It was all a lie. Islam. Christianity. The holy writings. None of it could be trusted.

Raina shuffled into the sitting room of the furnished flat they had rented, carrying a tray with a delicate silver tea service. His wife had been extraordinarily supportive through everything, which only deepened Shah's sense of guilt at having been led astray by the wanton seductress Gabrielle Greene.

Gabrielle was dead by his own hand, but her poison was still in him.

I will make it up to Raina, he promised himself, yet he knew not how.

"Atash," she clucked. "Drink some chai. It will calm your nerves."

He managed a wan smile. "Thank you, my wife."

She decanted a small amount of the amber liquid into a cup and passed it to him. He had never been much of a tea drinker. Coffee had always been his beverage of choice, an appropriately hyperactive drink for his hyperactive existence in New York.

Maybe it's time to turn over a new leaf, he thought. *A new drink to begin a new life.*

He took a sip. It was mildly spicy from the addition of zardamom pods and cinnamon, and just sweet enough to make him wish that it was more substantial.

This will take some getting used to.

He had just finished a second sip when a knock at the

door startled him. They were not expecting visitors. With the possible exception of his parents, who believed it was his place to visit them, not the other way around, no one even knew of the apartment.

He jumped to his feet in alarm, and nearly toppled over from the resulting head rush.

"Atash, calm yourself," Raina said. "It is only the groceries. I cannot make a home if I have nothing to cook. Finish your tea, then you can help me put things away."

Shah sat down quickly, fearing that he was about to black out, but the wooziness lingered. He tried to place the tea cup on the table, but misjudged the distance, spilling its contents onto the floor.

Behind him, he heard Raina speaking to the deliveryman. "You are early," she scolded, though not too harshly. "Five more minutes and he would have been out."

What?

He jumped up again, whirling toward the door, and then promptly collapsed onto the floor. He could feel the puddle of warm tea soaking into his clothes, but his limbs were completely unresponsive. A black fog was settling over him, but just before the light went out completely, he saw his wife and the man that she had just admitted to their apartment.

Her voice reached out through the ether. "Oh, Atash. You almost ruined everything."

Because I spilled the tea?

His thoughts were as muddled as everything else, and it took him a moment to connect what he had seen in that last glimpse before his eyesight failed, and what was now happening to him.

She drugged me. Raina drugged me.

"It was yours for the taking," she continued, only now there was a hard edge to her words, a tone he had never heard in all their years together. "We worked so hard to prepare the way. Oh, we knew you weren't ready, but that cretin Roche forced our hand, and then had the audacity to tell Jade Ihara about it before we could put him in the grave. But still, Gabrielle showed you such wonders. How could you do this to us? Why?"

The questions must have been rhetorical. There was no way he would be able to respond, and he knew she was not speaking to the man she had just ushered in.

Yet, in a way, she was. He had caught a glimpse of the visitor's face in the instant before the drug took away his vision. A face exactly like his own.

"You almost ruined everything, Atash," Raina repeated. "Fortunately, you can be replaced."

FACT FROM FICTION

We've always believed that the best stories are built on a foundation of truth, and this one is no exception. Now it's time to separate what is real from what we've made up.

Archimedes—We've only scratched the surface of Archimedes' genius. His discoveries, which include establishing the value of pi (the ration of a circle's circumference to its diameter), are the basis for calculus and physics, without which most of our modern scientific advances could not have been made. One scholar made the observation that, if more of Archimedes' writings had survived, we would already be living on Mars. Sadly, most of his writings were lost to history, the parchment books scraped clean and written over during the Middle Ages.

The Archimedes Palimpsest, mentioned in this novel, is real. It was discovered in a monastery just before World War I, the ancient Greek writing barely visible on the parchment which had been cleaned and resized, and used for a medieval prayer book. It has only been in the last decade that modern fluoroscopy techniques have made it possible to read one of Archimedes' most important works. The part about a Vault and a timelock that can only be opened every thousand years is our invention, but if Archimedes had wanted to create something like that, he probably could have.

The war machines described in the prologue and in the Arkimedeion museum, including the Archimedes Claw, used to pick up entire warships and then drop them down, smashing them to pieces in the harbor, are believed to be real. The heat ray, an array of parabolic mirrors capable of focusing the sun's light into a sort of laser beam for setting ships on fire, has long been attributed to Archimedes, but it is unlikely that he actually created such a device, or that it would have worked as suggested. In 2006 the MythBusters television program ruled the Archimedes Heat Ray "busted." In 2009, in conjunction with students from MIT, the show revisited the "myth" and found that, while it was technically possible to create such a device, it would have been of extremely limited usefulness in warfare.

The Arkimedeion Museum in Syracuse is a real place, but the layout of the museum and its contents are the authors' creation. Sadly a research trip was out of the question and descriptions of the facility are limited to a number of less than favorable visitor reviews, some of which complained that many of the interactive exhibits were not functional. As rule, we like to avoid presenting real world locations in a negative light, but those reviews seemed like an opportunity for a little exercise in "what if?"

Skulls—Strange elongated skulls found on the Paracas peninsula in Peru have long aroused the interest of UFO enthusiasts who see an astounding similarity to the shape of the heads described in most reports of encounters with the extraterrestrial "grays." One story, widely circulated on the Internet, mistakenly claims that DNA tests on the Paracas skulls indicate that they are not human. That story is a fiction, though not our invention. What is factual is that the skulls do exist, and are an example of what was once a widespread body modification technique practiced not only in South America, but all over the world, even well into the 20th century. And yes, elongated skulls were found in the Hal Saflieni Hypogeum on the island of Malta.

Certain cultures, probably for purely aesthetic reasons, would wrap the heads of infants tightly with blankets and ropes, or bind them to boards, in order to flatten and reshape the skull. Because the human head stops growing at a very young age, the desired effect can be achieved in a relatively short time, with no physical damage to the brain.

Many of the aforementioned UFO enthusiasts accept this explanation, but wonder if perhaps the reason these ancient people wanted to change the shape of their heads was to look more like their "gods" who they believe were actually alien astronauts. In the case of the Paracas culture, the same culture responsible for creating the Nazca Lines, large geoglyphs which can only be seen in their entirety from high altitude—a low flying spacecraft perhaps?—the question should not be lightly dismissed.

Phantom Time—The Phantom Time Hypothesis is real thing—that is to say, someone has proposed it, therefore the proposition exists. According to historian Herbert Illig, Holy Roman Emperor Otto II and Pope Sylvester II conspired to fabricate nearly three hundred years of history—corresponding to the years 614 to 911 CE—in order to place their respective reigns on the cusp of the new millennium, which it is supposed, would have given them a great deal of influence over faithful Christians. The primary evidence for Phantom Time is the adjustment made during the transition from the Julian to Gregorian calendar. Supporters of the hypothesis also claim that there is very little archaeological evidence that can be reliably dated to this period, and when challenged, call into question the accuracy of dating methods. They also correctly point out that most of what we know about the Middle Ages derives from written histories, many of which have a suspiciously fanciful flavor.

There is quite a bit of evidence against the hypothesis, but then that is exactly what we would expect from such a well-thought-out deception. The central argument however, namely the discrepancy in Pope Gregory's adjustment of the calendar in the year 1582, only works if we assume that Gregory was correcting for the accumulation of every extra leap year day added since the inception of the Julian calendar in 46 BCE. Since the purpose of the Gregorian calendar was to avoid confusion about when to celebrate Christian holidays, it is far more likely that Gregory's scholars would have chosen a more relevant starting point, such as the Council of Nicea in 325 CE, which established, among other things, the dates for those holidays.

While Phantom Time probably isn't a supportable proposition, it raises some interesting questions about the trustworthiness of history, particularly with respect to contemporary sources.

Fogou—Like skull deformation, the practice of creating underground chambers was ubiquitous in the ancient world. Many scholars favor a utilitarian explanation, and indeed, these chambers could have been used for food storage or a refuge from enemy attacks—survival bunkers for ancient preppers. Others believe they served a ritual purpose, a (figurative?) doorway to the Underworld or transition point to another realm. Neither explanation can be discounted simply because the cultures that made these chambers and tunnels left no written explanation for their purpose. From the fogous of Scotland, to the erdstall tunnels of Europe, to the kivas of the American southwest, these underground vaults remain a mystery that may never be solved.

Which brings us to….

Hal Saflieni Hypogeum—Until the recent discovery of Gobekli Tepe in Turkey, the megalithic temples of Malta were considered the oldest structures known to man, some dating back over 7,000 years. The Hypogeum is just a little more recent—the site has been dated to 4000 BCE—and is the only known subterranean temple from the prehistoric period, which makes its unusual acoustic design all the more intriguing. The auditory properties of the Hypogeum described herein are real, up to a point. Research has confirmed that the Oracle Room resonates at 110 Hertz, a frequency known to produce trance-like effects. That this was understood by architects living before the creation of written language is nothing short of amazing. And yes, as mentioned earlier, elongated skulls were discovered among the human remains buried in the Hypogeum.

Infrasound—The lower limit of human hearing has been established as 20 Hertz, though by the time most of us reach adulthood, the ability to hear lower ranges will have diminished considerably. (If you're curious about this, you can find phone apps, like the one Jade used, to produce a range of frequencies. The results may surprise and discourage). Any sound below 20 Hz is called infrasound, and while we cannot hear infrasound, it can produce unusual physical effects—ranging from nausea to extreme anxiety to outright panic. The connection between ghost sightings and infrasound in the 17-19 Hz range was first suggested in 1998, and ongoing research between infrasound and allegedly haunted houses has been very promising.

The idea that infrasound might be manipulated to produce very specific hallucinations, as described in this novel, is well beyond the limits of what is possible. For now.

Bell Rock—Located just south of Sedona, Arizona, Bell Rock is one of several magnificent red limestone buttes that tower over the desert landscape. It also happens to be the site of an "energy vortex," one of several purported to exist in the Sedona region. According to local lore and too many anecdotal reports to count, encountering a vortex may cause a wide range of emotional and physical reactions. Some feel rejuvenated. Other describe a strange humming sound. Still others report seeing strange lights in the sky. There are even stories about a gigantic alien spacecraft concealed inside Bell Rock. While the vault described in the story is completely fictional, the similarity between the effects of infrasound and the Sedona vortices is, to say the least, intriguing enough to explore in fiction. And if you ever happen to be in Sedona, maybe you'll get to experience a vortex encounter firsthand!

ABOUT THE AUTHORS

David Wood is the author of the popular action-adventure series, *The Dane Maddock Adventures*, as well as several stand-alone works and two series for young adults. Under his David Debord pen name he is the author of the *Absent Gods* fantasy series. When not writing, he co-hosts the Authorcast podcast. David and his family live in Santa Fe, New Mexico. Visit him online at www.davidwoodweb.com.

Sean Ellis is the author of several thriller and adventure novels. He is a veteran of Operation Enduring Freedom, and has a Bachelor of Science degree in Natural Resources Policy from Oregon State University. Sean is also a member of the International Thriller Writers organization. He currently resides in Arizona, where he divides his time between writing, adventure sports, and trying to figure out how to save the world. Visit him at www.seanellisthrillers.com.

Printed in Great Britain
by Amazon

62654970R00180